THE PARABOLIST

NICHOLAS RUDDOCK
THE PARABOLIST

DOUBLEDAY CANADA

Doubleday Canada and colophon are registered trademarks

Library and Archives Canada Cataloguing in Publication

Ruddock, Nicholas
The parabolist / Nicholas Ruddock.

ISBN 978-0-385-66873-6

I. Title.

PS8635.U34P37 2010   C813'.6   C2009-903966-4

This book is a work of fiction. Names, characters, places and incidents
are products of the author's imagination or are used fictitiously.
Any resemblance to actual events or locales or persons, living or dead,
is entirely coincidental.

Printed and bound in the USA

Published in Canada by Doubleday Canada,
a division of Random House of Canada Limited

Visit Random House of Canada Limited's website: www.randomhouse.ca

10 9 8 7 6 5 4 3 2 1

Cheryl,

to whom I and this novel
owe so much

Seek oneself, lose oneself in strange lands! But with a guiding line, with bread crumbs or white pebbles!

Roberto Bolaño, *The Savage Detectives*

Parabolist: noun

1. *one who speaks in parables.*

2. *a member of a splinter group of disaffected young poets in Mexico City circa 1975.*

3. *a practitioner of the art of concentrating multiple sources of energy into a single focus, illuminating or, if left unchecked, destroying everything in its path.*

t was well past three or four in the morning and she was married and far more experienced than he was and he couldn't remember half the things they did there in her bedroom on Roxborough Drive.

Oh Jasper, she kept saying.

Then there was a crunching sound in the gravel outside in the driveway, a car, and she got up and looked through the curtain.

Jasper, she said, oh my God, you've got to get out of here. Right now.

She panicked. She ran in circles around the bedroom, and then she ran into the adjoining bathroom and closed the door.

He stood for a second by the rumpled bed and then he took off. He reached down and grabbed his clothes.

He clutched them to his chest and ran naked out of the bedroom and down the stairs. Near the bottom, he vaulted over the mahogany banister. He slipped, he recovered, he put one elbow to the kitchen door and it flew open. It was dark in there but a dim light came up from the cellar. He stood there to breathe, to get his bearings. The kitchen door stopped its oscillation just in time.

He heard the turning of the key.

Honey, I'm home.

Those were the very words, it was hard to believe. His heart was pounding for the eleventh time that night. Quickly he ducked down onto the cellar steps and closed the door behind him.

The dog barked, a deep woof.

Hey there Brewster, the voice said.

He must have ruffled the dog's head in the hallway because Jasper heard the clinking of the collar, the tags. Then the kitchen light came on, a sliver across his knees. He heard water running upstairs in the pipes. Marnie was in the shower now. The refrigerator opened and closed and then Brewster came over to the cellar door and put his nose under it and snuffled.

Brewster, get out of there. Brewster drop that sock, come on boy, let's go upstairs.

The kitchen light turned off.

She shouted downstairs, Hey! You're home? I just got out of the shower, couldn't sleep, the humidity. Come to bed.

Flight cancelled, he said, fog.

Then, before her husband went up to the bedroom, damn it if he didn't activate the security system. Jasper heard his fingers tapping in the code in the front hallway. It was one of those very first alarms, primitive but effective, complete with flashing lights. Then he went upstairs with Brewster. His steps receded clump-clump, jingle-jingle the dog, and there Jasper was, all alone, halfway down to the basement. There was the side door, his best chance for escape. But now a red light flashed off and on, ominously, right by the lock.

He was trapped.

He sat on the steps and got dressed, minus the missing sock, and then he went all the way down to the basement and looked around. There was enough dim light from the windows but they too were all wired up. He picked up a flashlight on a bench. Nothing useful to be seen with that, just cobwebs. He went back up into the kitchen. The clock on the stove said 5:00. Then he heard the headboard groaning upstairs but it was hard to be jealous. The place was a bloody fortress in reverse and he had anatomy class in three hours so he was desperate.

Then he noticed it, the milkbox partway down the cellar stairs. A tight rectangle, maybe eighteen inches square. Even though it was small, it looked not impossible. Everybody used to slide in and out of those things when they were kids, and there was no wiring around this one, none at all.

Aha, the Achilles heel.

He opened the inside door of the milkbox and pushed on the outer door. It flew open with a bang that no one heard. Cool air rushed in. He was covered in sweat. He eased his head and shoulders in and braced his feet against the opposite wall and pushed. It was a very tight fit though, years of growth. Inch by inch he advanced and he swore he was almost there but it was no go. He went back to the kitchen. He looked around and there it was on the counter, a large can of Crisco, never opened. He took off all his clothes for the second time that night; the anticipation now was almost equal. Cleverly, he left Brewster's sock on the floor where it was. After all, it had been noticed. He was thinking more rationally now, like a seasoned criminal. He bundled up his pants, his shirt, his shoes and pushed them out through the milkbox into the free world. Bridges burned, he scooped handful after handful of Crisco and slathered himself neck to knee with it. He used it all. He put the empty can back in the basement, on the floor. Then he put his head and shoulders through the milkbox and again he pushed with his feet on the far wall and then bang-pop there he was, slithered and fallen on the driveway like a newborn. He almost shouted with pleasure but he didn't. He stood up and shivered. He put on all his clothes. He hopped from one foot to the other.

Maybe should have kept that sock.

Birds began to sing, cardinals. He set out in a lope like a wolf, but there was no way he'd get all the way home and back to school on time so he headed south, down into the ravine. He lay there, hidden from the roadside by a tree, and he fell asleep.

Then his inner clock kicked in. Maybe the traffic picked up or sunlight filtered through the trees. He made it to anatomy class just as Valerie Anderson, his lab partner, made the incision into the left wrist joint, and even though he had not slept more than an hour all night, being near Valerie Anderson was enough to keep him wide awake.

You smell good, Jasper, she said, almost like baking.

The cadaver lay there as always.

I'll be the assistant, he said. You cut, you be the surgeon.

Okay, she said.

They always took turns. First one of them assumed the role of the surgeon, the one who did the actual cutting, the peeling, the teasing of tissue. The other one held the retractors, kept things out of the way and held open the manual. The next day they switched. It was important to do it right, both jobs, to be careful. So he took the little hooked skin retractors and put them on each side of the incision Valerie had already made through the anterior aspect of the wrist. There was no bleeding, it was just formaldehyde that oozed out. He pulled apart the incision so she could see where she was going.

She was right, he smelled like Crisco. It wafted up from inside his shirt, heated to 98.6 degrees, body temperature.

Wait, he said.

He let go of the skin hooks and buttoned up the top of his lab coat.

That's better, Jasper, she said, now I can breathe.

Then she extended the incision so it ran all the way from the base of the thumb across the front of the wrist to the other side.

There, she said.

The flexor tendons, the radial and the ulnar arteries ran side by side, exposed.

You know what that is? she asked.

Like it says in the book, he said, the arteries, the veins, the tendons that flex the fingers. All laid bare.

She just looked at him.

I'll let that pass, she said.

Laid bare, he repeated.

It's the number-three method for committing suicide, this, the slashed wrist, she said.

First pills, then carbon monoxide, said Jasper, if I remember right.

Yes, but this way's not so easy, is it? I had to press hard to do that, to open the skin deep enough with this blade. And ever so sharp, Jasper, is this blade.

She made small circles in the air with the scalpel.

Ever so sharp and that's why teenage girls, they only have little scratches when they try it the first time. They use razor blades, that's all they have, a series of little scratches and maybe three or four drops of blood.

Poor things, he said, they get saved by ignorance.

By hesitation and by fear, she said.

By lack of physical strength, he said.

Lack of resolve more than anything, and thank God for that, Jasper, because they almost all get better in the long run.

Gestures. That's all. They're playing at it, those girls, said Jasper.

Men make gestures too, said Valerie Anderson.

Oh?

In the form of risky behaviour. Hold that back a bit more.

She bent towards Jasper Glass. She began to undercut the skin on the palmar surface of the hand. With the hooks, he pulled up and kept the tension constant and they proceeded that way until the whole hand was degloved. Three hours passed. Now and then his mind wandered from lack of sleep. It was a nice dissection they'd done.

Coffee? he asked.

Sure.

They washed off the stench of the formaldehyde and then they went down to the cafeteria. He bought two coffees and they sat together for lunch. She had hers from home, a brown bag.

I forgot mine, he said, or didn't have time to get it together. One of those things.

Jasper, she said.

She gave him half a sandwich, tuna fish.

Valerie Anderson had dark hair. During anatomy class she tied it back in a ponytail but now she let it down around her shoulders, and as usual everybody in the lunch room looked at her, and looked away, and looked back at her again.

The professor thought at first that Roberto Moreno should never have come to Canada. The young man was a fish out of water. For one thing, he looked different, with his thick, wavy hair combed back straight from his forehead. It had a slightly dampened look to it, slick, an effect he might have achieved with a hair product, though that would have been paradoxical because the rest of his presentation was essentially careless. Not in a slovenly way— he was clean—but the act of dressing was obviously an afterthought. Perhaps his hair had that shine naturally, the professor thought, but the professor had never been to Mexico. He couldn't compare that hair to anything he'd seen in France or Germany or Canada. Quite remarkable, the sheen it had, how dark it was yet how it reflected light.

He was skinny too, Roberto. When he arrived in mid-winter and moved into the basement of their neighbour's house, the professor and his wife were afraid he might perish from the wind and snow. Immediately, they looked through their sons' closets and took over to him, the first day he wandered out inappropriately—in his cotton trousers, a windbreaker and soft-soled brown leather shoes—a spare parka. Also, they took warm woollen mittens from the East Coast, the kind with just two fingers and a thumb.

Roberto Moreno put them on with a smile.

They found him quite engaging. He said something about lobsters, waved his gloved hands in the air, and they all laughed in a very friendly way.

They also took him galoshes.

You need these, June said, and she showed him how to put them on over his leather shoes, how to close the metal clips.

His English was surprisingly good. They were charmed by the boy, his self-effacing manner, the way he looked them directly in the eye.

Thank you, he said, come inside and meet my family, please.

That was how they met Roberto's uncle and aunt, who had rented the house next door and who, they understood, were acting *in loco parentis* for the young man. His parents had died, and the aunt and uncle had taken up the burden, or the pleasure as the aunt said, of raising Roberto for the past ten years. The uncle was a short and rotund man with a pencil-thin moustache, in the fashion, the professor later opined, of Latin Americans everywhere. He was a visiting professor from Mexico at the University of Toronto. As William Glass was himself a professor at the same university, that turned out to be a pleasant coincidence, yet as they talked they found that their interests were very different and therefore it was unlikely their professional paths would ever cross. For Julián Nájera was a medical man, sharply focused on the destruction of tumours by the lowering of temperatures to absolute zero. This was a new approach, he said, that he had stumbled upon by accident in Ciudad Juárez in the course of research in epitheliomas. William Glass's field of interest, on the other hand, was French idiomatic expressions which, he readily admitted, was—in the scientific sense—softer, more general and of little practical significance to anyone other than linguists, poets and writers.

An arcane field, the professor said, as though he were modest about his achievements, though in fact he was as passionate about idioms as any scientist could be about his subject, even if that scientist were on the verge of a great discovery, such as insulin or nuclear fission.

Ah, but Roberto is a poet, said the uncle.

Roberto has already had some success at his young age in Mexico City, said the aunt.

The professor and his wife were both impressed.

Poetry is a discipline for the young, or at least for the young at heart, isn't it? said the professor. Perhaps, Roberto, when my book is published, you would be interested.

Book? Roberto said, of course I would be interested in your book. I am interested in all books.

It was evident that that was not just politeness on his part. The young man truly loved the written word.

Parlez-vous français? asked William Glass.

Immediately Roberto responded in complex, grammatically correct French, but his accent was tinged with Spanish and thus grated on the professor's ear.

Really, Bill, June said later when he commented on the boy's accent.

Roberto then took off the lobster gloves that he had been wearing throughout the conversation.

Tell me all about your book, Professor, he said.

The Nájeras were also eager to hear, so in expectation they sat down together at the kitchen table and Silvana brought out some glasses into which she poured a clear liquid.

Tequila, she said.

They had three or four glasses each. The setting sun disappeared behind the curtains. Night fell.

William Glass explained that his book, with the dry but also direct title *A Living Collection of Idioms in French*, was to have been published five years ago by the small press at the University of Windsor.

Was to? said Roberto.

Well, it still is to be published, said the professor, but the ever-changing French language is so vibrant, as you probably know, that new idioms have kept coming at me, coming at me at such a pace that my book is rendered obsolete the moment I complete it. Thus I have been forced on several occasions to recall the manuscript. I start anew, I cull the dead, I introduce the newborn, and there are times, I confess, I despair that my book will ever see the light of day.

Of course, said Julián Nájera, a common fear among writers.

It's like coitus interruptus, said Roberto.

The tequila was long gone by then. They all laughed, however, because the effects were still with them.

Yes, said the professor, the production of a book is like the act of sex. At least here in Canada. I know nothing about books or sex in Mexico, but here I am robbed of pleasure just at the moment of fruition.

I think I can relate better to that than you can, said June.

That's something women know, all right, said Silvana.

Had Roberto Moreno's small joke about coitus inter-ruptus been in French rather than in Latin, Professor William Glass would have jotted it down immediately. He always kept a pocketful of small index cards at the ready and a pen or the stub of a pencil. He could have included Roberto's original observation in his compendium.

It qualifies as a freshly minted idiom, he said to June as they finally left the Nájeras' at midnight.

Don't be ridiculous, she said, you just sent in another version of your manuscript. That's the last thing you need, something brand new and not even French.

So they left the conversation about books, they left the spare parka, the lobster gloves and the galoshes with Roberto Moreno, and June and Bill Glass walked home through two concentric circles of light, yellow tinged, that met upon the melting snow—the yellow-tinged light from their two front porches, contiguous. They both commented, as they opened their front door, how pleased they were with their new neighbours.

Valerie Anderson first met Roberto Moreno in the after-hours poetry class at University College, as did Jasper Glass. They were medical students in their first year, but at that time someone in the upper echelons of the faculty determined that medical students needed a grounding in the classics of literature. Thus, the hope was, doctors would be sensitized to the Art of Medicine as well as to the Science. None of the students thought this was a bad idea. Indeed, Valerie Anderson's class was highly accomplished in the arts and counted, amongst its number, several classical musicians, three painters, a ballerina and even a trapeze specialist, as well as a secret writer who had already published a sestina in *Canadian Forum*, under a pseudonym.

So the English literature prerequisite was met with enthusiasm. Twice a week, in groups of ten or twelve, the medical students were assigned to classrooms on the west side of University College. There, at night, one graduate student or another stood before them and nervously attempted to explain the importance of Geoffrey Chaucer, Laurence Sterne, Robert Herrick, the Eliots—George and T.S.—and the list went on, until finally came the Canadian poets E.J. Pratt, A.M. Klein and P.K. Page. A motley selection indeed, based not on common sense or on the importance of the various works within the canon but instead on the nocturnal availability of teaching assistants, who, by virtue of demands put upon them by their own discipline, had narrowed their focus to such a degree that most of them seemed lost as individuals. They seemed unable to relate naturally to living human beings. Their thin voices fell at their feet like feathers. Valerie, Jasper, all bent forward at their desks in an attempt to hear.

The quality of teaching was a disappointment. Literature failed to come alive for the students.

Then, suddenly, the poetry section and, out of the blue, Roberto Moreno.

I am not your teacher, he said. I am replacing your teacher who has a fever, who is sick. Your teacher asked me to come to you tonight despite the fact that I have no qualifications at all.

Well, that was an honest and straightforward statement, and boldly stated too. Everyone sat up, curious. Everyone that is except Jasper's brother, John Glass, who was elsewhere, missing in action, absent. As often he was. But there was no roll call and no one missed John Glass, noticed or cared.

Tonight, Roberto Moreno said, I don't want to talk poetry here. Instead, we should repair to a café.

He used the word *repair,* a strange word in that context, and his accent was Latino, either Spanish or Portuguese.

As Valerie was the only girl in the class and as all the boys just sat there, she stood and said, Grad's Restaurant. Coffee and apple pie.

That was a bit of a joke because the apple pie at Grad's Restaurant was notoriously bad. The apples looked as though they'd been dipped in a fluorescent green syrup of liquid kryptonite. Only the crust was edible.

Okay, he said, then let us repair there, to your café.

When he said this, it was obvious that he was very young, the same age as they were, and he had a sweetness, a vulnerability. Valerie Anderson found him attractive. His hair was brushed straight back but it had a curl and a sheen to it as though he used Brylcreem, or brilliantine. But he didn't, she found out later. It was natural, the same as Japanese girls who twirl their shampooed hair on television, girls who sweep their glints of highlight back and forth for the camera. Though Roberto's hair was wavier than that, and it didn't reach down much past his collar.

When she reflected upon it, Valerie wondered if perhaps the course in English literature might have been better had it been taught by more-qualified professors. But those professors were not available in the evening. They were at home watching television or playing squash at the Granite Club on Bayview Avenue, or drinking with their cronies at the King Cole Room in the Park Plaza Hotel, five hundred yards from where the students were gathered.

It was just as well. The course might indeed have been better, but then she never would have met Roberto Moreno, so, for her, no matter how disappointed she was in the teaching, the poetry excepted, the course in English literature at University College turned out to be great. Outstanding, in fact. The most important experience of her young life.

Or was it? So many things happened to her afterwards, it was hard to be sure. Without the first blow from the chisel, what could the marble struck by Bernini ever have become? Nothing, nothing other than stone.

But that was a faulty metaphor, wasn't it?

Marble could never be anything but stone, whereas Valerie Anderson was a living and breathing organism. She was beyond the hand of any artist.

———

Bill and June didn't see much of their neighbours throughout the rest of the winter. If Roberto Moreno happened to be out shovelling snow, an activity he took to with alacrity and which he performed with precision, each snowbank cut like a knife edge, then Professor Glass waved to him when he came back from work in his Citroën and turned down the deeply rutted, ice-encrusted private driveway that ran the length of his house to his garage at the back.

But then spring came and it was natural to be outside, cutting the grass, weeding dandelions, watering the small plants that grew at the base of their mutual fence, so quite often their paths crossed.

Roberto wore a T-shirt or a sweater when he was out on the patio in the backyard. His aunt worked in the daytime packaging candies at a Laura Secord store on Eglinton Avenue, so Roberto was usually alone. If not reading at the patio table, he was writing. He preferred small pieces of yellow paper from a scratch pad. He often seemed a million miles away when he was composing his poems. He wrote ferociously, quickly, and the yellow papers fell at his feet and blew around the yard like bright leaves, but if he looked up and caught the professor's eye because of some movement made with a rake or the mower, he immediately stopped writing, came over to the fence, shook hands in a curiously formal way, and asked if the professor's idioms were under control. That was the expression he used, *under control*.

It must be like lassoing wild horses, he said, your idioms.

Then he gestured with his hand at the yellow scraps of paper that fluttered throughout his own yard, as though they were wild stallions and the rough patches of crabgrass over which they flew were the grasslands of Montana or Argentina.

One day, three of these scraps of poetry found their way through the wire fence and William Glass picked them up. They were written in Spanish, and though the connection between Spanish and French is close in many ways, he could make neither head nor tail of them. It was as if they had been written in code or shorthand, so he threw them back over the fence, respectfully, onto the grass at the Nájeras', and the next day, and the next week, they were still there, blown under the roses or caught in the far corner of the yard.

Ten medical students, including Valerie and Jasper, all went to Grad's Restaurant with Roberto Moreno on the night they met. Even though he was exhausted after the escape with Crisco, though he was a near-zombie on autopilot, Jasper never missed a class. And any time spent in the company of Valerie Anderson was a bonus. So he went. The class left through the southwest door of University College and walked as a group around King's College Circle and crossed College Street. At Grad's Restaurant, the students pulled together two tables and sat with their youthful substitute teacher, and after the arrival of coffee Roberto Moreno said, tell me who are your Canadian poets.

They put their heads together: Irving Layton, Margaret Avison, Michael Ondaatje, Margaret Atwood, Leonard Cohen, they said.

Is that all?

Valerie Anderson then spoke up and said, Al Purdy, Alden Nowlan, Raymond Souster, Gwendolyn MacEwen, George Bowering, Dennis Lee.

And he said good, good, and he wrote down all those names.

I have never heard of any of them, he said, forgive me.

Within several weeks, Roberto Moreno acquired all the books of all the writers mentioned at the restaurant. He acquired them but he didn't buy them. He stole them in groups of two or three at a time from the University of Toronto Bookstore, Coles on Yonge Street, the Book Cellar on Yorkville, Britnell Books on Yonge Street, or a used bookstore, a jungle of books with no apparent name, on Queen Street West.

The first words Jasper Glass said to Valerie Anderson the day they met were, oh, so they're bagged up, the bodies.

She didn't say anything.

Twenty metal tables lined the long room in two rows of ten, and on each table was a white plastic bag, lumpy, six feet long. Overhead, hanging lights drooped like the ones in pool halls, focused on whatever was below.

Okay, first job, unzip the bags, said the anatomy professor.

There were four students per body, two on each side.

His three companions just stood there so Jasper reached up, grasped the zipper with a flourish and pulled it down, all the way down. Then he pulled the two sides of the bag apart so they fell back over the sides of the table.

Hey, he said.

A male, overweight and very old, his skin grey-blue, naked.

They heard all the other zippers being undone.

They looked up and down the rows and saw the old, the sick and the grey, male and female in equal number, alternating.

Cadaverous, if you ask me, this guy, said Jasper Glass.

He could be anybody's grandfather, yours or mine, said Valerie Anderson.

Not exactly chiselled, whoever he is, said Jasper.

He put his hand on the abdomen, bloated with either fat or disease. He pushed tentatively upon it with his finger.

The young and the chiselled, they don't die too often, said Valerie.

Then the professor rapped on one of the metal tables and said, these bodies have been donated to science by their previous owners. Your job, over the next three months, sixteen hours per week, is to respectfully reduce them to their contingent parts. Inch by inch and then millimetre by millimetre. Thus, as physicians, you will have acquired an intimate first-hand knowledge of the miraculous, the intricate structure of the human body. And this knowledge of anatomy, needless to say, is critical to your development. Without this knowledge, you will be like explorers without maps, lost in the desert, doomed to make more false steps than true. To the detriment of all your patients. You will stare into the hot bright sun and fall to your knees.

I've heard he says the same thing every year, the bit about the hot sun, said Jasper.

I like it, I like what he said, said Valerie, it makes sense to me.

The professor came directly to them. He had a list on a clipboard.

Jasper Glass?

Yes, sir.

Are you related to the absent John Glass, by any chance?

He's my brother.

Valerie Anderson and Jasper Glass both scanned the room.

I guess he must have missed class today, perhaps he's sick, said Jasper. That happens to him sometimes.

It's an unfair load on his partner, Mr. Glass. He's aware of the five-thousand-word essay due later this year?

Yes, said Valerie, the history of medicine. We've started to think about it. So has he.

Mr. Glass's partner is not going to have an easy time of it, all alone, his tablemate *in absentia*.

No, sir, said Jasper. I'll keep my eyes peeled. He'll be here.

The professor turned away, rapped on the adjoining table and said, begin, young doctors. Follow the manual, it's foolproof. It's been field-tested here for fifty years. We've never lost a patient yet.

There was laughter then and they all set to work.

It's funny, said Jasper, I saw him outside ten minutes ago. It's not like he wasn't here.

So he vanished?

He's got a problem of some kind. It's up to him to solve it. What do you think of that, by the way? said Jasper.

What? she said.

The penis.

She looked at the cadaver, up and down, head to foot.

What do I know about bodies? she said.

He'd fallen for her already, after ten minutes in her company.

Okay then, let's go, let's start, he said.

They looked at the manual. Then they pulled the body to one side, log-rolled it so it was face down and started in on the buttocks. They first dissected the superficial nerves that spread like spiderwebs with the consistency of string. Their hands, by necessity, touched frequently within the flesh, flesh made slippery by the overly ample subcutaneous fat that rubbed off on their gloves and stuck piecemeal to their fingertips. Their man was significantly overweight, so they had a heavy go of it. There were two inches of glistening fat to hack through, down to gluteus maximus, the first muscle they'd ever seen, which rose up to them slowly as though from the underworld. They dissected tentatively as befit their novice status and then, more persuasively, they prodded with their fingers and cleaved tissue planes. Despite the clinical atmosphere, the white coats, the rubber gloves, the pungency of formaldehyde that pervaded every breath, Jasper found himself harbouring a desire for Valerie Anderson, upon this, the first day they met.

Here, hold that, she said.

He obeyed, the back of his wrist on hers as it worked away at some recalcitrant tissue.

If she warmed to him, some day in the back of his Volkswagen van, they could park anywhere, anytime on any weekday afternoon, make their separate excuses to all and sundry, insert the necessary two or three dimes at an anonymous meter on Hoskin or St. George or Huron Street, and then the two of them could slide through the side door and just do it, they'd go ahead without a word, lock themselves together like praying mantises or Velcro, the curtains of the van pulled tight against the sidewalk, the street, the whole city. They could embark on their own journey of anatomical discovery.

She must have known how he felt. She must have been aware of his longing. The pages of the manual flipped and flipped and the academic year advanced. They spent sixteen hours a week together. Constant desire eroded him. Daily longing displaced the apparent anatomical journey on which he was bound. They traced the course of the vagus nerve together, they pried the friable gallbladder from the undersurface of the liver.

He had a perpetual erection, an erection that impressed itself hopelessly upon the edge of the metal table where the body lay, and even upon the cadaver's innocent thigh, unyielding for hours as he leaned towards Valerie as though he were a necrophiliac.

Jasper, help me with this exposure, she said.

Upon reflection, he realized that his year-long obsession was the cause of his relatively poor grade in anatomy.

Jasper Glass: B–, posted on the board in the hallway.

When the unwitting object of his desire, Valerie Anderson, received an A+ for doing essentially the same work, he should have known she was not equally besotted. But hope sprung eternal in his breast. It wasn't until the fateful poetry class, until the night they met Roberto Moreno, when he observed with sorrow her sudden animation, her jacked-up interest, her hypervitality, it wasn't until then that he semi-admitted—for that was all he would ever do—that she was a lost cause, that he should set his sights elsewhere, that although she was as lovely as the rings of Saturn, he was but a sorry figure beside her.

Shabby, a poor man's Galileo who searched the sky with coloured pieces of glass, through a kaleidoscope, blind and foolish.

Their children were away from home. Both of them, Jasper and John, attended medical school in Toronto and they lived downtown. The house was quiet. Most evenings the professor sat in his study, book-lined wall-to-wall with the French classics alphabetically arranged, some doubled in translation. There, in that tranquil room, William Glass sorted through his shoebox of index cards, his idioms. He cross-referenced them. He shuffled them into categories and subcategories. Often, he composed letters to the University of Windsor Press, letters that queried their publishing schedule for the next quarter or raised issues about fonts, or suggested pagination requirements. Small but critical matters. Most of these letters he typed but never posted. He feared they might exasperate Louise Drabinsky, his editor at the press, a very clever woman but one who often sounded irritated on the phone when he called with his concerns. So he typed his letters, signed them with his fountain pen and filed them away in a thick folder that he kept for that purpose amongst his personal papers.

One afternoon, after several hours of such unsatisfactory activity, he pushed back his chair, and to clear his head from the excruciating minutiae, he began to walk vigorously throughout the house. That was his fitness regimen, up and down the stairs. He counted his steps out loud—one-two-three-four-five—and through all the rooms he walked briskly, through the second floor, the four bedrooms. The house was large, expansive, red brick, and on the exterior western wall, ivy clung. Over the course of this particular walk, he entered Jasper's deserted bedroom and looked out the window. There, on the roof of the Nájera house, on the roof where ice and snow still lay crusted and half melted, were two black squirrels enjoying the spring sunshine. He stopped to observe them. They must have chewed a hole under the roofline just above the eavestrough, for they ran playfully in and out of the attic and cavorted on the shingles and slipped into the eaves again before they scrambled back and disappeared. Their acrobatics were charming.

After that, it became a habit of Professor Glass's to observe them throughout the rest of spring. One of the squirrels developed an abdominal protuberance consistent with pregnancy and for a while she gave up her squirrelly antics and just lay there in the mid-afternoon sun, panting. She had a small tongue, pink. Then, early in May, his wildlife observations were rewarded with the sight of four tiny, hesitant baby squirrels crawling about in the eaves.

Over the weeks that followed, while an Arctic air mass hovered over the city and cold rain fell, the squirrel babies developed confidence enough to roll and tumble together, and it became a daily pleasure of the professor's to watch them and even record some measurements of their growth. For example, they seemed to give up feeding at the breast by the fourth week of their development. He often thought that, had he not been so skilled at languages, he could have been a biologist. He saw himself in a classroom wearing a white smock, with slides and a pointer.

Late one sunny afternoon when he walked into the bedroom to observe his four-legged friends, he glanced down into the neighbours' yard. There was Roberto, with a girl. Roberto had both his arms up and he was holding on to the lower branches of the cherry tree in the centre of the lawn. His feet were on the ground. Before him, with her back to the professor and her face thus obscured, knelt the young woman. She had straight black hair. At first glance, Professor Glass thought that she was adjusting his belt for him, or tying his shoes, or brushing dirt off his trousers. But then he noticed that both her hands were at the back of his jeans, upon his buttocks, and her head was bobbing slightly, slowly, in front of his waist and he realized with a shock that he was observing an act of fellatio. Quickly he averted his glance. He stood back from the window. Then he looked again.

He went downstairs to the kitchen and he said, June, June, come with me, come look.

Your squirrels?

No, no, he said.

Together they went back to their son's empty bedroom, and, standing back, he motioned with his arm.

Look out there, he said, into the backyard.

She peered out the window. Then she looked at him and said, well?

He looked out again and Roberto Moreno was now sitting down, reading a book on the patio, and the girl was sipping from a glass of water or lemonade and placing a sprig of some growth, perhaps a crocus or forget-me-not, in a small, clear vase.

Well? asked June again.

He was embarrassed and he thought, could I have imagined it?

But of course he had not imagined it. He was so taken aback by the contrast of what he had seen, so overt, and what June had seen, so innocent, that all he said to her was something ridiculous like, see what a good time Roberto is having?

She glanced at him as though he were daft and went back down to the kitchen.

When he was alone in the bedroom again and he looked out upon that scene of domesticity, the boy and the girl who sat together so primly and comfortably after such a daring outdoor activity, he mentally timed the number of seconds it had taken him to walk downstairs to fetch June, and then to return, not hurriedly, step by step up the stairway, steps one through nine—he counted them again—and then for the two observers to cross the bedroom and to look down from the high window. He wondered if it were possible, in that amount of time, for Roberto Moreno to ejaculate and for the girl, whoever she was, to disengage or whatever she did—hence the drink of lemonade—and then for the two of them to compose themselves so quickly, as they had apparently done. He was flabbergasted. Also, he was grateful that he had withdrawn from the window, for he realized that Roberto Moreno would have, at his spasming moment of culmination, rolled his eyes back, back in his head in such a way that he would have scanned the blank wall opposite, the red brick of the Glass house, and his eyes would have travelled farther up, up, up to the window at which the professor stood, transfixed, as transfixed as Roberto Moreno must have been himself, at his moment of release.

Luisa Sanchez did not go the airport with Roberto Moreno.

They sat together at one of the small tables inside Café Flores. They shared a *pastelito*. Coffee was free after the first cup.

I have my ticket, he said, the money is spent, the die is cast.

Roberto, she said and she leaned forward as she did so, Roberto, you and your stupid ticket, you are making a big mistake. Poets need their own habitat to breathe. A parabolist will die outside of Mexico, and be fore-warned, Roberto Moreno, that you will be dead for me the moment you leave. I don't really care for you any-way, I never did.

He thought about their lovemaking, the nights and mornings and afternoons in the bedroom she shared with her roommate.

Roberto, when flight number whatever-whatever-whatever you have, Aeroméxico, raises itself off the tarmac, nothing in my life will change, but you, Roberto, you will be dead. You need chaos, gaps, holes, heat to be yourself, you know that. Those are the last things you will find in Canada. You will be lost there, lost.

It was the first time she had ever spoken to him in this way. Usually she was morose, quiet, introspective.

When she finished her outburst, they sat in Café Flores for a while longer but they didn't speak. They picked at the remnants of the small pastry. She looked out the window at the passing hustle in the street and then she left. She didn't say another word. She just threw her purse over her shoulder and, instead of turning homeward as he hoped, for then he could have watched her from his vantage point until she disappeared and thus had her in his life for another two minutes, she turned the other way, instinctively.

———

At Grad's Restaurant, Roberto Moreno cut into his apple pie. They had bought him a piece and he ate it with gusto, as though there were nothing wrong.

Hmm, he said, there are no apples like this in Mexico.

I hope not, they said.

Then he asked, what groups of poets are there in Canada?

They had already named all the individual poets they could think of, those who wrote in English, although they qualified their response, saying they were medical students, that no doubt they were out of touch with the newest trends in poetry.

Yes, perhaps you are, he said, but tell me about groups or movements, poets who share a sensibility, a direction.

Well, they said, there's the Montreal poets. They were a group. They met and discussed their work. They critiqued each other and drank wine to excess on rue Chestnut, rue St-Denis, rue Guy.

Here in Toronto, said Valerie Anderson, as far as I know, poets are loners.

He looked at her and she looked back.

How strange, Valerie, said Roberto, because in Mexico City there are hundreds of poetry movements. Poets feed off each other, they achieve strength by numbers, wisdom from exposure to each other's work.

Here he began to speak less casually, as though he were assuming the role of a teacher, which in fact he was.

For example, he said, sipping his coffee with a grimace, I am a parabolist and within a few blocks, within my neighbourhood in Mexico City, there are many groups, subgroups, splinter groups and coalescing groups, groups that are not exclusive. It is possible for a poet to belong to more than one as long as their aims are not antithetical. So, in Mexico City, clustered around the area of the national university, as we are here in Toronto, we have, to name a few of the more prominent movements in our poetry—and here he began to walk his thumb along his fingertips to enumerate—all the usual political groups such as the Marxists and the Maoists, but we also have those who have rejected all of that, the concretists, the fluidists, the historicists, urbanists, imagists, antilyricists, adjectivalists, imitationists, infrarealists, reversists, phenomenologists, sensualists, fabulists, grammaticists, ellipticists, caesuracists, semicolonists . . .

It seemed Roberto could have gone on endlessly—his command of English was extraordinary—had the students not raised their arms and cried, almost as one, stop Professor!

Well, you see what I mean, he said.

Jasper Glass then said, Mr. Moreno, some of our Toronto poets get together and publish their work. The House of Anansi. Coach House Press.

Oh, that's what we do in Mexico City too. It's important for friends to publish each other's work. That's how something gets to be known, before it is recognized, before it rises like cream to the top of the bottle of milk.

Valerie Anderson asked Roberto Moreno if he could explain the term *parabolist* to them. The name he had used for himself, for his own work.

Parabolist? Well, class, you are scientists, you all know the shape of a parabola, how it reflects input to a central core, how it concentrates energy in its solar plexus, so to speak. A poet who is a true parabolist arranges words and ideas in such a way that the energy input burns. Then it explodes in the gut and the chest, where feelings are the deepest, where you can hardly breathe.

Whoa, they all thought.

Roberto Moreno laughed.

Do you believe that? he asked.

Then they noticed that the time for their class to end had long passed, and they all had chemistry lab in the morning. Everybody trooped out except for Roberto Moreno, Valerie Anderson and Jasper Glass. They were far too excited to sleep.

Let's go for a walk, they said.

So they walked all the way from College Street down Spadina to Dundas, then along Dundas to Markham Street, up Markham to College again, and by then it was nearly midnight and they had talked poetry for so long that Valerie Anderson's head had begun to ache.

I'm getting one of my migraines, she said.

How do you know, Valerie? asked Roberto Moreno.

I see wavy lines, a shimmer, then the headache starts. I have to go to bed. Sorry.

They flagged a cab right away.

Church and Isabella, please, Valerie said.

She lived in a high-rise, on the third floor, a sublet. At that hour, there were lots of young girls on Isabella Street, in tight leather boots as high as their thighs.

After they dropped Valerie Anderson off, Jasper Glass and Roberto Moreno closed down the night at the Silver Dollar on Spadina Avenue. They drank rye whisky in shot glasses and after that they walked a long distance in an extraordinary downpour, in a rain such as Jasper had never seen.

Like Mexico has come to Canada, Roberto, he said.

Eventually the night came to an end as it often does for poets, be it in Mexico City or in Toronto, in laughter, in oblivion, in the kind of delirious forgetfulness that was impossible, in retrospect, to ever forget, at least for Roberto Moreno.

He had much less to drink that night than Jasper Glass.

The only one who did go to the airport with Roberto, from the Zócalo square, was Isabela Cruz. She was just a friend but when she said she wanted to see him off, he was grateful for the company. He paid her fare on the bus both ways. She was very intense, too much so for his taste in ordinary times but on this, the occasion of his departure, her intensity seemed appropriate. She surprised him somewhat when she started to recite in a subdued whisper, as they sat together in the back of the bus, the entire unabridged version of her own *Words for a Departing Revolutionary.* The longer she read, the more animated and more vocal she became until, at the finale, as they pulled into the terminal, her voice rang throughout the entire bus like a volley of gunshots. Onomatopoeic, powerful, uncompromising. She was a parabolist all right, in the supreme sense of the word. By then many of the other passengers, unable to avoid hearing her, were in tears, and as they disembarked, they reached for her hand. Thank you, they said, thank you, as though they had received solace on the way to their own executions rather than entertainment upon leaving for a jaunt to Taxco. Isabela looked at them fiercely and she turned to him and said, Roberto, nothing like that could happen in Canada.

He didn't know what to say to her. Now he'd had two warnings. He took his suitcase from the rack and stepped down to the sidewalk and, from behind the window, she raised her fist in the air. Then the bus drove away and he walked into the terminal.

A few days after the poetry class, Roberto Moreno called Valerie Anderson. She was in the phone book. There were lots of Andersons but not too many *V*'s.

Perhaps we can spend the day together, he said.

Sure, she said, okay.

She had just finished another of the interminable sets of examinations they were subjected to at the Faculty of medicine, and there was a lull of a few days, a long weekend before the next semester was to begin. Clinical medicine, in hospitals. So it was a hiatus for her, the sun was out, and the cool rain that had settled in for much of the spring had taken the day off too.

We'll go to the island, she said.

The island?

He had no idea there were islands in Toronto.

So they took the subway to Union Station. The subway cars were crowded and they both hung on to the metal poles for support, and it was inevitable, the way the subway cars swayed on the turns, that they jostled each other and stood closer together than would have been natural otherwise.

At Union Station, they walked the rest of the way to the ferry docks. It was festive and crowded with children. There was a strong wind in the harbour, whitecaps slapped against the side of the vessel. *Sam McBride*, it said on the bridge, up high.

This is beautiful, he said, the air is fresh. I like the waves, Valerie.

She had sandwiches in a bag and a book of poetry and they went to a distant beach and put a blanket down on the sand. They looked out upon what might have been an ocean. Gulls circled, cormorants flew by, uninterested.

She read to him after their lunch.

Oh my girls, as you rush to me with your swift hullos
I see over your shoulders the years like a fascist army
Advancing against your love, burning your maiden
*   villages,*
I see your still minorities destroyed in lethal chambers
Your defenseless dreams shot backward into the pit,
And I see
The levelling down of all your innocent worlds.

That's by Miriam Waddington, she said.

Then the air cooled and they walked back to the ferry terminal. It was still only three in the afternoon. They returned to the city and walked along Eastern Avenue to the Beaches, and on the boardwalk they watched the dogs, and geese walked or teetered back and forth, and more small birds flew by in clusters. They went up Coxwell Avenue to Queen Street and along Queen Street to Kingston Road, nearly to the racetrack.

Hours passed. They sauntered as much as they walked and they visited several small bookstores and then a larger one, an emporium of some kind with books in Spanish. They stayed there a long time.

After they left, Roberto showed her three books.

Hasta el tornado, by Alfredo Reyes, he said, and this is *Corazón,* by Guillermo Pasqua, and *La paloma negra,* by Jorge O'Hara.

I didn't see you buy those, she said.

No, no, I just took them, he said.

All three books were thin, almost like wafers, and as he flipped the pages Valerie saw words widely scattered over the otherwise white pages.

Minimalists, he said, they're okay.

He had stolen the books even though she was there beside him the whole time and had seen nothing.

Why steal them? she asked.

He said he stole books out of habit, that he read them carefully and would sometimes return them if he liked the atmosphere in the bookstore.

It seems unfair to steal books from people who love books, from stores like that, she said.

It's unfair to charge for work that poets do for free, he said. In Mexico, no one pays for books. Everyone I know in Mexico steals books. Some have amassed vast libraries.

But someone must bring books to public attention, in bookstores, she said.

Valerie, he said, the whole point of poetry in Mexico, when published, is to be stolen. It is the highest accolade.

You mean no one sells books at all?

He laughed.

Well, yes, Octavio Paz sells books to the middle class. A parabolist, though, would not actually purchase a book by Octavio Paz. He would just take it from the shelf if it interested him.

She made a mental note to look up this man, Octavio Paz.

Are there female poets in Mexico City? she asked.

By then they had walked all the way back to Yonge Street and they went underground and waited for the next train.

Yes, he said, there are as many female poets as there are male poets. Some of them, of course, are parabolists. They hang out together. There is no difference, male or female, except for sex.

Do you mean gender? she asked.

No, I mean sex, poets often have sex together in Mexico.

They fall in love, she said.

That too, he said.

She said the only person she knew who stole books in Toronto, usually from the University of Toronto

Bookstore, was the brother of Jasper Glass, John Glass, and she felt that John Glass had some personal problems, including kleptomania.

Maybe it's different here, he said, but if this John Glass stole a book of mine, he'd be welcome to it.

Do you have a book published? she asked.

No, he said.

Is that part of parabolism, not to have a book?

It works out the same because parabolists are a lot like attack dogs and they are not popular with publishers.

Then Roberto said that one of the worst poems he ever wrote was published in an anthology of new poets and he was ashamed of it. The anthology was no good, and his own poem, the one they had chosen, was not totally serious. He was embarrassed by the whole affair.

That is my publication history, he said.

Do you know any famous poets? she asked.

No, not really, but there are some with a reputation. Perhaps, someday, Isabela Cruz, Roberto Bolaño. Fame, obscurity—for a poet it's almost the same thing, isn't it? Twenty years later, you never know.

So that is your milieu, so different from mine, she said.

They got off the subway at Eglinton, took the bus up Avenue Road to Glengrove Avenue and walked the short distance to Roberto's house. His aunt and his uncle were not home.

Valerie, would you like some lemonade?

Sure, she said, *limonada*.

They went out into the backyard, to the patio, with the full pitcher. He carried it carefully and put his new books down too, on the patio table. He fanned them out in an array like the tail of a peacock. Then he poured two small glasses of lemonade.

There, he said, these ice cubes, they rattle like a snake, don't they?

I've never heard a rattlesnake, she said.

It's a nice sound, really, he said. It means they don't want to hurt you, to touch you at all. Because if they do, they expend their venom, they have nothing left.

So they rattle in self-defence, she said.

Yes.

I never thought of it that way. I thought it was aggressive.

No, not at all, he said, it's more like a plea.

They stood close together as they had on the subway. The sun came back out, it was still warm, the wind had stopped entirely and Roberto took his shirt off, as he must have done in Mexico in such weather.

They leaned against each other and he was mostly skin and bone and ribs and they each drank lemonade and she felt as he brushed against her, on the outside of her hip, that he had an erection. But that was no surprise. He was like everyone else in that regard.

He moved against her and kissed her once on her forehead. Then he stopped and he went down to the tree in the yard. She thought it was a cherry tree.

Is that a cherry tree? she asked.

Yes, I think so.

The leaves had just started to come out. It was sparse and open back there and Roberto put his arms up and with both hands he clasped the lowest branch of the tree. His feet were still on the ground but his arms were high, as though he were hanging there.

Well, she thought, why not?

She looked around. All the houses, the red-brick one next door in particular that loomed close, there was no one there. The windows were blank, reflective.

She put down her glass of lemonade and walked to Roberto Moreno. She knelt before him on the ground. He looked at her but did not move. With her fingers shaking a bit, she opened his buttoned fly and with some difficulty extracted his penis through the opening she had created. Rigid, he was circumcised, that she knew, and she closed her eyes and put her lips, her mouth, her tongue over the tip of it, and as she had previously imagined but now actually did, she moved her head, her mouth back and forth, and pulled with her tongue and teeth over the glans, and it happened fast, she was surprised how fast. He ejaculated, she tasted it, the sudden warmth. She swallowed it and the whole episode lasted only ten or twenty seconds and throughout it all, Roberto said nothing, nothing at any rate that she could hear, but at the end he said, Val, Valerie.

She opened her eyes. His hands caressed her hair.

She put his softening penis back into his pants as though he were incapable of doing so himself, and perhaps he was. She buttoned his fly and got up from her knees and went back to the patio. She drank lemonade, she felt the taste of what she had done commingle and dissipate. Roberto sat down beside her. He laid his head on her shoulder. She started to read from one of his stolen books and he gently took it from her.

Valerie, I want to do the same for you.

Okay, but let's go inside for that, she said.

So she picked up the pitcher of lemonade and the ice cubes again rattled inside it—they still sounded like a snake—and just then the man next door came down into his yard with a rake in his hand. She said hello to him, she knew who he was. He was the father of two of her classmates. He said hello to her but maybe he didn't remember her. He looked at her as though he were confused, as if he'd both seen and never seen her before.

Well, she was in too much of a hurry to be concerned about that. She waved over her shoulder to him again, quickly, and she smiled, and then she went inside with Roberto Moreno.

In her fourth and final year of medicine, Marnie Kennedy picked out Jasper Glass, still just in his first year, to be her temporary lover. That was what she needed, something temporary, to while away the time.

She was in the library. She was walking through to the magazine rack, to the journals, when she saw him all by himself, studying with his feet up on another chair, and she'd seen him around before but it was only then, at that moment, that she realized how wistful and handsome he looked, and the thought occurred to her that she didn't need to be celibate for the whole six months just because her fiancé was away at Johns Hopkins, that she could exercise her natural desires and keep them strong, for Christian, by staying active in the sexual arena while he was away. Thus, when he returned for their wedding, already booked at Grace Church on-the-Hill just thirty-two weeks away, she would be prepared and ready and in no way falsely naive, or out of practice. It made no sense to her to have downtime. She was twenty-three years old. A waste, pining away by herself for that long. And she was confident that she could have Jasper Glass because she had never seen him with anyone but that dark-haired girl, whoever she was, and it was obvious the dark-haired girl had no interest in Jasper Glass as anything more than a friend.

So she went over to the table at which Jasper sat and said to him, touching the chair on which his feet lay, may I sit here?

He looked up. He knew her by her reputation for academic excellence—much praised—and for her undeniable beauty, and for the fact she was engaged to be married in the not-too-distant future. Her hair was very different from Valerie Anderson's, as day was to night. Blond ringlets fell to her shoulders. Her eyes were blue, as blue as his own, so looking at her was a bit like looking into a mirror.

Puzzled, he moved his feet for her.

Sure, he said, sit down. By all means.

He looked around at the empty tables.

What are you studying? she asked. Let me see.

She put her own books on the desk, beside his, as though she was settling in, and pulled Jasper's notes towards her.

Aha, the Krebs citric acid cycle.

It's tough going, said Jasper, I get stuck.

Where?

Right now, at the electron transfer.

Oh really? I'll show you, if you like.

Thanks, he said.

And he was grateful to her because he actually was stuck, but he was even more grateful for the attention bestowed upon him in that large, empty room by this girl whom he knew only from afar.

Jasper had his pen in hand and, anticipating instruction, he placed a new piece of paper on the table. Marnie leaned over, from his right side, her own pen poised, and as she did so he noticed that her breast, her left breast, came down directly on his right wrist, essentially immobilizing it.

She appeared not to notice. It must have been perfectly natural for her, he concluded. Obviously, she was at home in that body of hers, and for five minutes she drew equations for him, arrows that went in circles from acetyl-CoA to ATP and beyond, and the Krebs cycle became perfectly clear to Jasper Glass. He could tell how certain and confident she was of the science, though he was somewhat distracted by the softness of her breast and the slightly firmer nipple that grazed and flattened against his wrist repeatedly, up and down, an action that turned his thoughts at right angles to mathematics.

There, she said, get it?

She sat back up, the pressure disappeared.

He looked at her and down at his wrist and back at the paper, the drawings, the equations.

Show me again, he said, the part about ATP.

So she repeated the drawing, but this time her breast did not quite touch his arm. It hovered there a centimetre away, and Jasper accidentally moved his arm up into it.

Oh, sorry, Marnie.

As he said her name it felt foreign to his tongue yet a privilege.

Sorry? she said.

She hadn't noticed at all. She seemed oblivious to her own sexuality, which was strange because to him she was overwhelming. Maybe it had something to do with age and experience.

Take me to a dance on St. George Street, she said.

Me?

It's Friday night. Neither of us should be studying.

I heard you were engaged.

Yes, I'll be married in thirty-two weeks but that's thirty-two weeks away. A long long time.

She twirled her pen around in her hand and he wondered for the first time if maybe she was nervous too.

Where's your fiancé? he asked.

Johns Hopkins, Baltimore. A thousand miles away, the last time I checked.

They walked together up St. George Street in the dark. She had a dramatic coat of suede leather and she held his arm. At a large house north of Lowther Avenue, music was playing and they went inside.

Marnie, everybody said.

They ignored Jasper. All of them were older, but she stayed with him as though he was the sole focus of her interest and they danced, they close-danced, she pressed up against him as though she was not about to get married at all.

What's the name of the band? he asked.

I don't know, I don't care, she said. Oh, it's the Lotos Eaters.

What does your fiancé do? Jasper whispered into the side of her neck.

They were both sweating from the warmth, the closeness of bodies around them.

Tonight? I don't know. He's a biostatistician, a genius, she said.

Then they went into another room that was mostly, but not entirely, deserted. Two other couples were there, doing whatever they were doing by themselves. It was too dark to see. Jasper and Marnie lay down on a couch and at first he lay on top of her and they kissed for an hour and then they rolled on their sides and they stayed like that for another hour and then she rolled on top of him and they kissed some more. They never took off a stitch of clothing that night.

She drove him home in her car.

That was how it started. It came out of nowhere and it got crazy after that for thirty-two weeks, the kind of craziness that was fine with Jasper Glass but why she picked him, he never really knew. He never asked.

On the biochemistry exam a month later, he knew

the Krebs citric acid cycle perfectly. It was burned into his brain. All he had to do was close his eyes and he saw her hand, her pen, the paper, the equations, everything she did.

Jonathan Glass was called John by everyone who knew him and he ended up in the same medical class as his older brother, Jasper, because he was academically clever, very clever once upon a time although that time, unfortunately, did not last forever. His primary teachers advanced him because of his precocity. They "accelerated" him, as it was called, as though he were a racing car, not a human being.

You have a very intelligent and composed child, all the teachers said to his parents, William and June Glass.

So the Glass brothers, though fully fifteen months apart by birth, entered university on the same day, in the same faculty, in the same year as Valerie Anderson, and they were both enrolled in the English literature class, the one now taught by Roberto Moreno. John, however, decided not to attend that evening, unaware of the arrival of their new poetry teacher. Thus he missed out, to his lasting regret, on that pivotal occasion.

Brilliant though he had appeared to be as a child, he nevertheless accomplished the near impossible at the end of that year. He flunked out of the Faculty of Medicine. He failed, he flunked, whatever the past participle of that dreadful word is, and it was near impossible, that underachievement of his, because no one else had ever, within living memory, been cast out from the faculty without a second chance.

Partly, just partly, it was because of bellringers that he failed.

Bellringers. Another name for a particularly difficult exam in anatomy. Stations were set up in a large empty room, separate tables, and upon each table was a cadaver specimen, an unidentified body part that could be a cross-sectioned skull, a half-dissected pelvis, a foot from which all soft tissue had been removed, a small, staring eye like a child's marble, the coronal section of the cervical spine, the musculature of the lips of the oral cavity—anything at all as long as it was human and dead. Upon those myriad anatomical specimens, save the glaring eye, had been hung tiny numbered tags attached by string. One by one, the students were shepherded through in alphabetical order, including one very reluctant and pessimistic John Glass, pencils and paper at the ready. Each student had three minutes per station to identify the numbered tags, and then the bell rang, a tinny disconsolate sound, and on they moved to the next specimen, and were replaced, and moved on, and so it went until, an hour later, they were finished. But for the ringing bell, there was only the shuffling of feet, the sound of breathing, the scratching of pencil on paper and, very occasionally, an exclamation of puzzlement or dismay, for although every student had dissected a cadaver from head to toe, when the various organs were plucked from their usual cavities and laid bare upon a table, all landmarks vanished. They looked entirely different on their own, isolated and thus, to some, unrecognizable. It was so easy for a wrist to look like an ankle, a liver a spleen, a lung a kidney, the labia majora could well be mistaken for scrotum, and only the eye was instantaneously recognizable for what it was. The marks on bellringers were fearfully low for everyone.

That round thing, said John Glass, what was it? A swallowed marble?

A syphilitic eyeball, said Jasper, the pupil was irregular.

Yes, said Valerie, that was pretty straightforward.

It didn't look like an eye to me. I missed that one. And was that a gallbladder on the third table? Please say it was.

No, it was a normal ovarian cyst. They sit there, they can look like gallbladders. Vaguely.

Was that a fracture of the radius?

No, John, the tibia.

Was that a cross-section of the liver or the brain?

The one in the pickle jar? Spleen, I think. Someone with leukemia. Had you been in class, you might have known.

So John Glass did very poorly indeed. Some nights, in the Sigmund Samuel Library, he leafed through *Grant's Atlas of Anatomy* and looked at the pictures like a preschooler. With the names of everything written out, it seemed straightforward. But bellringer after bellringer, down he went. No surprise, after all the anatomy labs he had missed. He was in such a downward spiral that he saw himself, as he wrote in one of his poems, as a kamikaze pilot headed for some smoking funnel, hot steel blowing by his head.

That was an exaggeration, of course.

You're no spirit-wind, no kamikaze, Valerie Anderson said to him.

No?

No, the kamikaze were motivated by higher purpose.

And I'm not?

Not to my knowledge.

Well, said John, I read about one kamikaze pilot who returned to base nine times. They finally shot him. That's me in a bellringer.

Julián Gutiérrez Nájera was Roberto Moreno's uncle. He was married to Roberto's mother's sister, Silvana, and the two of them were childless until that night in February of 1964 when the train from Guadalajara to Ocatlán derailed and rolled down a steep embankment into a reservoir. Roberto was one of only eleven survivors. He was clinging to a log when he was found. The bodies of his parents disappeared downriver along with over two hundred others and no doubt they were swept out to sea, for they were never recovered. That is what the authorities said. As the Nájeras were Roberto's closest relatives, they stepped into the breach. It was the only thing to do and they never regretted it. Roberto was a charming boy even in the aftermath of the tragedy, stoic and sad and tough all at the same time. In school, his performance was well above average. At his parents' funeral, he gave a short oration of his own, which no one expected. After all, he was only ten years old and although no one remembered his exact words—he spoke in a strained voice but it was crystal-clear nevertheless—he made no reference to God or higher powers but spoke instead of Nature, how grateful he was to his mother and father for their lives, and for his life, and Roberto related the arc of his parents' existence, as the Nájeras recalled it, to trilobites and birds. It wasn't maudlin or sentimental at all. There were hundreds present who brought out their handkerchiefs and many of the women broke down completely, including Silvana. Then clods of earth were thrown down on the empty, symbolic coffins with an echo and a thump, much different in timbre, that thump, than the sound made when earth falls on coffins that are occupied.

Roberto cried. Silvana held him in her arms as they walked back to the car. They knew then that he was extraordinary and they made every opportunity to educate him. His own parents had not been able to afford books, but they had many. When it came time for him to go to university, he could have gone anywhere with the marks he had, but Silvana and Julián knew that he would make a fine engineer. They persuaded him to enroll in engineering school at the national university in Mexico City, despite his own desire to embark upon literature as a career.

Roberto, they said, look around you. Look at all the poets and writers, see how they live. You can write all you want as an engineer, in your spare time.

So he went into engineering and attended classes, or so they thought for some time, ignorant as they were about the difficulties of parenting. How everything can appear to be fine on the surface but underneath, where currents run deep, something entirely different is going on, another invisible world. For in fact Roberto never went to engineering school for more than a few weeks before he gravitated, like Newton's apple, back to the poets and the writers, the musicians, the actors, the film directors, the photographers who lived around the university by the dozens, hundreds really, men and women who led lives of marginality.

The Nájeras were understanding once they saw that he had made his choice.

Silvana, said Julián, pull yourself together and remember your dead sister, how she loved to sing and paint.

So they supported Roberto, enough to feed himself, to live a simple life.

Soon, they heard, he became a leader of what were called the parabolists but what they were, these parabolists, what they stood for, they had no idea. Roberto had difficulty explaining it in words they could understand.

It's a bit like focusing the heat of the sun through a magnifying glass upon the palm of your hand, he said.

Also, he continued, there are internal and external parabolists, and then there are the para-parabolists, poets who live and work on the edge of parabolism, who dip into it but who take it even further, where I don't want to go.

Oh, they said.

He spent, or misspent, the next few years surrounded by poets, by long-haired poets and by poets who shaved their heads, by down-and-out poets, poets who worked in bookstores and cafés, by boys with writers' bumps that bled on the third fingers of their right hands, and by girls, mostly beautiful and many of them anorexic, who moved with grace and jagged speed through the streets of Mexico City, their pencil stubs worn down by the passion of words.

Many times, when Julián or Silvana met him by chance on the street, he looked tired, as though he had been up all night. He was always enthusiastic, however, and they never feared that he had dropped into the netherworld of drugs. Then Julián received an offer from the University of Toronto to go to Canada for his sabbatical, for his work in cryotherapy for epithelial tumours. It was a splendid opportunity. They had to rent out their house in Mexico City, otherwise the trip would have been financially suicidal. They offered Roberto the chance to come along and they never dreamed he would accept their offer, though it was heartfelt from both of them, but he surprised them once again. Two months after their own arrival, there was Roberto Moreno at Toronto International Airport, smiling, standing with his two suitcases. One of them was so heavy, so full of books, that Julián had difficulty carrying it and wanted to hire a porter.

No, no, said Roberto, I'm okay with these. Let me take them myself.

He carried both of the suitcases to the parking garage. He said it was easier, with a heavy weight in both hands for balance, and indeed he managed the lengthy trip to the car without difficulty, even through the salt and slush and patches of ice that were so foreign to him.

After the first poetry class, after their long walk together, Jasper and Roberto Moreno dropped Valerie Anderson and her migraine headache at the corner of Church and Isabella.

Take something fast-acting, Jasper said to her. Don't let it take hold.

The streets were crowded at that hour with prostitutes, police cars, addicts, pimps, and lovers both homo- and heterosexual paired in shadows under trees. The two of them walked Valerie to the door and then returned to the waiting cab.

Roberto said, why does Valerie live in this district?

He must have feared she was supplementing her income with some activity in the sex trade.

Jasper laughed.

Valerie lives here because it's a good deal. She answered an ad in the student paper, the rent was low, it turned out to be a quiet building. That's all. Moreover, her roommate's hardly ever home.

No? Why is that?

Oh, she's got something going on with a plastic surgeon, an allergist, I forget which.

Valerie does?

No, no, the roommate, I can't even remember her name.

The cab pulled away. Jasper leaned forward to speak to the driver.

Bloor Street West, he said. But you know, come to think of it, Roberto, it's kind of hard to imagine an allergist with a sex life so it must be a plastic surgeon. Surgeons are restless, they prey on girls.

And then he added, it's a nice place, Valerie's.

As though he had been invited up, as though he had been there a hundred times.

You are not her boyfriend? asked Roberto.

I'm her lab partner in anatomy, said Jasper. We talk about things, that's all.

His own attraction to Valerie, his hesitant, his fruitless pursuit of her. He was totally in the dark when it came to Valerie Anderson, what she did for sexual expression, if she did anything at all. She had friends, all kinds of them, unusual ones, but she kept her own life so close to the vest that she remained to him an enigma despite the sixteen hours a week they spent together, breathing the same air. But the last thing Jasper Glass wanted to do was give Roberto Moreno encouragement of any kind. It wasn't that simple, because he liked them both. Roberto seemed one of the most open and friendly men he'd ever met, but Jesus, there was a wide field out there and why Valerie, he felt, why her? Roberto Moreno could pick and choose.

The cab turned onto Bloor and headed west.

Roberto, I'd stay away from her. I tell you, she's got a boyfriend in prison, he gets out in a week.

Roberto smiled at that, looked at Jasper Glass and said nothing.

Jasper glanced at the numbers that flicked past on the meter, three dollars already. Mentally, he shuffled through his wallet. He could afford it, almost for sure.

Roberto, he said, it's only midnight, let's go to the Silver Dollar.

What's that?

Just a place to drink, that's all. It's on me, a celebration.

A celebration? For what, Jasper?

For the poetry class, that's what.

But we never got started on the poems. But sure, let's go, let's see more of your city.

He didn't even ask about the boyfriend in prison, as though he didn't care.

At the Silver Dollar, the street was empty. Spadina Avenue, a few garbage cans, a cat, the neon sign that flickered half broken. Inside it was the same, almost deserted.

Jasper ordered rye whisky, two doubles.

This is Canadian whisky, he said, it's got a reputation for being a serious drink.

Like tequila, said Roberto.

He had perfect teeth that were revealed when he spoke, when he smiled like that.

I guess so, said Jasper, like tequila all right. Not that I've had much of that particular drink.

Keep the tab open, Jasper said to the waitress.

She wore a cocktail dress that was tight to her body, with spangles, and she was the only waitress on that night. It was dark inside.

As she made her way back to the bar, Jasper said, Jesus, Roberto, it's like the River Styx in here.

Yes, the River Styx, I know what you mean.

The rye whisky kicked in fast for Jasper Glass.

Roberto, you know I write music, I write all the words. That's why I like poetry. Music, poetry and music, they're the same thing.

The liquor seemed to have no effect on Roberto Moreno.

I agree with you, Jasper, one hundred per cent. But maybe, Jasper, he said, we're both being simplistic when we say that.

He kept repeating the name, Jasper, Jasper, as he talked.

Yes, Jasper said, maybe we are simplistic a bit.

He had no clue what Roberto Moreno meant.

You see, Jasper, when you have put the music into the skeleton of the poem, into its bones, then you have to cut it out, you have to cut it out, sever it, throw it away.

Throw it away?

Yes, it has served its purpose, Jasper. Take away the music, then you're left with a poem you are not ashamed of. They are not the same thing after all, music and poetry.

They drank for a minute in silence.

Odysseus, Odysseus, said Roberto Moreno.

Jasper thought he saw what he meant. Odysseus tied himself to the mast to avoid the beauty of music, to get to where he really wanted to go.

The mast, Jasper said, the beauty.

Exactly. But I tell you, Jasper, that is not my own theory alone but the theory of our group of poets. Parabolists.

The waitress materialized beside them and Jasper said, six more of these rye whiskys please, and she came back with them five minutes later and then vanished.

Time passed and the table wobbled and she came by with the tab and said, okay, you boys, closing time.

Roberto reached out his hand and took the bill and said, no, Jasper, on me. I will pay this bill.

Jasper tried to stop him but no matter what he said, Roberto would hear no more of it.

Roberto, Roberto, let's go to a place I know on Shaw Street. They serve liquor there still, there's no closing time. Well, sunrise.

Okay, said Roberto Moreno, whatever you like, that's okay with me.

It was pouring rain when they left the Silver Dollar, a downpour.

Tropical topical, Jasper said, I've never seen it like this.

He waved his arms in the air.

Tropical, yes, Roberto said, it rains like this at home.

They walked along College to Shaw Street. A police-man stopped them briefly at the corner of Bathurst.

Are you boys okay?

Then the policeman went away.

They found Shaw Street but they never found the after-hours club. Jasper seemed confused.

Oh well, he laughed.

They wandered for ten or fifteen minutes. Down came the pelting rain upon them and they were soaked head to foot, their hair plastered flat and it was so warm that finally Jasper pulled his shirt off. Then he sat on the curb beside the park that runs on the east side of Shaw Street. He still smelled like Crisco. His skin was soft and thick with it, like grease, twenty-four hours old now almost to the minute. Rain sluiced down on them and Roberto Moreno sat down too, on the curb.

Valerie Anderson, Jasper said.

Why did he say her name?

Their feet were in the gutter and the tropical topical rain washed over them and Jasper thought he saw some of his Crisco float down the storm drain, then down the Humber River to Lake Ontario.

Then his night went blank.

He woke up in his own bed, put there by some agency he could not remember. But it must have been Roberto Moreno. The rain, the downpour had had no effect at all on his skin, on the Crisco. His bedsheets were thick, twisted and coated with it, and great clumps of white paste were still stuck to his chest. Globs of it on his thighs. The clock on the dresser said noon. Already he'd missed anatomy, Valerie, the dissection of the brachial plexus.

Well, there was nothing he could do about it so he picked up his guitar and he played "*Oh the cuckoo, she's a pretty bird*." Then he played "Guantanamera" and sang with a fake Spanish accent.

Roberto Moreno, he thought, quite the guy.

He turned on the shower and it seemed to him, as he scrubbed off the last of the Crisco, that all songs he'd ever heard had something to do with desire.

Name me one song that doesn't. Even birdsong. Show me a poem without music.

He towelled off and, because he was a medical student, he knew he had a headache. He diagnosed it right there on the spot, a hangover from rye whisky.

He took two Aspirin and set out for school. There was still the afternoon.

Olé, he said.

Valerie Anderson stood by herself at the side of their mutual cadaver and waited. It was unusual for Jasper Glass not to be there. He was usually early, if anything, eager to talk, ready to go. Not only that, he had a ritual of sorts for the opening cut of the anatomical day. It involved a stance, a gesture with his arm, once or twice even a pirouette.

Let's not be tentative, Valerie, let's cut. He's already dead, right? One quick slice, like this, like this right over to . . . here. There! No screwing around, notice, that's how we do it. It's already done, look. You know, Valerie, many have commented on it, how we make a fine pair. Unlike our nervous Nellie friends across the table who are pussyfooting their way beneath the skin like trembling aspens. We are not like them at all! We are surgeons. These patients? They don't bleed, they ooze formaldehyde. Why hold back? Why hold back in this, Valerie, why hold back in anything?

She had to admit that when they had the chance to go to the Toronto General Hospital and sit in the observation room overlooking the OR, that's just how the real surgeons did it. They were fast, confident. So

Jasper was right. There was something to be said for speed and dexterity.

But by eight-thirty that morning, it was obvious Jasper was a no-show so she looked around for help. Wallace was also by himself. No surprise. His lab partner, John Glass, never showed up at all so Wallace, by necessity, had become skilled and independent.

She walked over to him.

Mind if I join you for this?

He looked up at her.

Golly, for sure, Valerie. No Jasper today?

Not today, it seems. I don't know where he is.

The two of them worked together. After an hour, they were right down to the brachial plexus, the tangle of nerves, arteries and veins that make up the axilla, the armpit. In a living person, of course, those arteries and veins would burst like geysers on any slip of the knife. Not here in the anatomy lab, though. The blood vessels of these dead ones, their bodies willed to science, had all been filled, by some mysterious process, with red and blue latex rubber. No longer could those vessels ooze, spray or pulse in hemorrhagic gouts of red. So Valerie held the retractors and time went by and Wallace teased out all the structures. They paged through the manual and read aloud to each other.

Now and then, in the quiet times, Valerie Anderson found herself thinking about parabolists. It seemed, if she understood it right, that to be a parabolist, you had to intensify your poetry, crank it up, make it hyper-real. Whatever that meant.

You think, Wallace, you think Roberto would like to see this?

This? These bodies? The new poetry teacher? asked Wallace.

Yes. This is about as hyper-real as it gets.

Anyone would be interested in this, Valerie.

Within a month, she knew they'd be inside the abdominal cavity. She and Jasper Glass and the others would then see the viscera, shiny, wet, slippery—the stomach, the bowels, the liver and spleen.

They'd get Roberto Moreno to come by, bend over and take a look inside.

Look, they'd say, there's realism. The heart and the lungs. This is what we are, we're animals. That's all we are.

But that would be concrete thinking, not deep at all. Certainly not parabolism. The sight of a dissected body likely would impress the young poetry teacher, but not in any metaphorical way.

Still, it would be interesting to have him there, to see what was once so vigorous, so alive, now dead and pulled apart and the students all standing around in lab coats, as Jasper had once said, like white crows on roadkill.

The phone rang at the University of Windsor Press. Professor Glass was convinced he could hear it ring two hundred miles away, but it sounded as close as the office next door. Though he had never met her personally, he imagined Louise Drabinsky in a sky-blue dress reaching for the receiver. She had an expectant air, or a puzzled one, or an irritated one. He wasn't sure.

Perhaps it's Professor Glass, she'd be thinking.

He always called her around the same time, four-thirty on Fridays.

She wore horn-rimmed glasses for all the reading she did. With contact lenses, her eyes would be bleary by this time of the afternoon. She would adjust the glasses on her nose. She'd have a Gilbey's when she got home, just like he'd have a beer or two. Maybe have the beer before, maybe that would be better for the courage he needed to summon up.

Needless to say, she wouldn't have his manuscript right in front of her. These days, she never did. It was tucked away in an office down the hall, almost ready for the final stage, for the printer. *A Living Collection of Idioms in French*.

Unfortunately, *Living* was the operative, trouble-some word. The constant turnover of idioms had been enough to drive them both a little crazy over the past five years. But that was how relationships grew stronger, in the professor's opinion. Under stress. Or duress. He wasn't sure if she felt the same way.

Louise, he'd say if she picked up the phone, listen to me. Take the phrase in English: *you can lead a horse to water but you can't make him drink*. We need this indexed, Louise, under five separate entries. *You, Lead, Horse, Water* and *Drink*. Otherwise a reader could miss it entirely. As it stands, my book is severely under-indexed, catastrophically so.

I understand your point of view, Bill, but if every idiom were so indexed, soon the index would dwarf the book itself. It would be ludicrous.

Louise, please. I understand the constraint of resources. I know that money is finite. I am a family man, I am familiar with budgets. But how can a serious scholar tolerate a shoddy index?

Bill, we have the resources to index that particular idiom only under *Horse* and *Water*. That's it. Don't ask me again.

The phone kept ringing. She must be out of the office. Was she out in the parking lot now, outside the press, with her sky-blue dress, getting into a Chevrolet? He couldn't be sure. The Detroit River would be sweeping past, a glinting silver-blue against the backdrop of Motor City.

On the twentieth ring, he hung up.

He'd call her back early Monday morning, catch her by surprise. Really, it was too bad she didn't speak French. She'd understand a lot better if she did. The French, they had their priorities straight, they didn't care about cost. Budgets went out the window when it came to the protection, the promulgation of their language. The French would throw money at his idioms as if those idioms were girls on stage at the Folies-Bergère.

Louise, he'd say. The French? Guess what! They bought a hundred thousand copies of my book!

Oh, God, if only that happened.

She'd be on top of the world then, Louise Drabinsky. She'd pick up on the first ring. There'd be a thrill in her voice.

Jasper Glass, Roberto Moreno's new friend, did not notice the disparity in consumption but he drank a lot more than Roberto the night they went to the Silver Dollar. Jasper ordered Canadian whisky, rye whisky, a drink that wasn't really to Roberto's taste. It was new to Roberto, it had a strange sweetness, so he just sipped from his glass to be polite and rattled the ice around. He was not in a mood for excess. Already the night had been wonderful. He had met a girl who reminded him in her physical appearance of Luisa Sanchez and he had discussed poetry with her and with her classmates. So, as they sat at the Silver Dollar, Roberto Moreno shifted and rotated full glasses of whisky towards Jasper.

Hey, Jasper, you drink this.

And Jasper did. He seemed glad to drink the whisky although he already looked so very tired, with dark circles under his eyes. But he summoned the energy from somewhere. He spoke about music and poetry and girls with an enthusiasm that was contagious.

In many ways, for Roberto, it was like being home in Mexico City, for there they spoke of exactly the same things, plus politics. But politics did not seem to be on the horizon here, at least with Jasper Glass and his friends. They seemed unaware of class oppression. So the two of them talked and the whisky came and went on the waitress's tray and all in all he might have had three drinks to Jasper Glass's eight or ten. Sometimes, while Jasper's lips moved and words tumbled from him, Roberto Moreno thought about Valerie Anderson, the girl they had dropped off in what appeared to him to be the middle of a sex district. Valerie Anderson of medium height and dark hair worn shoulder length, and, in contrast to the girls he had known in Mexico, girls who wore bright red lipstick and mascara of the blackest hue and who were as gaudy as tropical birds, Valerie Anderson wore no makeup at all. She dressed in the simplest way but exuded—he had felt it from across the table at Grad's Restaurant—a smouldering power and strength and conviction, a total respect for poetry, for the written word, for the emotional substrate that moved writers to write. Had he met Valerie Anderson under any other circumstance, when he was not in a professorial role, he would have told her immediately that she had made an extraordinary impact upon him. A beautiful girl with none of the painful mannerisms of most beautiful women, she moved and spoke as though she were unconscious of her effect on the world around her, or, if she were conscious of such an effect, as if she wished to negate it.

Then, as though in his increasing drunkenness he could read Roberto's mind, Jasper Glass leaned farther forward over the table at the Silver Dollar and mentioned her by name.

Valerie Anderson, he said, my lab partner. She really does have a boyfriend just released from prison.

Roberto almost laughed then, though he was touched by the transparent attempt to deflect his interest from Valerie Anderson, the boyfriend in prison being so ludicrous that even he, Jasper Glass, broke a smile when he said it. They dropped the subject as the waitress came around with the bill.

Closing time, boys, she said.

So they walked out into the night together and there was a downpour of rain as is common in parts of Mexico. It was quite familiar to Roberto, but Jasper Glass was flabbergasted by it—that was the word he used—he stood in the rain and waved his arms and he staggered in it and exclaimed how amazing it was, this deluge of water that came down with such force that even streetlights were invisible twenty yards away, isolating them from their surroundings as though they were on a stage set, and even more amazing was the fact that the rain did not spend itself quickly but instead, over the next two hours, increased in intensity and was accompanied by a dramatic rise in temperature. Not only did it look tropical but it felt that way too, a sodden warmth, an Amazonian jungle heat in the midst of a northern city. Later, they heard that the Don and Humber rivers had overflowed their banks for the first time since 1954, but no lives were lost on this occasion. At least not from flooding.

I know a place on Shaw Street, Jasper said, shouting over the noise of the deluge. We can get a drink there after hours.

So off they went. Jasper knew where he was going and they walked for half an hour or so until they came to a park where the trees shed water in rivulets and rivers of water percolated through the grass onto the roadway, and Jasper took his shirt off and swung it around his hips and tied it there and he started to sing "Guantanamera."

For you, Roberto, he said, laughing.

He had a nice tenor voice, though only snatches of it were audible through the rain. They stood directly under a street sign that said SHAW STREET.

Okay, Roberto, he shouted, not much farther now.

Then Roberto Moreno slipped and fell down and they both sat on the curb for a few minutes and Roberto noticed that Jasper Glass's torso was coated or encrusted with swaths of white cream. He looked at it, puzzled.

Don't worry, it's just Crisco!

Crisco?

Yes, he shouted almost straight into Roberto's ear. It's a type of shortening. We coat ourselves with it in Canada to squeeze through small openings.

A sexual lubricant? Roberto wondered.

But before Roberto could ask his friend anything further, Jasper shouted, jumped up and ran down and across the street as though possessed. He disappeared into the rain. Roberto followed. But the visibility on Shaw Street was terrible, down to zero, a streetlight broken or out of order. Perhaps there was a row of houses on the far side, in the shadows. Roberto wasn't sure.

Down came the rain harder. Roberto Moreno hit the curb on the other side of the street and nearly tripped. Jasper Glass was only five feet away, getting up from the ground now, crawling over a girl who lay half in, half out of the gutter. Her head was actually in the street and her dress was pulled up, torn. Water coursed around her, a river. She was not moving. And now, on the far side of the girl, a man clambered to his feet. He wore a T-shirt, his jeans were unzipped at the waist.

Violador, said Roberto Moreno.

Then he saw the man had a knife. Jasper must have seen it too because he backed off suddenly, away from the injured girl, and, in the midst of that tropical rain, Roberto Moreno suddenly felt at home. He laughed, he stepped forward and positioned himself beside the girl and in front of his new friend, Jasper Glass. The man in the T-shirt lunged at them both but was holding his knife like an amateur. He slashed it from side to side, and Roberto took just one more small step to his left, so now he stood directly over the girl. With one easy move of his right hand to his back pocket, he had his own switch-blade open. It took but a fraction of a second. Roberto's short blade twisted slightly as it took the *violador* in the chest and the lower ribs, and the blade kept going. It buried itself as though sucked in, until Roberto's hand struck hard against the heave of ribs and then his hand and the knife stopped. There was nowhere else for it to go. So Roberto Moreno waited a second or two, withdrew his knife, calmly, and waited like a matador for the effect of his thrust to become apparent.

At first, stunned, the rapist just stood there. Now Roberto could see his face. It showed surprise, not pain. The man dropped his useless knife and it fell on the girl's chest. It rolled away, flipped into the water by her neck, her head. Then he turned and walked up the road, slowly, step by slow step, north up Shaw Street.

Roberto followed but he was in no hurry. He turned into the first alley to the left and the rapist was already dead, face down.

There was nothing more to do. Roberto returned to Jasper Glass, to the girl, and the funny thing was that by then the girl was coming around but Jasper Glass had passed out. Jasper lay unconscious on the sidewalk beside her, curled up on his side.

Roberto pulled the girl out of the street, out of the curbside flood, leaving her on the sidewalk. He bent and whispered to her.

Then he lifted Jasper Glass up onto his left shoulder and walked like that all the way home. If it hadn't been for the rain, surely they would have been stopped by the police. At the corner of Shaw and College, Roberto laid his friend down beside a phone booth, propped him up, stepped inside and made the call to the authorities.

A girl on Shaw Street, he said.

He went through Jasper's wallet to find out where he lived. Then he picked him up again and off they went. They passed the Silver Dollar again, passed the flickering lights of Spadina Avenue.

Roberto was so impressed by his new friend, by his unarmed intervention in the rape, that he considered it an honour to carry him away from the scene of the battle. It reminded him of *Orfeo y Eurídice,* when Orpheo comes out of the underworld, the body of Eurydice in his arms.

Of course, Roberto knew that he had acted in self-defence that night but, as Jasper Glass later had no recall of anything that transpired, the rye whisky so strong,

Roberto did not enlighten him. The less said in those circumstances, the better. Canada was not Mexico, but police are police, they're much the same everywhere. They wouldn't be too happy with what they found on Shaw Street. But as he carried Jasper home, and it took two hours for him to do so, he thought carefully about the scene of the crime, the broken streetlight, the alley, the *violador*'s knife in the gutter, the girl, and there was nothing there to connect either of them to anything. Nothing at all.

It was at one of the poetry classes that John Glass first heard of Baudelaire's *Les fleurs du mal,* a passing reference made by Roberto Moreno. Because of that, from the next day on, he carried a tattered edition of Baudelaire wherever he went. It might have been the fatal blow for him, for his academic career, this Baudelaire. He'd already stopped going to all of his classes except embryology, a curious psychological quirk because embryology was difficult and tedious. It was perverse, the attraction he had to that minor course. It was self-destructive, the attention he paid to it.

Continual exposure to Baudelaire didn't help in any way either, other than to intensify his diffuse and pointless longing. And longing for what? He had no idea. Maybe the Glasses had a genetic flaw that prevented them from completing tasks. Look at his father.

Going to class? someone said to him near Hart House. Oh yes, he said.

But he didn't go. He always found something else to do.

Going to class? Valerie Anderson said to him outside the anatomy lab one day, just five minutes before it was to begin.

Maybe, maybe, he said.

Instead he went for coffee at Hart House and when he had finished three or four cups, the class was half over. What was the point in going then?

I'd like to attend class but I can't seem to do it, he said to anyone who asked.

Poetry was his seductress. He wrote it, he destroyed it, he morosed over it, he read it at all hours. He knew Margaret Avison, he had spoken to her personally, she made him feel as though he were a peer, an equal. He became peripherally involved with many of the poets who lived around the university.

One night, John Glass awoke after a party and found himself in Queen's Park. He had been asleep by a quince bush and with him was Gwendolyn MacEwen. She sat on the wet grass and held his head in her lap. She spoke to him and called him by an Italian name. That was all she did, nothing else. Maybe it was her, maybe it wasn't. Maybe it was just someone who looked like her. Anyway, she had dark hair and she bent over his face, that he knew.

He submitted poems to journals. They were all returned with scornful comments.

Sentimental, vainglorious, they've written to me. Look at this letter, Valerie, he said, what bullshit, editors.

What a life it was, really, the life of the artist. It was hard to go back to the science books after a night like that, after Gwendolyn MacEwen, and there were many similar nights and in fact most of his classmates looked upon John Glass as slightly crazy. They respected him nevertheless, despite his low marks. Most of them loved the printed word, they each had their own uncertainty and awkwardness, there was nothing they wanted to condemn.

But his closest friends couldn't let him slip to the wayside. One afternoon Valerie Anderson and Jasper Glass took him to Health Services. They were worried about him, about his mental health.

John, do you ever feel suicidal, do you have thoughts of self-harm? asked Valerie Anderson as they walked across the soccer field together.

Jesus, Valerie, laughed Jasper, he's my brother, I think I'd know.

Never, said John Glass. Trust me, I love this melancholy far too much to have it end unhappily.

Love it or not, there's something wrong with you, something holding you back. Go in, we'll wait out here. Get a diagnosis of some kind.

Inside, the nurse said, okay, Mr. Glass. Your turn, go on in.

The doctor sat in a swivel chair. He had a small desk up against the far wall and he swung around to look at John, who stood there, but the doctor remained in his chair.

What's the trouble?

I seem to have lost my energy, my drive. I can't seem to get to classes.

Take your pants off, your underpants too.

So John Glass did as he was told, though it was awkward to be fully dressed from the waist up and only socks below.

The doctor scooted over to him on his swivel chair and from his sitting position directly in front of the patient took John Glass's scrotum in his hand and lifted the testicles that lay within. He lifted them gently and rolled his fingers over them. He did this twenty or thirty times and he closed his eyes as he did so. After several minutes, he opened his eyes again and gazed directly at John's penis and lifted the shaft of the penis up, down and turned it sideways and held it in the palm of his hand before he looked up.

Cough please, Mr. Glass.

John coughed.

Thank you, let me see, let me see, said the doctor.

The doctor closed his eyes again and slid closer on his chair until John could feel his breath soft on his lower abdomen.

Then the man pushed back his chair.

You may get dressed, he said.

What about my heart, my lungs? I have a weight on my chest almost all the time, like an elephant's foot, a pressure feeling, said John.

You're a young man. Your heart and lungs are fine. They don't even warrant examination. Not like testicles, which at your age can harbour dangerous cancers and hernias. But you should know that. You're a medical student, correct? Medical students, Mr. Glass, are the worst, they worry about every disease they study. Be on your way. You're fine, you're normal, maybe even more so than average.

So that was what happened to Jonathan Glass at Health Services, and he went out none the wiser for it.

Well? said Valerie.

I'm fine according to the doctor, but all he did was hold my testicles for ten minutes.

Same guy I saw, I bet, said Jasper. Same exam I had when I tried out for the football team. That's all he did.

Women wouldn't put up with that, said Valerie. You should file a complaint with the College of Physicians.

No, said John, maybe it was okay. Normal enough, what do I know?

You don't know anything about life, you know nothing, said Valerie. They'll throw you out of medicine, John. You can't keep missing class.

Oh, I doubt that, Valerie, said Jasper. That's never happened. Once you're in, you're in. They always give you another chance, rewrites, supplementals, do it again.

Well, said Valerie, it's up to you, John. You're supposedly grown-up. But it makes me mad, a doctor like that who graduates from medical school, probably with honours, and then he practises like that. He doesn't ask you anything, he doesn't probe. There's nothing psychological, psychoanalytical to his examination. He couldn't give a damn about you, and meanwhile you're the one with the problem. You get kicked out of school, he rolls around in his swivel chair.

Well said, Valerie, said Jasper.

Hey, she said, Jasper, you know the project we have together? The history of medicine?

Oh, God yes, the five-thousand-word essay. It's a month away. We don't have to think about it for a long time. A week, two weeks, three, twenty-eight days even, then we throw it together. We can do it, Valerie, no sweat.

What essay? asked John.

The one you're supposed to do with your partner, with Wallace. You can write on anything. Pick your own topic. What I mean, Jasper, is why don't we do it on this?

On what?

The history of the physical exam. In particular, how it can be so poorly performed that it borders on abuse.

The history of medicine, Valerie, is not abuse. It's insulin, penicillin, Lister, Grant. It's got nothing to do with us, today.

Oh yes it does, said Valerie. You need to open your eyes. It'll take some work, some time.

Time together?

Of course time together. That's how it's supposed to be done.

Well, maybe I see what you mean then, said Jasper. Perhaps we could include, in our paper, something even more subtle than abuse. Such as, say, the history of the relationship between male and female medical students, how they are inevitably attracted to each other, how natural and wonderful that is. Part two: how desire can be repressed. Part three: how some medical women are unable to recognize their latent desires. That should really be our project, Valerie, yours and mine, together.

We'll take it on, Jasper, the abuse issue. I have a plan. It just came to me.

Wait, said John, I forgot my Baudelaire back there. Maybe Wallace and I can write about Baudelaire. Baudelaire must have had a disease of some kind.

I'm sick of Baudelaire, said Valerie. Those French poets will drive you deeper and deeper down. They run off my back like water, French poets.

Except for Rimbaud, said John.

Well, yes, except for Rimbaud.

John Glass went back to Health Services and picked up *Les fleurs du mal* where he'd left it. Sure enough, no one had touched it. It lay there on the side table.

The nurse said, I would have put it in a drawer but it didn't look like something anyone would take.

No, I guess not, said John. It's poetry, that's all it is.

At first, the night of the tropical rainstorm wasn't that much different from any other for the police. There was the usual run of minor accidents made worse by slippery roads. In fact there were two accidents at Spadina and College that could be blamed almost entirely on the rain. Water didn't drain off. It collected an inch deep over the metal of the streetcar tracks where the rails turned in half-circles. Twice, cars rode up on it and hydroplaned through the intersection. Twice, pedestrians were hit and the police were called, but as the night wore on, traffic diminished and there was time for more serious offences. It was always that way in any big city. No one killed anybody else at nine in the morning over bacon and eggs. They almost always waited until the wee hours, by which time personal imperfections, jealousy, desire, intoxicants, stupidity, all of them at once had time to build up, stew and then boil over.

The call about the sexual assault came in to the police dispatcher around three-thirty a.m.

A girl's been assaulted, probably raped, the voice said, on Shaw Street. She's lying there near the park.

The dispatcher noted an accent, something different about it, but there was so much background noise, probably rain off the roof of what might have been a phone booth, that he found himself shouting back into the phone.

Who's speaking?

Nothing but a dial tone.

The first squad car got to the girl within two minutes. Then an ambulance a few minutes after that, and five minutes after that, the dispatcher looked down the list of homicide detectives and put the call in to Andy Ames.

Andy? You're the man tonight? We got one. Rape–murder downtown.

You mean the girl's dead?

No, she's okay. The murder's someone else.

He was dressed in five minutes and gone. From Helendale Avenue down Yonge Street to College but, even with the windshield wipers maxed out, he had to pull over to the right and stop four times between Davisville and St. Clair in the dark section by the cemetery. He couldn't see, the water streamed down the windshield. Then it let up a bit. So it took him twenty minutes before he turned down Shaw, off College, and headed south, an hour still before daylight.

A cruiser blocked the road north of Queen, pulled half into an alley on the right side, its headlights on. He stopped his car in the middle of Shaw Street, did up his raincoat and stepped out.

He should have worn a hat. His head was soaked already but it was warm, crazily warm. He could have been anywhere in the southern hemisphere, the Oronoco River, somewhere like that, somewhere with parrots, steamy heat.

So what's up? he asked the constable who jumped out of the cruiser.

They had to stand close together to be heard over the din.

Down there, said the constable.

He pointed to the wash of headlights down the alley. A body lay thirty yards away.

Dead. I haven't touched him.

And the girl?

She's gone to hospital. She's okay otherwise, I think, cut on the head.

Where was she?

Farther down, on the sidewalk.

They walked into the alley. A sodden raccoon shambled past garbage cans, then the body of the man, face down on the asphalt. The constable pushed at the man with the toe of his foot.

You see what I mean? Dead. Guaranteed dead.

Detective Ames squatted by the body and felt for the carotid pulse.

Yes, I see what you mean. Let's flip him.

They rolled him over. No sign of rigor mortis, maybe thirty years old, a white male, his T-shirt rent in the middle and covered with blood. Ames put his finger through the hole, only half an inch in diameter, then lifted the shirt up and had a look. Despite the rain, the lights from the cruiser were enough to show the congealed blood, black-red, stuck like pudding to the chest, the abdomen, even down to the waist. The man's jeans were undone, the fly down.

Stab wound? asked the constable.

That's my guess, the heart, the aorta. He probably bled right out.

Related to the girl, unrelated?

Everything's related, that's the best rule. Everything, till it's proven not to be. So let's call an ambulance for this guy too, only this one's to the morgue.

He got back into his car. He had a hockey sweater on the back seat and he used it to dry off his hair. He flicked on the lights, watched the cruiser drive farther down into the alley, and he headed south, then left on Queen.

Someone had phoned in the crime and it sure as hell wasn't the man in the alley. So unless the girl was a killer armed with a sharpened stiletto, there were going to be complications here. Someone else was the murderer.

The emergency department was nearly empty.

It's quiet, the nurse said, the rain. There's a flood in the Don Valley.

That I can believe. I'm Detective Ames. You have the girl here, from Shaw Street?

That we do, in the back.

She smiled at the detective. Nurses and policemen, they always had a connection, something to do with the repetition, all the things they saw together.

You have a name for her? She okay?

The nurse looked at the chart and then turned it around and held it up for the constable.

Gwen O'Hara, he said.

Yes, and she is okay. She's regained consciousness.

Awake?

That's what I said.

She was sitting up when he half pulled the curtain back. A laceration on her right temple had been sutured and there was a bruise under her eye. Her hair was wet, pulled back and combed. Composed, more so than he would have thought. Sometimes though, composed and stunned, it was hard to tell the difference.

Detective Ames, he said.

Oh, police, she said.

He sat on the chair beside the bed.

Miss O'Hara, are you able to give me a statement?

I think so, she said, what I remember.

He took out his notepad, a pencil.

So start at the beginning, take your time.

I was walking north up Shaw Street.

At two in the morning, three in the morning?

I'm a student at Humber College, but I also waitress. Twice a week I moonlight. So I sometimes walk home late, it can't be helped. My head was down because of the rain, I couldn't hear a thing, the rain was heavy. A man came by me heading south. I had this feeling then, suddenly, like I was isolated, all alone. I turned to look, to check where he was, and he was right there, a foot behind me. I jumped a mile.

Can you describe him?

Five-ten, T-shirt, jeans, thirty, thirty-five, his hair matted down by the rain. Baby, he said.

Baby?

I couldn't say a thing, it was like my throat was closed. I turned around as fast as I could and started walking again but he grabbed me, my coat from behind.

Did he say anything else?

Down, get down on the sidewalk.

He forced you down?

Not really, I just went down. He had a knife in my face by then.

He was on top of you?

Not then, that was next. I thought, is this actually happening to me? and he said, baby. He said that over and over.

An accent?

No. Then he cut my face. Can I have a sip of that water?

She was composed, not stunned, but now she was beginning to lose it.

Water? Am I allowed to give you water, are you allowed water?

There was no one around. He handed her the half-full plastic glass from the bedside table and she sipped from it.

Thanks. Yes, I'm allowed.

Can you go on?

He pulled up my dress, it was so dark, he finished what he did but he went on for a long time and then he said something like, sorry about this, and he held the knife back up, over me.

He held the knife like this?

The detective held his arm up high as though to plunge down a knife, as in an Aztec sacrifice.

Yes, like that. He was going to kill me.

And then?

Then I felt this thump come out of nowhere, from the side, right across me. He was thrown off me. I looked up and there were two other guys standing there.

Out of nowhere.

I guess.

They rescued you?

For sure they rescued me.

Can you describe them?

They were really young, my age. They stood together, they were cocky. They actually laughed. They were poised in a way, it was strange, like they were untouchable.

They were drunk?

Maybe, I didn't care what they were. To me, they were angels.

Okay. I can understand that.

The man who attacked me got back on his feet, waved his knife and one of the boys, it must have been the one who pushed the man off me, he looked like he was coming from some kind of party. He was shirtless, covered with some kind of cream all over his chest, like Hallowe'en. Like a character in a play. But when he saw the knife, he backed right off. Then the other guy, shorter, darker, he laughed. When I heard him laugh, I thought, maybe I'll be okay.

Because?

I don't know.

Because he had a knife too?

I guess he did but I didn't see it.

What kind of knife?

He said to his friend, no, leave this to me.

Did he call his friend by name?

No.

He attacked your attacker?

No, he just stood there, right over me. He was the one attacked. I don't know what happened but the rapist dropped his knife. It actually landed on my chest and rolled off. I was conscious but I couldn't move, I couldn't speak.

She reached again for the water glass and he handed it to her. Her voice had a quiver in it now.

He walked away, the rapist walked away. I never saw him again.

What happened next, Gwen?

The guy, the dark one, bent down over me and said,

I barely heard him, stay there, don't move, we're calling the police for you, but we have to go. Something like that.

Did he have an accent, something not Canadian?

He could have spoken Chinese for all I cared.

You have some white stuff there on your neck, said the detective.

Oh?

Her hand moved upwards.

No, let me get that, he said.

He took a tongue depressor from the bedside table and gently skimmed off the trace of white matter that was smeared across her throat. He opened a small Baggie and scraped the thick white substance into it.

I'll keep this, he said. You think this could have come from your friend, the good Samaritan?

Maybe, she said. He was fast, he was that close. He was crazy to do what he did.

And then she started to cry.

There were a lot of things Detective Ames was comfortable with and a few things he wasn't. He picked up the Kleenex box, the hospital kind. Then he put it down. He saw the nurse go by and called to her. Then he turned to the girl.

Thanks, Miss O'Hara, that's enough for now. I'll talk to you again.

Okay, she said, that's okay.

The associate dean of the Faculty of Medicine, Dr. Hilger, a man with a distinguished European ancestry but also a man with a heart of ice and a face contorted by contempt for any student who stood shaking before him, sat and perused John Glass's sorry transcript.

Sit down, Mr. Glass, he said.

His face twitched with exasperation.

Glass, I cannot even say I am sorry, because when I take a look at your performance it calls into question the whole selection process we go through here at the University of Toronto, so abysmal are these marks, so catastrophically negative these evaluations from all your instructors, save one, that we cannot have you back at all. You are no longer a student in this faculty. Do not reapply. Your name is anathema here and will be so, I assure you, until the next millennium.

Sir, said John, please.

I am a busy man, Glass, you are dismissed.

Dr. Hilger stood up from the bureaucratic desk he occupied most of the day, while real doctors operated on real patients in real hospitals down the street, and John Glass thought, here is this intransigent man, my life seeping out of me and there he goes out the door. I am an ant to be stepped upon.

Sir, he said, please reconsider your decision. I merit another chance.

He started to speak rapidly as though speed could be more persuasive than logic.

I admit that in the past year I fell into a difficult crowd of friends, Dr. Hilger, dangerous friends within this same faculty, doctors-to-be with aspirations also in various arts. I have allowed myself to be led astray.

My marks have suffered, but they are not beyond salvation.

Glass, you are dismissed.

I beg you, look at my mark, Dr. Hilger, my mark in embryology.

The great man looked down again at the small folder on his desk that represented John Glass's academic life so far.

Embryology eighty-eight per cent, he said. Yes, Glass, such promise wasted on such a tiny and pathetic part of the curriculum. Embryology, a study I personally despise for its irrelevance to the practice of medicine, and had you ever become a doctor—which you will not, I repeat, you will not, Glass, perish the very thought—you could never have pursued a career in embryology anyway because your marks in biochemistry and physics and pathology and histology and anatomy are all less than eight per cent, by far the lowest marks ever recorded in a medical school anywhere in Canada, I am sure. Eight per cent. Unbelievable. Extraordinary. And, may I add, shameful. I call you Mr. Glass because you will never be Dr. Glass, or only over my dead body.

Dr. Hilger walked out of the room and his footsteps moved definitively down the hall and disappeared.

John Glass sat there for three minutes, stunned. A vise squeezed his chest.

Then he shouted out in a whisper, fuck you, fuck you, fuck you, but he didn't know to whom he spoke, to that great administrator who had just left, or to himself, to John Glass who sat there, a year's duration a fool.

He collected himself. He breathed as deeply as he could. He walked out from the lair of the monster into the sunshine of a May afternoon. It was blindingly bright, the same shocking brightness as when he was ten years old and he and his brother came out of the Nortown Cinema after a summer matinee. They shielded their eyes back then, the sudden heat and light washed over them while their brains and hearts remained inside, under the cool dark spell of film. Then, slowly, they became themselves again.

So it was on the day of his expulsion. He walked out into King's College Road. He could barely see at all, the trees not yet fully leafed, the high sun merciless, his eyes blurred by tears and everything that mattered to him was still back inside that cold brick building, where light was a rare, unaccustomed visitor.

Jasper was outside, waiting.

Well?

It's over, I'm finished.

No second chance, rewrites?

None.

Shit, they both said.

Jasper put his arm around his brother and they walked away together, John's last steps ever in that exact direction, away from the medical building.

Maybe there's a silver lining, Jasper said, maybe you should do something else anyway.

Sure. Like what?

Their steps took them to the pool hall, the one beside El Mocambo.

Rack 'em, they said, and as the red balls disappeared John Glass felt the oppressive weight lift off his chest.

I think I'll just finish the science part, the BSc, he said, then reapply some other place.

McGill, Jasper said, Montreal.

Yeah, why not. Better poets there too. Cheaper rent, rue Ste-Famille, rue Milton, I could do better there.

The Swiss Hut, poets who talk to each other. You'd like that.

Camaraderie, that's a French word, said John.

Exactly, said Jasper. I think this university was born without a heart.

How can that be, embryologically? said John.

You should know. You're the star in that.

Having no heart's impossible, it's incompatible with life, but I agree with you, Jasper, whatever heart there is on this campus is malformed.

Probably tetralogy of Fallot, said Jasper Glass, a congenital defect of some very serious kind.

John sank a red ball, a blue ball, another red.

So fucking true, he said.

He saw the poor children born like that, with tetralogy of Fallot, their misshapen heart valves, their arteries blowing and pumping blood in all the wrong directions, how their lips turned blue and their ribs rose and fell and their little arms waved in the air. Tears came to John's eyes again, but this time it wasn't self-pity.

They both put down their cues and walked out. They paid, but they didn't finish the game.

Valerie Anderson put her lemonade down in the kitchen and she and Roberto walked together into the living room, and without further ado she reached under her skirt and took off her underpants. She still had her book, Rimbaud's *Le bateau ivre,* in her hand when she sat down on the middle cushion of the couch, facing Roberto Moreno. She pulled her skirt up to her waist where it lay around her like a crumpled belt. Then she slid down, her buttocks on the edge of the couch, towards him, so now her feet were on the floor and she spread her legs wide apart. She surprised him again with her sexual audacity because up until then, until the cherry tree, she had been so exceptionally modest and circumspect, even distanced in the physical sense, and now her whole restrained persona had been blown away, what she had done, what she was doing, and despite the position she now assumed, naked from the waist down and on the couch, her feet also splayed, now her voice, which seemed disembodied, began to read from Rimbaud, as though Roberto Moreno were not in the same room, as though he were not looking directly at her. He could have been out by the cherry tree and she alone in the world. So he bent down and gently put his thumb inside her, slowly and carefully, and right away his thumb and his lower wrist were wet, and he dropped on his knees as she had done outside for him, and then he looked up at her, at her face, but all he could see was her book, her Rimbaud, and all he could hear was her voice.

Truly, I have wept too much! The dawns are grievous.
Every moon atrocious, every sun bitter:
Biting love has billowed me with drunken torpor.
O let my keel break! O let me go to the sea!

Then he put his hands on her thighs and his tongue inside her, as far as he could, and there was a slow, quiet buzz in the air as though his hearing was impaired and, despite the circumstances, despite the low sun that slanted in upon them and despite what he was doing to her, Valerie Anderson didn't alter her breathing or her words as far as he could tell, as he moved his tongue up, down and in

Of all the waters in Europe, I wish for
A black cool gutter where, in the embalmed twilight,
A crouched child, full of sorrow, abandons
A boat, a frail butterfly in May

until at last she took one hand off the book and put it on the back of his head, a guide with the weight of a breath of air, and she moved him, his neck was bent awkwardly then, so, with both hands, he raised her buttocks and he began to suck—the only English word for what he did— and she moved towards him and he noticed that now, at last, she had stopped her reading. In fact, had he not been there to support her, she would have fallen to the floor as did Rimbaud at last with a soft thump on the carpet to his right.

He heard her say to him, okay okay.

He put his thumb into her again. He felt her expand and squeeze simultaneously, and then she was on the floor and he pulled his pants down to his thighs and on the patterned carpet, blue and red, he entered her. Two, three strokes, that's all he managed before he pulled out. He came helplessly all over her, her stomach, her skirt, her blouse, and then they lay there tangled with sweat and they whispered together, Jesus, Jesus, it was more or less the same in both their languages, in English, in Spanish, the word Jesus, Jesus.

They had no idea at all in which language they spoke.

They lay there for what, five minutes, ten? They breathed on each other's hair.

Maybe the lemonade was spiked with something, Valerie Anderson finally said, I don't usually do these things.

My uncle made that lemonade, said Roberto.

So what does that prove? Perhaps he had designs on Silvana.

Roberto laughed.

Mexicans don't need alcohol for that, no matter how old they are.

Then Valerie picked up her small white underpants and put them on, still lying on the floor, and she lifted her hips and rolled her skirt back down and she looked very fetching, beautiful and at ease. Roberto too replaced his clothing. They went back outside and sat down on the patio, the small table now between them. Valerie stood up and from the pocket of her skirt she pulled out some pieces of paper, dog-eared pieces of varying thickness, white and off-white. They looked like they were used napkins from a restaurant dispenser, the silver kind.

Here's some poems you might like to read, not in Spanish, she said.

She looked through them for a minute, shuffled them, then picked out two and handed them across to Roberto.

Yours? he asked.

Well, yes, but they're only first drafts, they're not finished, they're spur-of-the-moment.

He looked at the first piece of paper and then turned it over because it was upside down. Then he began to read out loud and she looked away. For the first time that day she blushed.

> Desire crawls like a fire, calls to the wind
> and when you're not looking
> catches the window trim you sewed
> to keep the world from looking in.
> Why not begin pour the gas throw the torch in?
>
> Wood's not just for carving the saint's face,
> but for breaking and burning—we wash
> ourselves in the flame's flakes.
>
> We all eat from the tree,
> and it pleases me.

When did you write this? he asked her.
Yesterday, before today, she said.

First drafts are the best, he said, the most spontaneous. What do you think?

Just read the rest of the poem, she said, and don't read it out loud.

No matter how brazen she had been that day, under the cherry tree or on the couch when the Rimbaud toppled to the floor, Valerie Anderson never regretted anything she did with Roberto Moreno. Nothing, the whole time he stayed in Canada.

When he finished reading her poem, he looked up at her.

You're a natural, he said.

A natural poet? A natural disaster?

A natural parabolist.

Oh.

That's good, Valerie. It's a compliment. But be careful, no one can be a flat-out parabolist for long. It's way too intense. It eats you up and destroys relationships. It can be like napalm.

Then Roberto said, Valerie, what a good day we had today, didn't we, a very good day. Thank you for taking me to the islands out in Toronto Bay.

Hey, that rhymes, she said.

Now we are lovers, he said.

Yes, we are. Now let's go downtown. There are things I've got to do, said Valerie Anderson.

Julián and Silvana were concerned when they heard that Roberto had decided to come to Canada to join them, concerned that their lives and Roberto Moreno's would no longer be compatible. After all, for several years they had lived apart. Roberto's peer group in Mexico City appeared to be composed of the dregs of the intelligentsia—educated but unpublished poets—but there were also, among his close friends, visual artists who could afford neither paint nor canvas and who were therefore forced to make images only in their overcrowded heads, or with broken chalk on sidewalks, and there were classically trained musicians who had given up on Rodrigo and Ravel, who now played in repellent tunings that no Western ear could bear, and dancers, malnourished girls with no venue for performance but the lee corners of anonymous streets. Also acrobats, jugglers, unicyclists who spun to rhythms only they could hear. The Nájeras had met them all, before Roberto went to live on his own. These artistic youngsters were a penniless underclass, near destitute, only a friendly gesture or two away from being homeless. They all despised the bourgeois life, the life that Julián and Silvana Nájera led.

But Roberto himself was more accepting. He held negative views of no one, not even Octavio Paz who, because of his prominence in literary life in Mexico, was often ridiculed by radicals.

Roberto's attitude, his skills, his writing, what little they had seen of it, his politics, whatever sympathies he had, were inclusive rather than exclusive, even if at first glance they appeared dogmatic or unbending. Once you realized that, you found the real Roberto Moreno, his generosity, and that was the key to understanding him, to loving him the way they did.

Soon after he arrived in Toronto, they realized their fears were groundless. His behaviour in their house and their neighbourhood was impeccable. Yes, he developed friends in the same demographic as before— the unhappy poets in cafés, troubled girls from Jarvis Street, men from the Danforth—but he also acquired as friends a group of young men and women who were high achievers in the academic world, medical students at the University of Toronto. Two of these friends, Jasper Glass and his brother, John, lived right next door. Of course, Roberto had also had well-educated friends in Mexico City, but here in Toronto there were more of them and they had a lot of respect for Roberto. You could see it in the way they talked together, how they gravitated to him.

In Mexico, after the death of his parents, he had showed little interest in tidiness. Forever they were after him to clean up his room, pick up his socks, pick up his coloured pencils, pick up all the clothes thrown carelessly here and there. Books, books then appeared and multiplied as fast, Julián maintained, as fruit flies.

Perhaps there's something you can do with your deep cryogenics to keep his room neater, Silvana said to Julián.

Roberto's books were stacked everywhere, tilted, spilled. His entire room then resembled the aftermath of a volcanic explosion at Popocatépetl, with papers, recordings, mimeographs, drawings, manifestos—above all poetry books—pouring down from desk to floor like lava.

Julián said, I remember my room was a mess like that and look at me now.

And Julián was right, because in Canada, on Glengrove Avenue, Roberto Moreno became the model of behaviour, nearly.

One night Silvana came home after working a long shift at Laura Secord. She noticed a stain on the living room couch, on the middle cushion, at the edge. Also, there was a similar spot on the floor, directly below the cushion.

Oh no, she thought, this is a rented house.

She asked Roberto what had happened.

Oh, I spilled lemonade there. Sorry. But I've cleaned it up with soap and water. It should be fine when it dries.

Silly boy, she said, don't you know that an acidic fluid like lemonade requires baking soda?

No, he did not know that.

She added baking soda to a bowl of warm water and gave it to Roberto and he worked on the stain some more. When it dried, the couch, the rug, everywhere, there was no sign that anything had spilled at all.

Really, she thought, did the boy think she was born yesterday? She'd seen stains like that before.

Julián, dearest, she said, do you ever remember when we met, the very first time?

After he had seen Roberto Moreno hanging from the cherry tree and the girl who knelt before him, after he had called June up to the window to see, in fact, nothing at all, the professor went out to the yard with his rake and his pruning clippers. He liked to work up a healthy sweat in the garden.

Had he imagined it? And, if he had imagined it, what did that say about him, about his psychological state?

Roberto and the girl were just going inside. She waved to him in a most friendly way and showed no trace of embarrassment. The two of them did not reappear for a long time.

He worked away at the hostas, the lavender, the sweet woodruff, the ubiquitous goutweed they had planted on the advice of a horticulturist. Must have been a follower of the Marquis de Sade, that man. It was mostly this goutweed, a tenacious ground-covering plant that separated their yard from the Nájeras', and Herculean efforts were required to tame it, to beat it down. He tore away with his fingers at the gnarled roots deep in the earth.

It must have happened.

He had his quirks but hallucinations and visions were not among them. He was no Joan of Arc. He lived on no celestial plane. Joan of Arc's visions were, above all, chaste, weren't they? He was ashamed even to have thought of her. She had burned at the stake for the purity of her vision, whereas he felt lurid, embarrassed by what he had seen. Maybe it was a trick of the eye. *Trompe l'oeil.* Maybe Roberto had been hanging from the tree and the girl appeared to be down on her knees in front of him but she was actually ten feet away, digging at dandelions or at goutweed and reciting Wallace Stevens or Irving Layton, which made her head move up and down, and the angle from his observation post in the upstairs window was such that he conflated the two images. With the deep-seated prurience of his own nature, he had observed fellatio where there was naught but innocence.

Oh, enough of this, he thought, and he tore another wiry web of roots from the moist, forgiving earth.

He was down on his knees, as she had been. If June had seen it too, they could have discussed it the way they discussed everything, late at night. Jasper being Jasper, John with his head in the clouds, the idioms of Provence, everything was grist for the mill for their night-time conversations. The professor began to feel more composed. He turned his thoughts from Roberto Moreno and the girl to their own bedroom, June lying beside him in the night as they talked and talked as all parents did, the mahogany bed inlaid with mother-of-pearl. They slept and sometimes made love, almost always in the dark, and then he realized, had she seen what he had seen, he could have said to her, to June, wasn't that interesting, what people will do these days, outside?

June?

And she might have said, yes, dear, but I think it's something they do more of these days, oral sex. I read about it in *Maclean's*.

And then lovingly she might have turned to him and laid her head upon his chest.

He filled several bushel baskets with torn remnants of goutweed. He was satisfied with his physical exertions. His hands and fingernails were blackened. The side garden was now weed-free, immaculate. He stood up and stretched his back and as he did so, Roberto and the girl reappeared on the patio. They waved to him again and they sat down. They had books and appeared to be reading to each other in a very companionable way.

He looked at his watch, put the tools back in the garage, and went inside.

June, he said, I have to go down to Trinity. Somehow I forgot the papers for the Molière class. But first, I have to clean up. Look at these hands.

Oh, a real workman you are, she said, good job. I'll come down with you, Bill, if that's okay. Twenty minutes?

She had a white dress on with blue polka dots, a shapely one he had always liked. It had some looseness to it but it clung to her too, the way she wore it. The breeze caught the material and moved it around.

Sure, he said.

They got into the Citroën and she drove and they started out of the driveway. But the car made a *hump-hump* jerky movement.

June, he said, you need to be more definitive with the clutch.

They turned west down Glengrove and it was then that they saw Roberto Moreno and the girl with dark hair walking along the sidewalk, away from them, towards Avenue Road. She had her left hand crooked under his right arm, her shoulder against him. They were the same height.

In Mexico, the professor said, I would be a giant among men.

Physically, that would be true, said June, physically you would be a giant. Maybe they'd like a lift.

She pulled over and the professor rolled down the window to offer the two young people a ride.

We're on our way to the campus, he said.

Sure, that's great, they said.

They squeezed into the back seat together.

Professor and Mrs. Glass, said Roberto, I would like you to meet Valerie Anderson.

Oh, we've met before, Mr. Glass, said Valerie, the first day of school.

Then the professor remembered.

Oh yes, outside the library.

I'm Jasper's lab partner, Valerie said.

In the rear-view mirror, June looked at Valerie Anderson. She was extraordinarily pretty with dark eyes and high cheekbones and she appeared to wear no makeup at all, yet her cheeks were flushed with enthusiasm.

June turned her attention to the road again and *hump-humped* the car away from the curb.

A pleasure to meet you, she said. So you're in the boys' anatomy class.

Yes, and we're all in the same English lit class too, Jasper, John and I, said Valerie. And Roberto, he's the teacher now, so everybody knows everybody.

They drove down Avenue Road. They passed Upper Canada College and St. Clair Avenue. June asked Roberto what else he was up to.

I walk around the city and I write, he said.

Good, good, the Glasses said, and then the drive turned amicably quiet and they left the young poet and the medical student at Queen's Park, where it joined Hoskin Avenue. She pulled the car away from the curb smoothly this time.

Nice, aren't they, said June.

June, he said, and he reached over and touched her thigh, on the blue polka-dotted dress to get her full attention, I'm pretty sure I saw that young woman performing fellatio on Roberto this afternoon.

What? she said, you saw her what?

I saw her performing fellatio in the back garden, by the cherry tree. On Roberto. From the window in Jasper's room.

He leaned towards his wife when he said this and he felt the tightening pressure of the seat belt.

Really, June said.

She looked over her shoulder and accelerated into the next lane. They were still at Queen's Park, circling around the parliament buildings.

Really, she repeated, fellatio. You observed her performing fellatio from Jasper's window. Maybe you were mistaken, Bill. It might have been something else.

No, I saw her. She dropped on her knees in the garden.

June shifted into fourth.

Good for her, Bill, good for her, she said.

And then she realized she was in the wrong lane and they had to drive all the way up University Avenue back to Bloor Street, where she made an illegal left turn in order to get back to Trinity College.

One time out of a hundred, June said, you get caught for a move like that. Go for it, I say.

Well, guess what? Valerie Anderson said.

She had the brachial artery in her forceps and lifted it off and away as Jasper undercut it. There were all kinds of little branches that ran off down into the muscles of the forearm.

Snip snip, he said, snippety-snip, my dexterity is even more impressive as my experience grows. Make a mistake on this in the real world, then the fingers dry up and fall off. That's called a lawsuit. Here in our lab, though, we are protected. The litigious patient in this laboratory is a rarity.

Jasper, listen. The doctor at Health Services, the one who examined your brother? He's already been reported to the College of Physicians. He had a hearing last year.

He did?

Yes, and he was totally exonerated.

Keep pulling, keep pulling, Valerie.

I've started our project. It's time for you to get involved.

Our project?

I told you. The physical exam, how it can be abused. For our paper on the history of medicine.

The paper by you, by Valerie Anderson, you mean.

No, by both of us. You agreed. I talked to someone last night, she knows all about John's doctor. It's on the public record. He was brought before the college for fondling patients during physicals. Declared innocent of all charges. It would serve as a perfect introduction.

What's the point, if he's been exonerated?

Because it's not really about guilt, although that comes into it. It's also about the process at the college.

Jasper put his scalpel down carefully and looked at her.

Do you think, Valerie, do you still feel that we're going to have to spend a lot of time together on this? Just us?

It's a complicated issue. It won't be easy. Yes, it will take some time, some work together.

Well, that's all right with me then. The project's on. I will sacrifice my better idea. Do you remember it, my better idea?

Yes, said Valerie.

The attraction of medical students for each other, the denial of same?

Yes, said Valerie.

So when's our first move?

Tonight, if it's okay with you. Meet me at eight o'clock outside the library. We'll walk over to Jarvis Street.

Jarvis? You'll need someone with you there, Valerie. Lucky you asked, it's a dangerous area. I'm really quite indispensable to you, physically and intellectually. That's becoming more and more obvious, at least to me. You'll have to hold on to my arm the whole way. So who'd you meet last night? What got you going on this again?

A poet, Amber White. She had some haikus in at the journal. They were so good, I phoned her. She invited me over and we talked. I learned that she works as a court reporter at the College of Physicians so we started talking about medical cases, the whole process, and lo and behold, she was there. The case against John's doctor. We're going to her place tonight, you and I. She runs a shelter on Jarvis.

For the lovelorn?

No, Jasper, for girls, for young girls with nowhere to go.

What does that have to do with John? With our project?

Nothing.

Jasper Glass picked up the scalpel again. Then he leaned against the side of the metal table.

Okay, he said, you're the boss. But now I think you need to pull the elbow out more. Abduct it. Perfect, thanks. A shelter for girls. Where do all those girls come from, I wonder.

Everywhere, said Valerie Anderson. Everywhere and anywhere.

In Mexico City, Roberto Moreno fell into the company of political firebrands. These young men and women were controversial and disruptive within what is often thought, mistakenly, to be the tranquil, passive world of poetry. But in fact their world of poetry was the heart of darkness, riven with fissures, boiling with passions unbridled.

For example, his radical friends—they were para-parabolists by then—organized interruptions of readings by older poets. Even readings given by Octavio Paz, whom Roberto personally admired. But Octavio Paz had become conservative with age. Impolitely, the young writers shouted out their own words over his, they drowned him out. When they did, Octavio Paz stopped his reading, cleaned his glasses and started again. He was a dignified man. The organizers of the reading threw the young poets back into the streets. Octavio Paz did not agree with that, he wanted them to stay.

Did you shout out your words, Roberto, over his? asked Valerie Anderson.

No, said Roberto, I felt torn between my friends and my compassion. I actually applauded Octavio Paz. But there I was, thrown out anyway.

The headstrong young men and women of his circle plotted more extreme violations. Roberto sat in the corner and listened. These schemes included capturing Octavio Paz, stuffing him into the trunk of a car and killing him. But it never went beyond the plotting stage.

Here, in Quebec, said Valerie Anderson, the FLQ terrorists kidnapped Pierre Laporte, stuffed him into a trunk and strangled him.

Really? And he was a poet?

No, he was a politician. Still, he was an authority figure and in that way not unlike your Octavio Paz.

John Glass, Valerie Anderson and Roberto Moreno were walking up Yonge Street together. They picked their way between shoppers and pedestrians and never stopped talking as they went.

John Glass said, most Canadian poets don't address politics, except for Al Purdy and Dennis Lee.

Time will tell, said Valerie Anderson, a century may have to pass before we understand anything about our own poets.

In South America and in Central America, said Roberto, we writers excoriate the quintuple tyrannies of money, power, gender, language, and class. That's what we do.

Admirable, said Valerie, you care for the downtrodden.

You're lucky, you have lots to write about there, said John Glass. What about the personal lives of your friends? What else do they do?

They smoke cigarettes without filters. Especially the girls, said Roberto. You'd like them, I know you would.

I wish I had been born there, said John.

It's not so easy, you can starve. You can even die.

Roberto Moreno went on to describe how the poets of South and Central America came to the attention of authorities. In Mexico, in Chile, in El Salvador, he said, there came a knock on a door, or the door was smashed down by men in dark glasses, by death squads, by vigilantes or by criminals in uniform, and then there were circular rides in buses with blacked-out and duct-taped windows. There were football stadiums locked to the outside, bodies pushed from helicopters over the turbulent sea. So, if you appeared at readings by the very kind man Octavio Paz who might one day win the Nobel Prize, if you shouted him down as he spoke, if you wrote that you preferred death to the bended knee, that your allegiance was to the suffering of the poor and the disenfranchised, it gave you a far different outlook.

The imperfections of our society in Canada are more subtle, said Valerie. You don't see them here, they're papered over. Things happen here, though, on a personal level, that are as painful as they would be anywhere.

Politics was in our faces there, said Roberto. No one here is going to throw you over Niagara Falls for something you write.

So that's what Roberto Moreno was like in Mexico. Here, he wrapped himself in his winter coat and he read Canadian and British and American poetry. Valerie Anderson lay beside him dozens of times and he had no nightmares, joined no groups and attended no demonstrations.

Would you have strangled Octavio Paz yourself, she said, if you had kidnapped him and stuffed him in the back of a car?

They lay in bed, her head upon his chest. His voice reverberated through her, as though she listened through a drum.

No, he said, I would never have hurt Octavio Paz. I respected him. He was old, we were young, we were out of our minds.

But now you're only, what, twenty-one? she said.

She fell in love with him. For her, for her friends, he was always, in Canada, a redemptive force.

When Murlean Poirier left her home in Mattawa, Ontario, at eight in the morning, she had never heard of Amber White. Nor was she in any way more familiar with the concept of a women's shelter, a haven for street girls, than was Jasper Glass. Nevertheless, as she set out that morning and started to walk, that was where she was headed as sure as compasses spin and point to the North Pole.

The population of Mattawa was two thousand and eight people, and twelve of them were girls her age. She didn't talk to any of those girls. She was different, she had plans.

Ordinarily, she took the bus to school but today was special. She left early and walked all the way to Pine Street but then, at the schoolyard, with still no one else around, she just kept going. She had the little cotton carrying bag that she took to dance lessons. In it was a change of clothes, some underwear, two pairs of socks, a toothbrush, lipstick and forty-five dollars, all the money she'd saved up over the past two months. It seemed like a fair bit. She had a jump in her step.

Nerves? Maybe.

She got to Highway 17 by eight-thirty and walked south down the gravel shoulder. There was the usual wind from the west but it was warm. She didn't really need the windbreaker she had on, so she took it off, unwrapped the arms and tied them around her waist. She walked farther down the roadside towards North Bay, and when the last part of town dipped out of sight, she stopped and held out her thumb. This was the only iffy part, when she might be caught. But it worked out for her the way she had planned. It didn't take long at all.

He pulled over quite sharply. The car actually skidded a bit on the hardtop. She didn't have to run, she just walked quickly to the car, the right side, and already he'd leaned over and levered open the door halfway. A guy in shorts and a T-shirt but he looked okay.

Where you going, girl?

She bent down and looked in the car. She held the half-opened door in her right hand.

Toronto?

Well, hop in. I'm going as far as Sundridge, at least it's partway there.

Sundridge. That was past North Bay and that was good because after North Bay, there was no one she knew in the whole world.

Thank you, sir.

She slipped into the car, sat down and pulled the door closed. She put her bag on her lap.

Thanks, she said again.

It was the first time she had ever hitchhiked by herself.

No problem, he said.

He looked into his mirror and over his left shoulder and then turned back onto the road and accelerated. There was a truck with lumber on it coming down at them from behind.

Can't let that motherfucker get in front, he said. Sorry, I shouldn't have used that word, motherfucker. What's your name?

Heidi, she said, Heidi Chipman.

Heidi was the name of her dance teacher. Older, she already had kids of her own.

Well, Heidi, welcome aboard. I'm headed for Sundridge to trade in this lemon of a car.

Lemon? It seems to run okay.

I like your name, Heidi. Reminds me of Switzerland. Blond hair, really healthy girls, the Swiss. They drink milk, they yodel. What else do they do?

Not me, I don't yodel. I'm not Swiss.

You can put your bag there in the back, if you like.

He reached over to her and took the bag from her lap and swung it into the back seat.

Actually, she said, I think I need the bag, it's still cool in here.

She got up on the seat on her knees, retrieved the bag and sat back down with it.

There was silence for a while as the forest went by and the road went up and down the wooded hills. They passed over many small rivers and streams.

I always look for moose, I drive these roads. Can't be too careful. What's up in Toronto, Heidi?

Not much. Going to school, that's all.

Oh, what kind of school?

Hairdressing, beautician. That sort of thing.

Really? That's a tough business. Lots of those around, hairdressers. Even got one in South River.

I can do it, she said, it's something to do.

You got a place in Toronto, somewhere to stay?

An aunt.

That's great. Family, that's important.

He drove on without saying much more until they came to a gas station. He pulled over.

Gas up, take a leak, he said.

He got out of the car and he talked to the gas man and gave him money. When he came back, he had a magazine with him that he put down on the seat between them.

A lake opened up on the right and a float plane was taking off parallel to the road. It didn't take long before it was in the air and, almost immediately, it banked away to the south. It wiggled its wings.

See that wiggle?

Yes, she said.

That means his wife is watching the takeoff. He's saying hello, goodbye. I got my licence for that, too.

That's nice, she said, a nice airplane.

For half an hour they didn't talk, but now and then he whistled. Also now and then, he flipped a page in the magazine on the seat between them and took a look.

Heidi, you like these kinds of magazines?

She looked down. A girl smiled on the cover but she didn't have much on.

Not really, she said. I don't know much about it.

Girls make money posing for these pictures, he said, a lot more money than they make hairdressing.

She looked out the window. They were getting near North Bay. The road got rougher and there were a lot of potholes and dips.

Gotta watch what you do in here, he said, the road's been frozen and buckled and the bloody highway could care less.

He turned south at the intersection in North Bay

and continued down Highway 11. They passed a mall on the left.

See that? he asked. That's a strip joint.

It wasn't that far to Sundridge now, maybe half an hour.

Some girls who work in there, they're what's called naturalists. They take off their clothes because they believe in the natural world.

Oh.

Those girls are proud of themselves, Heidi.

What part of Sundridge you going to, the near part or the far part? she asked.

I'd do it for nothing if they asked me, he said.

The near part, the far part?

Sundridge? Smack in the middle. The car dealership, the pirates who sold me this.

So how long now, do you think? she asked.

See this twenty-dollar bill? Some guys leave tips like this for strippers and that's on top of what those girls make, whatever they make an hour. Not peanuts.

The car made a little swerve across the centre line but then he got it back on track. There was a green and white sign on the right side that said SUNDRIDGE 5.

I would never do that, she said.

He reached into his wallet and took out some more money and put it on the dashboard.

Look, he said.

There were two twenty-dollar bills there, brand new. She thought about the forty-five dollars she had saved up and how long that took.

I'll take you farther, Heidi, all the way to Bracebridge, if you want.

No thanks, this is far enough, thank you. We've come a long way already.

He slowed down when they got to the outskirts, to maybe half the speed limit, like he was dragging out the time he had with her. Finally, he turned into the parking lot of the car dealership, full of shiny cars and pickups, stopped, and they both got out.

Without saying goodbye, she walked to the side of the highway and put out her thumb. A half-hour went by. There were next to no cars going south. Waves of heat shimmered off the asphalt. A car with three men stopped but she waved them off.

Street-smart she was, street-smart.

Then, there he was again. He stopped his car right beside her.

Look, he said, brand-new car. I can take you to Bracebridge but then I got to get back.

No, thank you, she said.

Down the road, cumulonimbus clouds formed in the south, like cauliflower.

I won't talk like that anymore, Heidi.

He looked up at her from the driver's seat. She felt a drop of rain.

How long do we have? asked Jasper Glass.

All afternoon, as far as I'm concerned, said Marnie Kennedy, there's nothing pressing, till tonight.

Jasper laughed. Nothing pressing, he said.

He turned the van down Hoskin Avenue.

I know where to go, he said, Tower Road.

Tower Road? I never heard of it.

Maybe not but you've been there a thousand times. The laneway by Hart House. Right here.

He slowed the van on Hoskin and put on the right-turn signal. Then, with a break in the traffic, he turned into the small road that ran between the playing fields and Wycliffe College.

I didn't even know it had a name, Jasper, I thought it was just Hart House.

He pulled over to one side where there was space.

You get parking tickets here, you just throw them out, said Jasper, that's what I do. No repercussions.

One time I walked past here I heard madrigals, a harpsichord, a voice from over there, said Marnie.

She pointed to Wycliffe College.

The thing about madrigals, they're mostly about love, she said.

As she spoke, she was already unbuttoning her blouse.

Medieval love, courtly love, she said, and sex.

We'll get in the back, said Jasper Glass.

She climbed between the seats and he followed. He pulled the red and yellow curtains all the way around and they were in their private space. All they had back there was a mattress. She unsnapped her brassiere and the filtered sun spotted off her skin, her shoulders, her breasts. With the windows closed, soon it was so warm that any clothing at all was intolerable. She took off her skirt, her underpants, and she sat with her knees wide apart and looked at him.

Take off that stupid watch, Jasper.

I thought you said you had nothing pressing to do, Marnie.

A soccer ball deflected off the van and voices went by and three hours passed. They awoke in a pool of sweat. The sunlight was no longer as direct.

I can hardly breathe in here, said Marnie. Jasper, how long have we been here?

Jasper found the cast-off watch.

It's five o'clock. Day's almost gone.

Resuscitate me, Jasper.

What?

Resuscitate me, bring me back to life.

How do you mean?

He put one finger down between her thighs, between her labia minora.

No, she said, not like that.

She pushed his hand away.

I need you to breathe for me, as if I'm dead. I have an exam in three hours.

In CPR?

Yes, and the first thing they're going to ask is mouth-to-mouth. So resuscitate me.

I don't know how to do that. We haven't learned it yet. CPR is next year.

Try, just try.

He got onto his knees on the mattress beside her and

bent and put his mouth on hers. He blew as hard as he could.

Marnie laughed and turned her head away and said, no Jasper, that's no good, you have to pinch my nose closed. Otherwise, all that air just comes out.

She showed him how to pinch her nose with his fingers and how to elevate the angle of her jaw to better receive air from his lungs.

I love the colour of your hair, Marnie, though it's dark now with sweat, those ringlets.

Shut up, Jasper, you've got to be able to do this right. You never know. Now, I'll play dead, you breathe for me. You've got to get the air right down into my lungs. I am going to totally relax and die.

She swooned. He gently took her nose and pinched her nostrils together with the thumb and forefinger of his left hand. She was dead. He had no choice but to bend to her, to support her chin with his other hand, and then to form a sealed kiss upon her open mouth, and blow. As he did so, as he passed his breath into her, he looked down at her chest. It rose and fell in synchrony with his own expirations, her areolae, her pink nipples, her breasts, the sheen of sweat on her sternum.

She broke her mouth away.

There, you did it, that was good, she said. I guess I have time for once more, Jasper. Studying can be like this, you know, you have to do it over and over, to get it right.

She put her arms up around his neck and drew him down.

This is part of the exam?

No, the exam's over, I'm alive again. Thanks, Jasper, whoever you are. Whatever you are.

Valerie and Jasper walked to Amber White's together. A cool breeze from the north caught them by surprise, so they stepped briskly. Valerie hugged her arms to her chest.

Amber's a fine poet, said Valerie, but she makes her living, like I said, as a court reporter at the College of Physicians. She also runs a women's shelter, all on her own. She lives right next to it, on Jarvis.

It's getting dark. Take my arm, Valerie.

To his surprise, she did. She hooked her left hand into the crook of his right elbow but she didn't do anything else. She didn't move any closer to him, or change her tone of voice. Jasper knew if Marnie were there instead of Valerie, she would have closed the space between them and her arm would be around his waist. Not only that, she'd be reeling up against him as hard as she could, her hip on his. She'd look up at him and laugh, carefree.

I am besotted, I admit it openly.

With Marnie Kennedy?

Yes, I am besotted with her, but also with you. More with you.

Valerie laughed and said, you know about Roberto and me now, don't you?

Yes, said Jasper Glass. As I know about other disasters. The threat of nuclear holocaust, for example.

There's her house, the semi-detached one, red brick. Amber lives on the left side, the shelter's on the right.

She can afford that, both homes?

Barely, it runs on a shoestring.

And tonight, the purpose of this? Remind me.

She'll go over the hearing John's doctor had. She was there.

Those proceedings would be confidential, I would have thought.

Now they were only forty yards from Amber's house. Three girls sat on the near steps, smoking.

They must be in the shelter, said Valerie. They're younger than we are. I could volunteer here, you know.

That's crazy.

Valerie Anderson pulled her hand free and they walked up the steps to Amber's side and rang the bell.

She's over here in our side, one of the girls on the steps said. She said just come in, she's put on the kettle.

They sat with Amber White in the living room of the shelter. There was a couch, two armchairs, a desk, and on the wall a poster of a girl on a mountaintop, holding up her arms, triumphant.

Why did you become doctors? Amber asked.

I'm interested in social justice within the health care system, said Valerie Anderson. And we have a project to fulfill in that regard.

And you, Mr. Glass?

Oh, I share the same interests as Valerie, he said.

But not with the same passion, I detect.

Jasper laughed and said, touché, but I bring my own skill set to the project, if not the same ardour.

The problem is, said Amber White, that since I spoke to you, Valerie, I have changed my mind. I have little interest in your friend's case. I should have phoned you, but I didn't.

Oh, said Valerie.

All abuse is to be condemned, said Amber, but as a feminist, my priorities must entirely be women.

We saw your girls outside, said Valerie.

I offer them a semi-normal place to stay. It's all I can do.

She looked at Valerie Anderson.

When you phoned me, Valerie, I actually thought perhaps you could help me out, rather than the other way around. We're short of staff, it's all volunteer. You can imagine.

Jasper looked at Valerie.

We have exams coming up, he said, it's hard to find the time.

I was asking Ms. Anderson. You aren't allowed to work here, Mr. Glass.

Count me in, Amber, said Valerie Anderson. I can start tomorrow night.

Tomorrow night? asked Jasper.

Actually, you can study most of the time, said Amber. There's the desk. You're here only for emergencies.

Jasper looked at his watch. He walked to the window and looked out. Two of the girls were still sitting on the adjoining stoop, lipsticked, smoking. They saw

Jasper and waved and smiled. Then they spoke to each other and laughed and smiled back at him again.

Good, said Valerie, it's a deal. I'll bring my books.

On the way back to the campus, Valerie took Jasper's arm again.

I don't know what you agreed to back there, he said.

They cut across Queen's Park Circle on the south side of the parliament buildings. Lights from cars flashed across her face.

What about our project, he asked, the time we were going to spend together?

It's dead in the water, Jasper. This is far more important.

Valerie, will you ever, ever consider me?

No, never. But I love you. Anyway, you already have a girlfriend.

If you're referring to Marnie Kennedy, I don't have her, she has me. I keep her alive right now, that's all, said Jasper Glass.

Bill Glass leafed through the manuscript at least once a month, just to make sure his idioms were as fresh as possible.

No old lettuce wanted in the salad.

He was at the letter C: *C'est du gâteau*: it's easy, a piece of cake. *C'est la fin des haricots*: it's the last straw.

Then he heard a sound outside, a scraping sound, and he left his study to investigate. He walked into Jasper's bedroom and, looking down, he saw a man in the driveway. He had one of those long aluminum extension ladders held straight up into the sky but he faced away from the professor, towards the Nájera residence. He proceeded to plant the feet of the ladder carefully in the loose gravel, wiggle it back and forth and, when he was satisfied, he pulled quickly on the rope and extended the ladder to its fullest length. Then he let the ladder fall gently against the eaves of the Nájeras', right near the squirrel opening.

Oh no, not my squirrels.

Already today, he'd watched them for an hour. They'd seemed to flout gravity with abandon, the young ones. They jumped and spun and tumbled in a ball towards the end of the roof but they never fell. Really, it was quite a miracle of gymnastics.

June, come see, he had called.

When she looked out the window, she'd laughed with delight. He felt vindicated. This time, she had seen what he had seen.

Now he made his way downstairs and outside.

Excuse me, excuse me, but you're in my driveway.

Oh hello, the man said.

He was about six feet up the ladder by then, but he stopped and came down.

I'm sorry, I figured you wouldn't mind. It's the only safe place for my ladder, he said.

Yes the ladder, said Bill Glass, I do have issues with the ladder.

Well, your neighbours have a problem.

Oh?

Squirrels.

Squirrels? In the house? That sounds far-fetched, said Bill Glass.

I don't think so. They hear chewing noises in the night, from the attic. Keeps them awake, the gnawing. In this neighbourhood, that means squirrels. Other places, it's rats. They're lucky it's not rats.

Bill Glass thought of his little family under the roofline, the pleasant hours he had spent watching their antics.

Are you sure? he asked.

Oh yes. I'm sure, he said, I've been doing this for a lifetime, twenty years.

Then Bill Glass actually held the ladder to steady it, as if he were an accomplice, and the squirrel man climbed the ladder and peered over the edge of the eaves.

No doubt about it. The little pests are living here like it's the Taj Mahal.

Professor Glass shouted from below, will you be all right now?

Yes, yes, I got everything I need. Thanks. I just block it off, that's all. They go somewhere else.

Bill left the squirrel man and went inside. From his study, he heard the blows of a hammer, then again the metallic scraping, the jitter of the reverse-telescoping of the aluminum ladder, and all was quiet again.

He returned to Jasper's bedroom window. A grid of shiny grey metal now obstructed the entrance to what had been the squirrels' nursery. His squirrels.

He moved his gaze farther, down and to the right, where the cherry tree stood in the Nájeras' garden. There was no reason, this spring, to return to his vantage point again.

Two hours later, at dinner, Jasper was at home for once and the three of them sat at the table in the dining room.

Your father and I met a classmate of yours today, said June. We drove her and Roberto to the university.

Oh? said Jasper.

Yes, a nice girl. Valerie Anderson.

Oh, Valerie, said Jasper. My lab partner in anatomy. I love her, she is the epitome of heavenly beauty, she has the soul of an angel. And she is possessed as well of a fine mind.

Are you serious, Jasper? June asked. I never know with you.

I'm serious, I confess it. She's pretty controlled, though, and always on some mission of mercy or another.

Oh really, said the professor, you say she's pretty controlled? I agree with you on the pretty part.

What do you mean by that? asked Jasper.

Just a feeling I had. The way she related to Roberto Moreno, the way they interacted, they seemed very close. Not really controlled, that's not a word I'd use.

Jasper Glass said nothing.

Bill proceeded to carve the roast and all three of them remarked on how tender the beef was. June had taken a French cooking class at Cordon Bleu. No longer did they eat meat in the English manner. Now their beef was pink in the middle, in the French fashion, tender, more succulent.

I lost my squirrels today, said Bill Glass. God knows what becomes of them now.

They survive, said Jasper. They collect leaves. They build nests in trees, they scamper around the same. That's what squirrels do.

John Glass was the youngest person ever to be admitted to the Faculty of Medicine. It was a mistake, a travesty, because he was unprepared for it emotionally. He was just seventeen. He'd be finished at twenty-three. What would he know about life then? Not much.

Jasper and Valerie said that his problem was classic, that he was a textbook example of depression or anxiety, or both mixed together in a stew.

Read this article. This is you to a T, they said.

He agreed with them, but how did that help? It was easy for those two to be the cheerful diagnosticians. They had all the answers, sure, but that didn't make it any easier for him to be labelled. Valerie and Jasper, they coasted through life, as far as he could see. Beautiful, handsome, they had it all. They flew over the surface of life like skimmer birds. They were optimists, they didn't understand the powerful grip of melancholy, his closest companion. Day after day and night after night, John Glass sat in the library and leaned back in his chair and looked up at the lights and generally scanned the room, which was large enough to sit fifty students, each at a seat at one of the long tables, buffered from each other by piles of books.

As he did so, he imagined himself in a circus, lying on his back, his shirt removed, pegged down in the centre of the ring, his arms splayed and held by leather thongs fastened to his wrists and ankles, the big-top overhead, the tent full of paying customers. He lay on the sawdust floor and Dumbo the elephant walked in, trumpeted, spewed water, balanced on a ball, and then he approached John, curiously, his great head bedecked in red and gold, his tasselled tail flicking. There was no element of threat in what the elephant did. He lifted his right front foot and brought it down upon John's chest, but he did it tenderly and carefully as though he were full of concern, like a good physician, and he left it there, pinning John to the floor.

Then the master of ceremonies cracked his whip and the calliope played and the audience filed out and the two of them, Dumbo and John Glass, remained there, quite steadfast in their own way, unmoving for the entire school year.

After their first meeting at the shelter, Valerie Anderson came to know Amber White quite well. They shared a passion for reading and writing poetry. When Valerie was on duty, Amber often came over to talk.

One or two girls were usually there, lounging about, playing records, dancing by themselves. Then they'd pick up and leave and the house was quiet.

One evening, Amber asked, would you take a look at a poem of mine, an unpublished one?

Me?

Yes, you. Who else is here?

Amber pretended to look around the room.

I'm way too close to it, I've lost all perspective, she said.

Sure, Amber, I'd love to. Show it to me.

Amber went to her own side of the residence, and when she returned a minute later, she dropped a manuscript in front of Valerie. It thumped down and Valerie's tea jumped up and spilled into the saucer.

There, said Amber, this is what I mean. Just look at the first few pages. There's no rush.

Valerie read the title: *By Church and Isabella I Sat Down and Wept.*

Church and Isabella? That's where I live.

She instantly realized that the title of Amber's poem referenced an abused female writer, Elizabeth Smart.

It took Valerie Anderson three weeks of late-night reading to do justice to the imposing poem, to read and reread it, to assess its apparent simplicity and plumb its depths. She sat in the window of her apartment, overlooking the exact intersection of Church and Isabella, as she read it. The poem was 148 pages long, with few stanza breaks. She found it sturdy, proud, and the voice never faltered.

Amber, this has to be published. I wouldn't touch a thing.

Not a thing? What kind of reader are you? It's already been rejected twelve times.

Twelve times? To hell with them all then, we'll publish it ourselves. We'll start our own magazine, Amber. It's the only way to get this out.

That's a lot of work, just for me.

It's not for you, it's for the poem.

Okay then, it's for poetry. What'll we call it, the magazine? asked Amber White.

Valerie suggested that she'd take the alphabet *A* to *Z* and come up with twenty-six medical words. Amber could do the same with names of a purely feminist bent. Then they'd compare lists. If there was one word they shared, that would be the name of the new poetry magazine.

Should we publish work by male authors? asked Valerie.

There's no better way to make a feminist point, said Amber, so I'd say—yes.

That was as far as they got on the first day. Roberto Moreno came by to pick up Valerie and Amber got out the vacuum cleaner. One of the girls had failed to finish her chores.

Valerie and Roberto walked west on Wellesley, then up Church Street. Her mind raced *A* to *Z*. *Anthrax, Breast, Cadaver, Detox, Enucleate, Fallopia, Gallop, Hack, Incise, Jugular, Karyotype, Leech, Melancholy, Neoplasm, Ova, Push, Quanta, Reflux, Synergist, Truss, Ulcer, Viral, Wasted, X-ray, Yolk, Zygote.*

She wanted a title that would jump off the shelf, but when it came down to it, it was the work inside the journal that mattered. The editor of a poetry magazine!

She couldn't believe her luck. She couldn't believe her friendship with the poet Amber White.

You seem distracted tonight, Roberto said.

Sorry, she said, and she told him of the plans for the magazine and she ran through the names she was making up as she walked.

That's great, Valerie, great. Parabolism, here we come.

When Dr. Hilger banished John Glass from the Faculty of Medicine, he belittled John's lonely success in embryology. That was his privilege as associate dean in charge of discipline, but had John Glass been in Dr. Hilger's position, he would have been more circumspect. He never would have lashed out as the doctor had or subjected any student to public or private ridicule. And to boot, Dr. Hilger had failed to understand the significance of embryology.

John's textbook for embryology was small. It had a green cover and had been purchased third-hand and had been heavily used. The spine was broken.

The first owner's notations in blue and the second owner's notations in red already adorned the pages when John Glass opened it on the morning of the first class. And the lecturer, a charismatic man, the embryologist, large and bearded, stood before them at the lectern and stated, quite matter-of-factly, that they should be interested in his subject because they were all, once, themselves, embryos.

Silence filled the hall.

You are descended from embryos, he repeated.

More silence for the most part until someone made a sound like an ape. The teacher did not acknowledge it.

So a study of embryology is a study of our own physical genesis. But it's more than that, isn't it, students? For thoughtful men and women, as I hope you are, the study of embryology is also the key to unlocking the door to self-knowledge. Even the door to your own spirituality and faith.

What he said hit John Glass like a bodycheck in open ice. Why, of course! He himself was still an embryo emotionally and spiritually and that was the cause of his inertia, his malaise. Physically, he had grown into a boy-child and then a man, sure, but his physical growth was an illusion. Spiritually, he was undeveloped. In his knowledge of self, he was the size of a squash, a potato, a fourteen-week foetus.

Other students, upon hearing the lecturer speak of spirituality, immediately laughed and protested and shouted, Dark Ages! and, Science! Science! Darwin!

But the teacher held his ground. He raised the little green book as though it were a bible.

Doctors, he said, you wish to understand the human condition? Embryology is the key. Oh, you faithless who shout and mock the spiritual world, you to whom embryology is just another step in the curriculum, let me say this: you will study cell cleavages and that is all you will see. But open your hearts, my friends, and study the growth of the miraculous embryo and you will see much more than pale and stodgy cell clusters. You will see, for example, the first embryonic stem cells, the ones that form after conception, cells whose potential is so extraordinary as to defy belief. You will see how sadly limited we are, by comparison, now that we are grown to our adult, our mature state.

For pathetic indeed we are, he said.

He rose up on his toes when he said that and he raised his arms and he repeated himself.

Pathetic we are.

He slammed the book down on the lectern and all laughter and protest stopped. He turned off the lights. Slides flicked by one by one, and over the images John Glass heard the lecturer's voice and it went straight to his embryonic soul.

In the three nights before the anatomy exam, he studied embryology. Before physiology, he studied embryology. Before biochemistry, histology, pharmacology, pathology, before Christmas, before New Year's, before Rosh Hashanah, he opened his little green book and he saw himself, literally and figuratively, as first the totipotent fertilized ovum, then the sixteen-cell morula, as it was called at that stage, then the blastocyst, then the trophoblast. He drew in pen and pencil each one of those embryonic shapes, the cells dividing again and again but still part of a round and unified new human being that was, though very early, just like him. As he had been, once. His drawings were complex. The blastocyst looked somewhat like a golf ball but with deeper and completed dimples and suggestive grooves.

He made a folder of his drawings and handed them in. The teacher was impressed.

Glass, he said, you have restored my faith in young men and women.

Thank you, John said.

When he wrote the embryology exam, he placed first overall. It was almost unfair to the others, the knowledge he had accrued not only from the text but, in tandem, from the semi-ruined fabric of his own undeveloped life.

He could easily have scored 100 per cent but he settled for 88 per cent by not answering the last two questions. He hoped his teacher would recognize that his refusal to finish with total perfection revealed his profound understanding of spiritual ontogeny. His humility, his realization that he could be much more than just a collection of burgeoning cells.

In their third class with Roberto Moreno, they discussed the importance in poetry of that commonplace substance: water.

What brought it up? Keats's epitaph. He had requested that his gravestone remain empty but for the words *Here lies One Whose Name was writ in Water.* No name, no date, nothing but those heartbreaking words that recorded his impermanence, his anonymity and his regret.

Roberto Moreno mentioned Lorca, Octavio Paz, Gutiérrez, Shakespeare, Milton, Pratt and Birney. As a teacher, Roberto had to really bone up on the gringos that were on the course, but he did it.

Students, he said, it is impossible to avoid water when you read these poets.

Impossible also to avoid the shedding of tears, the running of blood. Byron swam the Hellespont, Shelley died at sea, Rosenberg was smothered in a shallow trench of mud. And all the Mexicans Roberto Moreno knew were the same. They had the same fixation with or attraction to water.

Tears and blood, said Roberto Moreno, tears and blood. Both have the same salt content as the sea.

John Glass arose from his seat and raised his arm.

Have you heard the story of the American poet Hart Crane and his so-called suicide?

There were a few groans from the class. Now they had to listen to one of John Glass's monologues on another obscure poet.

No, said Roberto Moreno, I haven't. Tell us about Hart Crane.

Hart Crane threw himself from the deck of an ocean-going vessel, said John Glass, and his act has puzzled those who care in the years since.

He committed suicide?

Well, that's the usual perception, said John Glass, but it's not mine. I'll tell you why. The act was observed by many of Hart Crane's fellow passengers. First, he strode to the rail, impassive. For a few minutes he stood there as did all the rest of his companions. The rolling sea was their tableau. Then he carefully removed his overcoat, folded it and placed it upon the deck, and in two quick steps was up and over the side. He was swimming in a trice, strong purposeful strokes away from the ship. Man overboard! his companions cried but the turning of the ship was so ponderous and shuddering that he was never seen again.

Well described, John, said Roberto Moreno.

He committed suicide then, said another student, that's obvious.

No, said John, I have thought about this. A lot. Everybody thinks of suicide, in one way or another it's a decision we all make. First, Hart Crane took off his heavy coat, a coat that would have helped him had suicide been his aim. Second, he swam with vigour, with intent. He must have either seen an island that was visible to no one else, or he heard a siren too beautiful to resist. Either way, Crane became one with water, our subject today, and saw it as his companion on whatever journey he took. It was not suicide. It was more like, well, confusion. It could happen to anyone.

The class was silent.

Where did this occur? asked Valerie Anderson.

The Gulf of Mexico. The water was warm.

Then someone said, go study that embryology, John.

There was much laughter.

Then Jasper Glass stood up and supported his brother's interpretation of the death of Hart Crane.

Confusion is much more prevalent than intended suicide, he said. It's universal.

Why do you care about this, John? asked Roberto Moreno.

Because I've made a study of suicide among writers. It came up in my research. For example, Virginia Woolf drowned herself in a river. She weighted her pockets with rocks and walked in. That was it. Had Hart Crane wanted to drown, he too would have weighted his pockets.

Where would he get rocks on a ship?

That's easy, he would improvise. He'd stuff his pockets with cutlery, with knives and forks and spoons, with silver from the kitchen.

Afterwards, John Glass left the class with Jasper and Valerie and Roberto.

Nobody really gets it, he said. It's so easy to be confused. Life is complex. More people kill themselves from confusion than from all the psychiatric diagnoses in the world.

And you, John, are you confused? asked Valerie.

Oh yes, sometimes I am. Not about this though.

Night shifts were the worst. Internal medicine, surgery, anaesthesia, emergency, it didn't matter what the discipline was. After eleven o'clock at night, it was the weirdest stuff that came down. So Abner Krank, twenty-nine years old, in his position as chief resident in psychiatry, 999 Queen Street, corner of Ossington where Ossington T-boned into Queen over the streetcar tracks, sat in the on-call office on the first floor of the mental hospital with a feeling of semi-dread as he waited.

One a.m. What would it be, sirens? Or the shuffling of feet, the ring of the phone, cries down the corridor?

He remembered once again the keening, the wail he heard one night while vacationing in France, in Castres, a cry that had haunted him ever since. Near asleep in the modest hotel that brushed up against the brown and murky river, he heard first the motor scooter, unadorned by a muffler and in full acceleration. It tore through the night street over cobbles, the revs thundered up against the walls, so close. He sat up in his bed. Then, in the aftermath came a strange heathen shout, primeval, a cry, a howl, as devastating a human utterance as ever a psychiatrist had heard. It lasted only ten seconds, no more, its source unknown, but he remembered it to this day.

Who knows, maybe that's why he went into this, psychiatry.

Regardless, any such noise tonight meant that he was going to have to do something. Intervene like the scientist he now was, juggle the Largactil. Praise be for Largactil, smack them with enough of that and peace was at hand in fifteen, twenty minutes.

Usually the police were involved. They came along because they were the only other nocturnal companions of the truly fucked-up, it seemed, the only ones who cared. Well, they didn't really care, in the emotional sense, any more than he did, but they both had jobs to do and these jobs were exactly defined. And if anything could be said about Abner Krank, it was that he was exact, exacting. On himself and on others. That's why he got through medical school easily, how he was accepted into his chosen field without any hesitation on the part of the Department of Psychiatry, and how he then became senior resident, vaulted over six other young doctors in the program.

He smiled. By now, though, he should have become used to night call. He should have been able to take it in stride. But he hadn't managed to do it, he always felt wired, jittery, insomniac.

He looked at his watch. Jesus, two-thirty and so far nothing?

It made no sense. Had he fallen asleep? No way.

He walked down the empty corridor to the lobby. Nobody there but a security guard.

What's up? said Abner Krank. I've never seen it so quiet.

Look out the door, Doctor, that's why. All the crazies, they're shut up inside. No one's going out in that.

Sheets of water streamed down the glass entrance door. Water had puddled inside, in the vestibule.

Funny thing, the guard said, it's raining like crazy and it's warm out there. Like Madagascar.

Oh, you've been to Madagascar?

No, no, just a figure of speech. You know, Doctor, hot and wet.

Then that's all you should say, hot and wet. Madagascar means nothing to me. It's not helpful to say Madagascar. Madagascar could be on the moon.

You say so, Doc, sorry.

Do we have an umbrella around here?

I think so, the Lost and Found, there's usually one.

Take a look, please. I'd like to go out, stretch my legs.

In this?

Why not? That's what umbrellas are for. I fancy a walk.

Yes sir, the guard said.

He went down the hall and came back with a black umbrella in his hand.

This should do, he said.

He handed it to the young doctor and watched him open the door and disappear into the rain. Even with the umbrella, the rain out there was coming down so hard that the doctor was going to come back looking like a drowned rat, and maybe a drowned rat from Madagascar. So the doctor didn't like to hear about Madagascar. That's his problem. Those Madagascar rats, they were the biggest rats in the world. They climbed up and down hawsers from ships anchored in Madagascar Harbour and they ran in packs. Probably they ran around in storms like this, just to wash off.

On Queen Street, Krank felt the rain pounding and the umbrella, as it turned out, wasn't a good one. Several of the thin metal struts were broken. But his head was dry. He turned east and walked the fifty yards to Shaw Street. He couldn't read the sign overhead but he knew where he was.

It was way too rainy, way too late for his favourite activity, following girls. No girls out in this, no one to watch. He liked the way they turned their heads to look at him and then, how they walked faster and faster. They had no idea who he was. They didn't know he was just testing the water.

He decided to go north on Shaw Street to Dundas, over to Ossington and then back to the hospital. He looked at his watch. 2:45. It was so uncommonly hot that he loosened his tie and undid the top button of his shirt. Already he felt clammy, half of it from the rain that leaked down from the crooked edge of the black umbrella, half from his own exertion. He could have a shower when he got back.

Weird, weird weather for Toronto.

Then he stumbled on them, maybe forty yards up Shaw Street. He had his head down and the umbrella low so he was only ten feet away. He almost tripped over them. They were having sex on the sidewalk, the man on top, and they were so into what they were doing he could have been a firetruck and they wouldn't have noticed. He stood there and the girl cried out.

No, she said.

She was bleeding from a cut on her head.

He quickly backed away a step or two and looked around. The park was shrouded on the other side of the street and on this side, row houses, all with little porches. He turned away and ran up the steps of the nearest one. There were no lights on, it was as dark as bats' wings where he stood.

Then he just watched.

It went on for quite a while. Now and then the rain intensified, and he could no longer hear anything over the rush of water down the eaves, the pelting on the street and on the sidewalk.

But he could see enough, the man's hips as they moved up and down.

Two, three minutes, five, how long was it? He didn't know.

Then a third and fourth person arrived on the scene in one hell of a hurry. Dr. Krank retreated into the recess of his porch. He pressed his back up against the wall.

The scene became a tumult of bodies and shouts came to him through the night. The rapist seemed to have been thrown off and then he was back on his feet and the two other men stood over the girl, guarding her.

There was a scuffle. He couldn't see much. He moved to the edge of the porch.

Then the original guy, the one in his white T-shirt, seemed to lose interest. He walked slowly up the street and out of sight.

The two men bent over the girl, now half on the sidewalk, half in the gutter. One of them walked away in the same direction the attacker had taken. Soon he was back. He looked calm, but by then his companion was lying motionless on the sidewalk too, side by side with the girl.

Injured? Krank couldn't tell.

The man who had returned crouched down. He put his arms around his companion and lifted him up easily. He slung him over his shoulder. He walked away into the night, north towards Dundas, his body angulated, skewed by his burden. The girl stayed where she was, motionless.

It was all over. He waited no longer than two minutes. Then he came out of the darkness and walked down to the sidewalk. She was breathing, the streak of blood still there on her forehead. Her dress was torn, her thigh exposed. It was too late for her, it had already happened. No point in walking farther now. He turned down Shaw Street and five minutes later he was back at the hospital.

Anything come up, anything for me? he asked the security guard.

No, nothing, Doctor, nothing at all. You're soaked through. How was the walk?

Hot and wet, like you said.

He shook off the umbrella and handed it back to the guard.

I slit the throat, said Jasper Glass.

He made his usual strong incision from below one ear down across the throat at the level of the larynx and continued up the other side, to the other ear.

There. No one lives through that, my friend, he said.

The usual formaldehyde ooze appeared and Valerie Anderson inserted the skin hooks. Then she pulled upwards as Jasper worked away under the chin.

Free it up there, she said. This will be the hard part, peeling off the face.

Oh?

The face, even when dead—it's still pretty personal. We've known our man for a month.

True, said Jasper, but once we get the skin off, it'll be a prehistoric mask, that's all. Nothing left but fat and muscles, like skinning a deer.

The soul of this body will be gone when we finish this step, gone forever, she said.

Not if we leave on the lips.

The lips?

The lips are the last refuge of the soul.

The eyes, she said.

No, it's the lips. Remember what it's like, Valerie, when someone dies on the ward? Pull harder there, outwards, that's better. Someone dies on the ward, one minute, no matter how sick they are, they're breathing. They've got the death rattle but they're still one hundred per cent alive. They have within them the spirit of struggle. Then they suddenly stop. Now they're dead, they're one hundred per cent dead. And their lips are purple, the lips are dead.

Jasper, it's the eyes that glass over. It's immediate. Shine a light in those eyes, they're dead, they're dry. That's how you make the diagnosis. No reaction to light. The eyes are the first to go.

The lips, he said.

Okay, we'll leave the lips on then, she said, it's fine with me.

They pulled the skin up over the chin and advanced upwards and Jasper carefully cut around the margins of the lips. They were just lying there then, loose on the face, so he tacked them down with four tiny sutures.

There, he said, lifelike indeed. I think I have a future in plastic surgery.

It's not too bad, Jasper, I admit. Pretty good.

Then they peeled back the skin of the cheeks, the nose, the temples, moving upwards as they did so.

The ultimate facelift, he said. I have removed all vestiges of age.

What do we do with this skin when we're finished?

Stretch it out, pin it to a basketball.

Jasper, she said.

He pressed himself up against the side of the table, the pressure still always there with Valerie, unabated.

Anderson, you know your name means son of Anders, and that's Danish. I'm partly Danish myself, the dour part of me, the deeply repressed, the psychologically twisted. Twisted like this face pinned on a basketball.

I haven't seen too much of that, your repressed side, she said.

But you have seen the longing side, the part that cannot bear love unrequited.

She laughed.

Yes, that I've seen, I've seen enough of that.

There was only the forehead, up to the hairline, to be released.

Don't laugh, he said. The Danish side of me is there but I admit, at the present time, it's overwhelmed by the Irish side.

I thought Glass was Jewish.

Well, it is Jewish some of the time but not for us. There's Jewish Glasses, German Glasses, Russian Glasses and Irish Glasses.

Beer glasses, shot glasses, she said.

Half-full, half-empty glasses, but statistically there are more Irish Glasses, Valerie, of which we Toronto Glasses form a tiny portion. But if you look at the Belfast telephone book or the Dublin book, you'll see more Glasses than Yeatses. We are not yet celebrated in literature, that's all. Well, that's not true, there's Seymour Glass, "A Perfect Day for Bananafish." By Salinger.

I haven't read that one, said Valerie Anderson.

Seymour Glass killed himself. Bang, a bullet right here, said Jasper.

He took the scalpel and thrust it through the flap of skin that already had been lifted from the right temple, pulled up like a tent by the skin hooks held by Valerie Anderson. It left a small hole, which he widened with his gloved finger.

There you go, Mr. Seymour Glass, he said, whatever reason you had, there's your bullet hole, in the right place.

Jasper, till now this has been a perfect dissection. Now you've messed it up.

All perfection needs a flaw to qualify, artistically, for the very perfection it seeks and embodies. You, for example, Valerie Anderson, have a slightly asymmetrical face.

Together they held up the peeled-off skin, raised it, stretched it out and looked at it.

There's no personality there at all, he said. The bullet hole makes no difference, Valerie. The thing about death, once it arrives, it's all over.

Then he rolled up the facial skin into a ball, as though it were pizza dough. He dropped it into the biological-waste container. It landed on nineteen other faces from nineteen other metal tables.

Thank God for the incinerator, he said.

Valerie looked at their cadaver.

Literally defaced, she said.

Valerie Anderson's and Jasper Glass's body was the only one left with lips. It was true, they agreed as they left the lab, that those tacked-on lips lent a touch of enduring humanity to it, however spurious.

Valerie and Amber met two days later for lunch at the Avenue Diner, on Davenport. It was crowded but they landed two seats side by side.

I can afford the salad, that's all I want, said Amber White.

So, said Valerie, let's look at the names. Show me yours first. This is exciting.

I kept it simple, straightforward. Like we agreed.

Amber pulled a piece of paper from her purse and handed it across the table.

Alice, Bosom, Coarse, Drama, Exit, Fork, Groove, Hamlette, Insideher, Justine, Kama, Leotard, Mensee, No, Ovum, Pent, Queen, Rent, Street, Touch, Undo, Vinculum, Wax, XX, Yen, Zipper.

Then they looked at Valerie's names and, from the lists, two similarities jumped out: *Breast* and *Ova, Bosom* and *Ovum.*

Men have breasts, don't they, said Valerie, however useless they are. The breasts, I mean, not men.

That's open to argument. But I agree, neither is gender-specific. So strike *Breast* and *Bosom,* said Amber White.

Then it's between *Ova* and *Ovum?*

I don't know, said Amber, what do you think? They're both pretty obvious. No one wants to be hit over the head with symbols.

So they settled on *Zygote.* It suggested burgeoning and fertility.

But that name sounds familiar to me, said Amber. There's already a magazine by that name.

So they looked at the lists again. They didn't want to give up the *Z*.

Zipper then, said Valerie, I like *Zipper*. It has an onomatopoeic buzz. You pull it down, you open it up, *Zipper* reveals.

They do us up, they undo us, said Amber.

Wherever there's a zipper, there's a woman.

Zippers on body bags too, the last step before the grave.

So that was it.

Zipper volume 1, number 1, was published three months later with the help of the Canada Council, the Ontario Arts Council, and the University of Toronto Medical Women's Bursary Fund for the Arts. It was amazing how fast it came together. The entire content of the first issue was *By Church and Isabella I Sat Down and Wept.*

Amber White, already quite experienced as a writer, nevertheless was proud to see her name on the cover. She turned to the opening lines

> *Buick Continental*
> *quasi sentimental*
> *masturbator*
> *pimp locator*

and they jumped off the page, they came at her like a cleaver, which was the metaphor Valerie used to describe Amber's work in her first editorial, on page 2.

Lines that worked like a cleaver. That's what all poets wanted.

The first issue of *Zipper* sold out. The two editors were amazed. Mind you, they had decided to print only two hundred copies and they had a lot of friends.

It's your poem, Amber, everybody's talking about it, said Valerie Anderson. I think we should jump on this opportunity.

Quickly, still under their own imprint, they published *By Church and Isabella I Sat Down and Wept* in book form. Softcover, a thousand copies this time. It too caught the public eye and was noticed by critics and brought Amber White a nomination for the Governor General's Award for poetry. So what if she lost in the long run. She didn't care.

Some of the work the two editors did for *Zipper* in its first year was unusual. They sent a letter to a misogynist poet in Montreal asking him for a telephone interview on the feminine mystique. He declined, but Amber and Valerie published his three-page refusal by breaking it up into lines and creating a found poem. It appeared years later in his collected works. They asked a Canadian female poet to comment on the apparent conflict of interest she had as a poet and as the wife of a diplomat in troubled countries. She responded with generosity, as they expected. Yes, there was a conflict. She sent six poems that, judging from the flora and fauna, had been written in the Amazon Basin, and had surely never been read over dinner tables in Rio de Janeiro. The journal also printed seventeen enigmatic Roberto Morenos, all titled after diptych street names: "Avenue Road," "Calle Rue," "Boulevard Street," "Parkway Crescent."

"Calle Rue" was later anthologized in *Best American Poetry*, where Roberto was mistakenly identified as a Mexican American living in Portland, Oregon.

How did that happen? asked Amber.

She wrote a letter to *Best American Poetry* and they offered an apology in the next issue, to appear in small print at the back. They would credit *Zipper* as the original source of the poem. Amber was mollified but it made her question her role as an editor. Why did she care? Did she think Roberto cared? Who owned poetry?

No one owned poetry. As long as it was out there, it didn't matter, it didn't need a leash.

Never mind, she told *Best American Poetry.*

Christian Foare, as Marnie Kennedy had said with her lips on the side of Jasper Glass's neck on the night they met, was a biostatistician, a mathematical genius, and her fiancé, her betrothed. He graduated with the highest honours from every school he attended, from North Toronto Collegiate to the University of Toronto to, finally, Johns Hopkins University, and it might have been a mistake in his personal life, this last posting, although as far as Jasper Glass could tell, Christian Foare knew nothing about Jasper Glass, nothing about what had transpired back in Toronto during the time he was away.

When Christian returned from Baltimore, he and Marnie Kennedy were married as planned at Grace

Church on-the-Hill even though her body was, figuratively speaking, still warm from the thirty thousand hands of Jasper Glass. As the families of the couple were well off, no wedding expense was spared. There were Lincolns and Cadillacs up and down the street by the church and later, for the reception, the Granite Club was jammed.

According to the *Toronto Star*, the bride was ravishingly beautiful, although all brides were so described by the *Star* society columnist, but in this particular case there had been no gilding of the lily, as revealed by the photographs taken of her, her white bridal gown, her smile.

In the background, the groom was quiet and dapper as befitted his position as the primary young biostatistician in all of North America, much sought after, again according to the *Toronto Star*, for his incisive understanding of meta-analyses, the significance of this or that, a skill for which he was about to be paid vast sums of money by drug companies who sponsored clinical trials. But he was also known, yet again according to the *Star*, for his absolute commitment to the truth. He would never warp figures one way or another, and should a drug prove no better than a placebo, then he would say so and it was back to the drawing board and millions of dollars lost for Ayerst or for Ciba-Geigy or for Boehringer. Christian Foare played squash and tennis, and after the wedding he and his wife honeymooned in Palm Beach, a honeymoon that Jasper Glass expected they enjoyed, but he heard nothing first-hand about it.

Nor did he wish to.

Then they returned, and Marnie started her internship at Mount Sinai Hospital, just one hundred yards away from where Jasper was still a medical student in the surgical rotation at the Toronto General Hospital. Christian Foare was away on business much of the time, to Boston, to New York or Rochester or Montreal, and, despite the fairy-tale life the newlyweds were embarking upon, Marnie Kennedy-Foare called Jasper up one day out of the blue and said she had a few hours off.

Where? he asked.

He was standing in the surgical lounge, leaning by the wall phone.

The interns' residence, 317.

Married quarters?

That's it, she said.

I'll be right over.

He asked Wallace, good old Wallace, to sit in for him on the gallbladder, holding retractors, something he was supposed to do in twenty minutes.

No problem, said Wallace. Thanks, Jasper, thanks a lot.

Wallace wanted to be a surgeon. He jumped at every chance.

Jasper had never seen Marnie before in whites, the official uniform that interns wore. He took off her lab coat first, the new name tag that said *Marnie Kennedy-Foare MD*, and her skirt next, but she did most of that herself. Then she was recognizably the same as ever. There was a photograph of the two newlyweds beside the bed, a photograph that tipped and fell face down when Jasper hit it with his hand half by accident. Marnie fell back on the bed and he ran his lips and his tongue down from her breasts to between her thighs.

Oh, Jasper, she said.

She pulled away and moved down into him simultaneously, in the same movement of her pelvis, a trick of hers that anatomically he could not explain.

Oh, Jasper, she said again.

Then they heard the hum of the elevator right next door and they both froze. He lifted his face and rested it on her left thigh. She lay there motionless. There were footsteps and then a key turned in the door.

This is impossible, she whispered.

They heard a soft whistling.

Oh Christ, Jasper, she said, you've got to get out of here. Fast.

She jumped up and ran around in circles but somehow she did it silently, she didn't make a sound.

More whistling came from the kitchen, recognizably Brahms' "Lullaby."

The window, she whispered.

He just stood there.

Jasper, the window.

She pointed, she had the sheet wrapped around her now, and Jasper stepped to the window and looked out. He saw a ledge about eight inches wide. It ran along the whole front of the building overlooking University Avenue, but at each end columns totally blocked it off. Dead ends.

Get out, she said.

Jasper almost said no and walked out through the kitchen but there was still something to be said for gallantry in this world, so instead he turned and kissed her. She pulled away.

Jasper, please, she said.

So now he was Cyrano de Bergerac. He'd go out in style. He slid the window up and, naked, he clambered onto the ledge. He looked down. He shuffled away from the window and pushed his back against the wall, firmly. It was concrete, warm, heated by the sun that had beaten down on it all afternoon. Three floors below were the sidewalk, the street, people walking. Ants, they didn't look like ants, he wasn't far enough up for that. But still, they looked small.

He heard a noise.

Her small hand darted out the window and a bundle of clothes was jammed down by his foot. A sharper gust of wind made him press back even harder against the wall. The clothes at his feet might as well have been a thousand miles away because there was no way he could bend down. The window beside him was still open.

He heard her say, a headache, a headache. They sent me home with oxycodone.

A low rumble of concern.

Can I get you anything?

No, no, just leave me here in the dark, pull the curtains.

Close the window?

No, please leave it like that. I need the air, Christian, I need the air.

Then he heard the curtains pulled, a swish.

A pigeon landed three feet to his left. It flew away again. A fresh blast of wind blew and all of Jasper's clothes, first the underwear, then the white shirt and then the pants, the socks, all of them pinwheeled into the air, spinning up and then, as though their parachutes had failed to open, the clothes plummeted straight to the sidewalk below.

Everybody down there looked up. A collective gasp arose that he could hear from his perch. They pointed.

Hey, are you crazy? they shouted. Don't jump! Take heart, young man, you have so much to live for!

A jumper, a jumper! Go ahead, jump!

Somebody laughed. A crowd of fifteen or twenty people had gathered. They peered up at him, a gargoyle on some ancient church facade.

Then he heard Marnie say, sorry, Jasper.

He heard a click as the window beside him closed.

That was it. He was on his own. He cupped his hands around his mouth to form a megaphone.

I can't take it anymore, he shouted.

That was a good line for suicides, a classic. He raised his arms in supplication.

No! Forlorn cries from concerned women floated upwards.

Wait, they shouted, we'll send someone up!

But that wouldn't do, would it? They'd come through Marnie's apartment, so again he raised his arms.

No, stop! I kill myself for all of you. A sacrifice!

He flapped his arms. He experienced a rush of fierce joy.

I am Icarus, Icarus! Yon sun has melted wax from these my faulty wings! I am doomed!

He pointed to the heavens but stood fixed upon the ledge. He could see people running now from all directions. It was time to change the pace, throw some guilt around.

You thrill-seekers, you ghouls! he shouted.

Sirens came from around the corner, 52 Division, a swarm of bright flashing lights in a cavalcade down University Avenue. Traffic peeled off to the side to let them through. Now there were hundreds of people gathered. They looked up at Jasper Glass and there was a damn good chance, he knew, that one of them would recognize him. Almost all the pedestrians in this area worked at the hospitals. He reached up carefully and pulled his long hair over his forehead. He covered his eyes as best he could and he twisted his mouth and face into a grotesque parody.

The Hunchback of Notre-Dame! he cried.

He knew it was a bit of a stretch. There was another collective gasp from the crowd.

No, they shouted, almost in unison, but at the same time he heard, jump, jump and hurry up about it, Chrissake.

A fireman with a bullhorn said, WAIT THERE, YOUNG FELLOW, THE NET IS ALMOST HERE.

No, shouted Jasper, death be my release from this bitter world!

Still, caution was his guide. He did not move. Five firemen raced from their truck with a landing net held between them like a trampoline. A calm descended upon him and he became aware of individual faces, hats, scarves, the shoulders of coats.

Then he saw him, his rival. Christian Foare. He had come out of the interns' residence, and Jasper saw him stop, caught in the hullabaloo. He watched him turn and look up. Their eyes met. Jasper looked away and waved his arms again, but words did not come to him this time, his throat was constricted and when he looked back down a few seconds later, Christian Foare had turned and was walking away. He never looked back and Jasper Glass watched him go.

WE'RE SENDING UP A COUNSELLOR, said the fireman.

The landing net was in place. Jasper Glass timed it perfectly. He launched himself up and out, high into the air, higher even than the ledge on which he perched, and still he flapped his arms as though in anticipation of flight.

Take this sinner! he shouted, and as he fell, the word *sinner* elongated itself behind him like a banner from his throat.

Screams from below drowned him out.

He landed dead-centre in the net. Strong young men threw a blanket over his nakedness. Then they rushed him to the ambulance and took him away.

That night Christian Foare came home from work after dark.

Marnie, he said, how's the headache?

Fine, she said, better, I lay there all afternoon. Whatever it was, it went away.

Hear anything about the fracas outside?

Fracas?

A man on the ledge outside, naked as a newborn. Fourth floor, right above our bedroom.

The fourth floor?

Right upstairs, he would have been right over your head.

No, Christian, she said. The oxycodone, I must have slept right through it.

Jumped into a net, I heard.

Well, she said, that's bizarre.

No kidding. Thank God we don't have to deal with stuff like that ourselves. We're moving to the new house soon anyway.

He put his arms around her and they never mentioned the jumper again.

Later Marnie wondered, did Christian Foare really love her that much?

What happened when he came out onto the street and looked up? Did he count the floors? Was his head so filled with equations that his brain counted one two three, yet his heart counted four? Did he really get it wrong? Had love fudged the numbers?

Love has a thousand faces, and most of them are blind.

Murlean Poirier wasn't back in the car for more than ten minutes before she realized she had made a mistake. It wasn't anything he said or did, he just stared through the front window and drove at exactly the speed limit. Before, he'd gone fast. She could see the speedometer from where she sat.

Why are you going so slow? she wanted to ask. She looked outside and tried to figure out what to do.

You said this car is new? she finally asked.

He perked up and slapped the dashboard with his hand.

Brand new, spanking new. Can't you smell it, Heidi? I love the smell, upholstery.

I feel I'm going to be sick.

What?

I'm going to throw up in your car.

Oh, Christ, no, don't do that.

He slowed right down. She opened her window as though to breathe fresh air. Then she bent over at the waist till her head was between her knees. She made a retching sound and heaved her shoulders. She sat back up and glanced at him. He was looking at her and then he looked at the floor to see what she'd done. She bent down again but all she could muster was dribbles of spit.

Jesus Christ, Heidi, hold on a minute.

She felt gravel under the tires.

Get out, quick, he said.

She had her bag in her lap. She opened the car door as soon as it stopped and jumped out.

There, she said, already I feel better.

They were on a straightaway. You could see a mile in each direction. Not many cars but enough to feel she wasn't all alone.

You mean you're okay now? That fast?

I'm okay now. I think.

Then hop back in, Heidi.

He never got out of the driver's seat. He just leaned over her way, towards the open door. He waved with his hand, beckoning her.

No, she said, the ride's over. It's your car that makes me sick.

You can't stay here, it's going to rain, it's going to pour. Look at the thunderclouds.

That's okay, I don't mind the rain. It's not cold.

She wanted to tell him to fuck off but she'd never used those words to a living human being. They were imaginary words for her. She went and sat on a rock. There were patches of sunshine and the rock was still warm.

He called her name one more time.

To hell with it, he said, I'm going home.

He U-turned, throwing up dust and small stones near her feet, and drove away. She counted to thirty and when she turned around, the road was empty.

She stood up and put out her thumb again. There was a bit more traffic but no one stopped right away so she had time to think.

She made up lists of things she didn't like, starting at the top of her own head. Her hair, too thin and brown like a mouse, there wasn't much she could do with it. Her eyebrows, her nose, her lips, her skinny chicken-bone chest though the breasts themselves, they were okay. The rough skin on the outside of her arms, dotted with tiny white spots. The doctor said there was nothing she could do about that, that everybody had it if you looked. Maybe that was true, maybe it wasn't.

School? Well, that was all right, she didn't hate it, she did pretty well.

When she turned sideways in the mirror, her stomach was flat, her legs were nice from all angles. Everybody said that.

Her mother, her father, her sister, the washing, the dishes, everybody lived with those, not just her.

On the other hand, she liked her new name a lot. Heidi Chipman.

Miss Chipman herself wouldn't mind, not that she'd ever know that Murlean used her name for a while. She did like Miss Chipman, though, she always had. How many years, those dance classes every Saturday? Nine years. After Miss Chipman had her second baby, she always asked Murlean to demonstrate the hardest moves.

Honey, you show them.

There was a bit of thunder far off.

Fuck off. Fuck off.

She said it ten or twenty times. It began to feel almost natural, the *f,* her teeth on her lower lip. Maybe she should have said it to him out loud.

The chief resident in psychiatry pronounced his name in the German way, *Kronk*.

Dr. Krank? everybody said as they looked at his name tag.

He corrected them ten times a day.

Actually, it's pronounced *Kronk,* please say Dr. *Kronk.*

He got off the streetcar on the north side of Queen Street, waited for the traffic to abate, and then crossed the road. Morning sunshine cast long shadows to his right. The Victorian building in which he worked, 999 Queen Street West, loomed over him, its cupola quiet now, but in the evening bats spilled from it. How fitting, they spilled in nervous clouds. Perhaps thousands of them, there were way too many to count. They swept like brooms across the sky, through insect-ridden air.

The on-call bedroom for the chief resident was up in that cupola. To get there, he had to climb the long staircase up and up, high into the oldest part of the building. It was the most medieval of the towers and other jagged eccentricities that grew from the roof of the mental hospital. The bedroom, at the very summit of the cupola, required a heavy metal skeleton key to open. It had no windows and the ceilings were at least twenty feet high. That was where he worked and slept, where he answered the phone, where he had casual sex with Anna, where he made his clinical decisions. If a new patient needed to be seen, down he went to the first floor, which was where he was headed now.

This was the worst rotation he had ever had. The endless locked wards full of psychotics so mangled within themselves that any attempt to communicate was ludicrous.

He looked at the admissions list. He read the summaries and at nine-thirty, half an hour late because they were medical students and they could wait forever as far as he was concerned, he walked along to the teaching unit.

Jesus, what kind of name was that last one? W.W.'s parents might as well have tied his hands behind his back.

Good morning, he said.

He was a nice-looking man, Dr. Krank, with curly dark hair. He always wore a white lab coat, buttoned up. It was considered professional to do so but, more importantly, he found that the material of the lab coat soaked up the mist from the injectable phenothiazines, the antipsychotics that floated through the air on the wards. Those drugs had a peculiar lasting odour. If he didn't wear the lab coat, then on his way home their miasma seeped out of him in waves.

Good morning, I am Dr. Krank, K-R-A-N-K, pronounced, as I have just said, *Kronk*.

He stood at the small green chalkboard that could be pushed around on wheels and then he wrote the address of the hospital, 999, in white chalk, large numbers that covered half the board. He realized, if he flipped it around, it would say 666. He resisted the temptation.

Okay, kids, listen. This is a public hospital. We do hard time here in the psychiatric rotation. It's part of our training. What do you think we see when we come here, as doctors? Ms. Anderson?

I expect, Dr. Krank, we see some very unfortunate people here.

She pronounced his name correctly.

Mr. Glass?

I agree with Valerie. Patients here would be at the end of their rope. Who would want to come here anyway, voluntarily?

John Glass was there only because Valerie Anderson had come over, knocked on the door and half dragged him along.

And you, Wallace Wallace?

Dr. Krank smiled as he said the name.

Psychotics, I expect. We'll see psychotics, said Wallace.

I thought you might say psychotics twice, Wallace Wallace, said Dr. Krank.

He looked directly at the girl, but she didn't laugh and neither did the other two. They didn't even break a smile and he realized that they must have heard that line many times already. He should have been smarter, he should have held off with his wit, been more subtle in his use of mockery.

What I meant was, you can say that twice, Wallace, you can say that twice because there are twice as many psychotics per square foot here as in any other psychiatric hospital in Ontario. Twice as many, three times, they pour out of the rooms when we go through the locked doors and Ms. Anderson is right, they are the most unfortunate people in our city.

He paused and looked at Valerie again.

Just walking into this building, you can feel the oppression, he said.

Maybe this particular girl, more than any other, could feel his personal suffering.

We can make it a bit better in here with our attitude, she said, a compassionate attitude.

He laughed.

I love you, you kids.

But of course he was thinking just of her. All three of the medical students heard the irony in his voice.

Well, he said, let's get down to the nitty-gritty.

He shuffled through his papers and separated one.

Here we go, a new admission, a suicide attempt. Mr. Smith. No one's seen him yet. He's been here overnight. So, what's important in the immediate evaluation of someone like this, someone in such a crisis that they attempt to take their own life?

Now that he was teaching, he felt better. He wasn't dealing face to face with hopeless cases, he wasn't writing orders for phenothiazines or restraints or blood work and he wasn't sitting up there with a lineup full of twitchers, Parkinsonians. All of those were far away, upstairs, and down here the girl with dark hair was interested, he could tell. She sat forward and answered right away.

The first thing to do is to assess the level of depression, whether they'd do it again.

Dr. Krank wrote LEVEL OF DEPRESSION on the board.

Good, Ms. Anderson, he said, and how would we assess that?

I'd just ask him, said John Glass, I'd ask him right out.

I'd take the patient's answers with a grain of salt, said Valerie, I'd assess his affect.

Dr. Krank looked down at his notes and then looked up.

What, he said, if the patient said he could fly, that he had wings? Is he manic? Delusional?

He wrote the words MANIC and DELUSIONAL on the board and he saw Wallace Wallace copy it down.

Yes, and equally, sir, family history needs to be explored, said Wallace.

Is that important? Family history? asked John Glass. I hope not.

Oh yes, said Dr. Krank, your mental state is often sealed somewhere in your genetic code.

Krank thought about his own mother for a tenth of a second and then he looked at his watch and already he'd been there twenty minutes. Christ, he had other things to do.

Listen, he said, I want you to copy down these words and then go see the patient. You'll have an hour. Valerie, you do the interview. You, Wallace, and you, John, this time you just sit there, observe. Don't overwhelm the patient by numbers. It's a simple enough rule in the psychiatric game. Then after lunch, Ms. Anderson and I, we get together and talk. We'll decide what to do. Next week it's your turn, Wallace, then John. Now, here are the things we need to ask the patient.

As he talked, he wrote down more key words on the board.

Has he been SLEEPING well? Does he have any evidence of HYPERSEXUALITY? Do you know what that is, Valerie?

Why did he say that? Why did he direct that question just to her? A mistake. It came out of him uncontrolled.

What I mean is, has our Mr. Smith been hearing VOICES, seeing what others do not see, does he get MESSAGES from the TV, from radio, does he have DELUSIONS OF GRANDEUR, special qualities? If he took DRUGS AND/OR ALCOHOL, then maybe the whole thing will blow over. Equally well, it could be the onset of a permanent SCHIZOPHRENIA, a life sentence. Anyway, Mr. Smith is here for three days on a Form 1, so that's the time frame we've got. Valerie, Ms. Anderson, back here in my office, one o'clock.

He picked up his papers, his briefcase and he left the room.

Talk about delusions of grandeur, said John Glass.

Typical psychiatric resident, full of himself, said Wallace Wallace.

How do people like that ever do anything for anybody? wondered Valerie Anderson. You know, there was a study of psychiatrists and it was found that eighty per cent chose their specialty because of vague inner turmoil, unhappiness, dissatisfaction. They're patients themselves, when it comes down to it.

That's the human condition for everyone, not just psychiatrists, said John Glass.

Let's go see our Mr. Smith, said Valerie.

They went down the hall to the admissions room. There was an orderly standing outside and they identified themselves with their name tags. He opened the door and in they went.

Jasper! said John.

Jasper Glass, said Valerie.

He lay on a small bed. He was in a patient gown, and over that a loose robe, a sickly multilaundered yellow. The room itself, threadbare by design, had no windows, no dangling cords, no obvious means for self-destruction. When he saw them walk in, Jasper Glass laughed and jumped up and hugged them all, one by one, even Wallace.

You look good, Jasper, said Valerie.

Great night's sleep in here. I feel good. How'd you know I was here?

Are you okay? she asked.

I'm fine, I'm fine.

We didn't know you were here, said Valerie. We're your interviewers. And, according to these notes, you are not Jasper Glass but Ebenezer Smith.

Yes, said Jasper, a new name I have forged during this unfortunate time. You might say it's a *nom-de-gloom*.

He's got forced speech, verbal salad, said Wallace Wallace. I read about that, it's a sign of real trouble.

It's a put-on, said Valerie.

According to these notes, Jasper, you claimed to be Icarus, that you could fly, said Wallace. No wonder you're here.

John Glass laughed. Icarus, he said.

But now, said Jasper, this particular Icarus needs to get out before untold damage is done to his reputation, to his career.

Run it by us, Jasper, said John. What happened?

It's simple. I jumped from a ledge. I failed a public suicide. Now, as the protocol goes, I'm under observation, lest the same urge strike me again. Lest I succeed.

Marnie? asked Valerie.

Why yes, said Jasper Glass, yes, Marnie was involved, though inadvertently, as a catalyst. To you fellow travellers I admit it, to others it remains a secret, just for us.

He put his fingers to his lips.

The four of them sat and talked for two hours. Then, when they had finished their interview with "Ebenezer Smith," the three medical students left. The orderly locked the door. Icarus sat on the threadbare bed and looked miserable.

John Glass and Wallace Wallace took the first street-car eastbound on Queen. Valerie Anderson, after she had eaten her lunch, a pastrami sandwich on rye with two accompanying plums, made her way to the office of the senior resident, Dr. Abner Krank.

There she found him leaning back in his chair with his feet up on the desk.

Ms. Anderson, he said, come in, come in. Please sit down. Good news, I've had a couple of cancellations.

She looked at him.

Cancellations?

I've got all the time in the world for you. For Mr. Smith, I mean.

The rape kit showed semen and motile spermatozoa from the vagina. The hair matchups were dead-on with the body that had been found in the alley, so there wasn't much left for the police to do. The rapist had been killed within minutes of the crime. The conclusion that had initially been drawn by Detective Ames, namely that death had been caused by a stab wound to the chest, was confirmed at autopsy. The knife blade pierced first the shirt, then the skin, then subcutaneous fat of which there was very little—the rapist was thin—then the intercostal muscles, the underlying pleura of the lung, then the pericardium and finally the wall of the left ventricle of the heart itself, a straight and deadly path with no clinical result possible other than certain death within a few minutes. The body in the alley, the rain that poured down upon it, the ooze of blood that turned black on the rubbled asphalt, all of it was soon reduced to a written record. In this one case, justice had actually been served, the police felt, meted out in quick and dramatic fashion. Privately, they were satisfied.

Between you and me, hats off to whoever it was, said the detective sergeant.

How hard should we look for the killer? asked Detective Ames.

Well, the proper answer to that is that every life is equally precious, Detective. Justice here, however, was spontaneous and vigilante in origin, and thus illegal. Theoretically, we still have a murderer to apprehend.

But the dead man had just raped and was about to kill the girl.

Allegedly raped. He was never tried for the crime. So as of now, he's innocent.

She identified him. The rape kit, it's open and shut, said Detective Ames.

True enough, but everyone is equal before the law. Need I repeat this again? The man who allegedly raped the girl and who allegedly held a knife to her throat with intent to kill may have had demons of his own, exculpatory demons that would have been taken into account by the mercy of the court in a trial he has been denied. Also, in our society, the last time I checked, the death sentence has been abolished.

Too bad, said Detective Ames.

Yes, we agree. Too bad. Interview the girl again, do what you can. It's a needle in a haystack. Have you canvassed the street yet?

No, not yet. That's on the list. I guess someone might have seen something, heard something, looked out the window, walked by.

That's what we need, an eyewitness other than the girl. Use your own judgment here, Detective, how to proceed, how hard to push. We've seen far worse crimes, I admit that.

So Detective Ames took the case file back to his desk and reread it for the third time. According to the girl, the young men who had stumbled upon the scene of the rape were not much more than twenty years old. The one who had actually knocked the rapist off the girl was thin and shirtless. He had light brown hair long enough to fall over his eyes. The other one, the one with the confident laugh and the redeeming knife, he was shorter, darker and more nonchalant.

That said, the rain was itself a barrier to vision. The streetlight was broken and whatever she thought she saw could have been shredded by any attorney. But there was one thing—the matter of the white substance that he himself had removed from her neck. He'd sent it to the lab that same night.

He leafed through the papers but there was no result from forensics. He made a phone call.

Just a minute, said the voice on the other end, yes, here it is. It's been analyzed. It's shortening.

Shortening?

Yes, Crisco. Where I come from, back 'ome, it's called Cookeen.

For baking?

That's the one, all right. Can be used as a sexual lubricant, I'm told, though personally I'm a K-Y Jelly man.

Thanks for that, said the detective.

He hung up the phone. A sexual lubricant. The autopsy report made no mention of any foreign substance on the genitals of the man in the alley. The rescuer then, two young men out in the middle of the night, one of them with Crisco. God knows what they were up to.

He wrote up a notice. It was the only thing he could think of doing. Anyone in the Toronto Police Force who had any knowledge of any criminal activity involving Crisco?

He sent it out to every division in the city and then he put the file away.

Ridiculous question, probably the most foolish one he'd ever asked.

June Glass became friends with Valerie Anderson over the summer. Valerie had begun seeing the boy next door, the Mexican boy, Roberto Moreno, and because it was summertime by then the two women ran into each other, first by accident and then, later, by mutual design. Mostly they discussed poetry, for poetry was June's great love in university, really throughout her whole life. Then they branched out to talk about generational differences, how for Valerie, for example, entering medicine as a profession was not extraordinary in any way. Opportunities were wide open for modern women like Valerie. Valerie must have felt that the world was her oyster when she was a teenager.

It was different for me, June said one day. I became more a clam than an oyster.

She went inside to her kitchen and reached for a bottle of sherry, came back out and poured them each a small glass, nearly to the brim.

I mixed up that metaphor, the clam and the oyster, she said, it didn't quite make sense.

I got it, said Valerie.

Bill had the job, I had the boys. That was basically it.

The male body, the female body, said Valerie. There's not a lot you can do.

She sipped from her glass.

Harvey's Bristol Cream, said June.

They were on the patio, a small bricked area by the garage, contiguous to the lawn. A large maple tree provided shade, and the crescendo and then decrescendo drone of cicadas filled the late-afternoon air.

How I love that sound, cicadas, June said. It pulls at my heartstrings more than any other sound I know. Like bagpipes.

She lit a cigarette, a du Maurier.

It's a mating call, according to the books, said Valerie.

According to the books everything's mating, as if that's all insects have an interest in.

Maybe it's a cry of existential sorrow. How would we know?

June exhaled smoke and laughed. Well, if we found cicadas reading *Being and Nothingness*, then we'd know, she said.

There's mating there too, in *Being and Nothingness*. There's sex, there's disappointment, said Valerie.

Forgetting insects for now, in the sphere of *Homo sapiens* I was the one who had the two children, said June, despite the fact that my academic credentials were actually, Valerie, between you and me, they were superior to Bill's.

They were quiet for a minute.

My advice to women, June said, is go for it all, do it all, do everything you want. Do everything you can because otherwise you'll have regrets. Actually, I suppose you have regrets no matter what you do in this world. Would you like another glass?

Sure, okay, said Valerie, thanks.

Bristol Cream, not bad in a pinch.

No, said Valerie.

A brown squirrel ran down the tree, spotted them and ran back up. June refilled the glasses.

Finally, Valerie, I got back into teaching when I was forty years old. Forest Hill Collegiate, which was good. It was a very, very good school, but it wasn't easy. It was nerve-racking.

Another cicada started up so they stopped and listened.

It's like a chainsaw, said Valerie.

Crickets rub their legs together, said June, but cicadas, they have a different trick, something they do with their bodies. You're right, it's more like a chainsaw, I guess, than like bagpipes. We're all the same, everything comes from our bodies, somewhere.

Instinctual machines, said Valerie. Our deepest emotions, stage-managed by some biochemical change, hormones, neural receptors.

Yes, said June. We think we have ideas and reasons for everything, but in fact we're driven by our biology.

Valerie didn't say anything. She knew that June Glass was not unhappy with her lot.

Girls, said June, when I was a girl I was a rocket ship. I was launched in a blue sky over Cape Canaveral, everything was fine and then bang! The secondary engines kicked in and instead of voooooooom . . .

She moved her right arm skyward and then slid it back down.

. . . I never truly escaped the surly bonds of earth at all.

Surly bonds of earth? asked Valerie.

A quote from an old poem. How we never escape ourselves, you know.

Oh, only mystics escape themselves, said Valerie. I'm not interested in mystics.

Sex, hormones, motherhood, said June Glass.

Then she stood up.

This bottle, Valerie, is empty but it was only a quarter full before anyway, so it's not like we've had a lot to drink.

No, not at all.

June went inside and when she came out she had a corkscrew and a bottle of Châteauneuf-du-Pape, and two tall-stemmed glasses.

I found some wine after all, she said. It's unusual for me to have so much time on my hands.

Me too, said Valerie, but it's rather pleasant, downtime.

These cicadas, said June, it's more like the rasp of a file than a chainsaw, come to think of it.

Then June laughed in a self-deprecating way.

Can you tell, Valerie, I used to write poems? A file, a chainsaw? Not for years now, I think I'm out of date.

You're a poet? That's great. Send us your stuff at *Zipper*. We'll have a look. I'll introduce you to Amber White. You can even be an editor, why not?

She struggled with the corkscrew and handed it to Valerie Anderson.

Here, you do this, you're the new generation.

Those were long days, summertime. Evening stretched out and assumed a life of its own, as if anything were possible.

———

All of Roberto Moreno's poetry sessions, his attempts to uncover truth and beauty within a contrived structure of words, his work with the medical students, all of it came about by chance. He never sought it out and in fact it came to him by painful circumstance. It would have been heartless for him to turn away and do nothing.

During his second week in Toronto, he left the house on Glengrove Avenue early in the morning and set out to explore the new city, as he had done every day, and this particular time he walked down Avenue Road to Eglinton, then over to Mount Pleasant, to Bloor Street, then over the bridge that crossed the valley to Danforth Avenue. By then it was noon hour, and the temperature had risen enough that he took off his coat and knotted its empty arms around his waist, and he thought, in his occasional loneliness, of Luisa Sanchez, her arms there instead. The remote solemnity she had, the distance she maintained even when they made love, her arms nearly as thin and yes, just as impersonal as the arms of his Canadian coat, a windbreaker.

A beautiful word in English, *windbreaker,* so functional yet so evocative.

As he proceeded, he saw in front of him, perhaps thirty yards away, a man who weaved rather than walked, who faltered and then fell to the ground. Several pedestrians circled round him, wary. They proceeded past, distancing themselves. The poor fellow was back on his feet by the time Roberto Moreno came abreast of him, and again he staggered, this time towards Roberto.

He would have fallen a second time had Roberto not grasped his arm and supported him.

Hey there my friend, Roberto said, are you all right?

No, he said, no, I'm far from all right.

Indeed his young face was covered in droplets of sweat and Roberto could feel, through the dampened shirt, how his body shook in fine spasms, as though he shivered, as though the temperatures hot and cold had clashed within him simultaneously and brought about a devastation.

Here, Roberto said.

He guided him through the door of a café that was close at hand. A booth was free. He half pushed him into one side, and then Roberto sat down across from him.

God, the young man said, I don't know.

He pulled loose papers out of his pocket and scattered them on the table. His hands trembled as much as his body.

I hope I haven't lost them, he said.

The waitress came over.

Coffee, said Roberto Moreno, we'll both have coffee.

Roberto picked up the papers, straightened them and placed them in the middle of the table.

Anything else? the waitress asked. Your friend looks as though he needs something else, maybe grilled cheese?

Grilled cheese, is that what you recommend?

Yes, grilled cheese and chicken soup for your friend. Not coffee.

Then bring soup and grilled cheese, but for me, just coffee, said Roberto.

As in Mexico, he appreciated the wisdom of waitresses, the welcoming warmth of cafés. He looked at his new friend more carefully, how thin he was. Two irregular purple spots on his forehead stood out from his pallor.

My name is Roberto Moreno, he said.

He held out his hand.

Stefan Grodzinski, and those are poems, those are poems, the young man said.

He pointed to the papers. Roberto picked them up again. "The Lotos-eaters," by Alfred Lord Tennyson.

I don't know what I'm going to do. I'm supposed to teach that tonight but I can't even walk. Medical students, medical students no less. What do they care?

Well they might care, if the poem is good. I don't know this poem. Why are you so sick?

Sick? I'm the world's worst fucking teacher. They fall asleep when I walk in the door. I'm turning beautiful poetry into death. I know it, I can see it.

I don't understand, said Roberto Moreno.

I'm dying, no one knows why. There's no way I'll ever eat that grilled cheese.

I can tell you're being hard on yourself, Stefan, said Roberto Moreno.

And so it was that, when she brought the food, Stefan left the sandwich alone but he sipped at the soup, and he and Roberto Moreno talked together about the particular poem that lay before them on the table.

It's a long one, you won't like it, it's dated in its style. I can tell, your accent, you'll find it a far cry from Spanish, from Lorca, as far as you can get.

Then he began to shake and shiver again. The soup was only half finished. He put his spoon down in it and left it there. Roberto picked up the grilled cheese. It was still warm and rather than waste it, he proceeded to eat it, and the waitress was right, it was good. It made him hungry for more.

You know, I can take your class for you, step in if you like, and no one the wiser, said Roberto.

He knew, when he said that, how unqualified he was in the eyes of the academic world.

You know English poetry?

I know poetry. I can read this, whatever it is, study it before class.

Okay, why not? I'm grateful, but you have only six hours.

Stefan looked at his watch and then he coughed and started to gag. He brought his paper napkin to his mouth.

Listen, I'll walk you home.

No, no. Don't bother, I'll make it.

How far?

Just around the corner.

Roberto beckoned to the waitress.

See? she said. I knew he'd like the grilled cheese. The cheddar's put colour in his cheeks. You go home to bed, my boy.

She put the bill on the table. Roberto counted out some money.

Thanks, she said.

Wait, the sick young man said. Here, you forgot the tip.

He pulled a five-dollar bill from his pocket.

I love you, he said to the waitress.

He appeared to be deadly serious.

Yes, we were born for each other, she replied.

She slipped the five-dollar bill back into his shirt pocket but he didn't notice. Out in the street, he seemed to regain some strength and they walked together north to Hurndale Avenue, where he lived on the second floor of a red-brick house. There were three book-lined rooms, a kitchen, a bathroom. He walked straight to the bedroom and lay down on the bed.

University College, Room 108, he said. Be there at eight. I'll be there next week, tell them.

Roberto took the poem and went into the kitchen. There was a black-and-white photograph on the wall beside the kitchen table, a photograph that appeared to be of a glass door with lettering. It was difficult to be sure, there were reflections of a street too, cars passing, a pedestrian, a flash from the camera. THE ROMAN SAUNA BATHS, that's what it said.

He went back to the bedroom but Stefan was asleep. He'd pulled the covers over himself entirely, even his head.

Stefan, he said.

Roberto pulled the blankets down far enough to ensure that Stefan's nose was not obstructed. The young poet looked more at peace now than he had in the café or on the street. His breathing was slow and even. Without closing the door, Roberto left the room, went downstairs and let himself out into the street. He looked at his watch and returned to Danforth Avenue at a brisk pace. He turned west, towards the university.

Two days later Roberto returned to report on the class. Stefan looked worse, asleep on his arms on the kitchen table.

It went okay, the class, said Roberto. They almost all showed up. That means you are a good teacher, not a bad one. You need to see a doctor, Stefan.

But Stefan refused.

I've seen them all, I've had a million tests. They've thrown up their hands, Roberto. They say to me: you've got something new, something not so nice. That's their diagnosis. I'm totally fucked, it's hopeless.

Roberto decided to watch over him as best he could. There seemed to be no one else in Stefan Grodzinski's life.

Within two weeks, the young man became bedridden, his sheets soiled and damp. Intermittent delirium crept in upon him. He was lucid one moment, deranged the next.

Roberto asked Valerie to come with him one night.

Valerie, please, I need your advice as a medical person.

At Hurndale Avenue, she looked at Stefan Grodzinski and tried to remember what he had looked like before, when he stood in front of the class. There wasn't much of him left.

Call an ambulance now, Roberto. He can't die like this even if he wants to.

They called the ambulance to Hurndale Avenue. He needed oxygen to breathe, and even then his efforts were pitiful and laboured. Over the next few weeks, the only visitors he had at the Wellesley Hospital were Roberto Moreno, Valerie Anderson and the Glass brothers.

Where's his family? asked John Glass. Where's the rest of his life?

After six weeks, Stefan was dead from his wasting illness and fevers. At the funeral, which took place in the cemetery on Mount Pleasant Avenue on a day with a dusting of snow, Valerie and Roberto and the Glasses, including June and Bill, were the only ones present. Together, they had made the arrangements.

For the second time in his life, in a graveyard, Roberto Moreno took a shovel in his hands. This time it felt smaller, and the few clots of earth he threw downwards were symbolic only. There were workmen standing by to finish the job.

Afterwards, June and Bill drove away and the others took the subway together downtown to Bloor Street.

We'll have a wake, Roberto said. He's got four or five beers in the refrigerator. That should be enough for us. Not much of a wake, but a wake.

They walked across the Bloor Street Viaduct towards Hurndale Avenue.

This bridge, said John Glass as he opened his arms expansively, is statistically the second-favourite spot in North America for suicides. Did you know that?

No, they all said.

Just behind the Golden Gate Bridge in San Francisco. Interesting that Stefan lived this close to it and never took advantage of it.

He never actually thought he'd die, said Jasper. He'd been alive all his life. It's the same for all of us. Besides, it's a long, long way down.

John Glass peered over the side of the bridge.

Sure, it's a long way down, he said, but ten seconds of free fall, full of expectation, I can imagine that. Wham. End of story.

Wordlessly they walked into Stefan's empty flat. They drank the four bottles of beer. Then they walked out and locked the door and as they went, Roberto Moreno carefully removed the photograph of the Roman Sauna Baths from the wall in the kitchen.

A memento, he said. We should have something tangible.

After that, despite his lack of qualifications, Roberto Moreno became the official replacement for Stefan Grodzinski. Under most circumstances, the University of Toronto never would have allowed him to continue. His age was against him, as was his lack of formal education. But there was in the air at that time an elixir of change, of experimentation, an openness, and of course the accolades he received right away from the students helped him.

The head of the department handed him the schedule for the class and the list of poems.

Read these, teach these, she said.

And he did read them. It was an eye-opener how cool they were in their temperament, these new men and women, these poets in English. Roberto felt he had to lower his thermostat to get through them, but he enjoyed it all, much more than he had expected. Financially, the money he was paid helped. He immediately signed the cheques over to his aunt and thus contributed to his upkeep.

At University College, with his medical students, he started a class tradition. At the end of each session they stood together.

To Stefan Grodzinski, said Roberto Moreno.

They raised their right arms as though they had glasses of wine and one of them, weekly in turn, quoted from the poem Stefan had handed to Roberto Moreno on the day they met in that warm and welcoming café. It was always the same two lines.

Courage! he said, and pointed toward the land,
This mounting wave will roll us shoreward soon.

That's a metaphor for death, said John Glass.

No, it isn't, said Valerie Anderson. It's about what it says it's about. It's about courage, about facing adversity.

Do you think, Valerie, said Jasper Glass, that those lines offer hope to those abandoned in love, encouraging them to persevere?

Yes, those lines offer such hope, to some people, she said.

First of all, said Valerie Anderson to Dr. Abner Krank in his sparsely furnished office, we found Mr. Smith's thought processes to be quite cogent.

She sat on one side of a grey metal desk, the psychiatric resident on the other. There was a framed print on the wall, a still life with flowers. He saw her look at it.

Manet, she said.

Yes, I brought it in to humanize the place, he said.

Actually, it was on the wall when he had arrived, peonies in a white vase, and because it was on the opposite wall he had looked at it for hours at a time before he moved it behind his desk and thus made it, for most of the time he spent in the office, invisible.

Mr. Smith has little to no recall of the actual incident.

Does he still have suicidal ideation, Ms. Anderson?

Dr. Krank imagined himself closer to Valerie Anderson, walking over to her side of the table and sitting there casually, his legs crossed. Her eyes were like limpid pools, limpid pools, dark and smoky, Cuban.

Do you speak Spanish?

No, she said, why do you ask?

Oh, no reason, he said, go on, go on.

Her breasts under the lab coat were neither large nor small.

Mr. Smith has no intent on suicide, nor has he formed a plan.

Auditory hallucinations? Delusions of grandeur? Icarus still falls from the sky?

No. All of that's gone. He's as rational this morning as you or I, Dr. Krank. Nor do we believe that he constitutes a danger to himself or others. In fact I think we have discovered the etiology of the whole affair.

She smiled. Her smile was eerily contagious and he felt his own lips start to curl upwards in imitation, though smiling was not flattering to him, the way it tightened his lips.

Oh? he said.

He rubbed away his smile with the back of his hand. He moved his fingers to his upper lip and massaged them as though deep in thought. She didn't seem to wear perfume but it was hard to be sure at this distance.

It's thanks to you, Dr. Krank, that we asked him about drugs and alcohol. As you wrote on the blackboard this morning.

Oh? he said again.

An hour prior to his bizarre behaviour, Mr. Smith ingested a hallucinogenic drug. By mistake.

Really, he said, by mistake. That's not unheard of.

Yes, possibly mescaline, possibly LSD. Can we tell with toxicology?

That's not in the budget, Ms. Anderson. Here at 999, we don't do toxicology on overdoses. We just guess from the history. May I call you by your first name, Valerie?

He leaned forward. With this girl, he could take a drug, any drug, a disinhibitory drug, a mad drug, a transforming drug, a drug that tore his clothes off, a drug that left him teetering on a ledge, as precarious as that other idiot, that Icarus.

And how did our Mr. Smith come by his mistaken drug, Valerie?

That's the embarrassing part for him. He bought it at a party on the weekend, on St. George Street, but didn't know what it was. Somehow, it fell into his trail mix. He noticed it at the last minute, but it was too late. He swallowed it at lunch.

Trail mix, he said, like granola.

He didn't see it among the raisins, the peanuts. I can see how it might happen. Anyway, lunch was the last thing he remembered until the landing net. He remembers the firemen, how they threw a blanket over him. Now, despite the gap in his memory, he seems normal, right back to normal.

Abner Krank stood and came around to her side of the desk. He bent down to her and she thought she heard him inhale above her head, deeply, through both nostrils. She sat back and didn't look up. He moved to the desk again and leaned against it, again half sitting. He looked at her intently. He seemed briefly confused and then he stared straight at her.

So we can rid ourselves of this young man, he said.

In my opinion, yes. Yes, we can discharge him right away. Get him out of the system.

He's a one-off, one-time psychotic then. Good. And follow-up?

The three of us will take care of that. John, Wallace and I, we can visit him a few times, send you a report.

Okay then, good work. I'll sign him out this morning. But one thing, the follow-up report, I want that done in person. And by you, Ms. Anderson. This is a serious case, it's garnered attention. Ebenezer Smith. Is he a Quaker or something?

No, no religion, she said.

He looked directly at her for a few seconds. Business-like, that's what she was. Doing her job and doing it well. Too many girls like this in medicine. She had her purse on her lap, a book poking out of it, a book with a pink cover.

So I guess that's all? she asked.

Well, there's no rush really, Ms. Anderson. It's quiet here. Cancellations, you know. What's the book about, that one?

He pointed to her purse. Immediately he saw her change. She pulled the book all the way out.

This one? It's poetry. Amber White. She's nominated for the Governor General's Award in poetry, for this very book. It's great.

Really. I've never heard of her. But I have to tell you, Valerie, I love poetry. Don't you? It speaks directly to me. There's no subterfuge in poetry.

Not in this poem, that's for sure.

May I see it?

She handed it to him and he opened it and flipped through the pages. Plenty of white space, that was good. A lot of short lines down the middle of the pages without any breaks. It wouldn't take long to read.

By Church and Isabella I Sat Down and Wept, he said. Beautiful, I love it. Can I borrow it?

Sure, she said. You can have it. Keep it, I have another copy.

No, no, I insist, I just want to borrow it. I'd like to give it back next week.

Okay, she said, that's fine.

Write your name here, on the inside cover. Write Valerie Anderson.

Her handwriting was quick and neat. He watched her leave the room and when she was gone, he stared at the blank wall opposite. Had she only looked back at him it would have been even more encouraging.

He looked at the back cover.

An uncompromising page-turner of a poem, replete with searing street sex. A harrowing cri de coeur *from Canada's foremost radical urban female warrior.*

On the book's spine, there was a zipper inside a parabola.

He swivelled in his chair and looked at the Manet. Too rich, too blowsy, too florid. Valerie Anderson. Someday, when he had the time, he wanted to write an article about the appreciation of physical beauty, its intoxicating effects. Perhaps there was some missing substance, a hormone that could be measured in the blood.

He placed his finger on the side of his throat and felt his carotid pulse.

Imagine the startlingly creative idioms that even now, June, even as we sit here, are springing *de novo* from the lips of Frenchmen.

As soon as he heard those words from his father, John Glass jumped up from the family dinner table.

Excuse me, he said, but tonight I have a date.

It was true. John was going out with Midori, the

Japanese girl he had met at the International Student Centre, at a poetry reading the week before.

His father didn't even notice what he'd said.

It could be a fisherman creating the idiom, June, lifting his net from the sea off Brittany. A cyclist straining for a mountaintop in the Pyrenees, a woman at her clothesline in Rouen, a commentator on television in Paris. And the common denominator? June? The common denominator is that I am here, in Toronto, and unaware. It's maddening. My book will suffer, not in the eyes of North Americans—but to the native French?

Yes, dear, John heard his mother say.

To the French, I will appear a colonial ass.

The keys to Jasper's Volkswagen lay on the hall table. What his brother didn't know wouldn't hurt him.

He poked his head back into the dining room.

I'm taking Jasper's van, he said.

Drive carefully, said June.

Had I found a French publishing house, perhaps we would be in France now. Provence, Normandy, Paris, paid for by Gallimard. Instead, Louise Drabinsky and the University of Windsor Press. My colleagues, I tell you, are not impressed. And my income from this project? June?

Zero, she said. Goodbye, John.

Yes, zero.

The van was a mess. There were papers all over the floor and the mattress in the back was covered with several haphazard blankets. It was Jasper's bedroom half the time. John had seen his brother and the blond girl, Marnie Kennedy, emerge from there late one afternoon.

In the lane off Hoskin Avenue. They both look tousled up more than a bit, and very relaxed.

Someday, he might get a vehicle like this himself. It was not impossible. He had his licence.

He turned the key in the ignition and the van started up though its body vibrated strangely before it settled down. He pushed the clutch carefully and felt around with the gearshift for reverse. It was a long driveway, a long way to back up.

He wiggled the gearshift.

Pretty sure that's reverse. There.

He adjusted the mirror. The hedge on the driver's side ran right to the sidewalk. He let out the clutch and this time back he went, slowly and carefully.

No one was coming from the right. He turned to look left, past the hedge, and accelerated slightly as he did so to get over the little hump of the sidewalk. But he overdid it with the accelerator and the VW jumped out onto the street with a *crump* sound. The little Fiat from down the street had smacked into his left rear bumper.

God.

Fortunately for John Glass, the Fiat was made of stern stuff and the old lady driving it was too. She jumped out like a teenager. She looked at her own car and then at the Volkswagen.

No report necessary, John, she said. Your fault. No damage to my car, we'll forget it. The paint's not even scratched.

The rear fender of Jasper's VW, however, had been crushed. It was pressed up against the tire.

Sorry, said John. I got distracted. The van just leapt out onto the street. Must be the clutch needs fixing. The car's possessed.

He managed to drive the van forward, back into the driveway, but he could hear and feel the tire grinding and he smelled rubber. Jasper would not be happy. In the garage, he found the hanging trouble light, a rubber hammer and a crowbar.

If you hear a noise, he said to his parents, it's just me, effecting a small repair on Jasper's van.

To which his father replied, Louise and I, we're like oil and water. Louise doesn't even speak French enough to know the difference between an idiom and a metaphor. Yet I'm fused to her like a Siamese twin.

John lay down on the gravel in the dark, his head under the rear fender. He took a few desultory swings at the indentation with the hammer, but he could get no purchase from where he lay. He sighed. He couldn't be any more useless.

Then he heard footsteps on the gravel and he saw running shoes off his left shoulder. He pulled himself out from under the van. There was his poetry teacher from next door, Roberto Moreno.

Hey, Roberto, he said, not making too much noise, I hope.

No, said Roberto, I was just curious. I heard the bang. You have a little problem there, John, I can see. Jasper's van, correct?

Correct. And he knows nothing about this. I need to fix it in a hurry.

They both sat down on the driveway. John Glass now had his back up against the car, Roberto Moreno leaned against the fence. The trouble light, which John had attached to the door handle, spot-lit them.

Cars are rare in Mexico City, in my circle of friends. Too expensive. But sometimes we would take an opportunity to drive one, said Roberto.

How do you mean, take an opportunity?

Well, if the keys were around, or if the car had been left running, we would take it for a short period of time.

Steal it?

Until the gas ran out. But we never left the neighbourhood. We drove in circles for the most part. You see, we never learned to drive, formally, so if we had a collision, we had to walk home.

That makes sense then, not to go too far, said John.

And sometimes, yes, our stolen car was then in turn stolen from us.

Roberto pointed his finger at John and crooked his thumb.

You mean at gunpoint? asked John Glass.

Oh yes, at gunpoint all right.

I don't know if that could happen in Toronto.

Oh yes it could, said Roberto. I have seen it with my own eyes. Not with guns, but the streets here in Toronto are dangerous.

They talked some more. Roberto Moreno told John Glass how he himself had not so much dropped out of engineering in Mexico as sifted out of it, like flour. How he had concentrated all of his attention on poetry rather than on his slide rule.

I stopped going to classes in engineering and it took me a long time to tell my aunt and uncle what I had done.

I'd like to drop out of medicine, said John Glass, but I haven't the decisiveness to do so.

They stood up and cast long shadows on the side of the house.

I think we need to jack it up and then support it with something safe, said Roberto.

When that was done, he slid under the car.

Now we hammer it back to its original shape, he said. You pull there on the outside, John.

Roberto Moreno struck repeatedly from below, using the rubber hammer.

I'm going to beat it all the way back, so the fender conforms to the wheel well, he said.

Yes, just beat on it until it conforms, said John Glass.

They laughed.

Roberto swung harder and harder and the echoes of his hammer reverberated off the Volkswagen, up and down and sideways against the canyonlike walls of both their houses. The blows tom-tommed down the street.

Roberto steals poetry books, said Valerie Anderson to John Glass, just like you do.

He does?

Yes. We took a walk through the Beaches, went into

a store and lo and behold, he had three books when we left. I never saw a thing.

Really.

He justified it, sort of. I'm not convinced.

After that revelation, John re-evaluated his own book-purchasing and -stealing policy. Perhaps, in Mexico City, thievery was a culturally acceptable way of building a library. Here in Toronto, however, the same practice was a serious offence. But still, John was limited in his resources and his appetite was at least as voracious as Roberto Moreno's, and the niggling thought of adding to his library without having to spend any money at all continued to be enticing. Taking medical books was out of the question. It was physically impossible to carry them off unseen. They were so bulky that he had to pay in cash and walk out, as best he could, with four or five of them piled high in his arms.

Now, however, he didn't feel quite as isolated. He was not alone in his craving for thin volumes. Early mornings, the university bookstore was not heavily staffed. Piles of identical books were stacked here and there according to discipline, but the poetry section and the fine literature section—novels, short fiction and criticism—were lined up on traditional bookshelves, and it was there that John Glass plied his trade. He depended upon his ski jacket, a black and loose affair into which he had sewn a tight belt just above the waist, a cinching device to support weight. He wandered through the poetry section and acquired, without cost, in alphabetical order, *The Circle Game,* by Margaret Atwood, *Procedures for*

Underground, by Margaret Atwood, *The Dumbfounding,* by Margaret Avison, *Touch,* by George Bowering, *The Energy of Slaves,* by Leonard Cohen, and *St. Martin's,* by Robert Creeley.

Satisfied with these, he picked up a 500-sheet package of yellow foolscap, the same paper favoured by his new mentor, Roberto Moreno. He looked at himself in a mirror on the wall and judged his ski jacket to be above suspicion.

Was it kleptomania? he wondered after he left.

No, kleptomaniacs stole spontaneously, irrationally. Kleptomaniacs stole silk stockings too slender to wear, lipstick in gaudy colours, silk scarves, double-A batteries, and *Good Housekeeping.* Kleptomaniacs did not go home and open up their stolen Baudelaire, as John Glass did every night and day, and read

> *What will you say tonight, forsaken soul,*
> *How will you speak, my long-since-withered heart,*
> *To her, the loveliest and most beloved*
> *Whose sudden grace has made you green again?*

A week later, at Britnell's bookstore on Yonge Street, he thrust into his coat *Rat Jelly,* by Michael Ondaatje, *Fovea Centralis,* by Christopher Dewdney, *Playing the Jesus Game,* by Alden Nowlan, and *The Whole Bloody Bird,* by Irving Layton.

After he left the store, he looked back. Was he being followed? A man with a shirt and tie. The man was back about fifty yards but he crossed the street at the same time John did. Then he walked briskly, with intent. He looked straight at John Glass.

John casually made the turn onto Scollard and then he ran, not wildly like a criminal but more like an athlete in training.

He kept his face impassive but his heart trip-hammered and the weight of the books shifted under his jacket. He was coming to pieces, literally. His torso bent forty-five degrees forward and skewed dramatically to the left at the same time, yet his legs still carried him, somehow, straight ahead.

At Bay Street he stopped and looked back. He adjusted his load of contraband. He caught his breath. No sign of anyone, no shirt-and-tie man.

Oh, the sheer beauty of escape from danger! How seductive it was! He fought it but, as usual, he lost and so was drawn back to Britnell's within the week. It was unnaturally hot that day. Sun poured through the windows from the west and the sales clerks took off their sweaters and touched the radiators and pulled their hands away in mock alarm.

We should never have turned on the heat, they said. Open the doors, get some of that fresh air in here.

John was drenched in sweat. At random, he opened a book.

> At first I thought that I would see
> How very cold the moon could be
> And then I knew that I could learn
> The icy coldness of the moon.

Tears came to his eyes. Valerie and Jasper would not understand those lines in a million years.

Two clerks came from the back of the store, one of them in a shirt and tie. Could it be him? No, he didn't think so but just in case he was a suspect, he immediately bought a small literary magazine for three dollars. It was the first cash he had paid for anything but foolscap in months.

Later, he showed the magazine to Valerie Anderson. They were sitting in the cafeteria where it was crowded, as usual, at lunchtime. Bodies were jammed in against each other by the low tables.

Look at this, Valerie, right on the first page. What's it say?

Supported by the Canada Council for the Arts.

No, right above that, what does it say?

She took the magazine. It was blue and there was a red Model T fragmented on the cover, very cool the way the red and blue shattered across each other.

Unsolicited manuscripts are discouraged, she read. John, *Zipper* would never do that. Unsolicited poems are the lifeblood of *Zipper*. We need welcoming magazines. Look what happened to Amber. Years and years of rejection before a small magazine changed her life.

Years and years of rejection, said John. I can relate to that.

You're not even twenty.

It begins in the womb, Valerie. You should know that. You studied embryology. Rejection starts at the moment of conception. It's inevitable.

Valerie popped the cork from the bottle of Châteauneuf-du-Pape and filled the wineglasses. June swirled it, tasted it. The light was beginning to fade, the backyards were quiet around them, one lawn mower in the distance.

Three hours later, they were still there. It was pitch black. Now it was Mouton Cadet they drank and the empty Châteauneuf-du-Pape bottle had rolled off to the side, against the garden rocks. June stood and on the fourth or fifth try, she succeeded in lighting a straw torch that was imbedded in the grass by the patio. A yellow flickering light cast itself about the yard.

That's better. My coordination's off a bit from the wine, I see. I almost can't keep my lighter straight. Where was I?

Something about your generation and sex, said Valerie Anderson. Now I hear crickets.

Oh yes. In our generation, for the most part we are very reticent in our sexual expression. We were shy. We are shy.

Most everyone is shy about sex, said Valerie, even the ones who pretend not to be. I'm shy, everybody I know is.

Well, my dear, I have to tell you that Bill, my husband, was by chance standing at the window the other day. You and Roberto were in the yard.

Oh, said Valerie.

And whatever he saw, or thought he saw, but if he saw what he thought he saw and if he saw what he told me, I have to tell you this: I wish I had been more like you. I wish I had been less reticent, less shy when I was younger. I wish I had felt more deeply, more provocatively, more out of control, that I could have thrown caution to the wind. Which in a way I'm doing now, by even mentioning this. God, I can hardly talk.

June, I'm afraid I know what you're referring to. Roberto and I, we had come to a stage in our relationship that . . .

Had you been drinking?

Lemonade, just lemonade. I had a physiological interest, June, in the process as I remember it, ridiculous though that sounds, the mechanics, the flow of it. I was curious about the physiological process. You laugh, I don't blame you. Yes, I admit it, June, I was a far cry from a scientist that day. It's confusing. Even worse to talk about it. I lost all sense of anything but the two of us, Roberto and me.

I understand, I think.

It felt preordained. No, I had not been drinking. But it was like drinking. It was an intoxication.

Certainly not shy.

No, I guess not. Well, I'm sorry the professor saw what he saw, but I'm not sorry for what I did. I have zero regrets about that. Zero.

I did it once, Valerie, in bed. I had the covers pulled over my head as though I were alone. Disembodied.

There you go, said Valerie, then you know.

The flickering light from the torch went out. They could no longer see each other's faces.

June started to recite. Her voice came out of the dark.

She had dark hair that framed her face, a moonstone
a perfect voice for poetry, for singing,
the girl
an actress less than half his age
restored his potency
(a coincidence, a coincidence)
he edited the poetry
tightened it up
smoothed out the libertine
and shivered at the harlot remarks she made
and asked her for rhyme, for control, for rhythm
which he found lacking
in her body
of work.

June's voice stopped.
Go on, said Valerie.

Oh, there were reservations
she had a mental twist
damaging in a young mother
it distracted him
(her white skin addictive)
from his translation of the Upanishads
from the soporific breezes of Palma, Majorca.

I think I get it, said Valerie.

Until that night in Barcelona
when she cleaved and broke
and fell through a skylight
down so many shards of glass
that wild swans stirred in their twenty-year sleep,
and the falcons, grounded, twisted under their leather
constraints
and even the bishops were rendered speechless
at the sight of the blood
from her glittering veins.

I get it, said Valerie. It's about Yeats. Who wrote that?

I did, said June. I'm drunk. I know I'm drunk but that poem came out effortlessly. Amazing I can remember all those words, so long ago.

The young in each other's arms, said Valerie, better than the young in the arms of the old.

I'll drink to that, said June.

There was barely enough light for Valerie to see June's white blouse, her arm moving up for a toast. Then the whiteness moved across the patio and bent down and kissed Valerie Anderson on the middle of her forehead.

I've had a really splendid time, Valerie, but it's bedtime for me. I'll call you a cab. I think I can dial the phone.

Good night, they both said at once.

Yes, good night, dear Valerie.

The police caught a break in the Crisco killing. Detective Ames came to work six weeks after the rape and the murder and there was a note on his desk: Call Sergeant Willis, something about Rosedale.

Rosedale? There's crime there?

He dialed the number.

Detective Ames from Homicide, he said.

Oh yes, Detective, I called about your note on Crisco. Well, believe it or not, we have something here. Pretty far-fetched. There was a break-in reported the night before your murder, on Roxborough Drive, and the burglar apparently squeezed through a milkbox to gain entry, thus bypassing the security system.

And?

The milkbox must have been too small. He used Crisco to squeeze himself through. It was smeared all over. Weird.

So it was a burglary then, break and enter?

Presumably, but the culprit didn't take anything. That was strange too. There was nothing missing, according to the householder. A Dr. Christian Foare.

Nothing at all, said Detective Ames.

There was a ruffling of papers over the phone.

No, nothing. Christian Foare. Oh, and there's a note here that he didn't tell his wife about it. He travels a lot, he didn't want to alarm her, etc. etc. Doctors, both of them. Maybe they don't know what they own, that's why nothing's missing.

Okay, thanks, said Detective Ames.

He took down the name and address and hung up the phone.

He drove up Mount Pleasant Avenue and, south of

St. Clair, turned east. It was peaceful and quiet in the residential enclave of Rosedale. Young girls, nannies he figured, pushed baby carriages on the sidewalks. They looked like Filipinas. They certainly couldn't afford property there, and neither could he. Maybe they did live there, though, these girls, their new lives down in basement rooms.

He pulled into the driveway and got out of the car. A big house surrounded by other big houses. He rang the bell and Christian Foare took him into the living room. There was no rug on the hardwood floor, just a sofa, a chair, a standing light.

Excuse the Spartan feel, said Christian Foare, we're new here.

Not together long?

No, just a couple of months.

So, the break-in, show me.

They walked into the kitchen and then down onto the cellar steps.

What happened was this, said Christian Foare. I got up one morning and the dog was whimpering at the cellar door. I looked down the stairs and the inner door of the milkbox was wide open. You can see I've nailed it shut since, closed it off with that metal strip, but then it was just an ordinary milkbox door and it was wide open. The outer door was closed tight, latched from the outside.

No one uses them to deliver milk anymore, said Detective Ames. They're museum pieces, like Model Ts. Drafty.

Right. So I went to close it and there was a sticky white substance all over it—it came off on my hands. Down in the cellar was a large can of Crisco. Empty. I went outside. As I said, the outer door was shut. So someone had broken in and then gone out the same way. It was frightening. I checked inside, I looked around but nothing had been taken that I could see. Marnie was still asleep.

She works late?

She's an intern at Mount Sinai. That's where she is now.

The report says you didn't tell her.

That's right. She's here by herself a lot. I've been away, she'd worry. I did ask her about the Crisco. She rarely buys it, I never do. Nobody's getting back in that way now so there's no need for her to know.

Maybe the burglar heard the dog and left, said Detective Ames. Did you keep the can?

I did, but she threw it out.

Too bad.

They walked back up the stairs into the kitchen.

On the windowsill by the breakfast table was a photograph of Christian Foare, thin with glasses, hair receding a bit, and a young woman standing together on a sand beach. A palm tree on the left, green-blue water behind, and they were both smiling at the camera. They were relaxed. She held up a glass to the photographer, a glass with a little umbrella in it. She had blond hair that was tousled in the wind and, in the photograph, she nearly blew her husband right off the beach. She was all you could see. He might as well have been another tree or deck chair. She had a soft drape of some kind, pink around her shoulders.

That's you and your wife? asked the detective.

Palm Beach, the honeymoon, said Christian Foare. That's Marnie.

Well, said Detective Ames, nice photograph. We'll see what comes of this. There's not a lot to go on, a break-in with nothing lost. We'll probably have to shelve it.

I understand that, said Christian Foare. I never thought you'd actually come out. I'm impressed by the thoroughness of the police.

You're a biostatistician, Dr. Foare?

That's right.

What do you think the odds are we catch this burglar?

One in ten thousand maybe, but it depends on many variables, I expect.

The odds aren't even that good, said the detective, not even one in a hundred thousand. Unless we catch them for something else.

Them? You mean there could be more than one?

No, just him. Sorry, him, whoever he is. He slips up somewhere else, then we tie it up that way.

If he slips on Crisco, you mean.

The detective laughed and that was the end of the interview. He returned to his car and drove back through Rosedale. By then school was out, and the sidewalks were busier. Kids with books in their arms pushed and shoved each other. The boys wore grey flannels, the girls those short, short skirts from private schools.

The next generation.

The discarded can of Crisco was found inside, at the bottom of the stairs. Break-out, not break-in, that's the way it looked to him. He'd seen it before. Someone locked inside by the security system.

The photograph. Her eyes, maybe it was just what he saw, what he read into it. Maybe it was nothing. But she had star quality, and sometimes that meant trouble.

Marnie Kennedy-Foare. He'd take the next step and check her out. No harm in that. Whoever went through her milkbox might well have been at Shaw Street the next night, saving Gwen O'Hara's life.

If it weren't for the murder, all of this would have been just a curiosity, something to laugh about. You'd have to be pretty desperate to use Crisco, anywhere, for anything other than pie.

He laughed. Pie.

So who would hang out with Marnie Kennedy-Foare? How old was she? Twenty-three, twenty-four? A hundred guys would hang out with her, you could see that from the photograph.

Someone in her class, someone nearby, someone she could spend time with and no one would even notice or care.

While her husband worked at the University of Toronto and Roberto Moreno taught poetry and explored the downtown streets, Roberto's aunt Silvana worked on Eglinton Avenue, at a candy store. The candy store was named Laura Secord, a famous name for Canadians, Silvana discovered, because in the war of 1812, when the American armed forces invaded Canada, it was Miss Laura Secord who walked with her cow, brazen as can be, right past the invaders. Thus Laura Secord gave early warning to her compatriots and to their Iroquois supporters in Upper Canada. The Americans, who had paid Laura Secord no attention at all, were then surprised to meet such organized resistance. They were not only thwarted in their plans but were roundly defeated. Many Americans were captured at the Battle of Beaver Dams in 1813.

What are beaver dams? Silvana asked Emily, her co-worker, her informant.

Emily and Silvana worked side by side most days, although Emily did not work Fridays. On those days she took care of her mother and the pace at the store became frenetic.

Beavers pile up mud and sticks, said Emily. They are famous for being industrious. They dam rivers, make ponds. Look.

Emily opened the cash register. It made a sound like a bell, and she pulled a nickel out of the drawer.

There, she said, that's a beaver. And on this side, the Queen of England.

Oh, the Queen I know, said Silvana.

Once again Silvana was pleased she had come here, to Canada, and had learned so many things.

She told Emily about the Alamo, how the Americans went to war against Mexico too.

The truth is, said Emily, in Canada no one remembers anything about Laura Secord anymore, or the War of 1812. All they know now are these candy stores.

Maybe that's better, said Silvana, your violent history now reduced to a box of chocolates.

What year was the Alamo?

1837, said Silvana.

She had studied Mexican colonial history so she had no trouble remembering dates. Also, in university, she had specialized in English, a fortunate choice as it turned out because now she could turn complex phrases in English and speak almost without an accent. Those two qualities had made her employable in Canada. On her third day in Toronto, as she walked along Eglinton Avenue just to get her bearings, she saw a sign in the corner front window of Laura Secord: HELP WANTED.

She went in and Mr. Crabtree hired her right away even though she did not have a social insurance number.

I believe in opportunities for immigrants, he said. I will pay you in cash, nearly the minimum wage but that means you pay no tax, so it's better for you. Keep it hush-hush from the others, please.

Yes, Mr. Crabtree. Thank you, she said.

Call me Gordon.

She was too formal in her upbringing to do that and she called him Mr. Crabtree all the time she worked there. But sometimes, when he was not there, Emily referred to him as Mr. Grabtree.

You mean Crabtree?

No, said Emily, Grabtree. Sometimes he grabs us.

Girls, girls, he says, and he touches us on the bum. Harmless? I guess it could be worse. We need the job, the hours are good.

Oh, said Silvana.

When Mr. Crabtree introduced her to Emily he said, this is Silvana, a lovely Latin lady who is joining us for the Christmas rush and then to Valentine's Day.

On the day she started, Silvana put on a hairnet and an apron, and the three employees stood behind the glass counter in which were displayed the many candies made by Laura Secord. Some of these were pure chocolate and others were filled with jellied centres, others with nuts. There were many designs. Chocolates were the same the world over, Silvana realized. For the most part, the women just opened packages of premade chocolates and displayed them artistically, but on occasion they were required to create special-order chocolates. For that job, Emily and Silvana each received special instruction from Mr. Crabtree, who the rest of the time sat in the back and worked his way through the cash receipts, inventory and expenses. They could hear him shifting in his chair, the rustle of paper, his voice on the phone.

Silvana was very happy with the job. They were still supplementing Roberto Moreno, and her modest income from Laura Secord meant that they could save money. They could live within their means.

Oh lady, lovely Latin lady, Mr. Crabtree sang every morning when she came into the store, stamping the snow off her feet.

He praised her in front of Emily.

Sales have improved since our Latin lady has joined us. More men are coming in, have you noticed?

And Silvana and Emily looked at each other because they had noticed no such thing.

Ten days before Valentine's Day, Mr. Crabtree came to her behind the counter and he spoke to her *sotto voce*. By then, he had started to call her Sylvie, as though she were French and not Mexican.

Sylvie, he said, this afternoon when Emily leaves for the day, perhaps you will stay behind? I will demonstrate the procedure by which we insert nougat into the centre of a preformed chocolate without disturbing the outer skin. It is a skill Marie and Emily already have. You, Sylvie, have the steadiest hands of the staff and I can see that you have the touch of an artiste.

Silvana was flattered by this assessment of her skill. The word *artiste*. She had always respected artists and so had her husband. It was one of the reasons they supported Roberto past his teenage years and continued to do so here in Canada.

Before Emily left, she looked at Silvana.

You are staying? Be careful, Silvana. Mr. Grabtree comes out after dark.

Once Emily was gone, he turned the dead bolt in the door and flipped the CLOSED sign so it faced the street.

Look, Sylvie, he said, the way the sun slants down on the work table at this late hour. That's no good for working with chocolate. Chocolate needs to retain its strength and not be softened by exposure to heat. Or to unmanaged heat, at least. So we close the blinds.

He did so and a dark shadow fell across the table. He lit a gooseneck lamp that was attached to the wall and stretched it out. Delicately then, he showed her, with a tiny blade, how to bisect the empty upper chocolate shell from its firm base.

Have you seen one of these? he asked. It's a surgical scalpel, number 12 blade.

With a small silver spoon, he heaped up crushed and creamy nougat and filled the little excised helmet of chocolate with it. Then, with his fingertips, immaculately clean, he carefully replaced it upon its base.

Now the next step, he said, the grand finale.

He picked up an instrument that looked like a pencil, a fine wire at its end.

It's electric, he said, you press on this small button, the wire heats up.

Sure enough, there was a cord from the base of the pencil to the wall outlet.

My own invention, he said. You won't find this anywhere else in the world of chocolate. It applies very localized heat. Just—so.

He held the red-hot wire a fraction of an inch from the divided surface of the chocolate and almost immediately the surface melted and the tiny crevice that had been there vanished. The nougat was now encased in milk chocolate.

Now, Latin lady, we must make forty dozen of these by next week and it will be your own special project. Try one for me.

It was five o'clock. Surely Julián was on his way home now on the subway, but the special hot-wire chocolatiering did not look all that difficult, though it did require a steady hand, so Silvana took an empty shell and, as Mr. Crabtree had done, inserted the scalpel blade on one side and, using mostly her wrist in a circular motion, easily divided it.

Good, very good, he said, and now the nougat.

She formed a tiny scoop of nougat on the silver spoon, but as she moved, it crumbled and fell off.

No, no, Sylvie, he said, not like that. Here, I'll show you.

He stepped behind her and put both arms around her. His arms and hers became as one. He did not touch her otherwise but of course the position they were in caused her some concern because of its suggested intimacy. But he proceeded, from behind, his hands on hers, to pile the nougat upon the spoon.

There, there, like that, he said in a soft voice, his breath on her shoulder.

Perfect, he said, and now the final step, the melding of the two.

She picked up the small electric pencil and activated it. The wire turned red. She placed the wire within a hair's breadth of the surface of the chocolate and began to move it slowly around the edge. She had to bend down slightly to do so.

Good, good, very good.

Then she felt it, the pressure from behind as he leaned into her.

Oh yes, he said, good, good, my lovely Latin lady, yes, yes.

His hands were still on hers. Silvana jerked herself forward. Then she drove the red-hot electric wire into the back of his hand. There was a sizzling sound like bacon fat.

He screamed and fell back from her.

Oh Mother of Jesus, he cried.

She turned to him.

Oh, I'm so sorry, Mr. Crabtree. Quick, put it under cold water!

She took him by the arm and half pushed him towards the washroom in the back. He was bent over now at the waist and moaning.

Cold water, cold water, she said.

Oh shit, shit.

Please, where is the first aid kit, Mr. Crabtree?

It was under the sink. He kicked at it with his foot and she pulled it out and opened it.

Sit on the toilet, Mr. Crabtree.

Carefully, she applied iodine to the oozing seared patch of flesh on the back of his hand. Then she applied some cream and gauze and wrapped the hand with it.

He kept moaning and rocked back and forth. He didn't look at her.

She applied tape to the bandage and patted it down gently.

There, she said, that's how we do it in Mexico.

——

Amber laughed.

He called me in. You should have been there, Valerie, it was really too much. He had our book, *By Church and Isabella*.

The president of the College of Physicians called you in? Your boss?

Yes, he'd read it. Or at least he said he did. He had it on his desk and he held it up in the air and then placed it down.

Really? What you write has nothing to do with your job.

They're very conservative. He was agitated. His secretary was there too. She was on my side, I could tell, but she couldn't say much.

What was she doing?

Taking notes. Like I usually do.

As though you were on trial?

Sort of, I guess.

What were his concerns?

Amber laughed some more. I'll try to remember, she said. Okay. First he said that the presence of a radical feminist with sexual and authority issues in the midst of a college hearing could distort the process.

That's ridiculous, said Valerie. No one would ever recognize you. How many people will actually read that poem?

None. That's what his secretary finally had the courage to say, but he said to her, you women defend each other, it's reflex for you to do so. She was quiet after that. Then, let me see—he said my book portrays women as disempowered and men as uniformly evil. And this is a new one, Valerie, wait for this—he thought the cover was sexually provocative.

The cover?

He said it was vaginal mucosa.

What? It's a retina. Can't they see the blood vessels? What did you say to that?

Nothing. They can think what they want. Oh, and finally he said, Ms. White, what would happen if there were a hearing coming to a conclusion within our chambers and suddenly there you are, up on your feet and shouting, as you do in your book, saying *stop stop you sons of bitches, listen to this woman, listen to her.*

And? asked Valerie Anderson.

To that I replied, I would never jump to my feet at the college.

You wouldn't?

No. It would be the end of me, the end of this shelter. I'd be on the street myself. I have no qualifications, I'm just a typist.

No just-a-typist could have written those lines, Amber. *Stop stop you sons of bitches, listen to this woman, listen to her.* When I read them the first time, Amber, I put the manuscript down. I went for a walk. I didn't take the elevator, I took the stairs. I went outside just to breathe.

The secretary picked up the phone in the outer office.

Faculty of Medicine, she said.

Yes, this is Abner Krank speaking, Dr. Abner Krank. I'm the senior psychiatric resident here at the university.

Yes?

I need to contact three students I had on rotation last week on an issue of some importance. Their marks, my evaluation. Somehow I neglected to get their addresses and their phone numbers.

Come by the office, said the secretary, I'll have the information for you. You'll have to come by in person. It's not information we're allowed to give out over the phone.

Yes, of course, I understand, he said.

It was easy after that, although he had one moment of consternation when he arrived at the registrar's office. Two police officers in uniform leaned over the counter. He eavesdropped while he sat waiting his turn.

They wanted the admission photographs of every student in the faculty.

I'm sorry, you'll need a court order for that, said the registrar.

The registrar must have been summoned from an inner office.

He spoke in a whisper yet Dr. Krank's hearing was excellent. His mother always said, Abner can hear a pin drop on a pillow a mile away.

Well, fancy that. A court order? Why here it is, said the older of the two officers.

He handed over a sheaf of papers. Then the registrar lifted the partition and ushered the policemen inside.

Dr. Krank stood up. It was his turn.

I phoned earlier, he said, but I don't have a court order.

He smiled what he thought would be interpreted as a conspiratorial smile, and he was right.

Oh yes, Dr. Krank, she said, that's okay. Really, you're faculty, aren't you? Of course you are.

He left the office in five minutes with the information he wanted on three pieces of paper. Well, one piece of paper really because the other two, the handwritten slips the secretary had supplied for the other two students, for John Glass and for the serious one with the thick lips, the double-barrelled Wallace Wallace—how did that one even get into medical school?—those two addresses he crumpled up in his right hand and discarded in a wastebasket by the door. Then he walked down the empty corridor towards sunlight, the setting sun.

He wasn't the type to get fixated on one part of a girl, her lips, her eyes, her hair, a dimpled smile, her hips, her breasts, the way she turned her head and smiled over her shoulder. No, he was a total-package person, he knew that, and when he first saw Valerie Anderson at 999 Queen Street with her well-meaning but simplistic friends, nonentities those two, when he saw her, Valerie in her total female package, he took a sledgehammer hit to the heart. Two weeks later he still felt sore from it. He couldn't shake her, the way she walked up the corridor at the end, how she resisted turning to look at him as he watched her go.

Even though he knew from his past experience how unwise it was to assume anything with girls.

What was he to do? The heart had its own habits. His past misadventures were not crimes, really. No one was hurt more than he was, emotionally. He'd taken therapy, he'd come out on the other side.

Madeleine, sweet Maddy. He'd never think of her again now. Well, maybe, the braces on her teeth.

He never did find out the name of the girl who lay there in the rain on Shaw Street. It wasn't mentioned in the paper. It's ironic, how close they could have been, had he left the hospital five minutes earlier.

Valerie was different from all the other girls, a tabula rasa, a doctor just as he was. That meant they would have so much more to talk about, not just problems and emotional issues. They were both doctors, or soon she was going to be one. They already shared so much. He would not cross the line with Valerie Anderson.

He was outside now. He unfolded the piece of paper he had been given and turned his back to the sun. The registrar's secretary had written *Valerie Jane Anderson, 75 Isabella #305*. Then the phone number.

He set out north around King's College Circle, under the bridge to Wellesley and headed east. He was on call tonight starting at eleven. Nothing would happen tonight. He'd be alone at 999, high up in the bat-filled cupola that loomed over the darkened grounds. Anyway, it took time to get to know a new girlfriend. There was no rush now. He had all the information he needed.

Wellesley. The most nondescript street in Toronto but it did provide the necessary access to Church Street going north so it was the route he took.

The Chinese grocery store–Minimart combo with the iron bars behind the glass windows? Like they expected break-ins every night? Didn't they think it out beforehand? It was impossible to clean those windows. Outside it was okay, but inside you'd need microinstrumentation or the hands of a Barbie doll to get the cloth between the glass and the vertical bars that pressed tight every four inches or so. Bars of a jail.

He went inside and bought some breath mints. Tic-Tacs. He always used three of those at a time.

It was clean enough inside the Minimart but outside, looking back in again, the windows were so heavily streaked with dust that the stacked cans could have been anything. Sardines, tuna fish, Oriental diced rat. He'd never go in there again without gloves.

Diced rat. He could make Valerie Anderson laugh with that line, as long as it came up naturally in conversation. Natural conversation, that was the key. That was what girls liked. He'd practised and practised and now he had it, the natural part, he had it down pat.

He used the dim light that filtered from the store to open the piece of paper again. Yes, 75 Isabella. He looked around and then he took out his wallet, folded the note and put it in with the dollar bills. He'd never lose it there. It would be a nice memento for them someday.

The usual on Church Street. He walked north until there it was, right on the corner, a high-rise. Now it was six o'clock. The timing was pretty good because everybody ate dinner. If she wasn't up in the apartment already, opening a can or slicing bread with her white fingers, the nails cut short like they'd all been taught in surgery, then soon she'd be walking home on the same route he'd taken. Tracing his own steps, remarkable as that would be.

So here he was, Church and Isabella, just like in the poetry book. He stepped into the phone booth on the corner, put in a dime and dialed. There was no answer. He checked the number, dialed again, same thing. A third time to be absolutely sure and it just rang and rang. If she'd been on the elevator or the stairs the first time, she would have answered by the third. So she wasn't home yet. One day he'd call the same number and she'd say, yes? He'd call her darling and it would all feel happy, normal.

She was probably studying with those doughheads. A lot of beautiful girls had no boyfriends. They scared them off. They were unattainable.

Then he saw her, halfway down the block, not alone. A man was with her. His heart jumped once in his chest. Quickly, he picked up the receiver again and he pretended to dial, he held the receiver over his face, more so than was perfectly natural, quite awkward really, but it offered him the disguise he needed. So he stayed like that. He opened and closed his mouth saying, oh yes, oh yes, into the mouthpiece, oh no oh no, I'll call you back tomorrow, Mother.

They approached, now only ten feet away. She glanced towards him so he turned slightly to the side, away from her. Thus he lost the opportunity to identify her companion. It could have been either of her two loser friends, or someone else, but when they walked past and he had another look, the guy was short, at least six inches shorter than he was. He himself was six feet two inches tall, a lot taller than Valerie Anderson. The two of them talked to each other in an animated fashion, as though they cared about the topic, as though they had a real stake in it.

He watched them as they entered the building together. The man held open the door for her. A gentleman, he bowed her in.

Valerie said to Roberto Moreno as they walked up the stairs, the man in the phone booth, did you see him?

Yes, I did, why?

I think that was Dr. Krank, the psychiatric resident we had when we got Jasper out of hospital.

He lives near here?

I don't know, maybe. I've never seen him here before. Maybe I'm wrong.

Abner stayed in the phone booth for another fifteen minutes and then he took the opportunity when it happened. An older lady fumbled for her keys at the entrance of Valerie's building and he ran over and held the door open for her.

Oh, thank you, she said.

Here, I'll take your groceries up.

You live here, young man?

She looked suspiciously at Abner and he could see the thick cataracts, dull and grey.

Sure I do, he said, upstairs.

Oh, good.

By then they were in the lobby. He pointed to the list of names.

Right there, that's me, he said. Now the groceries. Allow me, madame.

He pushed the button to the elevator. She handed him her bag.

What number, dear? he asked.

Once they were this old, calling them dear was okay. Before that, watch out. That came up in therapy.

I'm in 405, yes 405.

Right overtop of Valerie Anderson's, if the numbering was consistent. At the door to 405, the woman fumbled for the key and he took it from her and let her in.

There you go, he said, home sweet home.

Thank you, young man, you have been very kind. 405, she said.

He'd seen lots of old folks as patients, barely getting by, their minds half shot. The best thing to do was just to say, yes, yes, and think about something else.

He walked down one flight of stairs and though he knew it was madness to do so, he stood outside 305 for five minutes, motionless. He could hear them in there talking, their footsteps on the parquet floor. Laughter even.

Then he left and went quickly back to Wellesley Street. He turned into the convenience store, the one with the bars on the window. One more time in without gloves, it couldn't be helped.

I need a copy of these, he said to the clerk, right away if you can.

The old lady's keys jingled as he passed them over the counter.

Which ones? asked the clerk.

Do them all, said Abner Krank.

It took maybe five minutes. As soon as he paid for the keys, he ran all the way back to 75 Isabella. He used one of the new ones to let himself into the lobby. Then up the stairs to the fourth floor and another new one opened the door to 405.

Hello hello, he said.

Footsteps shuffled towards him from the kitchen.

It's me, he said, I forgot. I still had your keys.

Oh, she said, thank you. And who are you?

I helped you with the groceries. Remember?

It's dark in here, she said.

Oh, it's not bad, not bad at all, he said. You don't have to be able to see everything all the time.

In Mexico City, he and his friends carried knives and they did it purely for the protection of their physical bodies. It was illegal there to carry a weapon, but everybody had a switchblade, including all the girls they knew, and the police carried them too, as did the bus drivers, the tobacconists, the lottery sellers, the beggars, the lawyers on their way to work, nannies, mothers leaving hospitals with their babies, fathers playing soccer in the square, bouncing the ball off the back wall of Cathedral Santa Maria, *tap-tap*. Everybody had them. His knife, the one he took to Canada and the one that no one noticed in his luggage when he came through customs at Toronto International Airport, was a folding blade of the usual type that snapped open to fifteen centimetres with a touch of a button on the handle made of polished wood, inlaid with brass. He had never used it in Mexico. There, none of the vehement discussions they had about poetry ever became personal. No matter how much they despised intellectual posturing or sentimentality, it was their intellects that were at odds. Heated issues resolved themselves in a peaceful way, quietly, and poets who agreed among themselves separated into subgroups and splinter groups and newly coined groups, and those with whom they disagreed went their separate ways. They all had their magazines, their mimeographed pages, they warred over words and technique and style. But their knives stayed in their pockets.

Valerie Anderson was surprised when she found that Roberto Moreno carried a concealed weapon, as she called it, when she wrapped her arms around him and her hand felt it through the back pocket of his jeans.

You don't need that here, she said. No one has these in Canada. You risk being deported.

When he showed it to her, she flicked it open three or four times and touched the blade with her fingertip.

You could do surgery with this, she said, dangerous surgery.

That he had already once used it in Canada for dangerous surgery, of this Roberto made no mention.

After that conversation, Roberto stopped carrying the switchblade. He tucked it into the lowest drawer of his dresser and left it there until, one night, after his uncle had gone to bed, his aunt called to him and asked his advice on something that had happened to her at work.

I could never tell Julián, she said, because of his terrible temper. He would want me to quit my job.

He has a terrible temper?

Oh yes. When he was a young man he was a firecracker. Never towards me, Roberto, but to others, sometimes, he could be dark as midnight. He's stubborn as a burro with a grudge.

She explained to Roberto what Mr. Crabtree had done to her at work and what she had done, in return, to Mr. Crabtree.

Roberto was not like his uncle. He simmered rather than boiled.

Good for you, Aunt, it sounds as though you sent him a message, don't mess with me, don't mess with women, don't mess with Mexicans. I'm proud of you. What's your Mr. Crabtree's first name?

Gordon. Why?

Just curious, Aunt, just curious.

Thank you, Roberto, she said, for listening. I feel better now.

She went to bed.

Roberto Moreno reached for the telephone book and found that the only G. Crabtree did not live far from them. In fact, just around the corner, on Rosewell Avenue. What a coincidence that was. Roberto had probably already seen his aunt's employer in the course of his own neighbourhood walks.

He went upstairs to his room and removed his knife from its resting place. He flicked it open and closed and put it in the pocket of his hooded sweatshirt. Then he went out. It was not hard to find the Crabtree house, though some of the street numbers were not well illuminated. Maple trees hung dark and heavy from above, casting such shadows that even the three-quarter moon and the streetlight at the curb failed to penetrate the curtain of leaves. But he had a flashlight and when he arrived at his target, he walked nearly all the way to the front door, just to be certain the address was correct. It was.

A Chevrolet Malibu was parked in the driveway, ten feet from the front sidewalk. More remarkably, a woman stood in the front window of the house and he could tell, from the backlighting, that she wore something tight. A leotard maybe. She was exercising, yoga or tai chi or a variant of both, silhouetted in the window. At first, she was unaware of his presence, but as he flashed his light across the front of her porch, she stopped what she was doing. She looked right at him and, why not, he waved to her. She was only twenty feet away.

Must be Mr. Laura Secord's wife, he thought. Or daughter.

Surprisingly, she made a hesitant motion in reply, also a small wave of her right hand.

Then he walked over to the car. As though he were an inspector on an assembly line, he bent down before the front left tire. He was in deep shadow, not only from the tree but from a quince hedge close by. It took him only thirty seconds to methodically walk the four corners of the vehicle and insert his blade deep into each tire with a *thunk* and each time the swish of air rushed back against his knuckles as the car gradually staggered to the ground. He looked at her again and he waved again, not in any taunting way, just a wave, and he walked home. But, before that, before he left her sidewalk, he stretched his arms up high over his head and bent back, the only yoga move he knew. The Mountain, it was called.

It was his way of saying hello to her, that he was on her side. Hello, female Crabtree person, this was not done against you.

The next day, as a precaution, one that he knew he should have taken earlier, after Shaw Street, Roberto Moreno cleaned his knife fastidiously with rubbing alcohol. Then, from high up on the Bloor Viaduct, he dropped it all the way down into the Don River. Light glanced from it as it fell, as from a struggling fish.

There were no repercussions from the tire-puncturing, from the warning he sent. Perhaps she never reported it to the police. Perhaps she spoke to Mr. Crabtree and figured it out herself. At any rate, his aunt Silvana was never bothered again by Mr. Crabtree. She continued to work at the job she liked and never reported a problem again.

Roberto waited three weeks before he purchased a replacement weapon. This time, at a pawn shop at the corner of Church and Queen, he paid thirty dollars for a special one with a different design, one in which the blade leapt straight out from the front, rather than quartering in a quick circle from the side.

It seemed so direct, this new knife. It made a statement similar to the insertion a writer makes when he uses, at the end of a sentence, a colon:

Look at this, the new blade said, look at this carefully.

Roberto stood at the front of the class, as he did every Thursday evening at eight. He was clean shaven, neatly dressed in black trousers and a white shirt. All his students were there, sitting in a tight group at the front of the classroom.

Okay, my friends, he said. Tonight we will leave Al Purdy and Leonard Cohen in our wake and we leave Canada and the United States of America and England too, and we shall spend time in Mexico. What do you say?

Yes, said John Glass, yes to Mexico!

There was a murmur of agreement from everyone present, so Roberto Moreno went to the blackboard and quickly, from memory, he wrote in white chalk:

ANOTHER CONCERT IN THE GARDEN
It drizzled.
Sixty minutes is an inexhaustible orb.
Inside it, we tramp as mirror images.
Music's arrow
Penetrates me.

If I say corporeal, it answers tempest.
If I say ground, it answers why?

Our Mexico opens, a twinned bouquet:
The blues for having come,
rapture for being here.

I am undone in my own heart.

Is this on the course? asked Wallace Wallace.

No, Wallace, it's not on the course, but neither was Miriam Waddington. Besides as you know there is no course per se, there are no exams. You have all passed this course already, with A plus. I shall never stand in your way of becoming physicians. Let us move on. Class, what do you think? Read the poem carefully.

They all looked at the blackboard. In silence, they read the poem. Some of them moved their lips.

This poem seems very familiar to me, said Valerie Anderson.

Yes, thank you, Valerie. It is, in fact, an homage to a famous work by Octavio Paz. His title for his poem was "Concert in the Garden." This entirely different poem, "Another Concert in the Garden," was written by the prominent imitationist Raoul Mendoza. He is a first cousin to Octavio Paz. Actually, I think he is a first cousin once removed. As you can see from the similar title, Raoul Mendoza has made no effort to hide the source of his inspiration. He has trumpeted it to the world. You may recall, all of you, the night we met at

Grad's Restaurant, how I listed the many groups of poets who gather in Mexico City. Included in that list were the imitationists. They are, I believe, unique to Mexico.

Not true, said Jasper Glass, I've seen poems of my brother's that are highly derivative.

Jasper, said Valerie, that's not fair.

Derivative, said Roberto, is not the same as imitative. Derivative is a normal step for a young poet to take. To imitate, according to Raoul Mendoza, is not only to flatter but to expand thematically. It is a mature step by a confident, brazen yet respectful artist. But I must admit that before Raoul Mendoza began to imitate Octavio Paz, he was unknown.

How is this imitation actually done? asked John Glass.

The original poem is rewritten using synonyms. That's the core of the movement.

Plagiarism, said Wallace Wallace.

No, not at all. A great imitationist, as Raoul turned out to be, also adds a twist, as he did in this poem, that elevates it above and beyond the original. Or so many would say.

My recollection, said Valerie Anderson, is that there was no mention of the word *heart* in the poem by Paz. And the individual words are all different, anyway. Synonyms can never mean exactly the same thing.

Exactly, said Roberto. That was the discovery of Raoul Mendoza, and that is why we study him today, instead of Octavio Paz. In Spanish, it is even more beautiful. For example, the word *undone* in Spanish was *perdido*. Say *perdido,* class, together now.

Perdido, they all said.

I know that word, said Jasper Glass. I saw a movie, I forget the name but it was at the Revue Roncesvalles. Spanish with subtitles. A man walked in the desert. Sweat poured from under his hat. He kept walking and falling and the sun blazed high and finally he fell to his knees and said *perdido* five times, and five times the subtitle said *lost*. It did not say *undone*.

Translators can do whatever they like, said Roberto. They need only be true to their own concept of the original. That night at the cinema, obviously, Jasper, you were very observant. So, tonight's poem. Read it to us out loud, please, Wallace.

Wallace stood up and recited the poem in a very straightforward, flat voice.

That was a good reading, said Roberto Moreno, it dispensed with false drama. You did not wave your arms or let your voice roller-coaster. You did not bring attention to certain lines of the poem at the expense of others.

I think, said Jasper Glass, that "Another Concert in the Garden" is about an ophthalmologist—my clue is the word *orb* for eye—who one day looks into a patient's eye and imagines himself instead drawn into the soul. He walks along the arteries on the retina, here disguised as arrows, and then, like an insect in a carnivorous plant, the ophthalmologist gets undone, or lost, in his own heart, meaning his office, the medical building in which he works, which makes him fear that he is succumbing to the early onset of dementia.

Thanks, Jasper, said John Glass.

It's a concert in a garden, it drizzles but music is pervasive, said Valerie Anderson, it becomes all-encompassing.

The blues—melancholy—and rapture—joy—mingle together for they are one and the same, said John Glass, just two stops on the same continuum.

Perhaps there's a tent there, not mentioned, under which the musicians play in the rain, said Jasper. It's hard to play a guitar in the rain.

Jasper, asked Wallace Wallace, why did we save you anyway from the mental hospital? You are sabotaging this class.

There was silence in the classroom as only Valerie and John had knowledge of Jasper's escapade, his plunge to earth as Icarus. It had been kept a secret. Quickly, Wallace recovered from his mistake.

I mean, said Wallace, why can't Jasper take things more seriously? He will make all of us candidates for a mental hospital.

Let me say this, said Roberto Moreno, all contributions to the interpretation of a poem are welcome. Poetry is fraught with difficulty. Especially in translation. Some translators are equally at home in both languages yet others, including the maestro, Ezra Pound, could not speak any of the languages of China when he wrote his versions of the poetry of Li Po and Lao-tzu. So, if Jasper finds something amusing where no one else does, let it be.

May I add something? asked John Glass. I have trouble with the concept that we walk about in an inexhaustible eye, or orb, because, embryologically, the eye is an extension of the brain. Nowhere in the poem by Raoul Mendoza is there a mention of the brain.

Out in the corridor, a bell rang, signifying the end of the hour.

Roberto Moreno looked at Valerie Anderson.

Time to move on, he said. Next week, please bring in, students, some comments on these lines:

> *I put knowledge in my mouth but could not eat*
> *Despite the taste of powder cakes and sweetmeat.*
> *Then I learned a lesson in the People's Republik,*
> *With a startled heart and nervous stomach.*
> *I ran and swam the streets,*
> *Air and humidity beneath my feet.*

Oh, who wrote that? asked Wallace Wallace.

A girl I know, said Roberto Moreno.

He had the poem printed already, a copy for each of them. They handed the sheets around and then they all stood and raised their right arms for the toast.

Okay, said Roberto Moreno.

To Stefan Grodzinski, said Wallace Wallace.

In unison they recited the familiar lines from Tennyson.

> *Courage! he said, and pointed toward the land,*
> *This mounting wave will roll us shoreward soon.*

Class dismissed.

————

Bill, I wonder what the boys are up to, said June Glass. We don't see much of them anymore, do we.

No, we don't. They're grown up, for the most part. At least Jasper is. I don't know about John. His head's in the clouds. He's lost.

They were at the dinner table, each with a small pork chop, asparagus and a glass of white wine. Jasper had his own place now on Avenue Road, in the Hampton Court Apartments. John usually slept there too, on the couch. Now and then they came home for dinner, but rarely together and not tonight.

I fear, said Bill, that Louise Drabinsky is becoming vindictive. She can be frightening. She was short with me on the phone this afternoon. I'd had a few beers before I phoned and I couldn't say her bloody name straight. *Louise,* I tried to say, but it kept coming out *Louizze,* like I'd had a stroke. Just *Louizze.* Every other word was okay. The more I said her name, the more I heard something seeping into her voice. Disdain.

I've told you before, Bill, about your drinking. *Louizze. Jazzper.* Your tongue gets thick on the *s*'s. You've got to back off, Bill, and let the book go. How many times have we had this conversation?

I couldn't help it. Oh, she seemed happy enough at first. Bill, she said, Bill. She seemed delighted and it got me going. I dropped my guard. Louise, I read a new idiom today in *Paris Match,* it's too good to pass up. Can we slip it into the section on food? Of course then she had the same tedious complaint she always has.

Tedious?

Well, unimaginative, pedantic, bureaucratic, practical, call it what you will. Every time you want to make a substantial change in your *Idioms,* at this stage, the end-stage, it sets back the publication date by six months. Minimum.

She's right. You can't have it both ways.

I should have apologized and hung up the phone.

But you didn't.

No. I said, this idiom is so French, it can't be excluded. I want this book to be definitive, Louise, to sit there beside *Larousse.* The Glass book. Everybody will know it as the Glass book.

You said that?

Beurré comme un petit Lu. I forgot she spoke no French. Silence on the other end, I barged ahead, *beurré comme un petit Lu.* I was so very excited. Finally I remembered about her handicap in languages. Oh, Louise, I said, that means buttered like a biscuit, a butter-biscuit made in France. Even better, guess what that idiom means? I haven't the faintest idea, she said. It means, Louise, drunk or plastered. Put it in the Glass book and to hell with the publication date.

You actually said that?

Yes. I'm afraid so. It was then she changed. Or I thought she did. Your diction isn't quite right, she said. I threw caution to the wind. Louise, I said, I'm trying the idiom out, I've had a few drinks tonight to assess its accuracy. Tonight, I'm a buttered biscuit. Well, she said, buttered biscuit or not, now that you're on the phone, I have a bone to pick with you, I don't like that one about the velvet underpants. No one will like that one about velvet underpants.

Oh, said June.

She said it stopped her in her tracks. *Un petit jésus en culotte de velours.* Her accent was ghastly. Get rid of that idiom, Bill, she said. I was nonplussed, June. I didn't know what to say to her.

Well, Professor, she then said, you state, in your book, that this literally means a little Jesus in velvet underpants and that it means, idiomatically, delicious. That's all it means, delicious, for all those seven words in French?

Yes, Louise, I said, it's a fine example of the colour of the language, poetry really, the way it trips off the tongue. Or I said something like that to her and then I pronounced the phrase back to her in the proper accent. See? I said. But no, she didn't see.

Bill, she said, it strikes me that there are associations implied within that phrase that are not only the obvious ones, religious, but also there are sexual, even homosexual connotations implied.

That's news to me, I said, but even if so, would that be forbidden ground, Louise, in our book?

I hope you kept cool, said June, you didn't get flustered again. No *Louizze*s.

No, not at all. I was outraged but she never would have known. For once I had control. Guess what she asked me then.

I have no idea.

Bill, do you want me to index that phrase under Food, or under Sexuality and Depravity?

Are you pulling my leg, Louise? I said to her.

That particular idiom grates on me, she said, and will grate on many readers.

But Louise, I said, that's only because it's French and that's the point of the book, the whole point of our book is that it's French, it's different.

The French may be different, Bill, but how in the world could they come up with something like this, Jesus in velvet underpants, to mean delicious? Some dinner at Versailles perhaps? Bishops, cardinals, gourmands, a long table, footmen, candles, wine, pheasant under glass, they smile and bend their heads over the roasted bird and with a silver fork take a morsel and then they sit back and say, delicious, just like Jesus in velvet underpants? I don't like it, Professor Glass.

Well, I replied, we don't have to like it to include it. I heard it twice, at a monastery as I recall, and it has to stay in.

Bill, she said, what did they do to Jesus? Touch his velvet pants? What did they taste when they did that, what was so delicious?

I held firm on both of them, June, that one and the buttered biscuit too.

Louise cares about your book, Bill, she's passionate. That's obvious, that's good.

But do you think it possible, dear, that some of my idioms will bring disrepute down upon my head? Upon us both?

Hardly, Bill, they're not yours. You only write them down. They're like folk songs. They reflect a culture.

Sometimes, I wonder, why did I hang my hat on idioms? I might as well count angels on the head of a pin. Then there'd be no Louise Drabinsky.

I wonder what she looks like, your editor.

A vulture.

June laughed.

And I would be the carrion at her feet. My life has come to naught.

Don't be ridiculous. Look at our family, our children, if you doubt the purpose of your life.

I do think about that, June. And I remember, "He that hath wife and children hath given hostages to fortune; for they are impediments to great enterprises." I think our children have slowed me down, to be honest. No children, I'd be published long ago.

I can't take you seriously, she said. Every time you talk to that woman, you go off the deep end.

June, be honest. Do you think my book qualifies as a great enterprise?

She looked up and laughed.

Well, it's certainly a great enterprise of yours.

And your *Zipper*? How long have you been an editor there now, officially?

Three months, she said. *Zipper* has a chance for greatness. It's run by writers and dreamers.

The detective sat at his desk and looked at the photographs. There they were, his unusual suspect group of the day. All the medical students at the University of

Toronto. Four years of them, six hundred and forty faces caught in the innocent lights of a flashbulb.

They took the same kind of pictures at police college. His was at home in the bedroom, on the dresser, and yes, he didn't look much different from these kids.

He riffled through the photos like they were playing cards.

No shoulders smeared with Crisco.

He thought about all the faces, all the photographs he'd been given in his time, usually by parents. Those kids were young, self-conscious, at the most they offered a half-smile. Now they were gone somewhere, missing, presumed dead, on the run, whatever the case may be. The family pictures were always a couple of years out of date but they were useful nevertheless. Snapshots blown up and put on the backs of buses. CALL HOME, MIRANDA. But these were different. He knew where to find all these young men. This part was going to be easy.

Thanks again, he said to the officer who brought them over.

What's with these anyway? Looking for a physician?

A long shot, he said. Trying to find the accomplice to a murder. Remember Shaw Street?

He flipped through them one by one and cast aside all the black faces, the Chinese, the two Sikhs. And all the girls too. It didn't make much of a dint in the number.

There were also the four large group photographs, the whole class. He picked those up and went in to see the detective sergeant.

This is where we start, he said. With these, with Marnie Kennedy-Foare, with Crisco.

He flipped open his notebook.

One night Crisco in her milkbox, the next night Crisco on the neck of Gwen O'Hara, on Shaw Street. Pretty weird, it's hard not to make a connection. The rapist, he's found dead up the street. Justice is served, like we said, but still, if we find the milkbox guy, then we find his friend and that's the killer, the avenging angel, the absolutionist.

Makes sense to me.

The one consolation, going down this road, I guess when it's all done, we get to meet them.

Andy, there's no guarantee your man is here, in the Faculty of Medicine. In fact, it's far-fetched. They're serious students, they're not crazy night-walkers.

True, but you throw kids together, someone like Marnie, what do they do?

They have sex with each other, I guess, if they're like everybody else.

That's right, they form relationships. I'll check it out. It's a good place to start.

She's married.

Oh she is, she is. Her husband's got a head full of mathematics though, some kind of egghead. He I met, her I haven't. He's okay. Anyway, I narrow it down, get a name if I'm lucky, I show a few of these photographs to Gwen O'Hara, she blinks her eye, points her finger, the case is solved, onward and upward. All she has to do is twitch, she doesn't have to say a thing.

And the rapist, post-mortem, destroys someone else's life, said the detective sergeant.

It's a great job we have.

Run with it, Andy. It has to be done.

The next day, he waited until four-thirty before he went to Mount Sinai Hospital. The switchboard operator paged Dr. Kennedy-Foare and five minutes later there she was, the beach picture in real life. Blue eyes, blond hair pinned back and up, tufts of it flying here and there. She smiled and so did he. There was an immediate and undeniable warmth about her. She'd have no trouble with bedside manner, no matter what she went into.

He held up his badge.

Detective Ames, homicide, he said.

He still loved saying that.

Homicide? she said.

We're seeking your assistance in an investigation. May we talk?

She looked at her watch and she looked around.

The patient lounge is probably empty, she said.

Together they walked down a corridor. She pushed open a set of swinging doors and it was quieter. She opened another door and flicked on a light switch and they were in a cozy room, a kitchen table, a few chairs, a chesterfield.

Here, she said.

She angled two chairs from the table and they sat down.

Homicide, she said, you've got to be kidding. Something from the hospital?

No, no, he said, something that came up from a report your husband made, a break-in at your home some time back.

Oh, the milkbox.

She laughed like water bubbling over rocks. He could see she wasn't nervous at all.

Yes, she said, he told me about it the other day. He was impressed, how the police came out to the house. But he didn't say anything about homicide.

He didn't tell you about the break-in right away, when it happened?

No, he said I'd worry.

Again she laughed.

But I don't worry. Anyway, you'd need more than Crisco to get through that milkbox now. It's nailed and bolted shut. I live in a fortress.

Yes, I saw that. Anyway, Doctor, I have one or two questions. Is there any light you could shed on the whole matter of the burglary?

Light?

Any information you might have—independent information, information your husband may not be privy to—as to the identity of the person who came through the milkbox?

What do you mean?

Now she looked serious. She still wanted to help him. He could see that. She didn't look defensive at all, or withdrawn.

Well, Doctor, my interpretation of the milkbox, and the opinion of all of us down at Homicide, after due consideration, is that there is a strong possibility that the Crisco at the scene, in your milkbox, was used to egress the building rather than ingress it.

They practised sentences like that, the convoluted diction of interrogation, because in most people it led to confusion and confusion led to mistakes and mistakes led to confessions.

You mean leave rather than come in?

Yes. Someone in the house who wanted out and that was the only way to go.

Oh, that's impossible, she said, that's bizarre. Someone was home with me and when Christian came home, that same someone was trapped inside.

Exactly, he said. The Crisco was found inside the house afterwards, not outside.

She smiled at him, as probably she smiled at patients.

If I were squeezing through a milkbox, she said, and needed Crisco on the way in, I'd take it with me, inside, lest I be trapped.

So you didn't have a visitor, anybody with you that night?

No. I was alone with Brewster when Christian came through the door.

He made some notes in his notebook.

Brewster?

The dog, she said. But I don't understand where homicide comes into this.

We're trying to come up with a connection, your place and Shaw Street, a murder downtown. There was Crisco there too.

Crisco? It's laughable. It's everywhere, Crisco.

It wasn't laughable on Shaw Street, I can tell you that, Doctor. And, so far, your intruder's the only obvious common denominator.

She turned serious and stood up.

I'm sorry, I didn't mean to make light of anything. Good luck with your investigation, Detective, but I have to get back to work. I can't help you.

In his car, he sat and reflected. When she lied, what was it she'd said? He consulted his notebook. *I was alone with Brewster when Christian came through the door.* That's what the intelligent ones always did. They added that little bit of unnecessary information that turned the lie they were telling into the truth, the truth for them. *When Christian came through the door.* Sure, Marnie Kennedy-Foare was alone when Christian came through the door. Ten seconds earlier, probably not.

The real way to lie, or the real way to tell the truth, would have been the more natural, the expected, *I was alone all night with Brewster.* And that she couldn't say, or didn't.

Still, she had the bedside manner, the way she touched his arm when he was leaving.

He iced the investigative cake the next day. He walked into the cafeteria at the medical building well before lunch. He stood out, the only person there over thirty. The place was jammed and he didn't beat around the bush. He identified himself from table to table until he found the fourth-year students. Marnie's year.

Homicide, he said again.

Marnie Kennedy, you know her?

Sure we do. She's in our class, number one, the gold medallist. Sure we know her.

We're checking into her associates, her friends. She's not in any personal difficulty. Does she have a boyfriend, someone to whom she's close?

No, no, no, they all said. That's crazy. She's married now.

Then he went down through the years, one by one, and loyalty seeped away. Third year, second year, first year, he began to hear the same name all the time.

Oh, Jasper Glass, but I didn't say so. You didn't hear it from me.

Jasper Glass. Jasper Glass.

Okay.

When he went to see Gwen O'Hara the next day, he took just ten of the photographs with him. Just the right number, not enough to overwhelm her at all. She was waitressing the lunch hour at the Parrot, the new place on Queen Street. When the rush was over, she sat down across from him.

Here, Gwen, he said, take a look at these.

One by one, he flipped through them. The sixth one was Jasper Glass. He gave her five seconds with each.

Let me see again, she said.

He turned over the photographs in the same sequence.

A third time? she said. You're like a croupier, Andy, the way you snap them down.

Flip-flip-flip. There was somebody there she wanted to look at. He was sure of it. He was also sure that she too was going to lie to him, just like Marnie. It was lucky he wasn't just starting out, that he'd done this sort of thing lots of times before.

No, she said, my guys aren't there.

You're sure?

Positive.

Thanks, I'll come by again if something turns up.

Okay.

How are you doing?

I'm fine, pretty good. Where are these photos from?

Oh, just archives, he said, most of them.

Then he thought, what the heck.

Actually, all of these faces are from the Faculty of Medicine, here in Toronto. The first-year class.

Really, she said. Why pick them?

Oh, they're the right age, that's all. I can't see any of them flying through the night for you. Just a long shot.

Gwen O'Hara watched him leave.

One of her rescuers was the sixth photograph in the sequence, better looking than she remembered but unmistakable.

No way in the world was she going to turn him in, point the finger at that photograph and say, there he is, that's the man, there's the man who saved my life. He was untouchable and so was his friend, the one with the knife.

The police, they'd been nice to her, but they could spin their wheels for a long time on this one. Forever.

———

She called him late one night from her aunt's cottage in Muskoka.

Oh, Marnie, he said, hi.

Jasper, the police came by last week.

The police? What about?

They're looking for the guy who went through my milkbox. That's you.

They are?

Some connection with a murder on Shaw Street. What's that about, Jasper?

Shaw Street?

Shaw Street, Jasper, I don't even know where that is.

I know where it is, but I don't know anything about a murder there. Who came?

A policeman.

What did you say?

Nothing. There was nothing I could say without blowing us away. You and me.

A uniformed policeman?

No, a detective. Homicide.

Homicide? Jesus, I haven't got a clue.

Stay away from each other now, said Marnie, that's the best thing.

Oh, I don't know about that. I've done nothing wrong. Whatever tree they're barking up, it's not me. I am as innocent, Marnie, as a lamb. Trust me.

I do, Jasper, I do. Sort of.

Then they forgot about the homicide detective and they talked to each other's voices over the phone and she told him she was up there for three weeks, for the love of God, that sometimes she couldn't sleep—it was too hot, too humid—so in the middle of the night, last night, she got up and went down to the boathouse where in the loft there was a semblance of a breeze, and a mattress. She lay down by herself. She removed her pyjamas. The moon came through the open loft window by the lake, the mist rose up and even though she was still restless, Jasper, she said, finally, finally she fell asleep. Then hours later the sun came up, birds sang, warblers, and she stood naked in the open loft and dove into the lake, the water twenty feet deep and cool. She went skinny-dipping with no one else around, no one up yet in the early morning but her, and after breast-stroking and floating on her back for ten minutes she climbed out of the water onto the dock and then back up the ladder to the loft, where she lay flat and her bare skin dried in the air.

What about Christian?

Fast asleep up at the cottage. Recharging his brain. Nothing wakes him up.

Listen, Marnie, maybe the next night like that, we could get together. I could drive up.

Oh no, Jasper, don't do that. You never know what might happen. Especially now, with the police.

Then he heard the slam of a screen door in the background.

It's Aunt Audrey, she said, bye-bye.

She hung up the phone.

He remembered how she had said sorry, Jasper, how she had clicked the window shut and left him out there on the ledge to tumble from the sky. He forgave her. She was his first real lover.

For two weeks in Toronto the weather turned relatively cool and in the dissecting room, he and Valerie Anderson worked on the right leg of their cadaver. They began at the ankle, where it was easy—there were no muscles or fat to deal with, just tendons and ligaments and fine dissection—and they worked their way proximally into the calf, exposing the muscles as they went. Always, they had *Grant's Atlas of Anatomy* at hand.

So you think this is gastrocnemius, medial? he asked.

Yes, said Valerie Anderson.

Soleus here?

She looked at the picture in the book.

Definitely, or I think so. Pull it that way, there.

Later she said, sartorius?

Yes, that's it, it's long like a strap, it runs right up high. We'll have to extend the incision right up, there, to the inguinal ligament. It works with gracilis, which runs there, to the inner thigh.

He used the scalpel and ran the long incision farther up the inside of the leg.

Tra-la, he said.

Then together they undercut the skin to better view the bellies of the muscles.

Valerie?

Yes, Jasper.

Valerie, when?

When what?

When may I touch your enticing gracilis, even just by the knee?

It's my turn to cut now, she said, give me the blade.

On Thursday morning, in the cafeteria, he read in the *Toronto Star* that the upcoming heat wave, which looked like it was going to hit tomorrow, could quite possibly be a record-setter, that Ontario's electrical grid was going to be tested to the maximum, that the heat and the humidity were going to settle over the city in an L.A.-like smog, an inversion they called it. They even compared it to Mexico City. Seniors and those with chronic lung conditions were advised to stay indoors.

Okay, he thought, this is it. Here I come.

At four in the afternoon, he went out to the Volkswagen and turned the key. Nothing happened. He raised the hood. Everything there looked fine but damned if he could get a whimper out of the car and there was no one around to take a look at it. Everything was closed for the long weekend. But he knew Valerie was at home so he walked to her place and asked if he could borrow her Dodge Dart.

What for, Jasper?

Canoe trip overnight, Muskoka, rest and recreation in the great outdoors.

You can put a canoe on my car?

Sure, no problem. I got all the gear.

Okay, Jasper, but be careful, it's my mother's, not mine.

I know. Thanks, he said.

Then he briefly lost control because she was still the love of his life, unrequited.

Valerie, would you like to come along with me, camping?

It was hopeless. She was in love with Roberto Moreno and all she did was look at him in the same way she always did, bemused.

Don't forget the ENT exam, she said, Tuesday. Here's the keys. There's no gas, or next to none.

So he filled up the Dart at the Esso station on Oriole Parkway, drove up Avenue Road to Glengrove and there he took the only other thing he needed for the fruition of his plans—the canoe. His brother wasn't at home. The professor was there, though, working upstairs, and he was happy to come down. He helped Jasper lift the canoe and tie it to the roof rack. Then he put two paddles into the back seat of the Dart.

Beavertails, the professor said, poplar, one spare. Where's your tent?

I'll be sleeping outside, said Jasper, no need for a tent. The biting bugs are gone, the stars are now my canopy.

And your sleeping bag?

Also a frill, said Jasper, for a man of the north.

Then Roberto Moreno came out the back door of the Nájeras' house.

Hey, Roberto, said Jasper. It says in the paper it's like Mexico City here, an inversion, a heat wave.

In fact the humidity had already started to rise. He could feel himself sweating after the minimal exertion with the canoe.

Yes, said Roberto, you see, Jasper, Mexico City is surrounded by mountains, and the polluted air, which contains fine particulate matter, often hangs suspended over the city for weeks in an inverted bowl. It is a lot like breathing dirt. Hey, you have Valerie's car?

My Volkswagen won't start. I borrowed Valerie's just now.

That boat of yours looks like a hat on top of it, said Roberto.

Merci, said Jasper to his father, and *hasta la vista,* he said to Roberto and he pushed the thought of Roberto Moreno with Valerie Anderson, the two of them, their limbs wrapped together as tight as elastic, out of his mind where it had appeared spontaneously and unasked-for, and by the time he left the driveway, it was nine o'clock at night. The western sky turned orange and red and yellow, and now the whole world dripped with sweat. It was ninety-five degrees at least and the air smelled of gasoline and exhaust.

Roberto would feel at home in this all right.

There was no breath of wind. He drove up Avenue Road to the 401 and turned west in stop-and-go traffic. It took him forty minutes to get to the 400 and then he drove north in a long stream of cars with families, beach balls, bicycles and boats pulled behind cars, but it looked like the worst part of the traffic was over. Two hours to Highway 69. Then it was dark, the ropes from the canoe strung white in the headlights and bugs stuck dead to the windshield.

He stopped at a gas station. With sweeping arcs, he squeegeed the driver's side clean. He bought a cup of coffee. Then farther into the north and it was close to midnight when he finally pulled the car into a deserted gravel pit just north of Mactier. Someone had left an old refrigerator there, tipped over. He'd never stopped there before. The lake was just a hundred yards away through the woods, he knew that from the map. There had to be a path, lots of others must have parked here before. It was late enough in the season, he'd been right about that because there were no mosquitoes at all and it was easy to untie the canoe in the light spilled from the headlights, from the idling car. He turned the key and locked the Dart. He found the semi-broken trail that started where the gravel left off and with his small flashlight held in his teeth, he swung the canoe over his head and down the portage he went, the canoe an illuminated shell above him. Rocks and roots and boggy spots flashed under the wavering light. He saw the water through the gap in the trees. By the shore rocks, he flipped the canoe down, caught it on his knees and lowered it to the water's edge. His flashlight flickered and died.

It was humid all right. There were going to be a lot of restless sleepers tonight, not just Marnie Kennedy.

He waded in and submerged himself in the lake, held his breath, and when he broke the surface again, except for a few lights from late cottages in the distance, it was pitch-black, the Milky Way scrawled overhead. A loon called. It was transcendental, the whole scene. He felt giddy. He stepped into the canoe, knelt down and pushed off over the lake where the water was just like Jasper, like his name—like glass—and the canoe, cedar-strip, was the same blue-black as the night, invisible but for the spotted silver track it left behind, a surface turbulence. He knew more or less where he was going. A point of land surrounded on all sides by water, but it was farther than he thought, and the landmarks of the lake were so disguised by darkness that by the time he found it—the boathouse with the mahogany launch that lay dead-still inside—another hour had passed.

But there it was, just as Marnie had described it to him, the open loft window above, the rocks, the trees, the shadow of the cottage that loomed in the woods. One small yellow light barely filtered through the trees over the front door of the main building. The sign on the boathouse said SUMMERLEE. He laid off a few minutes just to appreciate it, the journey accomplished, as Horatio Nelson had laid off the shore of Spain before Trafalgar, waiting, contemplating the upcoming engagement of arms. Then he paddled as soundlessly as a watersnake or an Iroquois warrior on Sainte-Marie, and his paddle never left the water at all as he slipped it back and forth, a knife edge in the cool black, and the wooden gunwales of his canoe were silent, untouched, such was the skill of his paddling, when even the slightest rub would have sounded like cannonshot. He tied up to a ring on the dock.

Oh, the welcoming rings of summer.

He got out, he stretched his legs. All he had on was a bathing suit and it must have been two in the morning. The moon was up higher in the sky, now the stars were dimmed to a fraction of their former brilliance and the only way he could see to get up into the loft was by the vertical ladder nailed to the front of the boathouse, just where the dock ended, overlooking the open water. He gave the ladder a tentative pull. It was solid, nailed fast to the siding by what felt like four-inch spikes, the heads of large nails, its rungs smoothed by the passage of feet over the years.

Her feet.

Like a cat burglar, he climbed up and looked in. There she was, no more than four or five feet away but with the angle of the moonlight, the way it hit the doorway, there was just a rectangle of dim and diffused light and all he could see were her legs, bare naked, stretched towards him, and her left foot and knee were turned out and away, akimbo.

She lay on her back and he heard the soft to-and-fro of her breathing, deep in sleep. The rest of her, upwards from the thighs, was hidden by impenetrable darkness. With some difficulty, still on the rungs of the ladder, he stripped off his bathing suit, first one foot and then the next, and then up he went, low as he could go as he crawled on his knees over the transept into the loft itself. Then he crept towards her, silently, as far as her feet, and without so much as touching her with his hands, he placed his lips in a direct caress upon the instep of her left foot. No reaction, so profound was her slumber. Then he began to explore farther upon the map of her lower extremity, again his lips and now his tongue serving as sextant and compass and as he did so, he could not help but recall the anatomy that lay beneath the skin, so recently exposed in the laboratory with Valerie Anderson, and despite the erotic nature of his present progress, pages of *Grant's* flipped themselves open before him as, upon her toes one to five, he administered with his lips a gentle pull followed by a slow but definitive traverse along, yes, the first metatarsal bone, that was it, the sensitive inner arch of the foot, followed by small semi-bites, nibbles on the medial side of talus—he almost started to laugh—and then upon her medial malleolus, the guardian of the stability of the ankle joint, and next, that goal having been reached, he set upon a painfully slow but meticulous advance measured in micromillimetres up her calf, not forgetting the shy Achilles tendon nor the muscles soleus and gastrocnemius, whose soft bellies pushed back at him as he went.

Then there he was, at her inner knee, more pressure there, an escalation of force, for they had their history together, the two of them, a pattern to their lovemaking, no matter how spontaneous. They had roles well versed, and he kissed as slowly yet as powerfully as ever he had upon her medial collateral ligament, knee-high, the very centre, they felt, of an underappreciated erogenous zone, stimulation of which caused a reflex hip abduction, at least in her case, a quick and helpless opening of the thigh, which indeed it did again now, suddenly, as his tongue continued to impress itself upon her, mounting higher upon her slightly quivering leg and then, provoked equally by her stirring yet still-unconscious response and by his own mounting desire, he edged northward onto the low medial thigh where vastus medialis and quadriceps femoris shook beneath him like the trembling of small tectonic plates.

It was then that he felt her right leg, so far a passive spectator, stretch out and away, behind his left shoulder. Her breathing pattern changed as well. It quickened, as though roused from a surfacing dream. Then her left knee, from which his attention had just departed, came swinging down upon him, a hard push-thrust on his right arm, nearly a blow, intended to encourage him to move more centrally upon her but no, that was not to be. There was no rush. The milkiness of her thigh, upon which the admiring moon cast a shadow of his head, his hair, was so pure as to demand closer, even rapt, inspection. They had hours before dawn, there was no urgency as he kissed and slid past vastus medialis, then familiar sartorius and gracilis and up, up until finally there he was, as far as his journey could go, his mouth, his tongue pressed squarely upon the taut inguinal ligament, on the paper-thin skin of inner thigh as sensitive as a grace note in Mozart, on the pubis bone, on the mons veneris, and of course the left labia majora, whose soft warmth now impressed itself on his left cheekbone and ear.

Now she was fully awake. She put both her hands on the back of his head and quite roughly pulled him towards her, towards her midline anatomical structures, which had of course been his goal all along, but tantalizingly, he resisted her direction. He contracted his neck muscles in such a way that he was immovable. Her hands fell away, her fingers to the side of his neck. He looked up, but still only darkness. He could see nothing past her abdomen, her umbilicus, her epigastrium, just her ribs, which rose and fell like bellows, and then a thousand miles distant were the vague foothills of white, the dim outline of her breasts. After that, nothing. He felt as though he were the first explorer on Earth and she, Marnie, despite their familiarity, was now his *terra incognita*. So he paused in appreciation.

Hey, he whispered, it's me.

Yes, you, she said.

It was then that he knew, from the timbre of her voice, compromised though it was by the racking depths of her near fulfillment, that he had made a serious mistake.

This was not Marnie.

It was someone else, an interloper in her boathouse, escaped from the heat and from the unbearable humidity of the summer night, someone who had come here in perfect innocence to rest.

Oh yes, she murmured again, and again she used her hands to pry him towards her. He resisted, a centimetre away. He could be charged with sexual assault—or worse. Yet, at the same time, chivalry pounded strong within him. He could tell she wanted him, whoever she was, she wanted him, and so strongly did the seed stir within him that he lost his head. He obeyed the mute command of her hands and moved his mouth medially into her, his tongue upon her left labia minora, swollen and moist and she made a noise like *humph* and her pelvis rose and fell, her sacrum staccatoed first onto the thin mattress and then upon the wooden floor with such vigour that he feared splinters for her. He moved his hands to support her buttocks, larger than Marnie's. Oh, the violence with which she moved.

But then a godsend, he was saved from his predicament. He heard a different and more distant thumping. He drew back.

What was that? he asked, growling in a low register.

What, what? she said.

That noise.

Then they both heard it again, *thump-thump,* footsteps on the stairway, on the catwalk that came down from the cliff-side cottage and which entered the loft directly, straight from the elevated shoreline.

Heavy steps, and then a deep voice that said, Audrey? Audrey?

Oh, she whispered. Who are you?

He felt her pull away and the steps came closer. At the most, he had five seconds.

Please, she said.

He jumped up and turned from her and cast himself out through the opening and into the night, a swan dive he had practised for three years from the three-metre board at the athletic centre, male diving champion of the CIAU. Jasper Glass became a white arrow, he scythed through the northern air into Lake Joseph with nary a ripple or a sound, despite the penile erection that destroyed his symmetry. It might have been the best dive he ever made. Without resurfacing, he spun quickly underwater and backtracked into the protective darkness of the boathouse. He rose to the surface and clung to one of the bumpers of the launch.

Did I hear a splash? a male voice asked from upstairs, muffled by the ceiling, the floor that intervened.

No, no, she said, or if you did maybe it was a beaver.

Beavers, he said, those guys never stop working.

I don't know, I was asleep.

Just checking on you, he said.

I'm fine, she said, really.

You'll get a chill, Audrey, down here like this.

Not on a night like this.

No, I guess not, so damn hot.

Then his steps returned to the staircase and made their way back up into the forest, ponderously. All was still again. Jasper swam out of the depths of the boathouse to the dock and, still in the water, untied the canoe and swam away, the canoe roped behind him at the waist until he turned the corner at the point of land. Now he was exposed to the wide expanse of the lake but the dim light from the cottage was thoroughly blocked by trees. Up and over the gunwale he climbed and tumbled in. No longer did he care about the silence of strokes. He never looked back.

He paddled hard for half an hour. At shore he stepped out and briefly lost his balance on the rocks, but within a few seconds he had the canoe up on his shoulders. He half ran and half staggered through the still-total darkness up the scrabbled portage.

Valerie's car, everything fine.

He quickly dressed. He had sacrificed his bathing suit to the Goddess of the Boathouse, but that was okay. There was nothing to identify him. He roped the canoe into place, jumped in the car, floored the Dart and spun out of the gravel pit with stones flying everywhere, clattering off the chassis.

Calm down, he thought. If she was ever going to say something, she would have said it then, when he left her.

Help, help, she would have cried, and minutes later he would have heard the growling motor from the mahogany launch. Angry voices, male.

Drive south, he said out loud.

Highway 69 was empty. He turned on the radio. Chopin on the CBC, one nocturne after the other.

He rolled down the window. Night air whipped through his hair. After thirty miles he relaxed and thought about her again, the boathouse, whoever she was. Chopin filled the car, he turned the volume higher to offset the wind. A dark shape loomed in the middle of the road, scant yards away. The apparition was upon him and he hit it dead-on. His foot never reached the brake. There was a thump and a crunch and he was thrown hard, the seat belt vised against his chest, and the dark shape, whatever it was, starred the windshield and shattered it. And there he was, Jasper Glass, pinned by the monstrous weight that lay on his chest and also upon the mangled steering wheel that belonged to Valerie Anderson's mother.

The odour of beast and swamp and utter strangeness leached into his nostrils, his face.

He felt the Dart spin clockwise and stop.

The moose lay dying on top of him. Thousands of pounds of twitch and shudder that suddenly trembled some more, and then convulsed, but, as fortune had it on this occasion for Jasper Glass, the beast had catapulted backwards into the Dart and so was caught by the window frame. The large antlers and anvil-like hooves, splayed and jerking, death-dealing, were outside, jabbing only at air, at the shadows of rock and pine.

Broken, flickering headlights showed rock and grass. Jasper moved his right arm under the body of the animal. He could barely do so but he reached the ignition and turned off the key. Out went the headlights. There was a soft hissing from the engine. Through the blown front window, a trace of dawn scratched at the eastern sky.

His poor companion quivered one last time.

Jasper sat welded to the animal, the seat beside him wet, soaked with blood and the froth of saliva and what smelled like urine and feces. They were both covered with fragments of glass.

After about ten minutes in that uncomfortable position, he heard the brakes of a truck behind him and the opening and closing of a door.

A flashlight beam.

Jasper Glass and the moose glittered, as though crystallized.

The phone rang.

Dr. Krank? Third floor. Niki Pruss, she's rocking and picking at her skin and crying. She also attacked her roommate with an egg-salad sandwich.

Fifty milligrams of Largactil IM, he said. That should calm her down but if it doesn't, repeat it Q1H until she's totally snowed.

Yes, Doctor.

He could see her, the Filipina nurse, drawing up the Largactil. The big orderly held the patient still, embraced her even during the injection. Then he let her go. None of those nurses were big enough, maybe five-two he figured. They moved through the wards like humming-birds. Must be lots of mental patients too, where they come from, in Manila or Olongapo City, wherever. There had to be, it was pure stats. You had enough population, you had problems. So it's not like psychiatric care was new to them, the nurses, but the physical size of the patients here was different. Nurses had to be careful. Their wrists were the size of small sticks and just a snap, they'd break.

Lucky now, he didn't have to go down to the wards for the most part. He'd seen enough. He had all the doses down pat, it wasn't that hard to lay on the chemical straitjackets once you knew how, once you had confidence in the medication. When he first started, he always went with the lowest dose, to be careful. Now, fuck it, wham, just get it done. Get back to sleep. Who wants a second call, the same problem?

Anna was asleep beside him. Every Friday night now for the past six weeks, she hauled her cleaning stuff up the stairs, a bucket and a mop, and she did the floor and the bathroom. It took her ten minutes. The walls were so high, there was no point in wiping those down. They were twenty feet of flat institutional green. The bats were a ceiling away, hanging upside down under the ancient roof, digesting their mosquitoes and mayflies.

She smelled of Pine-Sol rather than perfume but he liked it. It was bracing to the nostrils, and she hadn't complained when he put his book down and unbuttoned her uniform for the first time.

Anna, it said on her name tag.

Five dollars? she said.

It was all over in seven or eight minutes. He gave her the money. It was the first time he'd paid for sex, but why not? A commercial transaction, one like any other, a service rendered. Emotionally clean. Sometimes he laughed out loud when he was by himself, when he thought of it.

Now, every Friday, when she had finished her shift, Anna finished it there with him. The two of them, in a calm way together, nothing really passionate about it, workmanlike. Whatever reason he had, she had her reason too. Five dollars was cheaper than dinner, it was quite a bargain. She got up early on those nights, afterwards, left at five in the morning and went back down the stairs. She used the mop all the way down, he could hear her, the bucket as it moved. When he got up two hours later, the steps were immaculate. She knew about thirty words of English, the rest was all in Romanian or some other eastern European language, something Slavic, guttural. Her breathing was as soft and as regular as a baby's and her back was turned as she slept.

He thought then about the new student, Valerie Anderson, about unbuttoning her white lab coat, how it would be different, how she smelled of soap or some other delicate scent. She would be shy, she wouldn't take the initiative in any way. Nor would she object.

His penis was now so hard he felt he could jam it through concrete. He peeled back the blanket but left it over her shoulders. He turned flat on his back. He tongued some saliva onto his left hand and he reached down and masturbated. The inevitable was upon him, he gave himself up and the semen shot back over his straining abdomen and his chest. It must have arced over his head too, in the dark, because he heard the dull *snick* as it hit the wall behind him.

He held his breath.

She moved in her sleep but didn't turn. He got up carefully and went to the bathroom. He unrolled toilet paper. Without turning on the light, he returned to the bed and wiped down the wall.

Sleep was easy after that. This time, he didn't even hear her leave.

After his expulsion from the Faculty of Medicine, John twisted in the wind for a few weeks and then took stock. First of all, there was no way he could tell his parents, so he swore his friends to secrecy.

Okay, they agreed, mum's the word.

Even Valerie Anderson said she would avoid breaking the news to June.

Sometimes, I guess, an omission or a white lie is a kindness, she said.

She was the weak link. His brother Jasper would never say anything, nor would Roberto Moreno.

Even if they drove red-hot splinters under my fingernails, said Jasper, my lips are sealed, blood brother. Anyway, you should just tell them yourself, right now. If you don't open up, nobody knows who you are, what you want, I've told you a million times.

John's bank account dwindled to a risible sum. His student loans were spent and gone. He had barely enough money for food, so he skipped both breakfast and lunch.

I am becoming wiry and quick, he said.

Everywhere he went, he walked or cycled. Then his bicycle, shoddy though it was, was stolen, and he reflected that the thief might well have hundreds of bicycles lined up somewhere, as he himself had books. He could hardly complain. He began to walk to his parents' house for meals even though it took him two hours to trek from the Hampton Court Apartments to Glengrove Avenue. The exercise helped him and, sometimes, something akin to happiness welled up within him as he walked through Eglinton Park, the closer he got to home.

He knew he had to knuckle down and get a job. But students in medicine had classes until the end of May, much later than all the other students at the university. All the plum jobs were taken. There were no postings on the boards at the colleges or in the newspapers.

Try taking out your own ad, said Valerie, you know, student looking for summer employment, that sort of thing.

He borrowed twenty-five dollars from Jasper and the next five days, in *The Globe and Mail,* a prospective employer could have read *Medical Student Seeks Summer Employ,* followed by John's name and phone number.

Medical student? said Jasper. Ex–medical student, more accurately. But I do like the use of *employ* as a noun, that's brave.

They were huddled over *The Globe,* sitting on the bench outside Hart House.

Well, who would hire an ex–medical student? asked John. No one.

True enough, said Jasper.

Besides, you never know. I have it in my heart to reapply or go elsewhere or do something vaguely medical, like physiotherapy, dentistry, lab technician, mortician, beautician. Podiatry.

Denturist, said Jasper. Purveyor of false smiles.

Yes, that would be fine, said John. Dentures fall from the palate as I do from the ranks of academia.

So, in print he masqueraded as a success, a work in progress, a medical student, and that was perfectly fine as his expulsion had not yet been made official. It appeared on no transcripts and no black crepe hung from his shoulders, no scarlet letter from his neck.

The advertisement he placed worked. The very first day, he received a call saying that, if he was interested, he could come in for an interview at the Roman Sauna Baths. It rang a bell for him. The photograph at Stefan's, the one that Roberto Moreno had taken as a remembrance.

The sauna baths, he said.

Yes. Bay Street south of College on the west side, just up from the tailors.

Okay, said John, I'll be right over.

The building was nondescript, two storeys. It looked like a small warehouse. The door on the south side was at street level and said, in understated smoked-glass writing, THE ROMAN SAUNA BATHS. He walked right by and missed it on his first pass, turned around and came back again. There it was, very discreet. He must have passed it hundreds of times without seeing it.

He went back to Bay Street and opened the smoked-glass door and a tiny distant bell rang. He saw, immediately before him, a long staircase that climbed quite precipitously, and at the top of the staircase was a landing, a turn, and a mirror placed on the far wall to reveal yet another staircase, equally precipitous, which rose farther and farther, to the second floor, as though in an exercise for perspective, seeking the vanishing point. Small wall sconces shed dim light on the stairs. The steps themselves were well kept, of polished wood, and their metal slip guards clicked slightly as he made his ascent.

At the very top, a window looked out upon Bay Street and on the right side of the landing he saw a Dutch door, the top half of glass, the bottom of wood, and at waist level, where the two parts of the door joined, was a small window cut in the glass, and a wooden platform that extended perhaps six inches both inside and out. A place for transactions, he assumed.

He knocked on the glass. Immediately a man appeared on the other side of the window and opened the door.

Mr. Glass, I presume.

None other, indeed. At your service, said John.

Come in, Mr. Glass.

There was a small office just ten feet away, a desk, a typewriter and a pot of coffee percolating on a small table. His host poured two cups.

Fresh these five minutes, he said. Sugar? Cream?

It was a delicious cup of coffee and the proprietor, who introduced himself as Bill Miskewicz, talked to John about the Roman Sauna Baths.

It's a place for men to come, John, to be quiet and discreet in an atmosphere of camaraderie, and without drugs or alcohol.

A club, said John.

Yes, in a way, but the membership is fluid. It's a cash organization, pay-as-you-go. And what we need is a doorman. Come take a look.

He showed John Glass around, first to a locker room and then to long corridors, and off the corridors were many small rooms sparsely but immaculately furnished with a bed and a clean sheet, a pillow, a small closet for clothes, a chair, a bedside table with a lamp.

They're all soundproofed, Bill Miskewicz said, so as to provide peace and quiet, privacy, away from the turmoil of the city, for our clientele.

And I shall have some peace there, for peace comes dropping slow, said John.

Exactly. Yeats. I think you'll fit in here.

Then he showed John the sparkling new and spotless sauna baths that gave the place its name, several of which filled the quadrangle surrounded by corridors that ran the circumference of the building.

So what do you think? asked Bill.

It looks very neat, well organized, said John, and little memory work required.

What you would do, if hired, said Bill as they walked back to the foyer, is this: an eight-hour shift. You man the door, take the cash, buzz in the gentlemen to the foyer, make them feel at home, direct them either to the locker room or the private rooms depending on their payment, and make sure each room is clean and prepared. Empty the ashtrays. And hand out towels too, for the sauna and the showers. It's that simple.

Who picks up the towels, who cleans the towels? asked John.

We have a service for that, the laundry's off-site. Just drop them in the hamper.

I'm very interested in the job, said John, if you're offering it to me.

Your being a medical student, that's perfect, said Bill, because just as in medicine, you understand, all transactions here are private and confidential. One of the tenets of our business, John, is that nothing goes beyond these walls.

Like the Masons, said John, or the IRA.

Well, I suppose, but about those organizations, I know very little.

My lips are sealed, I will take an oath, said John.

John, also I must tell you, frankly, this is an organization for homosexuals. We started this business for homosexuals to have a place to meet.

Far from the madding crowd.

As far as we can get, said Bill.

Well, said John, I am not a homosexual and have no such experience.

That's fine. I like you, John. I can see you have a rapport with people. If you'd rather not work in this environment, if you'd be uncomfortable, then I would understand and, with no hard feelings, we can end this interview. But otherwise I offer you the position.

Their speech was curiously formal and gentlemanly, as though they had subconsciously agreed on something. They were sitting in the foyer then. It was perfectly still in the building.

I accept, said John.

They stood and shook hands.

When do I start?

In one hour, if you can. The evening shift, four to midnight. I'll stay for the first few hours.

I'm dressed okay?

Yes, fine.

Okay, said John, I'll do it. But one more thing, Bill.

Yes?

I'm really an ex–medical student. I'm no longer in school.

Oh.

But I haven't given up, I'm reapplying.

What happened?

I felt out of place. I couldn't function. Academically, I fell behind.

That's a common story in university. You're still hired. Welcome to the Sauna Baths.

He came over to John and hugged him but there was nothing sexual about it. It reminded John of his own father. Even the man's name was the same.

Detective Ames got into his car on Helendale Avenue and joined the rush hour to work. All the way down, he reviewed the scenario he had constructed in his mind, the modus operandi of the quarry he sought. With, he admitted again, less than his usual motivation. Nevertheless, as an intellectual exercise, professionally, it was still rewarding.

First, there was Jasper Glass in the big house on Roxborough Drive, in the arms of the wayward Marnie Kennedy-Foare. That's a given. Then home comes the husband unexpectedly. Jasper somehow makes it into the basement, undetected. The alarm system is activated. What can Jasper do? Not much. Marnie could have come down a few hours later and let him out, but she didn't. So he Crisco'd his way out. He's home free. Next night, he comes out of nowhere and saves Gwen O'Hara down on Shaw Street. That's it. But it wasn't Jasper Glass with the knife, it was some friend of his, someone tougher, more capable. How hard could this be, finding this guy?

My money's on this fellow, first of all, he said to the detective sergeant.

He held up the photograph of Jasper Glass.

He doesn't look the type.

They both knew, after their cumulative experience

of forty-two years, that there was no type, no type for any kind of crime. But they still liked to make that observation.

I don't take him for the killer. He's the Crisco kid, the intervenor, the one who backed off from the knife. Call him whatever you like, he's the one who was with Marnie. Not that I blame him for that.

You showed this to the girl from Shaw Street?

I did and she lied. She flipped right by it. Then she went through them two more times to get a better look. Just like I expected.

No surprise.

She'll lie all the way to the Supreme Court.

What's her name?

Gwen O'Hara, a nice girl. A waitress.

Your girls are all nice girls, Andy. You always say that. Cross her off then, get to him some other way.

Or we just forget the whole thing and write it off. I don't see what we're going to gain from this, Ames said.

The detective sergeant looked at the photograph of Jasper Glass again.

We went through this before. Talk to Mr. Glass, find out who he spends his time with. It's some friend of his, it should be easy. Candy from a baby.

We got nothing on these two without Gwen's testimony, even if we find them.

So then we do the usual, Andy. Tell a few lies ourselves. That usually works, doesn't it?

Ames went back to his desk. He picked up an envelope on which he had written *Friends of Jasper Glass*.

He shook it and three black-and-white five-by-seven photographs fell out.

The first one, John Glass, obviously his brother. You could see the resemblance, though this boy was more serious. He looked at the camera as though he wasn't sure of anything. Laugh in the face of danger? Quick with a knife? Not this one.

He flipped to the next.

Valerie Anderson. With whom, according to his investigation so far, Jasper Glass spent half his time. What was it with these girls? They were supposed to be bookworms but they could have come from Hollywood casting. Well, it can't be her, she's female. Obviously.

The third one, Wallace Wallace. Now there's a possibility. A name like that? He might crack in an interview. He even looked like an egg, round head on top of a thick neck.

Without Gwen's testimony, right now they had nothing, that was true. But the two boys at the scene, Jasper Glass and whoever it was, they knew nothing about Gwen O'Hara. They didn't know who she was. All they knew was that they had stabbed and killed her attacker, left her there in the rain, called in the assault and disappeared. Which is exactly what he would have done too, under the circumstances.

The detective sergeant was right. The easiest and the most straightforward thing to do was to talk to Jasper Glass and tell the lie. And the lie was this: You, Jasper Glass, have been positively identified by the rape victim on Shaw Street. You've got no wiggle room, boy. She will testify in court.

Yessiree, that's it, that's the lie.

Then he wouldn't have to do any legwork. Jasper Glass would find it in his best interest to talk, once he weighed all the pros and cons, his career in medicine.

Wallace the one with the knife? He looked at the eyes of the young man in the last photograph. But his heart was hardly in it today. He put the Gwen O'Hara folder down and picked up another. There were lots of other cases that needed work, cases that featured real criminals.

Krank spotted her by chance on Devonshire Place, under the portico of Varsity Stadium. He wasn't dead certain it was Valerie but he followed her anyway and the girl with dark hair cut alongside the Buttery at Trinity College and turned in the door. When he followed her through, he saw her at a table, yes, it was her, Valerie Anderson, by herself.

She sipped a cup of tea, she read a book. It didn't look as though she was there for any particular reason. No one approached her and neither did he. He went back outside and stood out of the way, his back against a fence by the soccer field, and ten minutes later she came back out again and walked, without looking in his direction, down to Hoskin Avenue. He held back a hundred yards and thought that maybe he'd just take the rest of the morning off, see where she went, because his heart was actually pounding in his chest and it was tough to ignore that, he couldn't, the effect of adrenalin that coursed through his system, squeezed from those little glands just on top of his kidneys, as powerful a drug as any that he used in his psychiatric armamentarium. And quick, too, because the onset of adrenalin was immediate. Zero to sixty in microseconds. Whereas the antidepressants and the antipsychotics and the barbiturates he doled out took weeks to work, if they ever did.

She cut across Queen's Park south of the parliament buildings.

So she wasn't going home.

She walked along College Street and turned down Bay. Then she stopped by the doorway of a warehouse and leaned against the wall. He stood across the street from her and carefully examined a store window. As he had seen done in countless movies, he used the reflective surface as a mirror. She stood there for less than a minute before a young man came out of the door and greeted her.

He recognized the young man right away. John Glass, one of the two other students from 999.

Her boyfriend? Unlikely.

They headed north. She didn't touch John Glass or put her arm around him as they walked.

He crossed the street through sparse traffic and read the sign on the door.

THE ROMAN SAUNA BATHS.

Well, it takes all kinds.

He closed to within fifty yards as they walked north. If they turned around and saw him, so what? All he'd say is, oh hi, it's you.

Valerie Anderson and John Glass turned east on Wellesley, so possibly they were headed back to her place after all. They talked the whole time but she walked on the outside, by the curb, not on the inside where a woman should be. It looked like he was showing her something in a book. They both leaned forward as they walked and looked at something he held in his hands. That meant they didn't walk in a straight line, they wobbled along the sidewalk and nearly bumped into things.

They turned north on Church Street and came to her building. They went in. By that time, he had closed quarters to within twenty-five yards. Following them was a cinch, they never looked around. They were like children.

It was unimaginable that she'd have sex with John Glass now, in her apartment at this time of day. Maybe they studied together. But why would she waste her time like that?

He walked a block and walked back. They hadn't come out.

Shit.

He took out his own private set of keys and let himself in. The lobby was empty but for a pile of newspapers. He picked up one of those and put it down and waited for the elevator. The door slid open. Muzak. He got on and pressed the number 4.

For a minute he waited outside the old lady's door. All he could hear was TV, the volume high enough that he could make out every word, canned laughter, forced laughter.

He didn't knock, he didn't have to. He just let himself in and walked down the hallway past her kitchen.

She was in front of the TV, her back to him. That didn't matter, he could have walked right in front of her and what would she have seen? A shadow maybe, passing in front of the idiot box. Her neck was as thin as a chicken's and her head was bent forward. Osteoporosis, kyphosis, the usual old-lady neck. Snap it in half, none the wiser. He could walk out of there, the perfect crime, Raskolnikov.

He slipped behind her and went into the bedroom. It smelled like dust, baby powder, old violets, dry and airless, dark from the heavy curtains that covered the sliding-glass doors. No lock on those, it was broken. That was good, they were probably all broken like that, the whole building. He went out on the balcony, not even bothering to be quiet, and he looked down. They were right under him, sitting there.

I hear the kettle, Valerie Anderson said.

He pulled his head back. There was a scrape of a chair and Valerie Anderson must have gone into her kitchen. Then she returned.

I'm out of milk, sorry, she said.

He stood and listened to them for five minutes. All they talked about was books. Books, books, books and there was nothing very personal in what they said although they seemed at home with one another, at ease. Now and then they laughed but there was no hint of any intimacy in their interchange. Their intercourse. What a word that was. For all he knew, it was quite possible that she already loved him, Abner Krank, in her heart, spoken or unspoken.

The old lady, the old dear, turned off her TV. He stepped back into the closeness of her bedroom. He slid closed the balcony door and pulled the curtain back across and then the woman was in front of him. She shuffled towards the bed and sat down on it, five feet away. She sighed. She bent down to take off her shoes or her slippers, whatever you'd call those worn-out leather things on her feet.

All he did was walk out of the room. He didn't try to be quiet. She saw nothing, she heard nothing, and he closed the apartment door firmly with a click and left the building without seeing anyone else.

To be in Valerie Anderson's bedroom all he needed was a rope, maybe fifteen or twenty feet of it, and a pair of gloves. He could rappel down there as easy as pie. He could swing down like an orangutan. He could be a trapeze man. He could be her adamantine lover, the man she either dreamed of or never dreamed of, whether or not she knew or cared.

He'd give her a call first, though. Maybe that's all he needed to do, maybe he didn't have to run around like this, maybe already her heart was his. Maybe all he had to do was ask.

A string of thunderstorms went by. Murlean got soaked but she held out her thumb and twice she was picked up by families, mothers and fathers with carloads of kids.

We're only going five miles but no way can we leave you out there in the rain, honey, they said.

Murlean piled into the back seat with the children and the dogs and five miles later, out she went again, even in the crash of thunder.

Don't stand under trees, Heidi, they shouted to her.

The second ride dropped her at a gas station between Burk's Falls and Emsdale and she waited there for the storm to pass. It was black and furious and then eerily quiet in turns. Hardly anybody was on the road. When the lightning and thunder rolled away to the south, she left the shelter of the gas station and went back to the roadside. She felt she was like a wood chip in a stream, like *Paddle-to-the-Sea,* just rolling along as best she could. *Paddle-to-the-Sea,* that was a book she liked. The little carved canoe that bobbed along, on its own, all the way from Lake Nipigon to the Atlantic Ocean, downstream all the way.

Fuck you, she said again.

Now she had said it, she bet, fifty times. Practice makes perfect. What seemed strange an hour ago now tripped off her lips.

Finally, a trucker picked her up. By then, she was soaked on the side of the road.

He was carrying logs, so it took him a long time to stop. She had two hundred yards of running to get to the truck, but he met her partway with an umbrella. He held it over her head and they ran back together.

She looked sixteen, maybe, at the most.

Hop in, he said, and oh, watch out for the camera.

Then he ran around to his side, waited for two cars to go by, and then he opened the door and got into the driver's seat.

Whoa, he said, some storm.

He pulled the camera towards him a bit because the girl was dripping water.

I'm Heidi, she said.

You shouldn't be out there by yourself, Heidi.

Oh, I'm okay, so far so good, she said, thanks for the ride.

And she was okay too, the rain was warm and the cab of the truck seemed to be as good a place to be as any. He didn't talk as much as the first guy. Thank God for that.

Where you headed?

Toronto.

From?

North Bay.

I can take you as far as Barrie, a couple of hours, and then it's not far. How's your trip?

She settled back against the door and the seat and rearranged her hair.

Soaked, she said.

She smiled at him in a woebegone way.

I had a ride to Bracebridge, she said, but he changed his mind. He left me on the side of the road and went back. Then the rain came.

Before they got a few miles into their journey, just before Emsdale, there was a blockade of police cars and a sign that said ROAD CLOSED. A detour sign pointed right, to Highway 518.

So what's up? the trucker asked the policeman who waved them down.

Train derailed, overturned. There's hazardous material on the side of the road. Closed for at least twelve hours. You go over to 69, down there.

They went west on a smaller road, but it was still paved.

It'll take us a lot longer now, he said.

What's with the camera? she asked.

She picked it up and looked through it at the road ahead.

You just press that button there, he said, by your right thumb.

Murlean Poirier pressed it and it clicked. She jumped.

I might have just wasted one, she said.

You never know, he said, you never know it's wasted till it's developed.

She told him how she'd set out from North Bay and how she was going to stay with her aunt in Toronto and go to hairdressing school. He looked at her and Murlean could tell, the way he frowned, that he didn't believe her.

You're kind of young for that, he said.

Not really. My sister did it.

Your mom and dad know where you are?

Sure, it was their idea.

Then they should have put you on the bus, Heidi.

Eventually, they were at the junction of Highway 69 just south of Parry Sound. He stopped to make the turn. The sun was setting now, an orange red that mixed with the black of the storm clouds off to the north.

Tell you what, Heidi, I been thinking. Stay the night with us, with me and the wife. Foot's Bay, just down the road. Because I can tell you right now if I leave you by the side of this road, she'd never forgive me. Probably she'd come out in the car and pick you up herself. Then tomorrow, you and I, we get up at three or four in the morning and I take you straight to Barrie. You're there by six. It makes no difference to these logs.

Okay, that sounds fine.

An hour later, he pulled down a long driveway that turned in a big circle by a house in the woods. There was a lady outside, carrying in groceries.

This is Miss Heidi Chipman. I picked her up by the side of the road, he told his wife.

They were a quiet couple. They spoke very little, but they all had hamburgers and Murlean Poirier went to bed early. She was tired, more so than she had expected. She hung her cotton bag up in the bathroom to dry. At three the next morning there was a knock on her bedroom door.

Outside, it was still dark, hot and sticky and they drove down Highway 69. No one else was up. They had the windows open for air and he looked at her and she seemed lost in her own world. They could have been in Louisiana, on the bayous, the humidity so high within the heavy stillness.

Then the sky in the east started to turn pink, the way it often did in the summer. If it weren't for that little tinge of pink, the truck driver never would have seen the plume of steam that came off the grass on the far side of the road. From the east side, from about the only patch of grass between Mactier and Port Severn. The rest of the roadside for a hundred miles was solid rock, Precambrian

Shield, rock in jagged pieces or dynamited cliffs, huge rolling humps of it too, ground down from the ice age. Once or twice, right by the roadside, the water pooled into lakes or ponds deep enough to drown in.

It caught the trucker's eye, that little plume of smoke. He thought it was fire, although that was unlikely with all the rain. The ground was spongy with water, like muskeg, like peat.

He slowed down. A car was skewed off the road, half hidden by bulrushes and grass. The plume he'd seen rose up from the front of the car, from the radiator.

Whoa, you see that?

No, said Murlean.

He put on the air brakes and snapped on his flashers. When the truck stopped, he opened his door and ran across the empty highway. He heard her door slam too.

There was a small red car in the ditch ten yards off the shoulder. A Dart? It was hard to pick out exactly what it was because of the jumble of twisted metal at the front end, and a canoe, or half a canoe, tilted down over the windshield. Or what should have been the windshield.

He moved forward.

The missing half of the canoe lay in the bulrushes five yards away, towards the low spruce. The radiator, the front end of the car, was accordioned backwards, and stuck in the front window—where the window should have been—were the four legs, the hooves, the head and the antlers of a moose.

Where's the driver?

Heidi was beside him.

I don't know, he said.

He went closer to the driver's side, bent down and looked in. The side window was smashed and starred and jagged pieces of glass hung loose. It was still dark, the stench that rose from the front seat was terrible, the deepest swamp odour mixed with gas and oil. Steam-heat from the broken radiator. The driver's door was jammed. He pulled at it. Nothing—it was tight against the frame. With his elbow, he knocked out enough of the loose glass to put his head in. Someone was in there all right, tight behind the dead body of the moose.

Hey, he shouted, hey.

Hi, said a voice, I'm fine, I'm fine.

You sure?

I'm discomposed by this beast upon my lap. Is there anything you can do? This guy's got me pinned down.

Okay, listen, I'm going back to the truck, get the fire extinguisher. Heidi, stay here.

He ran back to the truck and returned with the extinguisher. He emptied it all over the radiator and the engine, half of which stuck up through the jagged hood so access was easy. The plume of steam hissed and diminished.

You know, said the trucker, there should be no moose down here. Too far south. There should be deer, that's all.

Tell that to this, my lap-friend, said Jasper Glass.

Heidi, go up, wait for the next car. But careful, don't go on the road.

You want the camera? she asked.

It was in the next few minutes that the driver of the truck would take the photo that would win the National

Magazine Award for photojournalism. He walked away from the wreck and pointed the Nikon at what used to be the front end of the Dart and took ten or twelve flashes. Then he took a few more from the side and from the back. Then, finally, he saw headlights coming down the road, and he saw Heidi wave the vehicle down. Naturally enough, a girl like that, the car stopped. After that another one.

The first photograph was the best. It showed the canoe, a Chestnut, tilted down and separated into two parts, twisted, smashed, ribs broken, gunwales splintered, but it was still nevertheless recognizable as an icon of the North. Under it, four stilled hooves and the rack of the moose, impaled in the window frame. The chassis of the Dart was tilted to the left. In the background, a line of dark trees stood out against the dawn and against the menace of the rock face that Jasper Glass had missed by three feet. It was a powerful picture, full of steam and fracture and death. Those were the words the critics used when he received the award. But really, it had been nothing but good luck. Heidi was the one who had remembered the camera. In fact, after the picture was developed, he wondered whether he was the one who took it. Maybe it was the girl, Heidi, running back with the camera. Maybe she stopped for a second and snapped it herself. He was never sure and by then he had no way to track her down.

An hour later it was extremely busy at the scene. The Jaws of Life first picked off the door on the driver's side and then extracted the body of the moose from the window. They left the animal in the roadside grass, his big horse-like lips and teeth torn away from the jawbone, a tongue, a mouthful of clotted blood. Police flashers went round and round. Dawn broke.

Finally, Jasper Glass stepped out of the wreck. He stretched, he bent over, he shook particles of glass from his hair.

Another half inch, the ambulance driver said, you couldn't have breathed. The pressure on your lungs would have been fatal.

Oh, I know, he said, it's my lucky day all right.

But he said that with a rueful air, as though he wasn't so sure.

Lucky or not, you're coming to the hospital to get checked out.

No, said Jasper Glass, I'm a doctor myself. Look at me.

He struck several dramatic poses. A karate stance followed by a pirouette followed by ten push-ups.

You see? There's nothing wrong. I'll get checked out at home.

Okay, said the ambulance driver, you promise to do that, I'll let you go.

But it was ten o'clock in the morning before the Ontario Provincial Police were finished with their paperwork.

Jasper, how you getting home? asked the trucker.

Good question. I guess I'll phone my brother.

I can take you to Barrie, you catch the bus. This girl's going too.

Okay, you're on.

They were dropped at the bus station in Barrie an hour later. On the Greyhound bus, the two of them sat together near the back. Within five minutes, Jasper had fallen asleep. Within another five minutes, his head lolled on Murlean Poirier's shoulder. She didn't move, even when her leg went numb. She stayed where she was until they pulled into the bus station, off Edward Street in downtown Toronto.

Hey, Jasper, she said.

He pulled his head up.

Sorry, Heidi.

That's okay.

He looked out the window.

Toronto, he said. I wasn't the best company for you, Heidi, your first trip to the big city.

This is the main bus station?

In all its glory.

She saw at least two hundred people from her window, standing or milling around. Most of them had bags and suitcases. She had no idea what she was going to do now that she was here.

Then they were off the bus and Jasper Glass took her by the arm. They moved out of the way, off to the side. Even though there was a small cut on the side of his forehead and a bruise on his cheek, he was far more handsome than anyone she'd ever met or seen in Mattawa.

Listen, Heidi, he said. I've got to run.

She looked around. Some of the buses had left and the crowd had thinned out.

Are you going to be okay?

Sure, she said, I got money.

You know where to go?

I got it in my purse, the address.

I'll get you a cab.

No, no, it's okay. I'll just take a walk, look around. My first time ever here.

She said that but she didn't feel like moving or looking around. The bus station was the only place she knew.

You're sure?

Yes, she said.

Tell you what, Heidi, I'll write my name and number down, you do the same. That way, you can call me anytime.

He wrote on a piece of paper and gave it to her.

Thanks, she said.

Now it's your turn, he said.

He still had his hand on her arm as though he wasn't going to let her go. She tore a piece of the same paper off and wrote down her name.

Heidi Chipman, she said out loud as she wrote. I'll call you, Jasper, I don't have my number yet.

Thanks, Heidi Chipman, he said.

He didn't look at what she'd written but he put it in his breast pocket.

Close to my heart. Well, now I'm off, I'm literally going to run. I'll give you a call.

He let go of her arm, smiled, and he did run, he jogged away from her, north up Bay Street. She watched him as he dodged his way through the dispersing crowd until he was gone. She stood there a few minutes, holding on to her bag.

Then a man was at her elbow.

Honey, you got a place to stay? he asked.

She looked at him.

My name's Mitchell, he said.

He held out his hand.

You're pretty. You shouldn't be here alone, he said.

Marnie's aunt Audrey came up from the boathouse.

I thought I heard the coffee perking away, she said.

Audrey, you look great, said Marnie.

I do?

Yes, your cheeks are red as apples. You must have slept well.

Thanks to you, honey. You're the one who told me how nice it is down there.

I almost came down myself, said Marnie. It was hot, close like an oven up here. I turned on the fan.

They poured two coffees and carried them out to the screened porch. They heard warblers from the woods.

Christian? her aunt asked.

Still asleep, recharging his brain.

Same with Jerry. He came down once in the night though, checked on me.

That's nice, said Marnie.

One of the best nights I've ever had. Marnie, how many nights have you spent there, this summer?

Oh, maybe three, let me think.

She counted on the fingers of her hand.

Yes, three, she said.

Anything happen down there, those nights?

Happen? How do you mean?

You hear anything, see anything?

No, nothing unusual. The water lapping. The moon in the sky. The loons.

You think the heat wave's over, Marnie?

Not yet, I can feel it even now.

Marnie got up and walked over to the screen and watched a ruby-throated hummingbird perch on a branch near the feeder. Then they heard the toilet flush and Jerry came out to the porch, his hair tousled. He rubbed his stomach with his hand and then he bent down and kissed Audrey, then Marnie, both on the forehead.

Girls, he said.

That's us all right, said Audrey. We're the girls.

Marnie excused herself and went back to the living room. Her mornings were the same every day. She read back issues of *The Lancet, The New England Journal of Medicine,* the *Canadian Medical Association Journal,* and *The Medical Letter.* Afternoons, down she went to the dock in her bikini and put up the umbrella and swam and read novels. Italo Calvino, Camus. It was the summer of serious reading for her, maybe the last chance she'd get before her life as a doctor became overwhelming.

Christian Foare stayed at his desk inside and worked every day on a paper he estimated would come to forty thousand words. After supper, the other three forced him to put that aside and play Scrabble or Monopoly.

I'll just put a house now on Park Place, said Jerry.

Damn you, Jerry, said Christian.

The summer was languid. It seemed endless, and even though Aunt Audrey spent all the remaining nights down in the boathouse, Marnie never saw her with quite those same red-apple cheeks again, the way she looked the first time.

Detective Ames was at the Parrot after lunch. Gwen O'Hara had finished her shift and she sat across from him, in the same seat she had sat in the time before.

I think we found him, he said, or at least one of them. Not the killer, mind you, the other one.

Really?

Yes, following trails the way we do, we get reports, hints, we track 'em down. People talk among themselves, you know.

I guess, said Gwen.

Would you take a look at a few more pictures?

Sure.

He took out more photographs, six this time. The last one in this sequence was Jasper Glass.

You showed me this one before.

I did?

Yes, and it's not him.

Actually, he's the one the talk's about. Maybe the night, the rain, the circumstances, they could have blurred your memory.

Andy, the night, the rain, the circumstances—it's all

seared on my brain. It's not him. This is not the kind of guy I would forget.

Without you, Gwen, we've got nothing on him, nothing on anyone.

You need me, then?

Pretty much. You're still the only eyewitness we have, the only link to the murder. But this guy, I have to tell you, it's still what we hear on the grapevine. Our sources have him there, pinpointed. But if you say no, off he goes.

Good, she said, that's the way it should be. This is a crime that shouldn't be solved.

On the other hand, it's funny how policing works. If a suspect, someone like this, even thinks he's been identified, then sometimes, bang, he confesses.

Well, he'd only confess if he'd been there.

He was there. This one here.

He held up the picture of Jasper Glass right in front of her.

Gwen, when I tell him you've identified him, who knows what he'll say?

Why are you telling me this, Andy?

Another waitress stopped at their table.

You guys want anything? Gwen?

No thanks, she said, we're just talking.

I'm explaining to you how it works, that's all, said Andy Ames. So you know how it's done. It's your case, after all.

Let me get this straight. You go to your suspect, whoever he is, this guy here, and you tell him I've identified him, even though I haven't?

That's it. Exactly. That's how it's done. It works.

I think I get the drift, she said.

Police work, it's simple psychology most of the time. Or game-playing.

Thanks, Andy, she said.

Okay, I better be going.

Do you need those pictures, Andy? You have copies?

We have copies, we have a million photographs. We have copies of a million photographs.

Then leave them with me. I'll try to jog my memory, just in case.

Any particular one you want?

No way. I'll take them all.

The last one?

She laughed and said, no, Andy, give me a break. I'll take them all. They all look fine to me. Maybe the rain, the circumstances, you know.

Gwen, keep all of these for two days. I haven't got the time or the inclination to work on them yet. But after two days, then my claws are out. Orders from on high.

Two days?

Did I say two days?

Yes.

Then there you go. Two days.

He phoned her at ten p.m. He still had her number from the registrar's office folded in his wallet.

She answered so fast he almost jumped. She must have been standing by the phone.

Hello, she said.

Hi, Valerie?

Hello?

He could hear music in the background, jazz piano.

Yes, Valerie, it's Abner.

Abner?

Abner Krank, from Queen Street.

Oh, Dr. Krank, she said, sure, hi.

You got Oscar Peterson on there?

Already he felt totally natural with her. He didn't have to plan what he said, which was good because the thing with his conversations in the past, they were never spontaneous enough. Words always seemed to bubble up slowly from his chest, as though through lava.

Actually, Joe Sealey, a tape, she said. So what's up?

He paused. He dug out the piece of paper he'd written a few things on, some phrases he could use.

Just a second, he said.

I thought maybe I saw you in the neighbourhood the other day. In a phone booth like Superman.

She laughed and he laughed. Happiness percolated up from somewhere in his chest when he heard her say the word *Superman* and apply it to him.

No, not me, that couldn't have been me, he said. I've never been there, not in my cape anyway. I don't even know where you live.

Church and Isabella, right on the corner. In the phone booth outside, I was sure it was you.

Valerie, Church and Isabella? Isn't that the same

intersection as the poetry book, the one you lent me? The one you signed?

That's it all right. Have you read it yet?

No, but it's next on my list. I can't wait, I read the first page. Terrific.

Another pause. He flattened out the piece of paper, which had curled up in his pocket. His palm was damp so his fingers stuck to it. He had to use the hand that held the receiver to peel the paper off.

Valerie, he said, this is Abner Krank.

What kind of idiot was he, reading the very first line to her for the second time.

I know, she said, you already said that.

Again she laughed and her laugh was a musical one, an accepting one. There was no mockery in it. She seemed to know already that he was nervous. God knows how many calls like this she'd received in her life.

He laughed too.

Huh-huh-huh, he said.

He was losing it. It sounded hollow this time, even to him. He looked at the paper again.

I'm wondering if you might like to go out this Friday, to a concert at Massey Hall.

You mean a date?

He heard the incredulity in her voice, the surprise.

Well, I guess, yes. That's what it would be. I'd pick you up at seven.

She didn't play coy or beat around the bush.

No, she said, I'm sorry but Friday's out. Really, Dr. Krank, I'm sorry.

Are you in a relationship, Valerie?

He'd predicted this, he knew what to say if she said yes.

Yes, she said.

We have so much in common, Valerie. It's hard to imagine anyone who shares as much as we do.

It hadn't come out the way he'd practised it. It was meant to be cool, sonorous, controlled, intimate, reassuring. Instead, he heard pleading.

Oh?

You know, medicine. We share an interest in that.

Oh, I see. I'm sorry, Dr. Krank, but that's how it is for me. I'm a lost cause for romance.

That's too bad, Ms. Anderson, he said. What should I do now?

He hadn't prepared that line, it just came to him. He was used to speaking in public, that was different. It was part of his job to stand up in front of people like Valerie Anderson and John Glass and when he spoke under those circumstances, they listened to him. They always did.

You seem like a nice enough guy, she said. It's a big world out there.

No, really, Valerie, I wonder what I will do now.

She hesitated and, for the first time, he felt the sway of the exchange move his way.

I don't understand, she said.

I'm sorry, sorry that I bothered you. I'm unsure as to what to do about it, that's all. What my options are.

But he wasn't unsure. He had it all figured out.

She said something that was meant to be nice and kind.

Thank you for calling me. I enjoyed our rotation together in psychiatry, but that's as far as I can go. I have a boyfriend. We're engaged to be married.

That wasn't true. She and Roberto had never discussed anything like marriage but she wanted to slam the door and slam it fast, without bruising fingers.

Goodbye then, Valerie, he said.

He hung up the phone and swept the useless piece of paper away into the basket. It was full of stupid platitudes.

What hobbies do you have Valerie? My mother was interested in that too.

He picked up the poetry book, her poetry book. Well, it was written by someone else, someone named Amber White, but there was Valerie Anderson's signature on the inside front cover and she was listed as the editor. So it was hers.

He liked the first part, so he read that again and then he riffled through the remaining 140 pages. He didn't have time for the whole poem, who would?

Lipstick
latex split
double-park
track-mark

Fuck it and fuck you too, Valerie, he said.
Plan B then.

———

Valerie Anderson and June Glass continued to meet every two weeks or so while the weather held. They drank French wine very slowly on June's patio, and as dusk fell they lit the kerosene torches and talked about the past. Mostly they spoke about events that had occurred to June before Valerie was even born, events June hadn't paid attention to in decades. In retrospect, over the course of all their conversations, June later realized that she had learned very little about Valerie Anderson, who seemed to be able to do a thousand things without falling behind at school. According to reports from Jasper, she remained at the very top of their class, academically.

I don't know how you do it, Valerie, said June.

I'm just lucky, I have an eidetic memory. Every page I look at is like a photograph. It sticks in my brain.

I've heard of that.

It fades after a while, after about a month. But by then the exams are already written. They can't take away my marks.

You're too modest, Valerie. It's not just your memory.

June found the attention from Valerie Anderson flattering, even exciting in a childish way. She was pleased that such a young and accomplished woman wanted to talk to her at all.

Actually, June, I consider you to be a role model, said Valerie.

Ridiculous.

No, no, you are remarkable, June, you have a real sensibility. You've lived a lot more than I have, that's for sure.

You know as well as I do that you can't judge the quality of a life by its length. Look at Keats, Chopin, Chekhov. I'd prefer to judge the quality of a life by love, by passion, and in that regard, dear, I'm afraid I fail as a role model. I haven't exactly leapt for the ring, have I.

Is that a circus metaphor?

I think so. On the trapeze. You stand on the platform, the ring swings by.

Well, I haven't even started up the steps to the plat-form, said Valerie. I've had it easy so far. Nothing much has happened to me.

And June Glass thought, could I not have had a daughter like this?

Tell me about your wedding, June, the details.

Just a minute, Valerie. I mentioned Chopin. He had tempestuous relationships with women. That means those women, those women of his were tempestuous too. They wore their hearts on their sleeves. I wish I could do that, that I had done it, that once at least, in love, I could have been blown right out of my socks. That I could cry and tear my hair out. Does that sound stupid?

Valerie laughed and said, there you go, June, that's why you're a role model.

My wedding, since you ask, our wedding was a bit of an underplayed event. Bill's parents were not even invited, they were *personae non gratae*. I'm not going to get into that. And my own parents, although present, were taci-turn to say the least and it was the smallest wedding on record. We had but one mutual friend there at Hart House for the ceremony. I did not wear a wedding dress in the classical sense. My suit, for that's what it was, was neither long nor white nor flowing but instead a simple stylish grey. My hat, dried flowers tilted to the side in the fashion of the time. I stood outside, afterwards, with my left hand tucked under Bill's arm. The wind, as I remember it, Valerie, that afternoon was strong enough to ruffle his hair. You can still see it in the one photograph we had taken. The same wind, the same photograph, pushed my skirt slightly off the vertical, towards him, against his leg and you could also see, from the lack of shadows on the ground, that the sun was absent that day, and the several pigeons who graced the roadway behind us formed the only welcoming party. That's all.

Go on, June. You have an eidetic memory that lasts a lot longer than mine.

Aided by the real photograph. Two or three pigeons and the bell tower of Hart House loomed behind us, a dramatic backdrop for our prosaic event. But in fact it was lonely, not celebratory, as though all my life I had waited for this and there it was, it was over. Afterwards we had a dinner of lake trout, peas and potatoes at the Royal York Hotel with my parents, the four of us. We stayed on, Bill and I, in the hotel, on the fifth floor for our one-night honeymoon. Were we like Chopin and George Sand? I don't think so. Emma Bovary? Anna Karenina? All those women drew from deeper wells than I.

Men wrote those novels, said Valerie Anderson.

The wine bottle had been emptied now.

Valerie, I always wanted a daughter. After Jasper, I knew our next child would be a girl. I felt it in everything

I did. I wanted a girl, I was one myself, I understood girls. Boys, I wasn't so sure. Witness Jasper and John. It became an obsession for me, nothing to be proud of, quite the reverse. As soon as I became pregnant, I began to refer to the new baby, invariably, as Julia. Feel her kick, Bill, I said, Julia has strong legs. And when she was born, she turned out to be John, whom of course you know. And here is the worst part of my eidetic memory: pathetically, when he was born a boy, I cried. And of course he cried. He was supposed to. A snowstorm darkened the hospital window which looked out over Bathurst Street. His crying and mine commingled. I tried to stifle my tears but I couldn't. My fear, Valerie, is that John heard me and registered my disappointment.

Studies would show that's extremely unlikely, said Valerie Anderson, though I know that's small comfort.

I rue those first moments with my son.

Think of all the unwanted girls like that, born all over the world even today. Orphanages full of girls, full of us, said Valerie Anderson.

Sometimes on those nights when they sat around and talked for hours in the shadowy light, the flames from the torches petering out, June Glass felt that Valerie Anderson was one of her own children. She let that feeling happen. There was nothing wrong with that, it was human nature to wish for things.

Look at all those passionate women, the ones in novels, the ones who wore their hearts on their sleeves. They all wanted something else, something other than the lives they actually had.

Krank had seen the street girls out there when he was in the phone booth. They were young, most of them, the ones that were close enough for him to see. If they were more than fourteen or fifteen years old, he'd be surprised. They bent down into cars like giraffes, and then they got into those cars and were driven away. They were going to get paid for sexual activity. Otherwise they wouldn't have been there, they'd have been out instead with chalk, playing hopscotch, skipping rope with their friends.

He looked at a few more pages. *By Church and Isabella I Sat Down and Cried.* Same sort of stuff, *bruise, semen, jit-jit-jit, smack, H, stroll.*

By midnight, he'd read most of the book, though not sequentially. He'd hopped around in it like a grasshopper.

How old was Anna, the cleaning lady. Thirty-five? Why should he pay her? What was he thinking?

If Gwen understood it properly, Andy had given her two days. But she didn't want to cut it fine, so she set out first thing the next morning.

She walked up McCaul Street to the university. She'd never been there before, only walked past. Now that she had a purpose, however, she turned north from College Street and went onto the campus.

She walked in a long oval around the soccer pitch and looked at the buildings. Students sat alone or in groups on the steps outside the library, and she went up to one of them and asked him where the medical building was.

Over there, he said.

It wasn't far away. It was a windy day and newspapers had been blown apart and pages scattered themselves under the parked cars and some of them flew in the air.

She entered the medical building and heard a noise, a clattering like a cafeteria. She walked in that direction and found herself in a lunchroom. There were boys and girls everywhere, eating their lunches out of bags and briefcases and everybody talked a mile a minute, so it was reassuring, she felt quite at home. It wasn't really much different from the Parrot, except for the briefcases and the white lab coats. Nobody over thirty, though.

She had one of the photographs that Andy had given her. She went over to a small table where students sat and handed them the picture.

I'm looking for this fellow, if you don't mind, she said.

One of them looked at the picture and smiled and handed it around. They all smiled and looked at her.

Jasper, they said, he must be around here somewhere. They craned their necks and scanned the room.

No, not here. Must be in anatomy.

Another boy stood up, a big guy with a friendly face. My name's Wallace.

He held out his hand.

Hi, Wallace, Gwen O'Hara.

I'll go get him. It's Jasper Glass. You wait here.

It's no trouble?

No, it's easy. He's just upstairs.

She sat down in one of the empty seats at the table and in five minutes, Wallace came back with the young man in the photograph.

There he was. Without the rain, the night, the so-called circumstances, there was no doubt in her mind.

Hi, he said to her, I'm Jasper Glass.

You look just like your picture, she said.

He had no idea who she was but she was a girl and she was pretty, a thin face, freckled. She looked a bit nervous. She showed him the photograph.

That's me. I'll just get us coffee.

They switched to a low table in the corner of the room and sat there for half an hour. They talked. Their knees almost touched. She told him how she remembered him from Shaw Street the night of the tropical rain, the night she was raped and almost killed, how he had come out of nowhere and saved her life.

Me? he said.

Yes, you. You were shirtless, covered with some kind of cream, you flew out of nowhere. You were with a friend.

I don't think so, he said.

Yet, as he spoke, the memory of the Crisco returned to him, the night of heavy drinking, the rain.

You were brave, she said.

I don't remember a thing, honestly. Not a thing. Anyway, if I ever did that, it was a reflex.

He looked puzzled, even amused by her story.

I think you saved my life, she said.

Gwen, I don't think this happened, that I can take credit for that. Attractive though it may be, the assumption of the mantle, your saviour, the damsel in distress, all of that, that would be right up my alley to take credit for it, but I didn't do it.

Oh yes, she said, it was you, and that's why I'm here. Jasper, listen.

Girls were always saying to him, *Jasper, listen.*

The police are going to be calling on you, tomorrow.

The police?

Within a day or two, yes, the police. A Detective Ames. He's actually a nice guy.

It's impossible, he said.

But of course Marnie had already warned him. The police were just coming closer now. It was all true.

Whoever was with you that night, he killed the rapist.

Killed him?

Stabbed him.

She started to cry very softly. She took a napkin from the holder and looked away.

The other man had a knife. It came down to a fight, one on one. All of us, really, we could all be dead.

Jesus, said Jasper Glass.

They're after him, whoever he is, and when they get to you, then they'll get to him. Do you understand? It makes no sense for either of you to get arrested.

Let's go for a walk, he said. We'll go for a walk.

He took her arm. They left the lunchroom and went outside.

There were some benches in front of Hart House and

they sat there and he found some crumbs in his pocket and sprinkled them for the pigeons.

He liked Gwen O'Hara. She was obviously spirited, resilient. He'd never seen her before in his life.

Jasper, they know who you are and they know you were there. So they're going to tell you I identified you. But I didn't.

You didn't?

No. I looked at your picture and I lied. Simple as that. Deny the whole thing, that's all you've got to do. That's why I came today.

It should be easy enough to say I wasn't there, said Jasper. I don't remember a thing. So as far as I'm concerned, I wasn't there. And, when I wasn't there, there was no one with me.

Good. Exactly. That's all you have to do.

Tell me about it, that night, how you remember it, he said.

You came out of the rain, knocked the man off, you jumped up and then you saw he had a knife. You backed off.

So I'm not the big hero.

Oh, I think you were, but your friend was there too. He took over. He had a knife and the fight lasted a few seconds.

You saw all that?

Yes.

So he acted in self-defence, whoever he was? If he was there?

Yes.

Jasper walked with Gwen O'Hara back to Queen Street and, by the time they hit Dundas, they were hand in hand. He couldn't believe it, but sex with this girl was not the first thing he had on his mind.

The one Abner Krank liked was blond and had her hair done up in pigtails and she was leaning up against the outside of a coffee shop. It was seven o'clock at night, still lots of daylight. He wasn't nervous at all. In fact, he felt clinical, that was the word for it, as though he were embarking on an experiment. Excited too, at the prospect of what might happen.

Hi, he said.

She looked at him. Blue eyes. She was chewing gum. Skimpy pink shorts, clean as clean can be, the blouse too, pink sneakers to match. Little white socks. The braids in her hair were damp. She must have just showered.

Hi, he said again, I'm looking for company. I'm thinking about half an hour.

Half an hour from now?

No. Half an hour of your time, now.

He had no idea what to say, what the language of the street was. But it didn't matter because she understood.

I'll have to talk to Mitchell, said Heidi Chipman.

There was a plate-glass window at the front of the coffee shop but she wasn't leaning totally on that. About half of her body was leaning on the adjacent brick part and she pushed herself off in the sinuous past-caring movement that only girls that age can make. She disappeared through the front door and all Abner could see then was reflections. He just stood and watched the street, the cars and trucks going by. He felt his wallet in his pants pocket. Fifty dollars all in tens. There was a limit to what he'd pay, but what the charge was, he didn't know.

In two minutes she came back out. Now she had with her a gold-sequined purse about the size of a wallet.

Mitchell says okay. Where's your car?

He hadn't thought of that. He'd expected a hotel nearby, a stairway, a corridor, a room. Then, he realized, if there were rooms there wouldn't be all those cars cruising by. It wouldn't be Church and Isabella. It would be an address, an apartment, a flat.

Listen, he said, wait for me, I'll get one.

I'll be here, she said, for maybe a half-hour, like you said.

Henry, I'm Henry, he said.

There's cars at Bay and Charles, she said.

She had a pretty smile.

What's your name? he asked.

Heidi.

It was only ten minutes before he was at the Avis dealer.

Small, mid-size, for three hours, he said.

He didn't care how big the car was as long as the front seat slid back. All cars had that.

He paid for it by credit card. He didn't want to be short of cash.

She was still there leaning up against the wall when he returned, but now she was smoking. Her head tipped up, smoke blew out from her lips in a stream. When he pulled over, she turned her head towards him. He reached over and unlocked the passenger door, pushed it half open.

You're almost late, she said. I was about to give up.

Get in, Heidi.

She slid in.

That's a nice purse, he said.

I like it, it glitters.

Is there a good place to go, somewhere you could recommend? he asked.

Maybe she'd like him for himself, the way he was, rather than for the money.

She laughed cheerfully and said, almost anywhere, drive around, take a look. It depends. This is a pretty nice car you picked up. Hope you didn't steal it.

He parked on St. Nicholas Street three minutes away, near the theatre. He checked the mirrors. No one nearby. An oasis of quiet in the heart of the city, St. Nicholas Street was, and until you looked around for it and found it, you never knew streets like this existed.

A delivery truck stopped half a block away.

He reached down under the front seat, pulled on the lever, and the seat slid back.

There, he said.

He took his wallet from his back pocket and gave her three tens. Then he put the wallet in the pocket of the windbreaker he had on.

Okay, he said. Now, Heidi.

First things first, she said.

She opened her gold purse and put the thirty dollars inside, closed the snap, put the purse down on the floor by her feet, and then she slid partway across, reached over with both hands and began to unbuckle his belt.

Maybe he could just have paid her twenty dollars.

She unzipped his trousers. He sat there motionless, his eyes on the rear-view mirror.

I guess this is what you want?

That's a start, for today, he said.

Why Henry, it looks like you're all ready.

Heidi Chipman bent down over his lap and took about one inch of his penis into her mouth. All he could see was the back of her head, her pigtails, the tight part in her hair.

He tasted like green hand soap. She went down to two inches, three inches.

It didn't take long, ten or twenty pulls with her tongue and lips and teeth and through it all he did nothing. Even though she ran her left hand over his thighs, his chest as she proceeded, he said nothing, but he shuddered at the end.

He pulled his clothes back together and drove her back to the coffee shop. For a moment, they sat in the front seat of the car. She took out a stick of Wrigley's Spearmint from her purse and put it in her mouth. She balled up the wrapping and dropped it on the floor. Then she jumped out and walked into the coffee shop. She didn't look back. In that respect, she was just like Valerie Anderson. It said in the pink poetry book that they wore those skimpy clothes like a uniform, like a butcher, a chef or an airline pilot. It was practical for the work they did.

Not likely to catch anything from oral sex, medically speaking.

Avis was closed so he slipped the keys into the return slot and started to walk to the subway station. Thirty dollars for that girl.

He patted his coat pocket.

Jesus Christ.

He patted it again and felt his pants, his shirt. He quickly ran back to the rented car but of course it was locked. He could see through the windows and there was nothing there.

She'd taken his wallet.

If Jasper Glass could kill himself, fall shrieking from the sky and get away with it, then so could he, figured John. He'd try it out, find out what it felt like. But he was going to do it alone, not like his older brother howling Icarus to the crowd, one eye on the landing net and the other on women.

Not that he'd actually go through with it. It was the process, not the end result, that would allow him to resonate with the lost, the forlorn, the woebegones, the depressives, the heartbreaking list of brilliant writers and poets who had preceded him across the River Styx.

He left the Sauna Baths at four a.m. after working overtime. He'd catnapped from two to four so he wasn't tired. He cycled down Bay Street on the new bicycle he had purchased with his first paycheque, all the way to the ferry docks. Maybe three cars passed him by. At that hour, streetlights had an irrational life of their own. They were red or yellow or green and they switched on and off of their own accord, cars or no cars. They went through their electronic motions, semaphore to the empty streets. No one watched, no one paid attention.

Courage, he thought, and he went through intersection after intersection at full speed. There was no point in stopping. It was downhill all the way to Lake Ontario.

Zoom, he said as he went through the King Street light. He felt the wind in his hair.

He waited at the bottom of Bay Street for two hours and took the first ferry to Ward's Island. It was good to be up that early. There was dew all over the seats on the upper deck and the water in the harbour was undisturbed, slick and smooth, a deep black. The low sun was in the east and he stood up and walked forward to the blunt prow of the *Sam McBride* and saw his own shadow cast upon the water.

This is what Hart Crane had seen when he jumped from the ship.

There were a few tourists and picnickers on board, but not many. They disembarked at the island and headed off to the west. Alone, he pushed his bicycle down the gangplank and then he walked—there was no rush—he took the small path that angled across to the open lake, to the beachfront, to the sand.

The rocks he brought along in his knapsack were heavy. Physically, he was as strong as ever, stronger with all the cycling he'd done. Maybe he should have even picked up a few more, just to be sure he had enough.

But there weren't that many in Trinity-Bellwoods Park, his source for stones. Path separators, with chipped white paint spattered over them. They were out of their element here too.

When he arrived at the beach, he sat at the water's edge. He looked out at the western horizon, flat and grey-black, still untouched by the rising sun. The sand was scuffed from the day before, a broken castle with a flag-stick made from a popsicle, its parapets pebbled and half crumbled. It still had some merit as a sandcastle. Someone could use it later as a starting point, so he walked around it, skirting the walls.

Virginia Woolf probably had a long coat for her rocks, not a knapsack like this. Well, he didn't think that mattered. It wasn't meant to be a historical re-enactment.

He walked straight out into the water. It was cold, as he expected, but not numbing.

It was a slow decline from the beach, the kind of shallow slant on which, in reverse, fish came out of the sea, walked on their fins, looked around and decided to stay. Now here he was, the reverse process.

He took a few more steps. The water was now over his knees. He stopped at when it reached mid-thigh. He adjusted the knapsack, hiked it up. He was reluctant to have the cold water hit his genitals but it had to be done. He shivered, then he was up to his waist, his chest, his shoulders. There were no waves at all, the lake was in a rare state of glassiness, a paralysis of its usual restless force. He couldn't have picked a better, more benign day.

From shore he must cut a ridiculous figure. His head, the top of his backpack, black against the grey nothing of the lake.

Farther, John? he said.

He took another step and the water jumped up to his chin.

Whoa.

He tried jumping but the rocks did their job all right, he was stuck there on the bottom. Like moon boots. Now he felt the not-so-subtle pressure on his lungs, the way his ribs needed to expand against the force of the lake to breathe, against the weight of the rocks on his back, no longer quite as heavy as they had felt before.

His left foot hit something.

Now he was really there. He could slip, then what?

Two more steps. The lake half an inch below his nostrils.

If a boat came by, the wake from it would wash his face for him, a lapping up and down, up and down. There was no such boat.

He tipped his nostrils down and felt the air stop. He opened his mouth. He stepped forward, deeper into the lake.

To hell with this. He took a quick and fearful step backwards and turned around, choked and spat out water. He bent forward, he pushed his upper body forward, afraid of the depth, the fathoms, the darkness that now lay behind him. He walked out of the lake.

Water streamed from him. It darkened the damp sand. He shrugged off the backpack, and lake water poured from it and pooled there. He sat down on terra firma. He removed his running shoes. He shook out the rocks onto the sand. Then his socks. He squeezed water from them too, wringing them out.

There you go. Experiment over. Fuck dying, it's not worth it. Leave it to those who have something to die for.

Heidi, you did good, you did real good today, said Mitchell.

I did?

Sure you did. Look at this.

He pulled cards and money out of the stolen wallet and put them all on the table.

There's not much there, she said.

That's true, what, twenty dollars. But Heidi, look at this.

He pulled out a small photograph and a driver's licence.

What did you say his name was?

Henry.

Well, Henry he's not. He's a doctor and his real name is Abner Krank. This, I bet, this is his mother.

There was a picture of a woman in a blue bathing suit, squinting into the sun, waist-deep in water. You could see the far shoreline, low pine trees.

He flipped it across the table to her.

Too old to be his girlfriend. Must be his mother. Heidi, how much you get in the car for what you did, ten dollars?

Actually, twenty.

I love you, Heidi, that's what I like about you. You I can trust.

He snapped his fingers and held out his hand.

She reached into her purse and brought out two of the three tens that Henry had given her. She passed them across the table.

Well, Heidi, with this little bit of information, this wallet, we just got some richer, you and me, because I make a phone call to Dr. Abner Krank, he pays me, he pays us, oh, one thousand dollars. Maybe two thousand, I can think about it.

Oh, she said.

You see?

I think I do, she said. You mean blackmail.

No, I do not mean blackmail, just a private arrangement. We just up the price for what you do, the service. It's legal. A thousand dollars instead of twenty.

I don't know, she said.

What do you mean, you don't know?

I'm not sure how friendly he'd be, Henry, paying that much.

That's his problem, not yours.

I hope, she said.

Don't worry, that's my job.

Mitchell put Abner Krank's wallet into the back pocket of his jeans.

Look, he said.

He slapped both his back pockets. He had two wallets, his own on one side, the stolen one on the other. He was balanced.

Okay, my young friends, said the anatomy professor, listen and listen carefully. Surgery is full of danger for the ignorant and the careless. Today, we will perform quite radical surgery upon these cadavers of ours. We are going to be handling different but equally sharp instruments as we open the thoracic cavity and the skull, both on the same day. One of these procedures, the opening of the thoracic cavity, will be performed in much the same way it has for centuries, by splitting the sternum by hand. With this.

He held up what looked like a large pair of wire cutters.

The cranium, however, is a different matter. For that, due to the strength and the thickness of the bone, we shall take advantage of electricity and use this, the oscillating saw.

It didn't look like a saw to Jasper Glass, certainly not the woodworking kind.

The goal of our procedure this morning is obvious to even the most obtuse of you. Though I see John Glass is missing, so that statement will not be put to the test.

Laughter erupted throughout the room.

Wallace, what is the purpose of our endeavour?

To gain access to the heart, the lungs, the ascending aorta, and the brain.

Excellent. True. I continue. Upon the living patient, the surgeon has many perils to face. He or she can puncture the thin membrane of the surgical glove and thus his, or her, living skin in many ways. A spicule of bone, a curved needle, the burn of cautery. What Canadian surgeon died of a wound infection incurred in the course of surgery, Ms. Anderson? And where?

Norman Bethune, in China.

Excellent. True. And the purpose of my lecture thus far is to caution you, young students, in your procedures this morning, not to make mistakes with sharp instruments.

Do not run with scissors, said Jasper Glass.

That's one simplistic way to put it. Thank you, Mr. Glass Senior, for your insight. Fortunately, these cadavers, already ravaged, do not carry within themselves living organisms and they do not pose, therefore, the same danger. Formaldehyde stings but it does not transmit, for example, syphilis or hepatitis B or both simultaneously, a deadly stew. I will now demonstrate, on this body, the proper way to expose the organs we seek. Please note the fastidious care I take, particularly with fragments of bone.

Ouch, said Jasper Glass.

Then there was a knock upon the door. The professor put down his tools and went out into the corridor.

Mr. Glass, he said upon his return, you are wanted outside. It's our lucky day.

So this is it, Jasper thought.

And he was right. It was the detective Marnie and Gwen had both predicted would find him, in the flesh at last.

He feigned surprise.

Homicide? he said. What the heck?

Let me cut to the quick, said Detective Ames. You have been identified, Mr. Glass, as a witness to a murder on Shaw Street.

What?

He was totally flabbergasted. He nearly fell back against the wall in the corridor. He'd practised it ten or twelve times.

Yes. A positive identification, Mr. Glass, iron-clad.

Then the policeman smiled for some reason.

And the murderer, our informant confirms, was in your company at the time.

You can't be serious.

To be frank, Mr. Glass, we have no issue with you, but we seek your help in identifying your friend.

That's crazy. Who could identify me? I wasn't there.

We have an eyewitness, a very reliable one. Perjure yourself at your peril, young man. I caution you.

It's impossible. I deny it totally and without reservation, Officer.

Then he was surprised. The detective did not pursue the matter any further. He just snapped shut his notebook, thanked him, said he might talk to him again, and he left.

Jasper returned to class.

What was that about? Valerie Anderson asked.

You won't believe it, a policeman. Something about a murder downtown, as if I might know something.

And?

And I don't. It's impossible.

Nothing is impossible with you, she said.

Nothing? You mean I can keep my hopes up? Valerie?

Hold the rib cage, she said.

By the time the two of them had plugged in the saw for the skull and were making the first cut, from behind both ears and arcing forward as though topping a hard-boiled egg, Detective Ames was back at the station. He went in to see the detective sergeant.

Our gambit didn't pay off. He denied it all. No memory of being there. Zero. No hesitation.

You told him about the positive ID?

It rolled off him like water.

Like he'd been warned?

You have to wonder.

Well, really, that's not too bad, said the detective sergeant. It's bad for the stats but not too bad for justice.

I could check out the rest of his friends, work backwards from there. I don't think it would be all that hard. One by one, you know.

But the girl, what's her name again?

Gwen O'Hara.

She doesn't make the ID, and your Jasper denies it all, then what are the chances the killer comes out and says, oh yes, that was me?

Zero. That's my guess, said Ames.

So we have nothing but the most circumstantial evidence. Crisco here, Crisco there, so what. Never fly in court.

So we drop it all?

For now. There's not much else to do. Let's sit on it, wait and see. Do something else. Oh, Andy, how often have you been talking to the girl?

To Gwen? A few times. I show her pictures, we talk.

I think you handled it right, this case, a good job. A credit to the force. It's nice to say that once in a while.

Thanks, said Detective Ames. By the way, Jasper Glass, his face today was covered with cuts and bruises, like he'd gone ten rounds with George Chuvalo.

Oh?

An accident up north, so he says. Ran into a moose. So he was punished after all, by God or by chance, by the dark of night, for whatever misdemeanours he might have committed. We're off the hook.

Back at his desk, he rearranged the case folder and one of the other photographs slipped partway out. Valerie Anderson. He looked at her for a full minute. He didn't mind a second look. Beautiful, dark, intense. If anything new came up, he'd talk to her. She'd have no axe to grind in this, no reason not to talk to him. Other than loyalty.

Marnie Kennedy-Foare. Valerie Anderson. Gwen O'Hara.

They were all nice girls, each in her own way. Like he said before, it was turning into one of those nice cases, the few and far between ones, the kind that ended the way they should. Everybody more or less happy, nobody going to jail.

Justice done, case semi-closed.

It was nine o'clock at night, a Thursday as usual, and they were in the classroom at University College.

Okay, said Roberto Moreno, this is the end of the second-last class this semester and it is, I'm sorry to say, my second-last class with you, my students. They have hired a real teacher for next term.

Wallace Wallace began to applaud and they all joined in. Then Roberto raised his arm.

Tell you what, he said, to hell with all these famous poets. Let's get down to one of our own, for our last class next week.

He walked about the class and handed out a mimeographed poem.

This is by Valerie Anderson, he said, for next time. But if any of you want to bring in work of your own, please do. We will look at everything, no matter how long it takes.

Then he stood at the front as he always did at the end of every class.

Two things, actually, for next time, my students. Read this poem by your classmate and come prepared next week for a discussion on at least this one poem. Also, before you go, write down these names. These are Spanish poets who write, of course, in Spanish and one day, perhaps, you will be in need of a poem in Spanish. It might save your life, like penicillin. These are some names you can seek out, should you tire of, say, Octavio Paz. I have included one Chilean, lest I be accused of bias.

On the blackboard he wrote the names: Gonzalo de Berceo, Juan Ruiz, Gil Vicente, Fernando de Herrera, Garcilaso de la Vega, Luis de Góngora, Lope de Vega, Gabriela Mistral.

How I love that last name, he said. A lyric poem in itself.

And lastly he wrote: Federico García Lorca.

These poets are not parabolists, he said, none of them are, and many of them are centuries old, as old as Shakespeare. But they are the building blocks of parabolism, of all modern poetry. Who cares if it's in English or Spanish or Farsi?

He looked around the room. No one cared. Everybody copied down the names dutifully. Then, after the toast to Stefan, they filed out of the class holding Valerie Anderson's poem. Some of them just folded it up and put it away. Others read it as they walked.

If you want me to be modern,
I'll have to cut my hair for
money, and I'll have to sell my
schoolbooks at a downtown
store. I have done these things
before. I have a piece of jewelry
of sentimental value. Do they
say sentiment is worth
anything anymore? Your
moods and new clothes are
too fast. I'm old fashioned. I
can't keep close. Between
rapture and collapse, I might
make it where you're going,
but I'll never make it back.

Haven't you something else to
show me, or to say? If you've
something modern, then you
may. I didn't understand. I said,
okay. Some finally fall from a
bout of ambition, pride or
timidity, inhibition. Me, I fell
from a mixed drink of all these,
coated my throat in gold leaf.

What's with the line breaks? Wallace Wallace asked
Valerie. What's with gold leaf?

It worked out well for John at the Sauna Baths. He
reported to work on time, never missed a shift, made
himself available if another staff member was sick and
he carried out all his duties in a highly organized way. It
seemed a total turnaround from his behaviour as a student. On his own, he developed a checklist and printed
up copies of it: cash, coffee, milk, sugar, towels, soap,
ashtrays, cigarettes (menthol, filter, non-filter), check the
sauna, the showers, the roomettes, razors, shampoo,
light bulbs, toilet paper, condoms, lubricant, Kleenex,
and in the end there were forty items on his list and, until
he had it memorized, he carried it around with him.

When the bell rang in the office, he returned briskly
to the glass window, to the Dutch door. He smiled a
welcome and ushered in the client or clients, as they
often came in pairs or groups, and sometimes they were

tipsy, dollar bills fell from their hands to the floor and they bent over laughing to pick them up, and soon they all knew John, they pleaded, John! when he confiscated alcohol, they said, John! when they paid or, Johnny! when they praised the quality and freshness of the Colombian coffee in the percolator and, oh, John! they said when they buried their faces, appreciative, in the aromatic towels and sometimes, even, which they knew they shouldn't, they called to him, John! through the open doors of their roomettes, Johnny! But on those occasions he always walked by, nor was he tempted to do otherwise for he was a staff member, the only one on duty in the evenings and nights and for some reason he found it an awesome responsibility, far more so than his responsibility had been as a medical student. The tight feeling in his chest disappeared. In the calm times, he wrote or read poetry. He never made an outgoing call, never stole even a cigarette or a quarter from the cash, and it would have been easy to do so. Even the tips went into the till.

His bank account thrived on his honesty and hard work. He had a key now to the smoked-glass door, and when he arrived, he walked his bicycle up the stairs and kept it propped against the wall in the office, near the coffee.

Keeping trim? they said to him. That's good, John.

He became a confidant, in a way like a priest, a confessor, as sometimes the clients of the baths came to him in his office and sat down and talked to him in such a way that he felt he could at last be a trusted recipient of a confidence and, yes, even the dispenser of grains of wisdom. They cried, they wondered if they would ever be loved by their nuclear families, their mothers and fathers and brothers and sisters, their aunts and uncles and nephews whom they carried on their shoulders, invisible burdens of disapproval.

There, there, John often said, there, there.

Then the outside bell rang and in came one or two more, the exchange of modest payment. They disappeared into their roomettes with the welcoming but somewhat, from the viewpoint of a former medical student, clinical-looking beds. Their belts and their clothes hung from hooks.

How do you know you only like women and girls? they asked him.

How do I know? I just feel it, he said. It's my history. I feel it in the core of my being.

Well, maybe you should feel this, they said, in the core of your being.

But he demurred and no one tried more than once but for a fellow with a German accent, Bavarian, who said to him, how do you know, John, how do you know without actual empirical experience?

Twice a week, three times a week, he was asked the same question by the same persistent young man, and he began to bring John small presents, books by Günter Grass and Heinrich Böll and other contemporary masters of collective guilt, of forlorn love gone awry.

You will like these novels, Johnny. They have nothing to do really with sex, certainly not with sex with men, but they do deal with repressed feelings, emotions and liberation in a personal sense.

John Glass shrugged it off. He understood that many of the clients at the Sauna Baths had been unfairly and harshly judged.

He augmented his income in another creative way. One day he was in Britnell's on his day off. He was in the poetry section, as usual, and had just placed *Civil Elegies and Other Poems,* by Dennis Lee, inside his ski jacket.

The proprietor came around the corner of the aisle.

Young man, he said.

Me?

Young man, I've noticed you here frequently. You have a passion for poetry, it seems.

John shifted his jacket and kept his right arm firmly to his side.

Yes, he said, I do, I love poetry.

We're looking for someone, the man said.

You are?

Yes, there's been a rash of thefts here recently.

Oh, said John.

A number of obscure but exceptional books stolen, and from this section, right here. We discovered it during inventory. Last week. Thirty-five books in the past year.

Thirty-five? Good Lord, had it been that many? He was unable to speak, he coughed, he choked, his confession stopped at his throat.

What I was hoping is that you would consider a position here. In security, so to speak, though never did I ever dream it would come to this. We would like someone to browse the store, keep an eye on things during busy times. I thought of you, you're here a lot, you might as well get paid. You don't seem to have a lot of money, correct me if I'm wrong.

Oh God, said John.

I beg your pardon?

No, said John, no I do not have a lot of money, and yes, I would love to browse your store. After all, I do it anyway.

Good, said the man, we'll shake on it.

He held out his right hand.

So did John, and as he raised his arm he felt *Civil Elegies* start to slip. Quickly, he pushed himself up against the bookcase on the right. *Civil Elegies* stopped its fall, pinned against his hip.

Welcome to Britnell's, the man said.

Despite hiring the young man as a security agent, Britnell's continued to lose the odd poetry book over the next few months. But John couldn't be on duty all the time, could he, and the lighting was bad back there, no windows, so, at the next inventory, when they discovered the ongoing loss of only *An Anthology of New York Poets* edited by Ron Padgett and David Shapiro, *Earth House Hold* by Gary Snyder, *Cairns* by Christopher Levinson, *O Taste and See* by Denise Levertov, and *Brébeuf and His Brethren* by E.J. Pratt, the staff at Britnell's considered the hiring of their new security man a success. The hemorrhaging of books became, they said, a mere flesh wound, an acceptable cost of business.

For the first time, with the money he made from his two positions, John actually purchased a book, *Contemporary German Poetry in Translation,* from his new part-time employer.

Thank you, John, for your business, they said.

No, thank you, said John.

To Helmut, he wrote in the front of the book, and he took it with him to the Roman Sauna Baths and presented it, the next evening, to the Bavarian man.

No hard feelings, Helmut, he said, but take this and seek solace in the written word. That's what I do, what I have done.

During his time in Toronto, Roberto Moreno received no word from his former lover, Luisa Sanchez. Upon his departure from Mexico City, she had said he would be dead for her. And so, apparently, he was.

Isabela Cruz, on the other hand, with whom he had never had a physical relationship, yet who had raised her fist to him from the airport bus in a gesture of solidarity, sent him a letter every week. Always the green and yellow stamp in the corner of the blue air-mail envelope. Poems, quatrains, sonnets of hers written in tiny crabbed letters. Of all the parabolists in Mexico City, she was the most productive. She wrote, she stood up and recited in cafés and on street corners while others slept in their beds or drank mescal or did whatever they did.

She wrote, *Roberto upon your return I will tear you*

in half with pleasure or crack your ribs with the strength of my joy.

To those letters, he had always responded in a lukewarm way.

I am finding it very interesting here, many new things have happened to me.

She was dismissive of his work as a poetry teacher in Toronto.

My God, Roberto, she wrote.

She was his only contemporary connection to Mexico City, so he savoured her letters for their rhythm, their atmosphere, the odd jotting of news they included. Also for the unrelenting and flattering optimism she had for herself, for Roberto, for parabolists in general, and, as the year wore on, he began to think of her more often.

It was inevitable.

Isabela, Isabela. The regular visits of the postman. When Roberto showed her letters to Valerie Anderson and translated them, as he invariably did, she did not seem to be jealous.

Roberto, she said, I love you. But if that woman were here I certainly would not pop her eyes out, despite the fact that she has stated that is what she would do to me, were she here with us. Are you sure you have translated her words exactly?

Roberto laughed and said, I'm afraid so, but Valerie, Isabela is all talk and she is not attractive like you, nor does she have your deep concern for others. Nor your dark eyes, nor your skin like cool silk.

Now you're talking like Octavio Paz or Pablo Neruda, Valerie said.

He touched her shoulder. Valerie put Isabela's most recent letter back on the table.

Roberto, she said, translate this poem of hers, this one. She must have jammed it in as an afterthought. Maybe we can use it in *Zipper*.

She pointed to a few words that curlicued around the corner of the page and spilled out onto the envelope.

Roberto looked and carefully translated the poem out loud.

> *Her fingers broke like sugar sticks,*
> *Then the wrist. You never thought the wrist.*

What do you think? Roberto asked.

I like it, Roberto, and it is good for *Zipper*. It's a cautionary tale about relationships, about love. It's not obvious, but it's there.

Once he knew Valerie's exercise routine, it was a lot easier. He didn't have to walk the streets behind her or go into the upstairs apartment or pretend to be anything but what he was. Three times a week for forty-five minutes at 5:15, Valerie Anderson jogged around King's College Circle. What could be easier? Most of the cars were gone by then so he parked without a problem on the left side of the road in front of the Sigmund Samuel Library and just sat there with a book or a magazine.

Within a few minutes, she started on her laps. She had a small carrying bag she left by the goalposts of the soccer pitch and she warmed up with some stretches. She was always alone. On each circuit of the field, she ran within three feet of his car and she came from behind him, counter-clockwise on the circle so she ran right past the door where he sat. He watched her through the side mirror as she approached and then he turned his head imperceptibly to the left and watched her go by, her dark hair in a ponytail for this aspect of her life, her sporting life. Her hair bounced up and down with each stride she took. Her hips were firm and compact, that was a good word for it—compact. She wore stretch pants, some kind of clinging material that all the girls wore with differing degrees of grace. Must be a sports bra, her breasts hardly moved at all.

She ran well, like an athlete. When she finished, she stretched again, picked up her bag and walked towards Hart House, and when she came back out twenty minutes later, her hair was wet and shiny and loose from the shower, and she must have smelled like soap, like shampoo, like conditioner, like the towel with which she dried off, no doubt the same kind of rough white towel they gave out to the men on their side of the separating wall, where he too showered after her workout.

Why not, she took twenty minutes, he took ten. But that was enough. He didn't follow her home anymore. There was a risk involved in that and he didn't want to push his luck. She'd seen him once, or thought she had.

So, after his shower at Hart House, he went back to 999 Queen Street, to his room with the high ceiling.

The wallet was a problem. He wasn't particularly concerned, he knew where it was. He rested on the bed, hands folded on his chest. It was a good position in which to plan.

Then the phone rang.

Dr. Krank? Switchboard. We had a few calls while you were out.

Wait, he said, I'll get a pencil.

Oh, you won't need that. It was just one person. She didn't leave a name or number. She'll call back.

Wildly, crazily, he thought, Valerie Anderson.

Doctor, she sounded about ten years old. But she wouldn't leave her name. Maybe your sister?

I don't know who it could be. Thank you, I'll just wait and see.

Heidi. He remembered her pigtails, the way they spread out from the back of her scalp. Quick tongue, quick little hands.

Then the phone rang again and the operator said, Doctor? A Mr. Mitchell for you. Can you take the call?

Yes, yes, he said. Hello?

It took some tracking to find you, Doctor.

I beg your pardon?

Once we found your wallet.

My wallet? You found it?

Yes we did. Actually, it was Heidi found it. I'm not sure where.

The man's voice was confident and jocular, as though

he were sharing a joke and as though he, too, Abner Krank, should start to laugh.

You're amused by this, Mr. Mitchell?

Amused? Oh no, I'm sorry, I know it's a serious matter. It has all your identification, Doctor, that's how we found you. Funny though, Heidi thought your name was Henry.

Krank said nothing. He was now sitting up on the side of the bed.

There's not a lot of money in your wallet, Doctor. Abner? I guess I can call you that?

Now he heard Mitchell laugh outright and take a drag on a cigarette. He heard the clanging of a streetcar, the iron roll of wheels.

Sorry, said Mitchell, there's a lot of noise at this end.

I'd like the wallet back, said Dr. Krank.

Of course. That's why I phoned. But I have to tell you that I'm as disappointed in you as I am with Heidi. What you've been up to, behind my back. She's my girl-friend too. I'm upset.

How much are you upset, Mr. Mitchell?

Krank heard the man whispering, probably the girl herself was jammed into the booth with him.

I'm upset a thousand dollars' worth, said Mitchell, and that's the cost of the return of the wallet.

Let me explain something to you, said Abner Krank. You have no bargaining power at all. That said, I'll give your girlfriend, my girlfriend too as you know, fifty dol-lars for taking my wallet. Not a penny more. It's the cards and the photograph I want, Mr. Mitchell.

It's Mitchell, not Mr. Mitchell. You think this nice lady in the bathing suit would like to know how you spend your money, Doctor?

Krank laughed.

Dead three years, he said, as you soon might be, Mr. Mitchell.

If that's a threat, Doctor, you should think twice.

Friday, said Dr. Krank, Friday's a good day for me. Outside the coffee shop at seven-thirty. I'll come by in a car, for Heidi. We'll do the same thing, Heidi and I, but this time I'll keep the wallet.

He hung up the phone.

Well, Mitch? said Heidi.

It didn't go quite right, said Mitchell.

How do you mean?

I don't know. He thinks he's smart, that's all. We'll see how smart he is Friday night.

I have to see him again? I don't like that.

You don't have to like it, Heidi. You just have to do it.

We'll have a party, Valerie Anderson said to Roberto Moreno, right here in the apartment, in celebration of the end of the year, the end of our poetry class.

The end of my professorship too. Good idea, said Roberto Moreno. We'll invite everybody. Make a list.

They wrote down names on one of his yellow pieces of paper.

Valerie Anderson. Roberto Moreno.

We'll invite those two for sure, even though they're staid and boring.

Amber White.

That accounts for *Zipper*. Now the poetry class.

Jasper, John, Wallace, Michael, Art, Sam, Mark. No more than that, just them.

What's the new girl's name, Jasper's girlfriend?

Gwen. He'll bring her, I expect. Put her down.

How many is that?

Eleven.

She tapped the paper with her pencil.

Then there's anyone from Amber's. Murlean's the only one there right now.

Murlean? You mean Heidi? She's got two names, that girl.

Murlean Poirier, write it down. That's her real name. We'll leave a note down there on the bulletin board. Anyone can come from the shelter, so there may be one or two more.

Friday at eight?

Sure.

Good, said Roberto Moreno, I'll get nachos, beer. Some limes. We'll pretend we're in Mexico.

Jasper was surprised when he picked up the phone and it was Marnie.

Hi, Jasper, she said, it's me, I'm back.

Marnie, great, how'd it go up there?

Hot, hot, she said. I was afraid you might come up.

His facial wounds from the moose had healed without a scar. The bruising had cleared after two weeks and it all seemed like light-years away, everything to do with Marnie Kennedy.

Any news from the police, Jasper?

Oh they came by. But that's old news, I'm in the clear. Something unrelated. A mistake on their part.

You sure?

Sure I'm sure.

Gwen O'Hara was asleep on the couch in the living room. They were in his place at Hampton Court. He could see Gwen from where he stood and, when he turned to his left, through the lace curtains he saw the odd car go by on Cottingham Street.

What rotation you on, Marnie?

Pediatrics.

Sick Kids?

Oncology. Those little kids, it's not great.

No, I wouldn't think so.

Jasper, I was thinking, I'd like to shake off the blues a bit, go for a walk. Rosedale Valley Road.

Now?

Yes, now. There's no better time.

It'll be dark in an hour, Marnie.

That's what I mean. There'll be nobody there. Under the cover of darkness, maybe something could happen.

Christian?

He's in Baltimore. At least he's on the plane. I actually saw it take off this time. I swear to God.

You're sure?

One hundred per cent. Meet me there, Jasper, it's no place for a girl to be all by herself.

Ghosts, highwaymen, goblins in the woods. We've been there, I know, said Jasper Glass.

But I like it there. It's frightening but exciting at the same time. Show up, Jasper, make sure I'm okay.

Where exactly, Marnie?

Maybe a hundred yards in, off Mount Pleasant? Under the light. You know, from before?

I don't think so, Marnie, I don't think I can do that.

Jasper?

It's different here now. I have a girlfriend, she's with me. Well, in the next room, sleeping. I can see her, she's on the couch.

Not Valerie, no way.

No, not Valerie. Someone else.

You're making this up, Jasper Glass. I know you, I wasn't born yesterday.

Cross my heart, the gospel truth.

I can't deal with this, Jasper, what you're telling me.

Sure you can, you're light-years ahead of me, Marnie. Another changing of the guard, that's all. You should know, you should be able to relate to this.

You've been my touchstone, Jasper Glass, believe it or not, she said.

I have?

Yes. Someone I can depend on.

They both laughed. He was thinking of Crisco, she of Icarus falling from the sky. Or maybe it was the other way around. Who knows.

Well, we have been pretty close, haven't we, he said.

Lots of fun, Jasper.

Then he heard the practical side of her kick in, the way it had before, when she was married and gone.

Let's hang up simultaneously, she said.

Okay, Marnie. But don't go out after dark. The sun sets early there, the trees are tall.

I won't, I promise.

Then the phone went dead. She'd beaten him to the punch with the hang-up. He knew she would. She was always a step ahead of him, emotionally.

Gwen O'Hara turned towards him from the couch and her eyes were open.

Changing of the guard? Don't go out after dark? What the heck does that mean?

Metaphors, that's all, like turning pages is a metaphor. We're moving on.

We?

You and I.

Who was that on the phone?

Marnie Kennedy, an old girlfriend. We're kind of out of touch now. She's married.

Good, said Gwen, that's the kind of old girlfriend I like. The out-of-touch and married kind. I hope she never phones again and if she does, Jasper, thanks for doing the same thing again.

I love you, she said.

He had to say it back to her, and he did. It wasn't difficult. He meant it. He was surprised, it was all turning out okay.

At six, showered and shaved, Abner Krank hopped on the eastbound streetcar at the corner of Ossington and Queen. There were plenty of empty seats but he chose to stand. He had everything he needed in his little sports bag. At the corner of Bay, he pulled on the bell-wire, the doors opened, and back he was, down into the street. He took a deep breath. It was getting dark. Pulse sixty-five.

It took him ten minutes to walk to the Avis dealer.

Small size, mid-size, it doesn't matter, he said.

He was too early for the appointment but not too early to reconnoitre, so he drove east on Carlton to Jarvis Street and turned left. A couple of blocks up, he saw them, Miss Pigtails herself and a young man walking north, towards the coffee shop. They were talking and oblivious so he drove past them once, circled the block and did it again. The young man was tall and scruffy looking, not particularly strong, too thin.

He had half an hour to spare, so after the wallet thieves went into the coffee shop, he drove farther up and parked on Isabella. The lights were on in Valerie's place, so far, so good. He had her poetry book in his bag. He planned to read a small part of it to her later, the *bend sinister my broken heart* part. He'd underlined and paper-clipped it. The book would fall open right at it and she'd get it right away. After all, she was the editor, she was more familiar with the passage even than he was.

He opened the bag beside him on the front seat, peeked in and there it was, the pink cover.

Heidi had a coffee, triple sugar, and looked at her reflection in the window. She more or less liked what she saw. The white blouse with the fake-fur trim, all of it spotless thanks to the washer and drier at the shelter, the hoop earrings, the white pants you couldn't see because she was sitting down. Same thing for the red boots. She held up the gold purse and turned it back and forth, the gold sequins. She didn't really have a lot of competition in the field, here on Jarvis. Most of the other girls were older. But she was worried about Henry and the wallet and not only that, she'd told Amber she'd meet her at eight, back at the shelter. They were going to walk together to the party at Valerie's.

She went to the bathroom. She always did that before she went to work. Then she lit a cigarette and went outside and leaned up against her spot on the front wall, in the pose she liked, right beside the alleyway that cut down to the back of the restaurant. There was Mitchell, she saw him poked out slightly behind a lamppost down the street. She saw the flash of his lighter. She almost laughed, except for being nervous, and she blew a few smoke rings in the air. The evening was so still they came out like doughnuts, and then the car came by and stopped.

Okay, my little sweetheart, said Abner Krank to himself in the driver's seat. He already had surgical gloves on and, in the carrying bag, he felt for the small instrument he'd brought along for the girl. Nothing mean or serious, just one of those steel walnut crushers, the kind you found in wooden bowls at Christmas. It was his own original idea. Corkscrews, those little skewers for shrimp, walnut crushers, kitchen things you never thought of at all, it was amazing what they could do. You just had to be creative.

As planned, he was quick. He didn't give her a chance to come over to the car. He jumped right out of the door on the driver's side and strode around the front. As soon as she saw him, she straightened up out of that cat pose she had, the one that had sucked him in in the first place.

Hi, Heidi, Heidi-hi, he said, singsong.

Henry, she began to say.

But that was as far as she got because with one fist he had her choked by the wispy fur collar and with the other hand, he grabbed the thin gold handle of her purse in the walnut crusher and also her thumb and the first two fingers of her left hand, because they were holding on to the purse. So far, perfect. She weighed one hundred pounds max. It was easy to actually push-lift her up against the brick wall and then swing her, in one move, around the corner into the alley. Judging by how far away Mr. Mitchell was, he had ten or fifteen seconds before he arrived on the scene, ten or fifteen seconds to make his point with Heidi alone.

Heidi-hi-hi-hi, he said again.

She smelled aftershave, a spray of saliva on her face. Peppermint.

Krank squeezed down with the walnut crusher as hard as he could. He didn't let go of her neck, though, so the scream that came out of her was muffled.

Her hand felt as though it were on fire or torn off or both.

Down the road the quickness of the attack took Mitchell by surprise. Shit. He tossed his smoke into Jarvis Street and started to run. Twelve seconds in the hundred-yard dash in high school but with each step he took now, the heels of his cowboy boots twisted.

It was a mistake, he'd never tried running in these before.

Heidi sort of collapsed and fell to her knees in the alley so Krank let her drop and bent down with her.

The wallet, Heidi, he said, letting go of her collar, her throat. My wallet.

All she did was cry his name two more times, Henry, Henry.

In this neighbourhood, a scream was like the barking of a dog, the clatter of a garbage can. It was background music.

He released the pressure and she dropped her purse. He picked it up. He didn't even have to open it to know the wallet wasn't there.

Well, the wallet was on its way, wasn't it? And there was something to be said for how he felt, the way he stood over her while she cried. No time to appreciate it though, time to be cool. Time for the main event.

He took the two-inch steel pipe, eighteen inches long, from under his jacket. He'd duct-taped one end of it for a grip. He stood with his back against the wall and waited by the corner. Mitchell came at full speed and made the turn and slipped on the heel of his boot and his right knee buckled. The last thing he saw was Heidi, bent over, still on the ground.

When it was all over, Detective Ames shook his head. He'd never seen anything like it.

So tell me, said the detective sergeant.

Okay, how's this: one psychiatric resident dead, one female medical student strangled, one pimp with his face caved in by a steel pipe, dead also, one Mexican visitor to our shores, nearly exsanguinated courtesy of the same psychiatric resident, one old lady innocently watching television, dead, and, lastly, nine statements from nine witnesses resulting in not even one charge that'll stick in court. It's unbelievable. One simple party gone to hell.

And the witnesses?

They're like bikers, or crackheads. None of them saw the same thing. Medical students, poets, a teenager from Jarvis Street, you'd think that with so many of them, it would be easy to piece it together.

Grind it out, Andy, grind it out.

Ames went back to his desk. He flipped through the forensic summary. Blood in the bedroom from five separate individuals.

The Mexican, Roberto Moreno. Blood on the floor, the bedspread, the sheets, even halfway up the wall where it splattered and sprayed. Arterial bleeding, like a pump. The girl, Valerie Anderson. Blood on the sheets, the floor. When Ames first saw her in real life that night, she didn't look a lot like her photograph, the one he'd seen earlier. She was barely alive, on oxygen. The ambulance attendants sprinted down the corridor with her, towards the elevator. He'd never seen a gurney go that fast. After her, another one just about as fast rolled along with the Mexican.

Wallace Wallace. Another med student. His blood was on the window out to the balcony, or what was left of the window.

Jasper Glass. This time it was blood instead of Crisco. But most of the blood was Roberto Moreno's. He was pretty much drenched in it, but it didn't slow him down. A few scratches. He led a charmed life, that one.

Abner Krank, the psychiatric resident. Not much blood lost but his black shirt was covered with multiple handprints of blood, fingerprints, palm prints from at least five individuals, many of them overlapped. It was hard to be sure which print came first. Cause of his death, broken neck, fracture-dislocation C_1–C_2. It would have been instantaneous. Too bad.

So there you go.

That was the hard evidence, but when he tried to piece it together from all the sources, it was a maelstrom. He couldn't pin anything down with certainty. So one more time, he decided to take it in chronological order, take what happened first, follow it along.

Even though the party at 75 Isabella was the main focus, it all started earlier, down at the coffee shop on Jarvis Street. The call for the police came in at 7:52, from the man behind the counter.

A girl just reported that someone is injured outside in the alley, he said. I haven't gone out to check yet, I'm not crazy.

When the police and the ambulance arrived, all they found was Mitchell Murray, on his back in the alley. The right side of his face was smashed in and the weapon used to do it, a steel pipe, was on the ground nearby. Vital signs absent, wallet missing.

Ames picked up the autopsy report.

The steel pipe had crushed through the nasal bone and shattered it. Then, next in line came the right maxillary bone and six teeth, the right maxillary sinus, the lower rim of the orbit, the eyeball itself half dislodged. Contusions in the frontal lobe of the brain. Cause of death: asphyxia, the jumble of teeth and blood and tongue that filled his throat and obstructed the airway. He probably took one deep breath, a reflex, and that was it. Choked on it all. If he'd fallen face down, Mr. Murray might have lived.

A mugging with a vengeance. That's what it looked like, superficially. But the level of violence was a surprise, overboard.

The coffee shop guy recognized the girl, Heidi Someone, but he had no idea where she lived.

She just came in running and crying, the one with pigtails. Someone's hurt in the alley, she said, call the police. Then she took off. I made the call. That's all I know.

It wasn't totally all he knew because, he told Ames, he came out from behind the counter after Heidi left, and he went outside and looked at Mr. Murray. He couldn't tell anything from the face, but the boots, he recognized those.

He used to sit in here and smoke and talk on the pay phone, like it was his office. Filled an ashtray an hour. Can't say I'll miss him. He's a pimp.

Heidi, she's his girl?

Right now, she's the one.

Ames himself was in the alley at 8:15. The steel pipe had rolled up against the wall and a pair of rubber gloves lay discarded on the ground.

So many people die in alleyways, maybe alleyways have a gravitational force of their own, he thought.

Bag those up, the pipe, the gloves, he'd said to one of the constables.

Next he reviewed the statements from Amber White and Murlean Poirier, a.k.a. Miss Heidi Chipman. After leaving the coffee shop, Heidi hurried to the shelter on Jarvis. She had plans to go to the party at 75 Isabella, from the frying pan into the fire, but when Amber White saw Heidi, she said no.

What time was it then? Just past eight o'clock.

Amber helped Heidi take off the torn blouse with the fur trim. She wiped Heidi's face with a washcloth, prepared an ice bag for her hand and cluck-clucked a bit.

Let me look at those fingers. And who the hell tore your collar? That Mitchell again? You can't go to the party, look at you. Want me to call the police? Did Mitchell do this to you, Murlean?

Amber had a special hatred for Mitchell Murray. She admitted to that but said that she couldn't have swung the pipe.

Detective, look at my muscles. They're for poetry, for typing. Someone struck a blow for women, though, I tip my hat to the result. Call me callous but I'm no murderer. At least not in alleyways, that's not my style. He was trouble for Murlean, she couldn't shake him off.

Murlean reported that she lay down on the couch in the living room with her swollen hand on her chest, held between two ice bags.

At 8:20, Amber set off up Jarvis Street, headed for Valerie's. That was okay, according to Murlean, to be left at the shelter, because even though she'd been invited to the party at Church and Isabella, she was half the age of everyone else who was going to be there. They were all medical students. What kind of music would they play at a party like that anyway? What would they do?

Lock the door, please, Amber said to Murlean when she was leaving.

She lay there on the couch at the shelter till ten o'clock. Then she roused herself and looked in the mirror and decided, okay, maybe I'll go to the party after all. She'd see Amber there, and Valerie. She freshened up and left. She was ice-bagged and her fingers were bruised and sore but otherwise she was none the worse for wear.

She hoped Mitchell was okay, but to be honest, she told Ames, she hadn't looked when she took off from the alley. She was scared.

On her way to the party, she kept on the far side of Jarvis Street, and when she looked across to where she had been attacked, it was dark, nothing there. Not even crime tape.

And the man who attacked you?

I have no idea why. He came out of nowhere. He hurt me, here.

And Detective Ames had looked at her hand. Two of the fingers were swollen to nearly double size. And the tip of one of them was sticking out to the side.

Let me see that, he said.

He took the girl's finger and gently pulled on it and there was a pop and the finger looked normal again, or at least straighter.

There, he said, it was dislocated. Nothing serious. I thought this party was full of doctors. Didn't they even look at it?

Not really, said Murlean. Mostly they read poems to each other. They're not real doctors yet, anyway. I'm not sure what they are.

He wrote that exact statement down—I'm not sure what they are—and in the weeks that followed, when it got confusing, he often went back to that phrase and reread it.

Then Murlean surprised him. She held up her hand.

The guy who hit Mitch? He's the same guy as did all of this.

She pointed to the bedroom.

So, eight p.m. Right on time, the poetry group minus Wallace Wallace and plus Gwen O'Hara arrived at 75 Isabella. They were rung in and took the elevator to 305.

Ames knew Gwen, they had a history together, an understanding. She was unlikely to lie to him directly. He trusted her, up to a point.

Roberto Moreno opened the door.

Hey, welcome, everybody, come on in, said Roberto. What's up these days?

Gwen said they kibitzed, the way you always did at parties. Jasper said something ridiculous, something like he was wandering around in an inexhaustible orb. Everybody laughed and Gwen handed Roberto some dried flowers.

Where's Wallace? asked Valerie Anderson.

Ames flipped to Wallace's testimony.

He'd been held up in the O.R., watching. The real doctors there had to fix a perforated bowel. It was too bad he'd missed the start of the party but he realized he might as well get used to having his plans messed up. Life of the surgeon, life of the surgeon-to-be. He arrived at 8:45, having run all the way to Valerie Anderson's, non-stop. What was it, ten blocks? As he came near the apartment building, on the south side of Isabella, however, he stopped.

He recognized someone in a car, parked by the curb.

Whoa, hey.

He did a double-take and walked back a few steps. Yes. He tapped on the passenger-side window.

Dr. Krank! he said.

At first the man didn't respond but then he turned his head.

Dr. Krank? Wallace Wallace, from 999.

The window was closed, so he didn't know if Krank had heard him. He tapped on it again.

Krank opened his door and got out of the mid-size and looked across the rooftop at Wallace Wallace.

Yes? he said.

It's me, Wallace Wallace, the medical student. From 999, remember? The case of the man who jumped off the intern's residence?

Oh yes. Hi.

Wallace thought in retrospect that something was weird about Krank, the way he hopped out of the car and stared across the roof at him.

Just in the neighbourhood, Doctor?

Checking it out. Maybe an apartment for next year.

You know what, Doctor? There's a party up here tonight at Valerie Anderson's. Why don't you pop up, come with me? You remember her, Valerie?

I don't get out a lot, the psychiatric resident said.

Studying, I bet, the college exams. All the more reason then. Come on, kick loose.

Later, when he looked back at the invitation he'd extended to the psychiatric resident, Wallace thought he had made a big mistake.

But Ames told him, relax. Dr. Krank would have done what he did anyway. He'd fixed on a plan and was not going to be stopped by circumstance. So your mistake was not a real mistake, it's just another way of the same thing happening, a variation.

Krank and Wallace went up together in the elevator.

Seems like a nice building full of apartments, this one, said Abner Krank, maybe I could live here, you never know, I've never been in a place like this. Nice elevator. Real nice, nice reflections, this mirror.

That's the way he talked, said Wallace. Words tumbled

out of him without meaning. I just thought he was excited, getting out to a party, you know.

They knocked on the door at Valerie's and Roberto Moreno took them right in.

This is Dr. Krank, Wallace said, I met him outside.

Roberto was, as usual, polite and reserved.

Hey, Valerie, said Wallace, look who's here.

For a tenth of a second, he told Ames, concern had crossed her face.

Oh, Dr. Krank, she said.

Then she said, Yes, yes, come in, come in.

Did I make a mistake? Wallace asked her in the kitchen a few minutes later.

Not really, Wallace, she said, it doesn't matter.

She put her hand on his arm. He remembered that because she'd never done that before, touched him.

So that's how Dr. Abner Krank arrived at the party. Obviously, it wasn't part of his plan, but he'd seen an opportunity and had been able to improvise.

Back to Gwen.

Roberto Moreno was very friendly to her, formal and old-worldly, she had said, in his approach and manners. Upon her arrival, he immediately took her around the small apartment. Together they admired some prints on the wall, a small painting.

Make yourself at home, he said.

Gwen thought Jasper's lab partner, Valerie Anderson, was very beautiful. Jasper had told her that, it was no surprise. Gwen, herself very pretty, said she felt plain by comparison. But so would any girl next to Valerie, it was not just her. The only other woman there was Amber White. It was mostly men, the medical world. Heidi hadn't arrived yet, she came late. Initially, Gwen felt awkward because the other guests all knew each other, but she settled into a conversation with Amber, a famous, or should she say notorious, poet. Gwen had heard of her through Jasper's mother, so they talked for twenty minutes about the literary magazine *Zipper*. Gwen had read a copy that was lying around at Jasper's. She admired the poetry, she said to Amber, because they weren't the usual la-di-da poems about sunsets and rain.

They have an edge, like a figure skate, said Gwen.

Then, about nine-thirty or maybe closer to ten, Gwen wasn't paying attention to time, Roberto clinked his glass with a fork and announced that Valerie Anderson, bad luck for her and for all of them, had one of her rare migraines.

She has gone to bed in the dark, he said. Don't worry, she will take some medicine and should be okay within the hour.

He put a sign on the bedroom door that said DO NOT DISTURB. Then he spoke to Jasper Glass.

You know what medicine she takes for migraines? She said it's in the bathroom.

I think so. I'll look through the medicine cabinet.

Jasper had seen it happen to Valerie once in a bio-chemistry exam, a pounding disabling headache, so much so that she laid her head down on the desk in the middle of Varsity Arena and then had to leave.

First she sees shimmering lines, then the headache starts, he said. It's no fun.

Okay, Mr. Glass, now your turn, Ames thought as he flipped through the files to find Jasper's.

In the medicine cabinet, Jasper found two tablets of plain Fiorinal. Also codeine 30 mg, four of those. He went to the kitchen, rinsed out an empty wine bottle and filled it with cold water. In the cupboard above the sink, he found a small glass. Then he went to the bedroom where Valerie lay face down on the bed, her earphones on, listening to something. He lifted up one side of them.

Fiorinal, codeine, which you want, Valerie? he asked.

Both, she said.

Her voice was muffled by the bedclothes.

He poured a glass of water for her and left the bottle on the bedside table.

Cold and fresh, he said, help yourself. It's right here. I'll open the sliding door for air.

Roberto Moreno came in and sat down on the side of the bed and stroked Valerie Anderson's dark hair.

Then Jasper left the room, but as he went through the doorway, he had to slide past the psychiatrist, Abner Krank, who peered into the bedroom.

Does she need any help? Krank asked.

No, it's under control. Nothing in your field anyway, Doctor. No demons at play, it's purely physical.

Then Wallace grabbed Jasper by the arm and whispered to him.

Jasper, I'm sorry, like I said to Valerie, I don't think I should have asked that guy here. He's a bit spaced.

No sweat, Wallace. What's it matter? Hey, every-one, keep on the music, laugh all you like, Valerie has earphones on. They block all noise. She'll be fine.

And in fact her absence didn't slow the party down, Jasper reported. By popular demand, first Amber read from one of the few cheerful sections of her long poem. Much applause ensued and Amber bowed. She was embarrassed by the attention. Then Roberto came out of Valerie's bedroom and read a poem she'd written, called "Trespasser Trespasser." Right after he finished his reading, the psychiatric resident jumped up and left. He thanked Roberto Moreno in a very perfunctory way and was out the door.

Reviewing all the notes, only Jasper, Roberto and Wallace Wallace even noticed him leave.

Did "Trespasser" tip Krank over the edge? Ames picked up his copy—the same one that had been read from and later discarded on the coffee table—and read her poem for the twentieth time since that night.

Trespasser Trespasser

> *I must wrap my heart in a cloth*
> *and put it away for a time. Now,*
> *there are things I can't enjoy*
> *that you take as given: first light through white pines,*
> *those heavy swaying gates—Trespasser, come closer,*
> *so I can see your face.*

Some very straight, some twisted beyond
any shape you have a word for,
some fallen and softening on the ground,
as soft as human skin, soft enough
for you to carve your initials in.

Abner Krank, with his carving knife, came to Valerie Anderson right after hearing this. Did the poem have anything to do with it? Does poetry have that kind of power? He put it away in the top drawer of his desk.

Nothing much appeared to happen at the party for half an hour. Nothing at the party itself, but upstairs in apartment 405, something did happen. And it took the police twenty-four hours to figure it out. In retrospect, not that it would have made any difference to the resident of 405, they could have gone up there later that night. After all, how did Abner Krank get to Valerie's balcony? With the rope, they figured he climbed up, one floor to the next, from the outside. It could be done, loop-dee-loop. But they never went up there that night, and the next day the old lady upstairs was discovered by her daughter-in-law. Stiff and dead in front of the TV, still on. A heart attack, a stroke, was the original diagnosis, but then the autopsy showed what— oh yes, a fracture-dislocation at C_1–C_2. Broken neck. You don't get injuries like that sitting in front of the TV. There was a *TV Guide* in front of her. She had the habit of crossing out what she'd seen with a felt pen, black line after black line down through the schedule. The last show she'd crossed out was at nine-thirty, Friday.

Gunsmoke. Time of death established, then, probably between ten-thirty and eleven. Forensics found fibres from the rope on the iron bars of the lady's balcony.

So Abner Krank left the party, went straight upstairs into her apartment and broke her neck from behind. Didn't even spill the old lady's tea. Then he took the tasseled rope from her purple Victorian curtains but he didn't use it to rappel on down. For that, he had a high-tech mountaineering rope complete with metal clips.

Down he went in the dark, balcony to balcony, one floor. Easy as pie. All the noise from the party and there she was, her earphones on, head down, Do Not Disturb. Perfect.

How long was he in there with her? Not too long, Ames hoped. At any rate, that's when the shit hit the fan.

Jasper Glass said that he said to Roberto, let's check on Valerie. Let's peek in.

It must have been past eleven o'clock by then.

But it was actually Amber White who looked in first because Roberto Moreno and Jasper Glass had to weave their way through the crowd, and Amber had the same idea at the same time but she was closer to the bedroom. In fact, she was leaning on the door talking to Gwen, so all she had to do was reach for the doorknob.

She half opened the door and looked into the dark of the bedroom.

Something moved. Yellow light filtered from the street. Shadows angled across the bed.

Valerie? Val? said Amber softly.

Amber screamed and ran straight into the bedroom but Gwen just stood where she was.

Paralyzed, Gwen?

I guess I was, Andy, I'm sorry.

It happens, he said, more often than not.

As fast as Amber ran into the bedroom, just as fast she came flying back out. She was slammed against the doorway as though flung by a catapult. Jasper Glass and Roberto Moreno then went by her at full speed. They were like one fused body and they both hit Amber on the way. They couldn't help it, she was taking up half the doorway.

I was trampled, she said, but at least it was by my friends.

Pretty much everyone was in agreement up to that point. Everybody agreed that Amber was the first one in and the first one out, all in a space of a few seconds.

Actually, John Glass said Gwen was in first, but he seemed to be in his own world, John Glass.

Amber said, he was on top of her, I screamed at him but he slammed me back with his arm.

Detective Ames flipped a few more pages of testimony.

According to Jasper, and to quote him almost exactly, as he came into the bedroom at warp speed, he blew by the shelter lady and there was someone dressed in black on top of Valerie Anderson, half turned his way. He threw himself forward but only half hit his target and slipped and fell from the edge of the bed to the floor. Valerie was face down, naked for the millisecond he saw her. He looked up from the floor and saw the fucking psychiatric resident, those were the words he used, coming down with his knife towards Valerie, her back, her neck.

Amber heard Roberto Moreno shout, *violador*! He was half a step behind Jasper and threw himself across his girlfriend and the knife that was meant for her caught him in the upper arm with such violence that he was spun off the bed. He fell on top of Jasper Glass, the two of them jumbled up on the floor.

Gwen was in the doorway still and she was then brushed aside by Wallace.

Ames picked up at the beginning of Wallace's statement. It wasn't really a statement, it was a rant.

Wallace said he saw Roberto Moreno lying on top of Jasper Glass. Blood from one of them hissed up against the wallpaper. He could actually hear it, he said, it was arterial bleeding, a pumping hiss. Then he looked at the bed. Valerie was naked, not moving at all, face down. The guy in black, the guy he had invited to the party, was standing up on the far side of her, near the sliding balcony door. He had no clothes on from the waist down.

Wallace was stocky, six feet tall, and it was hard for anyone else to see around him, so when the other witnesses said they saw nothing, Ames believed them.

We heard the breaking of glass, said Gwen O'Hara.

That must have been when Roberto Moreno, with his one good arm, picked up the wine bottle from the bedside table and broke it, transforming it into a weapon. Wallace saw him do it and Amber confirmed it. They both mentioned the bottle, which was found under the bed when it was all over, jagged and dangerous. No sign that it had been used, however. The only bit of blood on it was Roberto's.

Wallace said Krank looked down at Valerie Anderson. Krank still had his knife but after slicing Roberto, he seemed in no rush.

He didn't give a shit about Roberto, Jasper or any of them. Or me. We were out of the picture, we were nothing to him, Wallace said.

Nothing? asked Detective Ames.

Yes, said Wallace. All Krank cared about was her.

Gwen said she heard Jasper say, go Roberto, now!

Roberto Moreno rose to his feet with the neck of the shattered bottle in his hand, but then he just slid back down to the floor, beside Jasper Glass.

He never moved again, said Amber, and Gwen, Jasper, Wallace and John all said the same thing.

Wallace reached down to the bottom of the bed and took a tangled and bloody white sheet from the mess and threw it over Valerie Anderson. It slipped off her and fell to the floor at Abner Krank's feet. The psychiatric resident saw it fall and looked at Wallace for the first time.

Leave the girl alone, said Abner Krank, you dumb fuck.

Wallace then stepped between Valerie and Abner Krank. He had to push Krank back a step to do so.

I saw the knife, he said, but I didn't care about it.

Violador, he said.

He didn't speak Spanish but he'd heard Roberto Moreno and understood.

Violador, confirmed by three others. No one else would have said that except Roberto, and he was unconscious.

Wallace hit Abner Krank with his fist straight into the chest, just once. Krank flew back through the balcony door, breaking it into shards of glass. He fell out onto the balcony and his knife, the knife for roasts and girls, fell to the bedroom floor.

That gave everybody else a chance to do whatever they did. And that's where the testimonies became impossible to follow and why he, Detective Ames, had no charges to lay.

Murlean Poirier said Abner Krank flew through the door like he was hit by a bazooka.

Jasper Glass said that although he was on the floor on the far side of the bed, still trying to get out from under Roberto Moreno, Abner Krank flew away from him like part of the expanding universe. He was on his way past Pluto.

What did you do after that, Jasper? Detective Ames had asked.

I tore off a piece of the sheet and tied it up high around Roberto's arm. He was still bleeding from his arm.

And what had Wallace then told Ames?

Wallace admitted hitting Krank all right, knife or no knife. Wallace had nothing but his fist, no weapon. Why would he have a weapon? Something just came over him, he had no sense of personal fear, he felt nothing but overwhelming outrage. He was outside the rational world.

Roberto Moreno was bleeding and Valerie was on the bed and Wallace could have killed the man a thousand times, a thousand times over and if it weren't for Gwen O'Hara, who grabbed him, he would have finished the job himself.

He might even have done it despite Gwen O'Hara, he might have been the one who shook Gwen off and grabbed the piece of rope and slung it around the fucker's neck and tied it to the balcony stanchion and threw him over the edge. It might have been him, he had the strength to do it, he could have raised the whole building and slammed it down on the son of a bitch. He wasn't sure if he had done it, but he could have. Anybody who loved Valerie Anderson would have done it. The only difference between him and all the others at the party was his physical strength.

We all killed the bastard, we all killed him, I killed him, he said.

I didn't know you loved Valerie Anderson, said Detective Ames.

We all loved her. Arrest us all, but take me first.

Krank must have been stunned after he was hit, after he went through the door and fell to the balcony floor. Wallace said he went to him, put his foot hard on his chest, like they do up north with fish on the bottom of the boat, to keep him from thrashing.

Murlean, Amber, John Glass, who knows who else held him down, who sat on his legs and pinned him there. Everybody might have done it at once.

No, not Amber.

Amber said she rushed over to Valerie and Valerie wasn't breathing. She turned her over. A thick velvet rope was wrapped around Valerie's waist and a cord, a ligature like a shoelace, encircled her neck. Amber couldn't get her fingers under it. She panicked, looked down to the floor and grabbed a sharp fragment of glass and, trembling, cut the cord.

I cut my own hand too, I cut Valerie.

She then covered up Valerie and lay down beside her on the bed.

Gwen ran into the kitchen and called the police.

Wallace had Krank pinned down outside. Gwen found the climbing rope and she began to tie it around Krank's arms, his chest. John Glass helped, he held the legs.

They were like pistons, he said.

Tie him up tight, Gwen said, for God's sake don't let him loose.

Amber called out to Jasper, please, she's not breathing.

All Amber could do was dab at the small cut she'd made on Valerie's throat.

Jesus Christ, said Jasper Glass.

Jasper said he was helping tie up the rapist by then.

Don't let go of this, he said to Gwen. And to John.

John and Gwen do not remember receiving that advice. They held the rope of their own accord, they both said.

Jasper went to Valerie and held her nostrils closed with his fingers. He lifted her jaw and applied his lips to hers and blew. He remembered the practice session, how Marnie's chest rose and fell, as did Valerie's now.

That's all I did for the next ten minutes, he said, until she breathed on her own.

Roberto lay senseless in the corner the whole time, they all said.

Then came the finale. Somehow, the psychiatric resident got a loop of the rope around his neck. No one could remember how. No one said they'd been the one to put it there. The next moment, and this was something they all saw, Krank was back up on his feet, spinning wildly, his arms still tied down, off balance, out of control.

Then, nine witnesses agree, Abner Krank threw himself over the balcony.

No one saw how it happened, how the rope got stuck on this end, how he ended up hanging from the third-floor balcony, swinging in the air. Wallace and John Glass went and looked over the edge.

Jesus, they both said.

Or said they said.

The detective flipped his notes to Valerie Anderson. She still hadn't given a complete statement. According to the doctors, she wasn't ready. All she had said was one word.

Roberto.

So that's the way it was. A hundred more pages of interviews but it was all the same.

I didn't see, I don't know, it might have been Wallace or Jasper or John or all three of them who tied him up but the hanging, that happened by itself.

He went back to the detective sergeant's office.

The way I see it, you sift through all this, this is how it came down. Abner Krank is in the bedroom with Valerie Anderson. Amber looks in, she screams. She runs in and is thrown back, a piece of fluff. Enter Jasper Glass, he throws himself at the rapist. Second time for him, same move. Roberto Moreno right on his heels. Funny, it's like Shaw Street all over again. But this time Moreno goes to his girlfriend. Krank has the knife, he brushes away Jasper Glass. He couldn't care less about Jasper Glass, he swings the knife down at Valerie. She's the one he wants. The Mexican puts his arm up and catches the full force of it. Down through triceps, the brachial artery to bone. Then Mr. Wallace. He does what he does, one punch but with the force of righteous fury behind it. Abner Krank, the rapist, goes back through the window. He lies there on the balcony, stunned. After that, suicide or murder, take your pick.

What about the Mexican? asked the detective sergeant.

ICU for three days. Then, when I finally spoke to him, surprise surprise—he remembered nothing. Well, nothing after he fell from the bed.

I don't see murder here anyway, even if it was.

No, said Detective Ames, neither do I.

The two men twirled their pencils. They were comfortable together.

One funny thing, between you and me, is the handprints on the victim's black shirt, said Detective Ames.

Oh?

We identified all the prints. It wasn't easy with all that blood, but we did it. Large palm prints, left and right.

Wallace, Amber White, John Glass and, despite the fact he was nearly dead in the corner, Roberto Moreno. Figure that one out. And Jasper Glass—he's always there at the edge of everything—two prints right smack on the centre of the chest.

So what are you saying?

More went on than we'll ever know. The nearly dead man, the exsanguinated Roberto Moreno, rose from the corner and managed to get to the rapist. Don't ask me how. Talk to them all twenty times, you get the same thing, like it was all rehearsed, every word perfect, every one of them. What do they remember? Everything and nothing. Mostly contradictions. Even Gwen. And get this, don't forget, they're a poetry group. A *poetry group*.

He laughed and consulted his notes again.

Parabolists, they're a bunch of parabolists, what-ever that means. Gwen told me that, so I asked her what it meant.

And?

She really had no idea. Something about catching the rays of the sun, letting them focus and burn. Something about love. Some concept of Roberto Moreno's.

Sounds like bullshit to me.

Maybe. But they're all still alive, aren't they? How did the Mexican get out to the balcony? Three pints of blood, he lost. Sounds pretty damn focused to me.

It was quite a year, an epoch really. How long was it? Fifteen months, twelve months, what does it matter, the exact number of months since Roberto Moreno arrived and Bill and June Glass spotted him outside in the snow. They took over the lobster gloves, the parka, and after that it wasn't too long before they met Valerie Anderson and they never, as parents, expected to be so intimately involved in the lives of their children but it worked out that way. With *Zipper* taking off the way it did, it was a personal revelation for June herself, a focus for her passion. How she became an actor at last on the stage of poetry. She never would have dreamed it possible. But then came winter into summer and the cascade of misfortune that followed. Jasper footloose as always, John his academic struggles, and lastly what happened to Valerie Anderson. Who would ever have thought that possible?

For the first time in a long while, months and months, Valerie Anderson called June Glass.

Can I come over?

Oh God, yes, Valerie, she said.

They sat outside in the backyard, alone together in the penumbra of the silver maple. A shuffle of leaves up to their ankles in the late afternoon. Valerie had a sweater on, as did June Glass. The wind was from the north, winter loomed in the grey-soled clouds as they hastened overhead. Next door, the accountant collected leaves under the cherry tree, his presence a reminder of the departure of the Nájeras, the parting glass of tequila June and Bill had shared with them.

There were no yellow papers, no crumpled poems to be caught in the tines of rakes.

June saw that Valerie Anderson was cold. She had her

arms held tight to her chest. She got up and put her scarf around Valerie's neck where there was still a visible scar, a blue-red thin linear crease to which Valerie seemed to pay no attention.

June, she said, Roberto has now gone too, last week.

Her voice was thin, barely audible, but much improved from what it had been after the attack.

Gone?

June was only half surprised. She had known for some time, from the boys, that Roberto Moreno's passport from Mexico had expired.

I thought he would have said goodbye to me, June said.

I know, Valerie said.

June shifted her chair closer.

But ever since the end of the poetry class, Valerie said, Roberto was restless. He was writing fewer and fewer poems and he took long walks to the Danforth by himself.

And, she went on to say as June bent her head closer to hers, still those letters came, more often than before from that woman in Mexico City, Isabela Cruz.

His platonic friend, as I recall, said June.

Yes, said Valerie, that's the one.

Valerie said she felt a curious kinship with this unknown Mexican girl.

I feel no jealousy at all, she said. Or I don't think I do.

What sort of things did she write? said June.

Oh, Roberto translated them, things like *on the roof-tops here the smog is like sulphur, the laundry yellowed.*

As though to induce nostalgia?

No, said Valerie, I don't think there was any such intent. She's a parabolist, that's all. That's what parabolists write about. Anything really.

That's pretty mild, rooftops, smog.

There was more than that. Once she got going, look out. You saw the poem in *Zipper*.

Yes, I certainly did, said June.

Then Valerie recounted how she had sat down with Roberto Moreno and said to him, go ahead, Roberto, I know you have to leave, I'm okay here now.

And?

Well, now his plans are to get his landed immigrant status from there, from Mexico City.

Dear dear, June Glass thought.

Her mind travelled through space at thirty thousand feet and landed on the tarmac on the high Mexican plateau and she thought about Roberto Moreno, in his own environment. His turf, where the rays of the equatorial sun powered down.

He'll come back, June said. It's far more exciting here.

Valerie smiled a wan smile.

Tell me your news, June, Valerie said.

Wait, Valerie, can you have wine?

She nodded assent, and June went into the kitchen and came back out with a Côtes-du-Rhône, maybe a third of the bottle left. She poured two small glasses. By now the accountant had finished his yardwork next door and a profound silence descended on the neighbourhood, so rare.

No cicadas now, said Valerie.

They raised their glasses to each other.

John's back in medical school, June said.

Valerie jumped in her chair.

What?

Yes, it's true, he's back in.

Impossible, said Valerie.

It took him forever to tell us, Valerie. His expulsion, his job at the sauna baths, all quite a shock for us as you can imagine. Anyway, we accepted it. That's what parents do. But then, as I understand it, the doctor who expelled him came to the baths one night and said, you look familiar to me, young man. You are the embryologist. Yes, said John, I am the embryologist, how can I help you, sir? On this occasion the expeller of my son did nothing but take the key to his roomette, but a week later he appeared again and said, Mr. Glass, for now I know it's you, I have reviewed your file. I'm anxious that my academic life, my family life, my time here at the baths do not intersect in any way. Do you understand? Of course, said John. And the doctor went on to say that his lives were compartmentalized, separate and mutually exclusive. To which I understand John said, Doctor, rest assured that I have taken an oath of confidentiality and I would never under any circumstances disclose matters of privacy. Moreover, I do not think it of any importance. Thank you, Mr. Glass, said the expeller, you have brought my heart full ease. And, I must say, John, I find your ethics of the highest order, an important quality in a physician. You should reapply sometime if you wish, Mr. Glass, he said. And

John let it rest for a month but then he did, he reapplied and just yesterday, otherwise you would already have heard, Valerie, his acceptance came in the mail. Mind you, he has to repeat the whole year.

Valerie laughed for the first time in ages and said, including embryology?

Yes, including embryology.

After that, Valerie Anderson and June Glass discussed *Zipper,* how their intention was to continue their editorial duties with Amber White, how they expected to maintain or even extend its seminal role in Canadian poetry.

Of course, we'll miss Roberto, June said, till he's back.

Then they were silent.

So, Valerie, what do you think?

About what?

Everything, Valerie, everything.

I don't know, June. I'm only twenty-one.

Well, I'm forty-eight and I don't know either.

The bottle of wine had enough left for a few drops each. June shared them carefully, drop by drop.

There, she said, so that's that. Finished.

Jasper Glass was alone in the anatomy lab. He stood at the foot of their cadaver. Now it was nothing but a skeleton, but it wasn't one of those perfect Hallowe'en ones like the skeletons they used for teaching, perfect, smooth and white. Instead, their body, the one he had shared with Valerie, looked abandoned. The scalp and upper cranium were levered back upon the table. The lips Jasper had so carefully sutured into place were still there but they had dried out and thinned, hardened like worms. And the massive opened rib cage, from which the heart and lungs had been dissected and removed, lay wrecked and ragged as though a hurricane had blown through it. Tendrils of dry flesh hung from the remnants of ribs.

Thanks, old fellow, he said.

He patted the nearest foot, what was left of it.

Then he turned off the light and left the room.

The phone rang, the professor jumped.

Maybe it was Louise Drabinsky with good news.

On the other hand, maybe not.

Bill let the phone ring and ring and ring and ring. He sat there, sure it was her. Someday, he'd know what to do, but not quite yet.

ACKNOWLEDGMENTS

I wish to express my gratitude to the following:

For editing in the first instance and throughout the year of writing, Cheryl Ruddock.

For first reading, Nora Ruddock and William Ruddock.

For her poetry, Jessica Ruddock, a.k.a. Koko Bonaparte.

For help in French translation, Isabelle Pinard and Nora Ruddock; in Spanish, Luisa Perez.

Thanks to Jeffrey Wyndowe, Jim Colby, Michael Ruddock, James Ruddock, David Ruddock, Frank Ruddock, Michael Gillies.

For laughing at the right places, for shaking their heads and publishing my short stories in the last five years, Robert Martin, Anne Simpson, Sabine Campbell, Richard Cumyn, Veronica Ross, Mark Anthony Jarman, Anita Chong, Benjamin Wood, Kent Bruyneel, Rick Maddocks, Christine Dewar, Priscila Uppal, Barry Callaghan, Nina Callaghan.

For encouragement at the University of Guelph, Jane Urquhart.

For representing me, Martha Magor and Anne McDermid of Anne McDermid Associates.

Thank you to Doubleday Canada, to the Random House design team and to Susan Burns. Thank you in particular to Senior Editor Nita Pronovost who brought *The Parabolist* to the finish line with such decisive wisdom and panache.

The City of Toronto is the only true living character in this book. Any other semblance to reality is a coincidence A few buildings and streetscapes have been altered or shifted counter-clockwise for the purposes of plot. The medical curriculum has been warped to suit the fictional circumstances.

Thank you as well, in absentia, to my parents, William Ruddock and June Strickland, whose love of literature started it for all for us.

PERMISSIONS AND CREDITS

Grateful acknowledgment is made to the following:

Charles Baudelaire, excerpt from "What Will You Say Tonight," from *Les fleurs du mal,* translated by Richard Howard (Boston: David R. Godine, 1982). Reprinted by permission of David R. Godine, Publisher, Inc. Translation copyright 1982 by Richard Howard. Reprinted with permission.

Excerpt from *The Savage Detectives* by Roberto Bolaño. Copyright © 1998 by Roberto Bolaño. Translation copyright 2007 by Natasha Wimmer. Reprinted by permission of Farrar, Straus and Giroux, LLC.

Koko Bonaparte, excerpt from "The Annunciation," unpublished poem, 2009.

Koko Bonaparte, excerpts from "A Little Bit of Learning," "So I Go" and "Tried to" from the CD *Koko Bonaparte,* Wild Whip Records, 2008. Reprinted with permission.

Koko Bonaparte, "Trespasser Trespasser," unpublished poem, 2009.

Arthur Rimbaud, excerpt from *The Drunken Boat,* excerpt translated by Isabelle Pinard and Nora Ruddock.

Margot Ruddock, excerpt from *The Lemon Tree* (London: J.M. Dent, 1937).*

Alfred Lord Tennyson, excerpt from "The Lotos-eaters," from *Poems to Remember* (Toronto & Vancouver: J.M. Dent & Sons, 1951).

Miriam Waddington, excerpt from "Girls," from *Collected Poems* (Toronto: Oxford University Press Canada, 1986). Reprinted with permission.

W. B. Yeats, excerpt from "The Lake Isle of Innisfree," from *Poems to Remember* (Toronto & Vancouver: J.M. Dent & Sons, 1951).

*All attempts at tracing the copyright holder were unsuccessful.

All other poetry appearing in the novel and not listed here is written by the author.

NICHOLAS RUDDOCK's writing has been published in *The Dalhousie Review*, *The Antigonish Review*, *Fiddlehead*, *Prism International*, *Grain*, *sub-Terrain*, *Event*, and *Exile*. His short story "How Eunice Got Her Baby" was published in the Journey Prize Anthology in 2007, and the Canadian Film Centre has made a film adaptation, narrated by Gordon Pinsent. Ruddock is a family physician. He lives in Guelph, Ontario.